VALENTINE PONTIFEX, THE LONG-AWAITED CULMINATION OF ROBERT SILVERBERG'S MAGNIFICENT MAJIPOOR TRILOGY:

"Silverberg, in *Lord Valentine's Castle*, introduced the sprawling planet of Majipoor... through the eyes of an innocent: a deposed king stripped of his memory, seeing the several alien races and delicately eerie overgrowth of his home planet as if for the first time.... *Majipoor Chronicles* used the... device of an experience recorder to give us a time-lapse picture of Majipoor through the centuries. Now *Valentine Pontifex* whirls that cumulative information into action, the lazy pace through time and space giving way to a dance of conflicting emotions and political intrigue. Both the world and Lord Valentine have matured, and the trilogy becomes whole in a way that the form rarely achieves."

—*Village Voice*

"There's an almost symphonic grandeur to the thoughtful way Silverberg weaves the strands of the story together, effortlessly juggling the various motifs, while enchancing the central characters' solidity. Taken as a single work, the trilogy must now be judged the best of its type since Zelazny's classic, Hugo-winning *Lord of Light*."

—*Publishers Weekly*

. . . and for *Majipoor Chronicles:*

VALENTINE PONTIFEX

Robert Silverberg

BANTAM BOOKS
TORONTO · NEW YORK · LONDON · SYDNEY · AUCKLAND

*This low-priced Bantam Book
has been completely reset in a type face
designed for easy reading, and was printed
from new plates. It contains the complete
text of the original hard-cover edition.*
NOT ONE WORD HAS BEEN OMITTED.

VALENTINE PONTIFEX

*A Bantam Book / published by arrangement with
Arbor House Publishing Company*

PRINTING HISTORY
Arbor House edition published October 1983
A Main Selection of Science Fiction Book Club.

Bantam edition / November 1984

*Bantam Books are published by Bantam Books, Inc. Its trade-
mark, consisting of the words "Bantam Books" and the por-
trayal of a rooster, is Registered in U.S. Patent and Trademark
Office and in other countries. Marca Registrada. Bantam
Books, Inc., 666 Fifth Avenue, New York, New York 10103.*

PRINTED IN THE UNITED STATES OF AMERICA

O   0 9 8 7 6 5 4 3 2 1

for
KAREN
SANDRA
CATHERINE
JERRY
CAROL
ELLEN
DYANNE
HILARY
DIANA
—*bulwarks in a season of stormy weather*

...*I live in mighty fear that all the universe will be broken into a thousand fragments in the general ruin, that formless chaos will return and vanquish the gods and men, that the earth and sea will be engulfed by the planets wandering in the heavens. ...Of all the generations, it is we who have been chosen to merit this bitter fate, to be crushed by the falling pieces of the broken sky.*

—SENECA
Thyestes

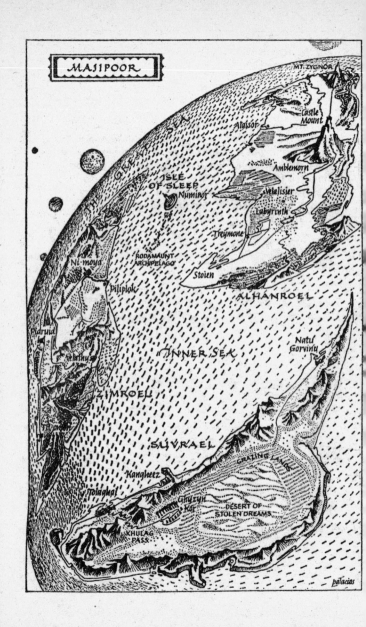

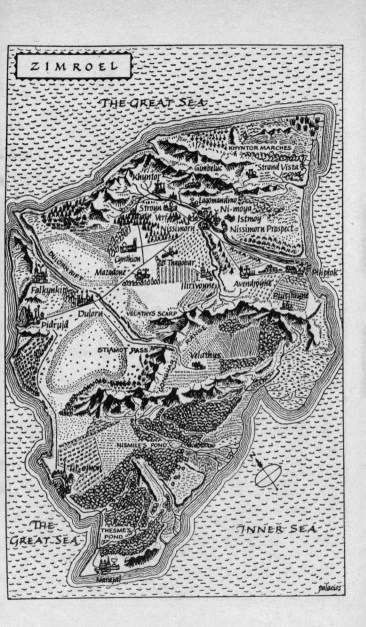

CASTLE MOUNT AND GLAYGE VALLEY

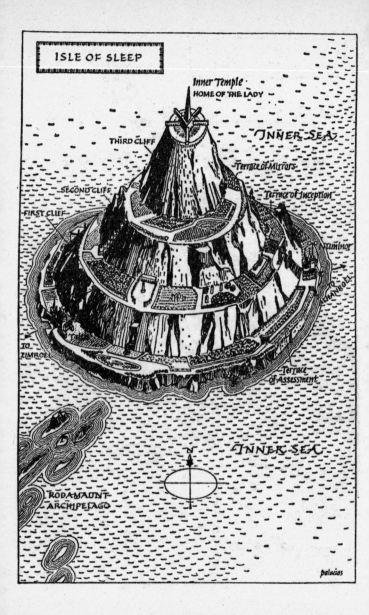

ONE

The Book
of the
Coronal

1

Valentine swayed, braced himself with his free hand against the table, struggled to keep himself from spilling his wine.

This is very odd, he thought, this dizziness, this confusion. Too much wine—the stale air—maybe gravity pulls harder, this far down below the surface—

"Propose the toast, lordship," Deliamber murmured. "First to the Pontifex, and then to his aides, and then—"

"Yes. Yes, I know."

Valentine peered uncertainly from side to side, like a steetmoy at bay, ringed round by the spears of hunters.

"Friends—" he began.

"To the Pontifex Tyeveras!" Deliamber whispered sharply.

Friends. Yes. Those who were most dear to him, seated close at hand. Almost everyone but Carabella and Elidath: she was on her way to meet him in the west, was she not, and Elidath was handling the chores of government on Castle Mount in Valentine's absence. But the others were here, Sleet, Deliamber, Tunigorn, Shanamir, Lisamon and Ermanar, Tisana, the Skandar Zalzan Kavol, Asenhart the Hjort—yes, all his dear ones, all the pillars of his life and reign—

"Friends," he said, "lift your wine-bowls, join me in one more toast. You know that it has not been granted me by the Divine to enjoy an easy time upon the throne. You all know the hardships that have been thrust upon me, the challenges that had to be faced, the tasks required of me, the weighty problems still unresolved."

"This is not the right speech, I think," he heard someone behind him say.

Deliamber muttered again, "His majesty the Pontifex! You must offer a toast to his majesty the Pontifex!"

Valentine ignored them. These words that came from him now seemed to come of their own accord.

3

"If I have borne these unparalleled difficulties with some grace," he went on, "it is only because I have had the support, the counsel, the love, of such a band of comrades and precious friends as few rulers can ever have claimed. It is with your indispensable help, good friends, that we will come at last to a resolution of the troubles that afflict Majipoor and enter into the era of true amity that we all desire. And so, as we make ready to set forth tomorrow into this realm of ours, eagerly, joyously, to undertake the grand processional, I offer this last toast of the evening, my friends, to you, to those who have sustained me and nurtured me throughout all these years, and who—"

"How strange he looks," Ermanar murmured. "Is he ill?"

A spasm of astonishing pain swept through him. There was a terrible droning buzz in his ears, and his breath was as hot as flame. He felt himself descending into night, a night so terrible that it obliterated all light and swept across his soul like a tide of black blood. The wine-bowl fell from his hand and shattered; and it was as if the entire world had shattered, flying apart into thousands of crumbling fragments that went tumbling crazily toward every corner of the universe. The dizziness was overwhelming now. And the darkness—that utter and total night, that complete eclipse—

"Lordship!" someone bellowed. Could that have been Hissune?

"He's having a sending!" another voice cried.

"A sending? How, while he is awake?"

"My lord! My lord! My lord!"

Valentine looked downward. Everything was black, a pool of night rising from the floor. That blackness seemed to be beckoning to him. Come, a quiet voice was saying, here is your path, here is your destiny: night, darkness, doom. Yield. Yield, Lord Valentine, Coronal that was, Pontifex that will never be. Yield. And Valentine yielded, for in that moment of bewilderment and paralysis of spirit there was nothing else he could do. He stared into the black pool rising about him, and he allowed himself to fall toward it. Unquestioningly, uncomprehendingly, he plunged into that all-engulfing darkness.

I am dead, he thought. I float now on the breast of the black river that returns me to the Source, and soon I must rise and go ashore and find the road that leads to the Bridge of Farewells; and then will I go across into that place where all life has its beginning and its end.

A strange kind of peace pervaded his soul then, a feeling of wondrous ease and contentment, a powerful sense that all the universe was joined in happy harmony. He felt as though he had come to rest in a cradle, where now he lay warmly swaddled, free at last of the torments of kingship. Ah, how good that was! To lie quietly, and let all turbulence sweep by him! Was this death? Why, then, death was joy!

—*You are deceived, my lord. Death is the end of joy.*

—*Who speaks to me here?*

—*You know me, my lord.*

—*Deliamber? Are you dead also? Ah, what a safe kind place death is, old friend!*

—*You are safe, yes. But not dead.*

—*It feels much like death to me.*

—*And have you such thorough experience of death, my lord, that you can speak of it so knowingly?*

—*What is this, if it is not death?*

—*Merely a spell,* said Deliamber.

—*One of yours, wizard?*

—*No, not mine. But I can bring you from it, if you will permit. Come: awaken. Awaken.*

—*No, Deliamber! Let me be.*

—*You must, my lord.*

—*Must,* Valentine said bitterly. *Must! Always must! Am I never to rest? Let me stay where I am. This is a place of peace. I have no stomach for war, Deliamber.*

—*Come, my lord.*

—*Tell me next that it is my duty to awaken.*

—*I need not tell you what you know so well. Come.*

He opened his eyes, and found himself in midair, lying limply in Lisamon Hultin's arms. The Amazon carried him as though he were a doll, nestling against the vastness of her breasts. Small wonder he had imagined himself in a cradle, he thought, or floating down the black river! Beside him was Autifon Deliamber, perched on Lisamon's left shoulder. Valentine perceived the wizardry that had called him back from his swoon: the tips of three of the Vroon's tentacles were touching him, one to his forehead, one to his cheek, one to his chest.

He said, feeling immensely foolish, "You can put me down now."

"You are very weak, lordship," Lisamon rumbled.

"Not quite that weak, I think. Put me down."

Carefully, as though Valentine were nine hundred years old, Lisamon lowered him to the ground. At once, sweeping waves of dizziness rocked him, and he reached out to lean against the giant woman, who still hovered protectively close by. His teeth were chattering. His heavy robes clung to his damp, clammy skin like shrouds. He feared that if he closed his eyes only for an instant, that pool of darkness would rise up again and engulf him. But he forced himself toward a sort of steadiness, even if it were only a pretense. Old training asserted itself: he could not allow himself to be seen looking dazed and weak, no matter what sort of irrational terrors were roaring through his head.

He felt himself growing calmer after a moment, and looked around. They had taken him from the great hall. He was in some brightly lit corridor inlaid with a thousand intertwined and overlapping Pontifical emblems, the eye-baffling Labyrinth symbol repeated over and over. A mob of people clustered about him, looking anxious and dismayed: Tunigorn, Sleet, Hissune, and Shanamir of his own court, and some of the Pontifex's staff as well, Hornkast and old Dilifon and behind them half a dozen other bobbing yellow-masked heads.

"Where am I?" Valentine asked.

"Another moment and we'll be at your chambers, lordship," Sleet said.

"Have I been unconscious long?"

"Two or three minutes, only. You began to fall, while making your speech. But Hissune caught you, and Lisamon."

"It was the wine," Valentine said. "I suppose I had too much, a bowl of this and a bowl of that—"

"You are quite sober now," Deliamber pointed out. "And it is only a few minutes later."

"Let me believe it was the wine," said Valentine, "for a little while longer." The corridor swung leftward and there appeared before him the great carved door of his suite, chased with gold inlays of the starburst emblem over which his own LVC monogram had been engraved. "Where is Tisana?" he called.

"Here, my lord," said the dream-speaker, from some distance.

"Good. I want you inside with me. Also Deliamber and Sleet. No one else. Is that clear?"

"May I enter also?" said a voice out of the group of Pontifical officials.

It belonged to a thin-lipped gaunt man with strangely ashen skin, whom Valentine recognized after a moment as Sepulthrove, physician to the Pontifex Tyeveras. He shook his head. "I am grateful for your concern. But I think you are not needed."

"Such a sudden collapse, my lord—it calls for diagnosis—"

"There's some wisdom in that," Tunigorn observed quietly.

Valentine shrugged. "Afterward, then. First let me speak with my advisers, good Sepulthrove. And then you can tap my kneecaps a bit, if you think that it's necessary. Come— Tisana, Deliamber—"

He swept into his suite with the last counterfeit of regal poise he could muster, feeling a vast relief as the heavy door swung shut on the bustling throng in the corridor. He let out his breath in a long slow gust and dropped down, trembling in the release of tension, on the brocaded couch.

"Lordship?" Sleet said softly.

"Wait. Wait. Just let me be."

He rubbed his throbbing forehead and his aching eyes. The strain of feigning, out there, that he had made a swift and complete recovery from whatever had happened to him in the banquet hall had been expensive to his spirit. But gradually some of his true strength returned. He looked toward the dream-speaker. The robust old woman, thick-bodied and strong, seemed to him just then to be the fount of all comfort.

"Come, Tisana, sit next to me," Valentine said.

She settled down beside him and slipped her arm around his shoulders. Yes, he thought. Oh, yes, good! Warmth flowed back into his chilled soul, and the darkness receded. From him rushed a great torrent of love for Tisana, sturdy and reliable and wise, who in the days of his exile had been the first openly to hail him as *Lord* Valentine, when he had been still content to think of himself as Valentine the juggler. How many times in the years of his restored reign had she shared the mind-opening dream-wine with him, and had taken him in her arms to draw from him the secrets of the turbulent images that came to him in sleep! How often had she given him ease from the weight of kingship!

She said, "I was frightened greatly to see you fall, Lord Valentine, and you know I am not one who frightens easily. You say it was the wine?"

"So I said, out there."

"But it was not the wine, I think."

"No. Deliamber thinks it was a spell."

"Of whose making?" Tisana asked.

Valentine looked to the Vroon. "Well?"

Deliamber displayed a tension that Valentine had only rarely seen the little creature reveal: a troubled coiling and weaving of his innumerable tentacles, a strange glitter in his great yellow eyes, grinding motions of his birdlike beak. "I am at a loss for an answer," said Deliamber finally. "Just as not all dreams are sendings, so too is it the case that not all spells have makers."

"Some spells cast themselves, is that it?" Valentine asked.

"Not precisely. But there are spells that arise spontaneously—from within, my lord, within oneself, generated out of the empty places of the soul."

"What are you saying? That I put an enchantment on myself, Deliamber?"

Tisana said gently, "Dreams—spells—it is all the same thing, Lord Valentine. Certain auguries are making themselves known through you. Omens are forcing themselves into view. Storms are gathering, and these are the early harbingers."

"You see all that so soon? I had a troubled dream, you know, just before the banquet, and most certainly it was full of stormy omens and auguries and harbingers. But unless I've been talking of it in my sleep, I've told you nothing of it yet, have I?"

"I think you dreamed of chaos, my lord."

Valentine stared at her. "How could you know that?"

Shrugging, Tisana said, "Because chaos must come. We all recognize the truth of that. There is unfinished business in the world, and it cries out for finishing."

"The shapeshifters, you mean," Valentine muttered.

"I would not presume," the old woman said, "to advise you on matters of state—"

"Spare me such tact. From my advisers I expect advice, not tact."

"My realm is only the realm of dreams," said Tisana.

"I dreamed snow on Castle Mount, and a great earthquake that split the world apart."

"Shall I speak that dream for you, my lord?"

"How can you speak it, when we haven't yet had the dream-wine?"

"A speaking's not a good idea just now," said Deliamber firmly. "The Coronal's had visions enough for one night. He'd not be well served by drinking dream-wine now. I think this can easily wait until—"

"That dream needs no wine," said Tisana. "A child could speak it. Earthquakes? The shattering of the world? Why, you must prepare yourself for hard hours, my lord."

"What are you saying?"

It was Sleet who replied: "These are omens of war, lordship."

Valentine swung about and glared at the little man. "War?" he cried. "*War?* Must I do battle again? I was the first Coronal in eight thousand years to lead an army into the field; must I do it twice?"

"Surely you know, my lord," said Sleet, "that the war of the restoration was merely the first skirmish of the true war that must be fought, a war that has been in the making for many centuries, a war that I think you know cannot now be avoided."

"There are no unavoidable wars," Valentine said.

"Do you think so, my lord?"

The Coronal glowered bleakly at Sleet, but made no response. They were telling him what he had already concluded without their help, but did not wish to hear; and, hearing it anyway, he felt a terrible restlessness invading his soul. After a moment he rose and began to wander silently around the room. At the far end of the chamber was an enormous eerie sculpture, a great thing made of the curved bones of sea dragons, interwoven to meet in the form of the fingers of a pair of clasped upturned hands, or perhaps the interlocking fangs of some colossal demonic mouth. For a long while Valentine stood before it, idly stroking the gleaming polished bone. Unfinished business, Tisana had said. Yes. Yes. The Shapeshifters. Shapeshifters, Metamorphs, Piurivars, call them by whatever name you chose: the true natives of Majipoor, those from whom this wondrous world had been stolen by the settlers from the stars, fourteen thousand years before. For eight years, Valentine thought, I've struggled to understand the needs of those people. And I still know nothing at all.

He turned and said, "When I rose to speak, my mind was on what Hornkast the high spokesman just had said: the Coronal is the world, and the world is the Coronal. And suddenly I *became* Majipoor. Everything that was happening everywhere in the world was sweeping through my soul."

"You have experienced that before," Tisana said. "In dreams that I have spoken for you: when you said you saw twenty billion golden threads sprouting from the soil, and you held them all in your right hand. And another dream, when you spread your arms wide, and embraced the world, and—"

"This was different," Valentine said. "This time the world was falling apart."

"How so?"

"Literally. Crumbling into fragments. There was nothing left but a sea of darkness—into which I fell—"

"Hornkast spoke the truth," said Tisana quietly. "You *are* the world, lordship. Dark knowledge is finding its way to you, and it comes through the air from all the world about you. It is a sending, my lord: not of the Lady, nor of the King of Dreams, but of the world entire."

Valentine glanced toward the Vroon. "What do you say to that, Deliamber?"

"I have known Tisana fifty years, I think, and I have never yet heard foolishness from her lips."

"Then there is to be war?"

"I believe the war has already begun," said Deliamber.

2

Hissune would not soon forgive himself for coming late to the banquet. His first official event since being elevated to Lord Valentine's staff, and he hadn't managed to show up on time. That was inexcusable.

Some of it was his sister Ailimoor's fault. All the while he was trying to get into his fine new formal clothes, she kept running in, fussing with him, adjusting his shoulder chain, worrying about the length and cut of his tunic, finding scuff marks on his brilliantly polished boots that would be invisible to anyone's eyes but hers. She was fifteen, a very difficult age for girls—*all* ages seemed to be difficult for girls, Hissune sometimes thought—and these days she tended to be bossy, opinionated, preoccupied with trivial domestic detail.

So in her eagerness to make him perfect for the Coronal's banquet she helped to make him late. She spent what felt to him like a good twenty minutes simply fiddling with his emblem of office, the little golden starburst epaulet that he was supposed to wear on his left shoulder within the loop of the chain. She moved it endlessly a fraction of an inch this way or that to center it more exactly, until at last she said, "All right. That'll do. Here, see if you like it."

She snatched up her old hand-mirror, speckled and rusty where the backing was wearing away, and held it before him. Hissune caught a faint distorted glimpse of himself, looking very unfamiliar, all pomp and splendor, as though decked out for a pageant. The costume felt theatrical, stagy, unreal. And yet he was aware of a new kind of poise and authority seeping inward to his soul from his clothing. How odd, he thought, that a hasty fitting at a fancy Place of Masks tailor could produce such an instant transformation of personality—no longer Hissune the ragged hustling street-boy, no longer Hissune the restless and uncertain young clerk, but now Hissune the popinjay, Hissune the peacock, Hissune the proud companion of the Coronal.

And Hissune the unpunctual. If he hurried, though, he might still reach the Great Hall of the Pontifex on time.

But just then his mother Elsinome returned from work, and there was another small delay. She came into his room, a slight, dark-haired woman, pale and weary-looking, and stared at him in awe and wonder, as though someone had captured a comet and set it loose to whirl about her dismal flat. Her eyes were glowing, her features had a radiance he had never seen before.

"How magnificent you look, Hissune! How splendid!"

He grinned and spun about, better to show off his imperial finery. "It's almost absurd, isn't it? I look like a knight just down from Castle Mount!"

"You look like a prince! You look like a Coronal!"

"Ah, yes, Lord Hissune. But I'd need an ermine robe for that, I think, and a fine green doublet, and perhaps a great gaudy starburst pendant on my chest. Yet this is good enough for the moment, eh, mother?"

They laughed; and, for all her weariness, she seized him and swung him about in a wild little three-step dance. Then she released him and said, "But it grows late. You should have been off to the feast by this time!"

"I should have been, yes." He moved toward the door. "How strange all this is, eh, mother? To be going off to dine at the Coronal's table—to sit at his elbow—to journey with him on the grand processional—to dwell on Castle Mount—"

"So very strange, yes," said Elsinome quietly.

They all lined up—Elsinome, Ailimoor, his younger sister Maraune—and solemnly Hissune kissed them, and squeezed their hands, and sidestepped them when they tried to hug him, fearing they would rumple his robes; and he saw them staring at him again as though he were some godlike being, or at the very least the Coronal himself. It was quite as if he were no longer one of this family, or as if he never had been, but had descended from the sky to strut about these dreary rooms for a little while this afternoon. At times he almost felt that way himself—that he had not spent these eighteen years of his life in a few dingy rooms in the first ring of the Labyrinth, but indeed was and always had been Hissune of the Castle, knight and initiate, frequenter of the royal court, connoisseur of all its pleasures.

Folly. Madness. You must always remember who you are, he told himself, and where you started from.

But it was hard not to keep dwelling on the transformation that had come over their lives, he thought, while he was making his way down the endless spiraling staircase to the street. So much had changed. Once he and his mother both had worked the streets of the Labyrinth, she begging crowns from passing gentry for her hungry children, he rushing up to tourists and insistently offering to guide them, for half a royal or so, through the scenic wonders of the underground city. And now he was the Coronal's young protégé, and she, through his new connections, was steward of wines at the cafe of the Court of Globes. All achieved by luck, by extraordinary and improbable luck.

Or was it only luck? he wondered. That time so many years back, when he was ten and had thrust his services as a guide upon that tall fair-haired man, it had been convenient indeed for him that the stranger was none other than the Coronal Lord Valentine, overthrown and exiled and in the

Labyrinth to win the support of the Pontifex in his reconquest of the throne.

But that in itself might not have led anywhere. Hissune often asked himself what it was about him that had caught Lord Valentine's fancy, that caused the Coronal to remember him and have him located after the restoration, and be taken from the streets to work in the House of Records, and now to be summoned into the innermost sphere of his administration. His irreverence, perhaps. His quips, his cool, casual manner, his lack of awe for coronals and pontifexes, his ability, even at ten, to look out for himself. That must have impressed Lord Valentine. Those Castle Mount knights, Hissune thought, are all so polite, so dainty-mannered: I must have seemed more alien than a Ghayrog to him. And yet the Labyrinth is full of tough little boys. Any of them might have been the one who tugged at the Coronal's sleeve. But I was the one. Luck. Luck.

He emerged into the dusty little plaza in front of his house. Before him lay the narrow curving streets of the Guadeloom Court district where he had spent all the days of his life; above him rose the decrepit buildings, thousands of years old and lopsided with age, that formed the boundary palisade of his world. Under the harsh white lights, much too bright, almost crackling in their electric intensity—all this ring of the Labyrinth was bathed in that same fierce light, so little like that of the gentle golden-green sun whose rays never reached this city—the flaking gray masonry of the old buildings emanated a terrible weariness, a mineral fatigue. Hissune wondered if he had ever noticed before just how bleak and shabby this place was.

The plaza was crowded. Not many of the people of Guadeloom Court cared to spend their evenings penned up in their dim little flats, and so they flocked down here to mill aimlessly about in a kind of random patternless promenade. And as Hissune in his shimmering new clothes made his way through that promenade, it seemed that everyone that he had ever known was out there glaring at him, glowering, snickering, scowling. He saw Vanimoon, who was his own age to the hour and had once seemed almost like a brother to him, and Vanimoon's slender almond-eyed little sister, not so little anymore, and Heulan, and Heulan's three great hulking brothers, and Nikkilone, and tiny squinch-faced Ghisnet, and the beady-eyed Vroon who sold candied ghumba root, and

Confalume the pickpocket, and the old Ghayrog sisters that everyone thought were really Metamorphs, which Hissune had never believed, and this one and that one and more. All staring, all silently asking him, *Why are you putting on such airs, Hissune, why this pomp, why this splendor?*

He moved uneasily across the plaza, miserably aware that the banquet must be almost about to begin and he had an enormous distance downlevel to traverse. And everyone he had ever known stood in his way, staring at him.

Vanimoon was the first to cry out. "Where are you going, Hissune? To a costume ball?"

"He's off to the Isle, to play ninesticks with the Lady!"

"No, he's going to hunt sea-dragons with the Pontifex!"

"Let me by," Hissune said quietly, for they were pressing close upon him now.

"Let him by! Let him by!" they chorused gaily, but they did not move back.

"Where'd you get the fancy clothes, Hissune?" Ghisnet asked.

"Rented them," Heulan said.

"Stole them, you mean," said one of Heulan's brothers.

"Found a drunken knight in an alleyway and stripped him bare!"

"Get out of my way," said Hissune, holding his temper in check with more than a little effort. "I have something important to do."

"Something important! Something important!"

"He has an audience with the Pontifex!"

"The Pontifex is going to make Hissune a Duke!"

"Duke Hissune! Prince Hissune!"

"Why not Lord Hissune?"

"Lord Hissune! Lord Hissune!"

There was an ugly edge to their voices. Ten or twelve of them ringed him, pushing inward. Resentment and jealousy ruled them now. This flamboyant outfit of his, the shoulder chain, the epaulet, the boots, the cloak—it was too much for them, an arrogant way of underscoring the gulf that had opened between him and them. In another moment they'd be plucking at his tunic, tugging at the chain. Hissune felt the beginnings of panic. It was folly to try to reason with a mob, worse folly to attempt to force his way through. And of course it was hopeless to expect imperial proctors to be patrolling a neighborhood like this. He was on his own.

Vanimoon, who was the closest, reached toward Hissune's shoulder as though to give him a shove. Hissune backed away, but not before Vanimoon had left a grimy track along the pale green fabric of his cloak. Sudden astonishing fury surged through him. "Don't touch me again!" he yelled, angrily making the sign of the sea dragon at Vanimoon. "Don't any of you touch me!"

With a mocking laugh Vanimoon clawed for him a second time. Swiftly Hissune caught him by the wrist, clamping down with crushing force.

"Hoy! Let go!" Vanimoon grunted.

Instead Hissune pulled Vanimoon's arm upward and back, and spun him roughly around. Hissune had never been much of a fighter—he was too small and lithe for that, and preferred to rely on speed and wits—but he could be strong enough when anger kindled him. Now he felt himself throbbing with violent energy. In a low tense voice he said, "If I have to, Vanimoon, I'll break it. I don't want you or anybody else touching me."

"You're hurting me!"

"Will you keep your hands to yourself?"

"Man can't even stand to be teased—"

Hissune twisted Vanimoon's arm as far up as it would go. "I'll pull it right off you if I have to."

"Let—go—"

"If you'll keep your distance."

"All right. All right!"

Hissune released him and caught his breath. His heart was pounding and he was soaked with sweat: he did not dare to wonder how he must look. After all of Ailimoor's endless fussing over him, too.

Vanimoon, stepping back, sullenly rubbed his wrist. "Afraid I'll soil his fancy clothes. Doesn't want common people's dirt on them."

"That's right. Now get out of my way. I'm late enough already."

"For the Coronal's banquet, I suppose?"

"Exactly. I'm late for the Coronal's banquet."

Vanimoon and the others gaped at him, their expressions hovering midway between scorn and awe. Hissune pushed his way past them and strode across the plaza.

The evening, he thought, was off to a very bad start.

3

On a day in high summer when the sun hung all but motionless over Castle Mount, the Coronal Lord Valentine rode out joyously into the flower-shimmering meadows below the Castle's southern wing.

He went alone, not even taking with him his consort the Lady Carabella. The members of his council objected strongly to his going anywhere unguarded, even within the Castle, let alone venturing outside the sprawling perimeter of the royal domain. Whenever the issue arose, Elidath pounded hand against fist and Tunigorn rose up tall as though prepared to block Valentine's departure with his own body, and little Sleet turned positively black in the face with fury and reminded the Coronal that his enemies had succeeded in overthrowing him once, and might yet again.

"Ah, surely I'd be safe anywhere on Castle Mount!" Valentine insisted.

But always they had had their way, until today. The safety of the Coronal of Majipoor, they insisted, was paramount. And so whenever Lord Valentine went riding, Elidath or Tunigorn or perhaps Stasilaine rode always beside him, as they had since they were boys together, and half a dozen members of the Coronal's guard lurked a respectful distance behind.

This time, though, Valentine had somehow eluded them all. He was unsure how he had managed it: but when the overpowering urge to ride had come upon him in midmorning he simply strode into the south-wing stables, saddled his mount without the help of a groom, and set out across the green porcelain cobblestones of a strangely empty Dizimaule Plaza, passing swiftly under the great arch and into the lovely fields that flanked the Grand Calintane Highway. No one stopped him. No one called out to him. It was as though some wizardry had rendered him invisible.

Free, if only for an hour or two! The Coronal threw his head back and laughed as he had not laughed in a long while, and slapped his mount's flank, and sped across the meadows,

16

moving so swiftly that the hooves of his great purple beast seemed scarcely to touch the myriad blossoms all about.

Ah, this was the life!

He glanced over his shoulder. The fantastic bewildering pile of the Castle was diminishing rapidly behind him, though it still seemed immense at this distance, stretching over half the horizon, an incomprehensibly huge edifice of some forty thousand rooms that clung like some vast monster to the summit of the Mount. He could not remember any occasion since his restoration to the throne when he had been out of that castle without his bodyguard. Not even *once*.

Well, he was out of it now. Valentine looked off to his left, where the thirty-mile-high crag that was Castle Mount sloped away at a dizzying angle, and saw the pleasure-city of High Morpin gleaming below, a webwork of airy golden threads. Ride down there, spend a day at the games? Why not? He was free! Ride on beyond, if he chose, and stroll in the gardens of Tolingar Barrier, among the halatingas and tanigales and sithereels, and come back with a yellow alabandina flower in his cap as a cockade? Why not? The day was his. Ride to Furible in time for the feeding-time of the stone birds, ride to Stee and sip golden wine atop Thimin Tower, ride to Bombifale or Peritole or Banglecode—

His mount seemed equal to any such labor. It carried him hour after hour without fatigue. When he came to High Morpin he tethered it at Confalume Fountain, where shafts of tinted water slender as spears shot hundreds of feet into the air while maintaining, by some ancient magic, their rigid shapes, and on foot he strode along the streets of closely woven golden cable until he came to the place of the mirror slides, where he and Voriax had tested their skills so often when they were boys. But when he went out on the glittering slides no one took any notice of him, as though they felt it rude to stare at a Coronal doing the slides, or as though he were still somehow cloaked by that strange invisibility. That seemed odd, but he was not greatly troubled by it. When he was done with the slides he thought he might go on to the power tunnels or the juggernauts, but then it seemed just as pleasing to continue his journey, and a moment later he was upon his mount once more, and riding on to Bombifale. In that ancient and most lovely of cities, where curving walls of the deepest burnt-orange sandstone were topped with pale towers tapering to elegant points, they had come to him one day long ago when he had been on holiday alone, five of them, his friends, and found him in a tavern of vaulted onyx and polished alabaster, and when he greeted them with surprise and laughter they responded by kneeling to him and making the starburst sign and crying, "Valentine! Lord Valentine! Hail, Lord Valentine!" To which his first thought was that he was being mocked, for he was not the king but the king's younger brother, and he knew he never would be king, and did not want to be. And though he was a man who did not get angry easily, he grew angry then, that his friends should intrude on him with this cruel nonsense. But then he saw how pale their faces were, how strange their eyes, and his anger left him, and grief and fear entered his soul: and that was how he learned that Voriax his brother was dead and he had been named Coronal in his place. In Bombifale this day ten years later, it seemed to Valentine that every third man he met had the face of Voriax, black-bearded and hard-eyed and ruddy-faced, and that troubled him, so he left Bombifale quickly.

He did not stop again, for there was so much to see, so many hundreds of miles to traverse. He went on, past one city and another in a serene untroubled way, as if he were floating, as if he were flying. Now and again he had an astounding view from the brink of some precipice of all the Mount spread out below him, its Fifty Cities somehow visible every one at once, and the innumerable foothill towns too, and the Six Rivers, and the broad plain of Alhanroel sweeping off to the faraway Inner Sea—such splendor, such immensity. Majipoor! Surely it was the most beautiful of all the worlds to which mankind had spread in the thousands of years of the great movement outward from Old Earth. And all given into his hand, all placed in his charge, a responsibility from which he would never shrink.

But as he rode onward an unexpected mystery began to impinge upon his soul. The air grew dark and cold, which was strange, for on Castle Mount the climate was forever controlled to yield an eternal balmy springtime. Then something like chill spittle struck him on the cheek, and he searched about for a challenger, and saw none, and was struck again, and again: snow, he realized finally, sweeping hard against him on the breast of the frosty wind. Snow, on Castle Mount? Harsh winds?

And worse: the earth was groaning like a monster in

labor. His mount, which had never disobeyed him, now reared back in fear, made a weird whinnying sound, shook its heavy head in slow, ponderous dismay. Valentine heard the booming of distant thunder, and closer at hand a strange cracking noise, and he saw giant furrows appearing in the ground. Everything was madly heaving and churning. An earthquake? The entire Mount was whipping about like a dragon-ship's mast when the hot dry winds blew from the south. The sky itself, black and leaden, took on sudden weight.

What is this? Oh, good Lady my mother, what is happening on Castle Mount?

Valentine clung desperately to his bucking, panicky animal. The whole world seemed to be shattering, crumbling, sliding, flowing. It was his task to hold it together, clutching its giant continents close against his breast, keeping the seas in their beds, holding back the rivers that rose in ravening fury against the helpless cities—

And he could not sustain it all.

It was too much for him. Mighty forces thrust whole provinces aloft, and set them clashing against their neighbors. Valentine reached forth to keep them in their places, wishing he had iron hoops with which to bind them. But he could not do it. The land shivered and rose and split, and black clouds of dust covered the face of the sun, and he was powerless to quell that awesome convulsion. One man alone could not bind this vast planet and halt its sundering. He called his comrades to his aid. "Lisamon! Elidath!"

No response. He called again, and again, but his voice was lost in the booming and the grinding.

All stability had gone from the world. It was as though he were riding the mirror slides in High Morpin, where you had to dance and hop lively to stay upright as the whirling slides tilted and jerked, but that was a game and this was true chaos, the roots of the world uprooted. The heaving tossed him down and rolled him over and over, and he dug his fingers fiercely into the soft yielding earth to keep from sliding into the crevasses that opened beside him. Out of those yawning cracks came terrifying sounds of laughter, and a purple glow that seemed to rise from a sun that the earth had swallowed. Angry faces floated in the air above him, faces he almost recognized, but they shifted about disconcertingly as he studied them, eyes becoming noses, noses becoming ears. Then behind those nightmare faces he saw another that he knew, shining dark hair, gentle warm eyes. The Lady of the Isle, the sweet mother.

"It is enough," she said. "Awaken now, Valentine!"

"And am I dreaming, then?"

"Of course. Of course."

"Then I should stay, and learn what I can from this dream!"

"You have learned enough, I think. Awaken now."

Yes. It was enough: any more such knowledge might make an end of him. As he had been taught long ago, he brought himself upward from this unexpected sleep and sat up, blinking, struggling to shed his grogginess and confusion. Images of titanic cataclysm still reverberated in his soul; but gradually he perceived that all was peaceful here. He lay on a richly brocaded couch in a high-vaulted room all green and gold. What had halted the earthquake? Where was his mount? Who had brought him here? Ah, *they* had! Beside him crouched a pale, lean, white-haired man with a ragged scar running the length of one cheek. Sleet. And Tunigorn standing just to the rear, frowning, heavy eyebrows contracting into a single furry ridge. "Calm, calm, calm," Sleet was saying. "It's all right, now. You're awake."

Awake? A dream, then, only a dream?

So it would seem. He was not on Castle Mount at all. There had been no snowstorm, no earthquake, no clouds of dust blotting out the sun. A dream, yes! But such a terrible dream, frighteningly vivid and compelling, so powerful that he found it difficult now to return to reality.

"Where is this place?" Valentine asked.

"Labyrinth, lordship."

Where? The Labyrinth? What, then, had he been spirited away from Castle Mount while he slept? Valentine felt sweat bursting from his brow. The Labyrinth? Ah, yes, yes. The truth of it closed on him like a hand on his throat. The Labyrinth, yes. He remembered, now. The state visit, of which this was, the Divine be thanked, the final night. That ghastly banquet still to endure. He could not hide from it any longer. The Labyrinth, the Labyrinth, the confounded Labyrinth: he was in it, down in the bottommost level of all. The walls of the suite glowed with handsome murals of the Castle, the Mount, the Fifty Cities: scenes so lovely that they were a mockery to him now. So distant from Castle Mount, so far from the sun's sweet warmth—

Ah, what a sour business, he thought, to awaken from a dream of destruction and calamity, only to find yourself in the most dismal place in the world!

4

Six hundred miles east of the brilliant crystalline city of Dulorn, in the marshy valley known as Prestimion Vale, where a few hundred families of Ghayrogs raised lusavender and rice on widely scattered plantations, it was getting to be the midyear harvest season. The glossy, swollen, black lusavender pods, nearly ripe, hung in thick clusters at the ends of curving stems that rose from the half-submerged fields.

For Aximaan Threysz, the oldest and shrewdest of the lusavender farmers of Prestimion Vale, there was an excitement about this harvest like nothing she had felt in decades. The experiment in protoplast augmentation that she had begun three seasons back under the guidance of the government agricultural agent was reaching its culmination now. This season she had given her entire plantation over to the new kind of lusavender: and there were the pods, twice normal size, ready to be stripped! No one else in the Vale had dared to take the risk, not until Aximaan Threysz had checked things out. And now she had; and soon her success would be confirmed; and they would all weep, oh, yes! when she came to market a week ahead of everyone else with double her usual volume of seed!

As she stood deep in mud by the edge of her fields, pressing her finger-ridges into the closest pods and trying to determine how soon to start the picking, one of her eldest son's boys came running up with a message: "Father says to tell you he's just heard in town that the agricultural agent's on his way from Mazadone! He's reached Helkaplod already. Tomorrow he'll ride to Sijaneel."

"Then he'll be in the Vale by Twoday," she said. "Good. Perfect!" Her forked tongue began to flicker. "Go, child, run back to your father. Tell him we'll hold the feast for the agent on Seaday and we'll begin the harvest on Fourday. And I want the whole family to gather in the plantation house in half an hour. Go, now! Run."

The plantation had been in the family of Aximaan Threysz since Lord Confalume's time. It covered an irregularly triangular area that stretched for five miles or so along the banks of Havilbove Fluence, jigged in a southeasterly way down to the outskirts of Mazadone Forest Preserve, and swung by roundabout curves back toward the river to the north. Within that zone, Aximaan Threysz ruled as lord absolute over her five sons and nine daughters, her uncountable grandchildren, and the twenty-odd Liimen and Vroons who were her farm-hands. When Aximaan Threysz said it was seedtime, they went out and seeded. When Aximaan Threysz said it was harvest time, they went out and reaped. At the great house at the edge of the androdragma grove, dinner was served at the time Aximaan Threysz came to table, whenever that time happened to be. Even the family sleeping schedules were subject to Aximaan Threysz's decrees: for Ghayrogs are hibernators, but she could not have the whole family asleep at once. The eldest son knew he must always be awake during the first six weeks of his mother's annual winter rest; the eldest daughter took command for the remaining six weeks. Aximaan Threysz assigned sleep-times to the other family members according to her sense of what was appropriate to the plantation's needs. No one ever questioned her. Even when she was young—an impossibly long time ago, when Ossier was Pontifex and Lord Tyeveras had the Castle—she had been the one to whom all others turned, even her father, even her mate, in time of crisis. She had outlived both of those, and some of her offspring as well, and many a Coronal had come and gone on Castle Mount, and still Aximaan Threysz went on and on. Her thick scaly hide had lost its high gloss and was purplish with age now, the writhing fleshy serpents of her hair had faded from jet black to pale gray, her chilly unblinking green eyes were clouded and milky, but yet she moved unceasingly through the routines of the farm.

Nothing of any value could be raised on her land except rice and lusavender, and even those were not easy. The rainstorms of the far north found easy access to Dulorn Province down the great funnel of the Rift, and, though the city of Dulorn itself lay in a dry zone, the territory to its west, amply watered and well drained, was fertile and rich. But the district around Prestimion Vale on the eastern side of the Rift was another sort of place entirely, dank and swampy, its soil a heavy bluish muck. With careful timing, though, it was possible to plant rice at the end of winter just ahead of the spring floods, and to put in lusavender in late spring and again at the end of autumn. No one in the region knew the rhythm of the seasons better than Aximaan Threysz, and only the most rash of farmers would set his seedlings out before word had come that she had begun her planting.

Imperious though she was, overwhelming in her prestige and authority, Aximaan Threysz nevertheless had one trait that the people of the Vale found incomprehensible: she deferred to the provincial agricultural agent as though he were the fount of all knowledge and she the merest apprentice. Two or three times a year the agent came out from the provincial capital of Mazadone, riding a circuit through the swamplands, and his first stop in the Vale was always Aximaan Threysz's plantation. She housed him in the great house, she broached the casks of fireshower wine and brandied niyk, she sent her grandsons off to Havilbove Fluence to catch the tasty little hiktigans that scurried between the rocks of the rapids, she ordered the frozen bidlak steaks to be thawed and roasted over logs of aromatic thwale. And when the feasting was done she drew the agent aside and talked far into the night with him of such things as fertilizers and seedling grafts and harvesting machinery, while her daughters Heynok and Jarnok sat by, taking down notes of every word.

It mystified everyone that Aximaan Threysz, who surely knew more about the planting of lusavender than anyone who had ever lived, would care a straw for what some little government employee could tell her. But her family knew why. "We have our ways, and we become set in our ways," she often said. "We do what we have done before, because it has worked for us before. We plant our seeds, we tend our seedlings, we watch over the ripening, we harvest our crop, and then we begin all over in the same way. And if each crop is no smaller than the crop before, we think we are doing well. But in fact we are failing, if we merely equal what we have done before. There is no standing still in this world: to stand still is to sink into the mud."

So it was that Aximaan Threysz subscribed to the agricultural journals, and sent her grandchildren off now and then to the university, and listened most carefully to what the provincial agent might have to say. And year by year the method of her farming underwent small changes, and year by year the sacks of lusavender seeds that Aximaan Threysz shipped off to market in Mazadone were greater in number than the year before, and the shining grains of rice were heaped ever higher in her storehouses. For there was always some better way of doing things to be learned, and Aximaan Threysz made sure she learned it. "We are Majipoor," she said again and again. "The great cities rest on foundations of grain. Without us, Ni-moya and Pidruid and Khyntor and Piliplok would be wastelands. And the cities grow ever larger every year: so we must work ever harder to feed them, is that not so? We have no choice in that: it is the will of the Divine. Is that not so?"

She had outlasted fifteen or twenty agents by now. They came out as young men, brimming over with the latest notions but often shy about offering them to her. "I don't know what I could possibly teach you," they liked to tell her. "I'm the one who should be learning from you, Aximaan Threysz!" So she had to go through the same routine again and again, putting them at their ease, convincing them that she was sincerely interested in hearing of the latest techniques.

It was always a nuisance when the old agent retired and some youngster took over. As she moved deeper into vast old age it became ever harder to establish any sort of useful relationship with the new ones until several seasons had gone by. But that had not been a problem when Caliman Hayn had turned up two years ago. He was a young human, thirty or forty or fifty years old—anyone short of seventy seemed young to Aximaan Threysz these days—with a curiously blunt, offhand manner that was much to her liking. He showed no awe for her and did not seem interested in flattering her. "They tell me you are the farmer most willing to try new things," he said brusquely, no more than ten minutes after they had met. "What would you say to a process that can double the size of lusavender seeds without harming their flavor?"

"I would say that I am being gulled," she said. "It sounds considerably too good to be true."

"Nevertheless the process exists."

"Does it, now?"

"We're ready to put it into limited experimental use. I see by my predecessors' files that you're known for your willingness to experiment."

"So I am," said Aximaan Threysz. "What sort of thing is this?"

It was, he said, something called protoplast augmentation, which involved using enzymes to digest the cell walls of plants to give access to the genetic material within. That material then could undergo manipulation, after which the cellular matter, the protoplast, was placed in a culture medium and allowed to regenerate its cell wall. From that single cell an entire new plant with greatly improved characteristics could be grown.

"I thought such skills were lost on Majipoor thousands of years ago," Aximaan Threysz said.

"Lord Valentine has been encouraging some revival of interest in the ancient sciences."

"Lord Valentine?"

"The Coronal, yes," said Caliman Hayn.

"Ah, the Coronal!" Aximaan Threysz looked away. Valentine? Valentine? She would have said the Coronal's name was Voriax; but a moment's thought and she recalled that Voriax was dead. Yes, and a Lord Valentine had replaced him, she had heard, and as she gave it more thought she remembered that something odd had happened to that Valentine—was he the one who had had his body exchanged with another man's? Probably that was the one. But such people as Coronals meant very little to Aximaan Threysz, who had not left Prestimion Vale in twenty or thirty years and to whom Castle Mount and its Coronals were so far away that they might just as well be mythical. What mattered to Aximaan Threysz was the growing of rice and lusavender.

The imperial botanical laboratories, Caliman Hayn told her, had bred an enhanced clone of lusavender that needed field research under normal farming conditions. He invited Aximaan Threysz to collaborate in this research—in return for which he would agree not to offer the new plant to anyone else in Prestimion Vale until she had had the chance to establish it in all her fields.

It was irresistible. She received from him a packet of astonishingly immense lusavender seeds, great shiny things as big around as a Skandar's eye, and planted them in a remote corner of her land, where there was no likelihood of their cross-pollinating with her normal lusavenders. The seeds sprouted rapidly and from them came plants that differed from the usual kind only in having stems of a thickness two or three times normal. When they flowered, though, the ruffled purple blossoms were enormous, as broad as saucers, and the flowers brought forth pods of awesome length, that at harvest time yielded huge quantities of the giant seeds. Aximaan Threysz was tempted to use them for the autumn planting, and cover all her acreage with the new kind of lusavender in order to reap an amazing bumper crop next winter. But she could not, for she had agreed to turn most of the oversize seed over to Caliman Hayn for laboratory study in Mazadone. He left her enough to plant perhaps a fifth of her land. This season, however, she was instructed to mix the augmented plants among the normal ones to induce interbreeding: the augmented characteristics were thought to be dominant, but that had never been tested on so large a scale.

Though Aximaan Threysz forbade her family to speak of the experiment in Prestimion Vale, it was impossible for long to keep the other farmers from learning of it. The thick-stemmed second-generation plants that sprang up everywhere on her plantation could hardly be concealed, and in one way and another, news of what Aximaan Threysz was doing spread through the Vale. Curious neighbors wangled invitations and stared at the new lusavender in amazement.

But they were suspicious. "Plants like that, they'll suck all the nourishment from the soil in two or three years," some said. "She keeps it up, she'll turn her place into a desert." Others thought the giant seeds surely would yield tasteless or bitter lusavender-meal. A few argued that Aximaan Threysz generally knew what she was doing. But even they were content to let her be the pioneer.

At winter's end she harvested her crop: normal seeds, which were sent off to market as usual, and giant ones, which were bagged and set aside for planting. The third season would tell the tale, for some of the big seeds were of the pure clone and some, probably most, were hybrids between normal and augmented lusavender; and it remained to be seen what sort of plants the hybrid seeds would produce.

In late winter came the time for planting rice, before the floods arrived. When that was done, the higher and drier lands of the plantation received the lusavender seeds; and all through the spring and summer she watched the thick stems rising, the huge flowers unfolding, the heavy pods elongating and turning dark. From time to time she broke open a pod and peered at the soft green seeds. They were large, no question about that. But their flavor? What if they had no flavor, or a foul one? She had gambled an entire season's production on that.

Well, the answer would be at hand soon enough.

On Starday came word that the agricultural agent was approaching, and would arrive at the plantation, as expected, on Twoday. But the same report brought puzzling and disturbing news: for the agent who was coming was not Caliman Hayn, but someone named Yerewain Noor. Aximaan Threysz could not understand that. Hayn was too young to have retired. And it bothered her to have him vanish just as the protoplast experiment was nearing its end.

Yerewain Noor turned out to be even younger than Hayn, and annoyingly callow. He began at once to tell her how honored he was to meet her, with all the usual rhetorical flourishes, but she cut him off.

"Where's the other man?" she demanded.

No one seemed to know, Noor said. Lamely he explained that Hayn had gone off without warning three months ago, saying nothing to anyone and dumping an enormous administrative mess on the rest of the department. "We're still figuring it all out. Evidently he was mixed up in a bunch of experimental studies, but we don't know what sort or with whom, and—"

"One of them took place here," said Aximaan Threysz coldly. "Field testing of protoplast-augmented lusavender."

Noor groaned. "The Divine spare me! How many more of Hayn's little private projects am I going to stumble into? Protoplast-augmented lusavender, is it?"

"You sound as if you've never heard the term."

"I've heard it, yes. But I can't say I know much about it."

"Come with me," Aximaan Threysz said, and marched off, past the paddies where the rice now stood hip-high, and on into the lusavender fields. Anger sped her stride: the young agricultural agent was hard pressed to match her pace. As she went she told him about the packet of giant seeds Hayn had brought her, the planting of the new clone on her land, the interbreeding with normal lusavender, the generation of hybrids now coming to ripening. In a moment more they reached the first rows of lusavender. Suddenly she halted, appalled, horrified.

"The Lady protect us all!" she cried.

"What is it?"

"Look! *Look!*"

For once Aximaan Threysz's sense of timing had failed her. Most unexpectedly the hybrid lusavender had begun to throw seed, two weeks or more ahead of the likely day. Under the fierce summer sun the great pods were starting to split, cracking open with an ugly sound like the snapping of bones. Each, as it popped, hurled its huge seeds almost with the force of bullets in every direction; they flew thirty or forty feet through the air and disappeared in the thick muck that covered the flooded fields. There was no halting that process: within an hour all the pods would be open, the harvest would be lost.

But that was far from the worst of it.

Forth from the pods came not only seeds but a fine brown powder that Aximaan Threysz knew only too well. Wildly she rushed into the field, paying no attention to the seeds that crashed with stinging impact against her scaly skin. Seizing a pod that had not yet split, she broke it open, and a cloud of the powder rose toward her face. Yes. Yes. Lusavender smut! Each pod held at least a cupful of spores; and as pod after pod yielded to the heat of the day, the brown spores hovering over the field became a visible stain on the air, until they were swept away by the lightest of breezes.

Yerewain Noor knew what was happening too. "Call out your field hands!" he cried. "You've got to torch this stuff!"

"Too late," said Aximaan Threysz in a sepulchral voice. "No hope now. Too late, too late, too late. What can hold the spores back now?" Her land was infected beyond repair. And in an hour the spores would be spread all through the Vale. "It's all over with us, can't you see?"

"But lusavender smut was wiped out long ago!" Noor said in a foolish voice.

Aximaan Threysz nodded. She remembered it well: the fires, the sprayings, the breeding of smut-resistant clones, the roguing out of any plant that held the genetic predisposition to harbor the lethal fungus. Seventy, eighty, ninety years ago: how they had worked to rid the world of that blight! And here it was again, in these hybrid plants. These plants alone in all Majipoor, she thought, were capable of providing a home for lusavender smut. Her plants, so lovingly grown, so skillfully tended. By her own hand had she brought the smut back into the world, and set it free to blight her neighbors' crops.

"Hayn!" she roared. "Hayn, where are you? What have you done to me?"

She wished she could die, now, here, before what was about to happen could unfold. But she knew she would not be that lucky; for long life had been her blessing, and now it was her curse. The popping of the pods resounded in her ears like the guns of an advancing army, rampaging across the Vale. She had lived one year too long, she thought: long enough to see the end of the world.

5

Downward Hissune traveled, feeling rumpled and sweaty and apprehensive, through passageways and liftshafts he had known all his life, and soon the shabby world of the outermost ring was far behind him. He descended through level after level of wonders and marvels to which he had not given a second glance in years: Court of Columns, Hall of Winds, Place of Masks, Court of Pyramids, Court of Globes, the Arena, House of Records. People came here from Castle Mount or Alaisor or Stoien, or even from impossibly distant and supposedly fabulous Ni-moya on the other continent, and wandered around dazed and stupefied, lost in admiration of the ingenuity that had devised and constructed such bizarre architectural splendors so far underground. But to Hissune it was only the drab and dreary old Labyrinth. For him it had neither charm or mystery: it was simply his home.

The big pentagonal plaza in front of the House of Records marked the lower limit of the public zone of the Labyrinth. Below, all was reserved for government officials. Hissune passed beneath the great green-glowing screen on the wall of the House of Records that listed all the Pontifexes, all the Coronals—the two rows of inscriptions stretching up virtually beyond the reach of the keenest eye, somewhere far up there the names of Dvorn and Melikand and Barhold and Stiamot of thousands of years ago, and down here the entries for Kinniken and Ossier and Tyeveras, Malibor and Voriax and Valentine—and on the far side of the imperial roster Hissune presented his credentials to the puffy-faced masked Hjorts who kept the gateway, and down he went into the deepest realm of the Labyrinth. Past the warrens and burrows of the middle bureaucracy, past the courts of the high ministers, past the tunnels that led to the great ventilating systems on

which all this depended. Again and again he was stopped at
checkpoints and asked to identify himself. Here in the imperial sector they took matters of security very seriously. Somewhere in these depths the Pontifex himself had his lair—a
huge spherical glass globe, so it was said, in which the crazy
old monarch sat enthroned amidst the network of life-support
mechanisms that had kept him alive far past his time. Did
they fear assassins? Hissune wondered. If what he had heard
was true, it would be merely the Divine's own mercy to pull
the plug on the old Pontifex and let poor Tyeveras return at
last to the Source: Hissune could not understand what possible reason there could be to keep him living on like that,
decade after decade, in such madness, in such senility.

At last, breathless and frayed, Hissune arrived at the
threshold of the Great Hall in the uttermost depths of the
Labyrinth. He was hideously late, perhaps an hour.

Three colossal shaggy Skandars in the uniform of the
Coronal's guard barred his way. Hissune, shriveling under
the fierce supercilious stares of the gigantic four-armed beings,
had to fight back the impulse to drop to his knees and beg
their forgiveness. Somehow he regained a shred or two of his
self-respect, and, trying his best to stare back just as
superciliously—no easy chore, when he had to meet the gaze
of creatures nine feet high—he announced himself as a
member of Lord Valentine's staff, and an invited guest.

He half expected them to burst into guffaws and swat
him away like some little buzzing insect. But no: gravely they
examined his epaulet, and consulted some documents they
held, and favored him with great sweeping bows, and sent
him onward through the huge brass-bound doorway.

Finally! The Coronal's banquet!

Just within the door stood a resplendently garbed Hjort
with great goggling golden eyes and bizarre orange-daubed
whiskers sprouting from his rough-skinned grayish face. This
astonishing-looking individual was Vinorkis, the Coronal's
majordomo, who saluted now with a great flourish and cried,
"Ah! The Initiate Hissune!"

"Not yet an initiate," Hissune tried to tell him, but the
Hjort had already swung grandly about and was on his way
down the center aisle, not looking back. With numb-legged
strides Hissune followed him.

He felt impossibly conspicuous. There must have been
five thousand people in the room, seated at round tables that

held a dozen or so each, and he imagined that every eye was fastened on him. To his horror, he was no more than twenty paces into the room when he heard laughter beginning to rise, softly at first, then more heartily, and then waves of mirth that rolled from one side of the room to the other, crashing against him with stunning impact. He had never before heard such a vast roaring noise: it was the way he imagined the sea to sound as it flailed some wild northern coast.

The Hjort marched on and on, for what seemed like a mile and a half, and Hissune grimly marched on behind him through that ocean of merriment, wishing he were half an inch high. But after a while he realized that these people were laughing not at him but at a pack of dwarfish acrobats who were attempting with deliberate clownishness to form a human pyramid, and he grew less uneasy. Then the high dais came into view, and there was Lord Valentine himself beckoning to him, smiling, indicating the empty seat close by his side. Hissune thought he would weep from sheer relief. Everything was going to be all right after all.

"Your lordship!" Vinorkis boomed. "The Initiate Hissune!"

Hissune sank wearily and gratefully into his seat, just as an enormous round of applause for the acrobats, who were done with their act, resounded in the hall. A steward handed him a brimming bowl of some glistening golden wine, and as he put it to his lips, others around the table lifted their own bowls in a salute of welcome. Yesterday morning, during the brief and astonishing conversation with Lord Valentine in which the Coronal had invited him to join his staff on Castle Mount, Hissune had seen a few of these people at a distance, but there had been no time for introductions. Now they were actually giving him greeting—him!—and introducing themselves. But they needed no introduction, for these were the heroes of Lord Valentine's glorious war of restoration, and everyone knew who they were.

That huge warrior-woman sitting beside him was surely Lisamon Hultin, the Coronal's personal bodyguard, who, so the story went, once had cut Lord Valentine free of the belly of a sea dragon after he had been swallowed. And the amazingly pale-skinned little man with the white hair and the scarred face was, Hissune knew, the famous Sleet, juggling tutor to Lord Valentine in the days of exile; and the keen-eyed, heavy-browed man was the master archer Tunigorn of

Castle Mount; and the small many-tentacled Vroon had to be
the wizard Deliamber; and that man hardly older than Hissune
himself, with the freckled face, was very likely the onetime
herdboy Shanamir; and that slender, dignified Hjort must be
Grand Admiral Asenhart—yes, these were the famous ones,
and Hissune, who once had thought himself immune to any
sort of awe, found himself very much awed indeed to be of
their company now.

Immune to awe? Why, he had once walked up to Lord
Valentine himself and shamelessly extorted half a royal from
him for a tour of the Labyrinth, and three crowns more to
find him lodgings in the outer ring. He had felt no awe then.
Coronals and Pontifexes were simply men with more power
and money than ordinary people, and they attained their
thrones through the good luck of being born into the Castle
Mount aristocracy and making their way through the ranks
with just the right happy accidents to take them to the top.
You didn't even have to be particularly smart to be a Coronal,
Hissune had noticed years ago. After all, just in the last
twenty years or so, Lord Malibor had gone off to harpoon sea
dragons and had stupidly gotten himself eaten by one, and
Lord Voriax had died just as foolishly from a stray bolt that
struck him down while he was out hunting in the forest, and
his brother Lord Valentine, who was reputed to be fairly
intelligent, had been witless enough to go drinking and
carousing with the son of the King of Dreams, thereby letting
himself be drugged and wiped clean of his memory and
dumped from his throne. Feel awe for such as those? Why, in
the Labyrinth any seven-year-old who conducted himself
with such casual regard for his own welfare would be regarded
as a hopeless idiot.

But Hissune had observed that some of his early irreverence seemed to have worn away over the years. When one is
ten and has lived by one's wits in the streets since the age of
five or six, it is easy enough to thumb one's nose at power.
But he no longer was ten, and he no longer roved the streets.
His perspective was a little deeper these days: and he knew it
was no small thing to be Coronal of Majipoor, and no easy
task. So when Hissune looked toward that broad-shouldered,
golden-haired man, seeming both regal and gentle at once,
who wore the green doublet and ermine robe of the world's
second highest office, and when he considered that that man,
only ten feet from him, was the Coronal Lord Valentine, who

had chosen him out of all Majipoor to join this group tonight, he felt something very like a shiver traveling down his back, and he admitted finally to himself that what that shiver was was awe: for the office of the kingship, and for the person of Lord Valentine, and for the mysterious chain of happenstance that had brought a mere boy of the Labyrinth into this august company.

He sipped his wine and felt a warm glow spread through his soul. What did the evening's earlier troubles matter? He was here now, and welcome. Let Vanimoon and Heulan and Ghisnet eat their hearts out with envy! He was here, among the great ones, beginning his ascent toward the summit of the world, and soon he would be attaining heights from which the Vanimoons of his childhood would be altogether invisible.

In moments, though, that sense of well-being was completely gone from him, and he found himself tumbling back into confusion and dismay.

The first thing that went wrong was nothing more than a minor blunder, absurd but forgivable, scarcely his fault at all. Sleet had remarked on the obvious anxiety the Pontifical officials displayed every time they looked toward the Coronal's table: plainly they were madly fearful that Lord Valentine was not sufficiently enjoying himself. And Hissune, newly radiant with wine and gloriously happy to be at the banquet at last, had brashly blurted out, "They ought to be worried! They know they'd better make a good impression, or they'll be out in the cold when Lord Valentine becomes Pontifex!"

There were gasps all around the table. Everyone stared at him as though he had uttered some monstrous blasphemy— all but the Coronal, who clamped his lips together in the manner of one who has unexpectedly found a toad in his soup, and turned away.

"Did I say something wrong?" Hissune asked.

"Hush!" Lisamon Hultin whispered fiercely, and the mountainous Amazon woman nudged him urgently in the ribs.

"But is it not so that one day Lord Valentine will be Pontifex? And when that happens, won't he want to install a staff of his own?"

Lisamon nudged him again, so emphatically that she all but knocked him from his seat. Sleet glared belligerently at him, and Shanamir said in a sharp whisper, "Enough! You're only making it worse for yourself."

Hissune shook his head. With a trace of anger showing beneath his confusion he said, "I don't understand."

"I'll explain it to you later," said Shanamir.

Stubbornly Hissune said, "But what have I done? To say that Lord Valentine is going to be Pontifex some day, and—"

With deep frost in his voice Shanamir said, "Lord Valentine does not wish to contemplate the necessity of becoming Pontifex at this time. He particularly does not wish to contemplate it during his dinner. It is something not spoken of in his presence. Do you understand now? Do you?"

"Ah, I do now," said Hissune miserably.

In his shame he wanted to crawl under the table and hide. But how was he supposed to have known that the Coronal was touchy about having to become Pontifex some day? It was only to be expected, wasn't it? When a Pontifex died, the Coronal automatically took his place, and named a new Coronal who would himself eventually go on to dwell in the Labyrinth. That was the system: that was the way it had been for thousands of years. If Lord Valentine disliked the idea of being Pontifex so much, he might better have served himself by declining to become Coronal; but it didn't make sense for him to close his eyes to the succession law in the hope it would go away.

Though the Coronal himself had maintained a cool silence, great damage surely had been done. To show up late, then to say the wrongest possible thing the first time he opened his mouth—what a woeful beginning! Could it ever be undone? Hissune brooded about it all through the performance of some terrible jugglers, and during the dreary speeches that followed, and he might have gone on agonizing over it all evening, if something far worse had not happened.

It was Lord Valentine's turn to make a speech. But the Coronal seemed strangely remote and preoccupied as he got to his feet. He appeared almost to be sleepwalking—his eyes distant and vague, his gestures uncertain. At the high table people began to murmur. After an awful moment of silence he started to speak, but apparently it was the wrong speech, and very muddled besides. Was the Coronal sick? Drunk? Under some sudden malign spell? It troubled Hissune to see Lord Valentine so bewildered. Old Hornkast had just finished saying that the Coronal not only governed Majipoor but in some sense *was* Majipoor: and there was the Coronal a moment later, tottering, incoherent, looking as though he was about to topple—

Someone should take him by the arm, Hissune thought, and help him to sit down before he falls. But no one moved. No one dared. Please, Hissune begged silently, staring at Sleet, at Tunigorn, at Ermanar. Stop him, someone. Stop him. And still no one moved.

"Lordship!" a voice cried hoarsely.

Hissune realized it was his own. And he went rushing forward to seize the Coronal as he dropped headlong toward the gleaming wooden floor.

6

This is the dream of the Pontifex Tyeveras:

Here in the realm that I inhabit now, nothing has color and nothing has sound and nothing has motion. The alabandina blossoms are black and the shining fronds of the semotan trees are white, and from the bird that does not fly comes a song that cannot be heard. I lie on a bed of soft gentle rubbermoss, staring upward at drops of rain that do not fall. When the wind blows in the glade, not a leaf flutters. The name of this realm is death, and the alabandinas and semotans are dead, and the bird is dead, and the wind and the rain are dead. And I too am dead.

They come and stand about me and they say, "Are you Tyeveras that was Coronal of Majipoor and Pontifex of Majipoor?"

And I say, "I am dead."

"Are you Tyeveras?" they say again.

And I say, "I am dead Tyeveras, that was your king and that was your emperor. See, I have no color? See, I make no sound? I am dead."

"You are not dead."

"Here on my right hand is Lord Malibor that was my first Coronal. He is dead, is he not? Here on my left hand is Lord Voriax that was my second Coronal. Is he not dead? I lie between two dead men. I also am dead."

"Come and rise and walk, Tyeveras that was Coronal, Tyeveras that is Pontifex."

"I need not do that. I am excused, for I am dead."

"Listen to our voices."

"Your voices make no sound."

"Listen, Tyeveras, listen, listen, listen!"

"The alabandinas are black. The sky is white. This is the realm of death."

"Come and rise and walk, Emperor of Majipoor."

"Who are you?"

"Valentine that is your third Coronal."

"I hail you, Valentine, Pontifex of Majipoor!"

"That title is not yet mine. Come and rise and walk."

And I say, "It is not required of me, for I am dead," but they say, "We do not hear you, king that was, emperor that is," and then the voice that says it is the voice of Valentine tells me once more, "Come and rise and walk," and the hand of Valentine is on my hand in this realm where nothing moves, and it pulls me upward, and I drift, light as air floating on air, and I go forth, moving without motion, breathing without drawing breath. Together we cross a bridge that curves like the rainbow's arc across an abyss as deep as the world is broad, and its shimmering metal skin rings with a sound like the singing of young girls with each step I take. On the far side all is flooded with color: amber, turquoise, coral, lilac, emerald, auburn, indigo, crimson. The vault of the sky is jade and the sharp strands of sunlight that pierce the air are bronze. Everything flows, everything billows: there is no firmness, there is no stability. The voices say, "This is life, Tyeveras! This is your proper realm!" To which I make no reply, for after all I am dead and merely dreaming that I live: but I begin to weep, and my tears are all the colors of the stars.

And this too is the dream of the Pontifex Tyeveras:

I sit enthroned on a machine within a machine, and about me is a wall of blue glass. I hear bubbling sounds, and the soft ticking of intricate mechanisms. My heart beats slowly: I am aware of each heavy surge of fluid through its chambers, but that fluid, I think, is probably not blood. Whatever it is, though, it moves in me, and I am aware of it. Therefore I must surely be alive. How can that be? I am so old: have I then outlived death itself? I am Tyeveras that was Coronal to Ossier, and I touched once the hand of Lord Kinniken when the Castle was his, and Ossier only a prince, and the second Pontifex Thimin had the Labyrinth. If that is so, I think I must be the only man of Thimin's time who is yet alive, if I am alive, and I think I am alive. But I sleep. I dream. A great stillness enfolds me. Color seeps from the world. All is black, all is white, nothing moves, there is no sound. This is how I imagine the realm of death to be. Look, there is the Pontifex Confalume, and there is Prestimion, and there is Dekkeret! All those great emperors lie staring upward toward rain that does not fall, and in words without sound they say, Welcome, Tyeveras that was, welcome, weary old king, come lie beside us, now that you are dead like us. Yes. Yes. Ah, how beautiful it is here! Look, there is Lord Malibor, that man of the city of Bombifale in whom I hoped so much, so wrongly, and he is dead, and that is Lord Voriax of the black beard and the ruddy cheeks, but his cheeks are not ruddy now. And at last am I permitted to join them. Everything is silent. Everything is still. At last, at last, at last! At last they let me die, even if it is only when I dream.

And so the Pontifex Tyeveras floats midway between worlds, neither dead nor alive, dreaming of the world of the living when he thinks that he is dead, dreaming of the realm of death when he remembers that he is alive.

7

"A little wine, if you will," Valentine said. Sleet put the bowl in his hand, and the Coronal drank deeply. "I was just dozing," he muttered. "A quick nap, before the banquet— and that dream, Sleet! That dream! Get me Tisana, will you? I have to have a speaking of that dream."

"With respect, lordship, there's no time for that now," said Sleet.

"We've come to fetch you," Tunigorn put in. "The banquet's about to begin. Protocol requires that you be at the dais when the Pontifical officials—"

"Protocol! Protocol! That dream was almost like a sending, don't you understand! Such a vision of disaster—"

"The Coronal does not receive sendings, lordship," Sleet said quietly. "And the banquet will start in minutes, and we must robe you and convey you. You'll have Tisana and her potions afterward, if you like, my lord. But for now—"

"I must explore that dream!"

"I understand. But there lacks the time. Come, my lord."

He knew that Sleet and Tunigorn were right: like it or not, he must get himself to the banquet at once. It was more than just a social event; it was a rite of courtesy, the showing of honor by the senior monarch to the younger king who was his adopted son and anointed successor, and even though the Pontifex might be senile or altogether mad the Coronal did not have the option of taking the event lightly. He must go, and the dream must wait. No dream so potent, so rife with omen, could simply be ignored—he would need a dream-speaking, and probably a conference with the wizard Deliamber also—but there would be time to deal with all that afterward.

"Come, lordship," Sleet said again, holding his ermine robe of office out to him.

The heavy spell of that vision still clung to Valentine's spirit when he entered the Great Hall of the Pontifex ten minutes later. But it would not do for the Coronal of Majipoor to seem dour or preoccupied at such an event, and so he put upon his face the most affable expression he could manage, as he made his way toward the high table.

Which was, indeed, the way he had conducted himself all throughout the interminable week of this official visit: the forced smile, the studied amiability. Of all the cities of giant Majipoor, the Labyrinth was the one Lord Valentine loved least. It was to him a grim, oppressive place that he entered only when the unavoidable responsibilities of office required it. Just as he felt most keenly alive under the warm summer sun and the great vault of the open sky, riding in some forest in heavy leaf, a fair fresh wind tossing his golden hair about, so did he feel buried before his time whenever he entered this cheerless sunken city. He loathed its dismal descending coils, its infinity of shadowy underground levels, its claustrophobic atmosphere.

And most of all he loathed the knowledge of the inevitable destiny that awaited him here, when he must succeed to the title of Pontifex at last, and give up the sweet joys of life on Castle Mount, and take up residence for the rest of his days in this dreadful living tomb.

Tonight in particular, this banquet in the Great Hall, on the deepest level of the gloomy subterranean city—how he had dreaded that! The hideous hall itself, all harsh angles and glaring lights and weird ricocheting reflections, and the pompous officials of the Pontifical staff in their preposterous little traditional masks, and the windy speechmaking, and the boredom, and above all the burdensome sense of the entire Labyrinth pressing down upon him like a colossal mass of stone—merely to think of it had filled him with horror. Perhaps that ugly dream, he thought, had been a mere foreshadowing of the uneasiness he felt about what he must endure tonight.

Yet to his surprise he found himself unwinding, relaxing—not precisely enjoying himself at the banquet, no, hardly that, but at least finding it within his endurance.

They had redecorated the hall. That helped. Brilliant banners in green and gold, the colors emblematic of the Coronal, had been hung everywhere, blurring and disguising the strangely disquieting outlines of the enormous room. The lighting too had been changed since his last visit: gentle glowfloats now drifted pleasantly through the air.

And plainly the officials of the Pontifex had spared neither cost nor effort in making the occasion a festive one. From the legendary Pontifical wine cellars came an astounding procession of the planet's finest vintages: the golden fireshower wine of Pidruid, and the dry white of Amblemorn, and then the delicate red of Ni-moya, followed by a rich, robust purple wine of Muldemar that had been laid down years ago, in the reign of Lord Malibor. With each wine, of course, an appropriate delicacy: chilled thokkaberries, smoked sea dragon, calimbots in Narabal style, roast haunch of bilantoon. And an unending flow of entertainment: singers, mimes, harpists, jugglers. From time to time one of the Pontifex's minions would glance warily toward the high table where Lord Valentine and his companions sat, as though to ask, *Is it sufficient? Is your lordship content?*

And Valentine met each of those worried glances with a warm smile, a friendly nod, a lifting of his wine-bowl, by way of telling his uneasy hosts, *Yes, yes, I am well pleased with all you have done for us.*

"What edgy little jackals they all are!" Sleet cried. "You can smell the worry-sweat on them from six tables away."

Which led to a foolish and painful remark from young Hissune about the likelihood that they were trying to curry favor with Lord Valentine against the day when he became Pontifex. The unexpected tactlessness stung Valentine with whiplash effect, and he turned away, heart racing, throat suddenly dry. He forced himself to remain calm: smiled across the tables to the high spokesman Hornkast, nodded to the Pontifical majordomo, beamed at this one and that, while behind him he could hear Shanamir explaining irately to Hissune the nature of his blunder.

In a moment Valentine's anger had ebbed. Why should the boy have known, after all, that that was a forbidden topic of discussion? But there was nothing he could do to put an end to Hissune's obvious humiliation without acknowledging the depth of his sensitivity on that score; so he let himself glide back into conversation as though nothing untoward had happened.

Then five jugglers appeared, three humans, a Skandar, and a Hjort, to cause a blessed distraction. They commenced a wild and frenzied hurling of torches, sickles, and knives that brought cheers and applause from the Coronal.

Of course, they were mere flashy third-raters whose flaws and insufficiencies and evasions were evident enough to Valentine's expert eye. No matter: jugglers always gave him delight. Inevitably they recalled to his mind that strange and blissful time years before, when he had been a juggler himself, wandering from town to town with an itinerant raggle-taggle troupe. He had been innocent then, untroubled by the burdens of power, a truly happy man.

Valentine's enthusiasm for the jugglers drew a scowl from Sleet, who said sourly, "Ah, lordship, do you truly think they're as good as all that?"

"They show great zeal, Sleet."

"So do cattle that forage for fodder in a dry season. But they are cattle nonetheless. And these zealous jugglers of yours are little more than amateurs, my lord."

"Oh, Sleet, Sleet, show more mercy!"

"There are certain standards in this craft, my lord. As you should still remember."

Valentine chuckled. "The joy these people give me has

little to do with their skills, Sleet. Seeing them stirs recollections in me of other days, a simpler life, bygone companions."

"Ah, then," Sleet said. "That's another matter, my lord! That is sentiment. But I speak of craft."

"We speak of different things, then."

The jugglers took their leave in a flurry of furious throws and bungled catches, and Valentine sat back, smiling, cheerful. But the fun's over, he thought. Time for the speeches now.

Even those proved surprisingly tolerable, though. Shinaam delivered the first: the Pontifical minister of internal affairs, a man of the Ghayrog race, with glistening reptilian scales and a flickering forked red tongue. Gracefully and swiftly he offered formal welcome to Lord Valentine and his entourage.

The adjutant Ermanar made reply on behalf of the Coronal. When he was done, it was the turn of ancient shriveled Dilifon, private secretary to the Pontifex, who conveyed the personal greetings of the high monarch. Which was mere fraud, Valentine knew, since it was common knowledge that old Tyeveras had not spoken a rational word to anyone close upon a decade. But he accepted Dilifon's quavering fabrications politely and delegated Tunigorn to offer the response.

Then Hornkast spoke: the high spokesman of the Pontificate, plump, solemn, the true ruler of the Labyrinth in these years of the senility of the Pontifex Tyeveras. His theme, he declared, was the grand processional. Valentine sat to attention at once: for in the past year he had thought of little else than the processional, that far-ranging ceremonial journey in which the Coronal must go forth upon Majipoor and show himself to the people, and receive from them their homage, their allegiance, their love.

"It may seem to some," said Hornkast, "a mere pleasure jaunt, a trivial and meaningless holiday from the cares of office. Not so! Not so! For it is the person of the Coronal—the actual, physical person, not a banner, not a flag, not a portrait—that binds all the far-flung provinces of the world to a common loyalty. And it is only through periodic contact with the actual presence of that royal person that that loyalty is renewed."

Valentine frowned and looked away. Through his mind there surged a sudden disturbing image: the landscape of Majipoor sundered and upheaved, and one solitary man desperately wrestling with the splintered terrain, striving to thrust everything back into place.

"For the Coronal," Hornkast went on, "is the embodiment of Majipoor. The Coronal is Majipoor personified. He is the world; the world is the Coronal. And so when he undertakes the grand processional, as you, Lord Valentine, now will do for the first time since your glorious restoration, he is not only going forth to the world, but he is going forth to himself—to a voyage into his own soul, to an encounter with the deepest roots of his identity—"

Was it so? Of course. Of course. Hornkast, he knew, was simply spouting standard rhetoric, oratorical noises of a sort that Valentine had had to endure all too often. And yet, this time the words seemed to trigger something in him, seemed to open some great dark tunnel of mysteries. That dream— the cold wind blowing across Castle Mount, the groans of the earth, the shattered landscape—*The Coronal is the embodiment of Majipoor—he is the world—*

Once in his reign already that unity had been broken, when Valentine, thrust from power by treachery, stripped of his memory and even of his own body, had been hurled into exile. Was it to happen again? A second overthrow, a second downfall? Or was something even more dreadful imminent, something far more serious than the fate of one single man?

He tasted the unfamiliar taste of fear. Banquet or no, Valentine knew he should have gone at once for a dream-speaking. Some grim knowledge was striving to break through to his awareness, beyond all doubt. Something was wrong within the Coronal—which was the same as saying something was wrong in the world—

"My lord?" It was Autifon Deliamber. The little Vroonish wizard said, "It is time, my lord, for you to offer the final toast."

"What? When?"

"Now, my lord."

"Ah. Indeed," Valentine said vaguely. "The final toast, yes."

He rose and let his gaze journey throughout the great room, into its most shadowy depths. And a sudden strangeness came upon him, for he realized that he was entirely unprepared. He had little notion of what he was to say, or to whom he should direct it, or even—really—what he was doing in this place at all. The Labyrinth? Was this in truth the

Labyrinth, that loathsome place of shadows and mildew?
Why was he here? What did these people want him to do?
Perhaps this was merely another dream, and he had never
left Castle Mount. He did not know. He did not understand
anything.

Something will come, he thought. I need only wait. But
he waited, and nothing came, except deeper strangeness. He
felt a throbbing in his forehead, a humming in his ears. Then
he experienced a powerful sense of himself here in the
Labyrinth as occupying a place at the precise center of the
world, the core of the whole gigantic globe. But some irresistible force was pulling him from that place. Between one
moment and the next his soul went surging from him as
though it were a great mantle of light, streaming upward
through the many layers of the Labyrinth to the surface and
then reaching forth to encompass all the immensity of Majipoor,
even to the distant coasts of Zimroel and sun-blackened
Suvrael, and the unknown expanse of the Great Sea on the
far side of the planet. He wrapped the world like a glowing
veil. In that dizzying moment he felt that he and the planet
were one, that he embodied in himself the twenty billion
people of Majipoor, humans and Skandars and Hjorts and
Metamorphs and all the rest, moving within him like the
corpuscles of his blood. He was everywhere at once: he was
all the sorrow in the world, and all the joy, and all the
yearning, and all the need. He was everything. He was a
boiling universe of contradictions and conflicts. He felt the
heat of the desert and the warm rain of the tropics and the
chill of the high peaks. He laughed and wept and died and
made love and ate and drank and danced and fought and rode
wildly through unknown hills and toiled in the fields and cut
a path through thick vine-webbed jungles. In the oceans of
his soul vast sea dragons breached the surface and let forth
monstrous bleating roars and dived again, to the uttermost
depths. Faces without eyes hovered before him, grinning,
leering. Bony attenuated hands fluttered in the air. Choirs
sang discordant hymns. All at once, at once, at once, a
terrible lunatic simultaneity.

He stood in silence, bewildered, lost, as the room reeled
wildly about him. "Propose the toast, lordship," Deliamber
seemed to be saying over and over. "First to the Pontifex, and
then to his aides, and then—"

Control yourself, Valentine thought. *You are Coronal of
Majipoor.*

With a desperate effort he pulled himself free of that grotesque hallucination.

"The toast to the Pontifex, lordship—"

"Yes. Yes, I know."

Phantom images still haunted him. Ghostly fleshless fingers plucked at him. He fought free. *Control. Control. Control.*

He felt utterly lost.

"The toast, lordship!"

The toast? The toast? What was that? A ceremony. An obligation upon him. *You are Coronal of Majipoor.* Yes. He must speak. He must say words to these people.

"Friends—" he began. And then came the dizzying plunge into chaos.

8

"The Coronal wants to see you," Shanamir said.

Hissune looked up, startled. For the past hour and a half he had been waiting tensely in a dismal many-columned antechamber with a grotesque bulbous ceiling, wondering what was happening behind the closed doors of Lord Valentine's suite and whether he was supposed to remain here indefinitely. It was well past midnight, and some ten hours from now the Coronal and his staff were to depart from the Labyrinth on the next leg of the grand processional, unless tonight's strange events had altered that plan. Hissune still had to make his way all the way up to the outermost ring, gather his possessions and say goodbye to his mother and sisters, and get back here in time to join the outbound party—and fit some sleep into the picture, too. All was in confusion.

After the collapse of the Coronal, after Lord Valentine had been carried away to his suite, after the banquet hall had been cleared, Hissune and some of the other members of the Coronal's group had assembled in this drab room nearby. Word had come, after a time, that Lord Valentine was recovering well, and that they were all to wait there for further instructions. Then, one by one, they had been summoned to the Coronal—Tunigorn first, then Ermanar, Asenhart, Shanamir, and the rest, until Hissune was left alone with some members of the Coronal's guard and a few very minor staff people. He did not feel like asking any of these subalterns what the appropriate thing for him to do might be; but he dared not leave, either, and so he waited, and waited some more, and went on waiting.

He closed his eyes when they grew raw and began to ache, though he did not sleep. A single image revolved endlessly in his mind: the Coronal beginning to fall, and he and Lisamon Hultin springing from their seats at the same moment to catch him. He was unable to shake from his mind the horror of that sudden astonishing climax to the banquet: the Coronal bemused, pathetic, groping for words and failing to find the right ones, swaying, teetering, falling—

Of course a Coronal was just as capable of getting himself drunk and behaving foolishly as anyone else. One of the many things that Hissune's illicit explorations of the memory-readings in the Register of Souls during the years he worked in the House of Records had taught him was that there was nothing superhuman about the men who wore the starburst crown. So it was altogether possible that this evening Lord Valentine, who seemed so intensely to dislike being in the Labyrinth, had allowed the free-flowing wine to ease that dislike, until, when it was his turn to speak, he was in a drunken muddle.

But somehow Hissune doubted that it was wine that had muddled the Coronal, even though Lord Valentine had said as much himself. He had been watching the Coronal closely all during the speechmaking, and he hadn't seemed at all drunk then, only convivial, joyous, relaxed. And afterward, when the little Vroonish wizard had brought Lord Valentine back from his swoon by touching his tentacles to him, the Coronal had seemed a trifle shaky, as anyone who had fainted might be, but nevertheless quite clearheaded. Nobody could sober up that fast. No, Hissune thought, more likely it had been something other than drunkenness, some sorcery, some deep sending that had seized Lord Valentine's spirit just at that moment. And that was terrifying.

He rose now and went down the winding corridor to the Coronal's chambers. As he approached the intricately carved door, gleaming with brilliant golden starbursts and royal monograms, it opened and Tunigorn and Ermanar emerged, looking drawn and somber. They nodded to him and Tunigorn, with a quick gesture of his finger, ordered the guards at the door to let him go in.

Lord Valentine sat at a broad desk of some rare and highly polished blood-colored wood. The Coronal's big heavy-knuckled hands were spread out before him against the surface of the desk, as though he were supporting himself with them. His face was pale, his eyes seemed to be having difficulty focusing, his shoulders were slumped.

"My lord—" Hissune began uncertainly, and faltered into silence.

He remained just within the doorway, feeling awkward, out of place, keenly uncomfortable. Lord Valentine did not seem to have noticed him. The old dream-speaker Tisana was in the room, and Sleet, and the Vroon, but no one said a thing. Hissune was baffled. He had no idea what the etiquette of approaching a tired and obviously ill Coronal might be. Was one supposed to offer one's kind sympathies, or to pretend that the monarch was in the finest of health? Hissune made the starburst gesture, and, getting no response, made it again. He felt his cheeks blazing.

He searched for some shred of his former youthful self-assurance, and found nothing. Strangely, he seemed to be growing more ill at ease with Lord Valentine, rather than less, the more often he saw the Coronal. That was hard to understand.

Sleet rescued him at last, saying loudly, "My lord, it is the Initiate Hissune."

The Coronal raised his head and stared at Hissune. The depth of fatigue that his fixed and glassy eyes revealed was terrifying. And yet, as Hissune watched in amazement, Lord Valentine drew himself back from the brink of exhaustion the way a man who has caught a vine after slipping over the edge of a precipice pulls himself to safety: with a desperate show of unanswerable strength. It was astonishing to see some color come to his cheeks, some animation to his expression. He managed even to project a distinct kingliness, a feeling of command. Hissune, awed, wondered if it might be some trick they learn on Castle Mount, when they are in training to become Coronals—

"Come closer," Lord Valentine said.

Hissune took a couple of steps deeper into the room.

"Are you afraid of me?"

"My lord—"

"I can't allow you to waste time fearing me, Hissune. I have too much work to do. And so do you. Once I believed that you felt absolutely no awe of me at all. Was I wrong?"

"My lord, it's only that you look so tired—and I'm tired myself, I suppose—this night has been so strange, for me, for you, for everyone—"

The Coronal nodded. "A night full of great strangenesses, yes. Is it morning yet? I never know the time, when I'm in this place."

"A little past midnight, my lord."

"Only a little past midnight? I thought it was almost morning. How long this night has been!" Lord Valentine laughed softly. "But it's always a little past midnight in the Labyrinth, isn't it, Hissune? By the Divine, if you could know how I yearn to see the sun again!"

"My lord—" Deliamber murmured tactfully. "It does indeed grow late, and there is still much to do—"

"Indeed." For an instant the Coronal's eyes flickered into glassiness again. Then, recovering once more, he said, "To business, then. The first item of which is the giving of my thanks. I'd have been badly hurt but for your being there to catch me. You must have been on your way toward me before I went over, eh? Was it that obvious I was about to keel over?"

Reddening a little, Hissune said, "It was, lordship. At least to me."

"Ah."

"But I may have been watching you more closely than the others were."

"Yes. I dare say you may have been."

"I hope your lordship won't greatly suffer the ill effects of—of—"

A faint smile appeared on the Coronal's lips. "I wasn't drunk, Hissune."

"I didn't mean to imply—I mean—but that is to say—"

"Not drunk, no. A spell, a sending—who knows? Wine is one thing, and sorcery's another, and I think I still can tell the difference. It was a dark vision, boy: not the first I've had lately. The omens are troublesome. War's on the wind."

"War?" Hissune blurted. The word was unfamiliar, alien, ugly: it hovered in the air like some foul droning insect looking for prey. War? War? Into Hissune's mind leaped an image eight thousand years old, springing from the cache of memories he had stolen in the Register of Souls: the dry hills of the far northwest ablaze, the sky black with thick coils of rising smoke, in the final awful convulsion of Lord Stiamot's long war against the Metamorphs. But that was ancient history. There had been no war in all the centuries since, other than the war of restoration. And scarce any lives had been lost in that, by design of Lord Valentine, to whom violence was an abomination. "How can there be war?" Hissune demanded. "We have no wars on Majipoor!"

"War's coming, boy!" said Sleet roughly. "And when it does, by the Lady, there'll be no hiding from it!"

"But war with whom? This is the most peaceful of worlds. What enemy could there be?"

"There is one," Sleet said. "Are you Labyrinth people so sheltered from the real world that you fail to comprehend that?"

Hissune frowned. "The Metamorphs, you mean?"

"Aye, the Metamorphs!" Sleet cried. "The filthy Shapeshifters, boy! Did you think we could keep them penned up forever? By the Lady, there'll be a rampage soon enough!"

Hissune stared in shock and amazement at the lean little scar-faced man. Sleet's eyes were shining. He seemed almost to welcome the prospect.

Shaking his head slowly, Hissune said, "With all respect, High Counsellor Sleet, this makes no sense to me. A few millions of them, against twenty billions of us? They fought that war once, and lost it, and however much they hate us, I don't think they're going to try it again."

Sleet pointed toward the Coronal, who seemed barely to be listening. "And the time they put their own puppet on Lord Valentine's throne? What was that if not a declaration of war? Ah, boy, boy, you know nothing! The Shapeshifters have been scheming against us for centuries, and their time is at hand. The Coronal's own dreams foretell it! By the Lady, the Coronal himself dreams of war!"

"By the Lady indeed, Sleet," said the Coronal in a voice of infinite weariness, "there'll be no war if I can help it, and you know that."

"And if you can't help it, my lord?" Sleet shot back.

The little man's chalk-white face was flushed now with excitement; his eyes gleamed, he made tight rapid obsessive gestures with his hands, as though he were juggling invisible clubs. It had not occurred to Hissune that anyone, even a

High Counsellor, spoke so bluntly to Coronals. And perhaps it did not happen often, for Hissune saw something much like anger cross the face of Lord Valentine: Lord Valentine who was reputed never to have known rage, who had gently and lovingly sought even to win the soul of his enemy the usurper Dominin Barjazid, in the last moments of the war of restoration. Then that anger gave way to the dreadful weariness again, which made the Coronal seem to be a man of seventy or eighty years, and not the young and vigorous forty or so that Hissune knew him to be.

There was an endless moment of tense silence. At length Lord Valentine said, speaking slowly and deliberately and addressing his words to Hissune as though no one else were in the room. "Let me hear no more talk of war while hope of peace remains. But the omens were dark, true enough: if there is not to be war, there is certain to be some calamity of another kind. I will not ignore such warnings. We have changed some of our plans this night, Hissune."

"Will you call off the grand processional, my lord?"

"That I must not do. Again and again I've postponed it, saying that there was too much work for me at Castle Mount, that I had no time to go jaunting about the world. Perhaps I've postponed it too long. The processional should be made every seven or eight years."

"And has it been longer than that, sir?"

"Almost ten. Nor did I complete the tour, that other time, for at Til-omon, you know, there was that small interruption, when someone else relieved me for a while of my tasks, without my knowledge." The Coronal stared past Hissune into an infinitely remote distance. He seemed for a moment to be peering into the misty gulfs of time: thinking, perhaps, of the bizarre usurpation that had been worked upon him by the Barjazid, and of the months or years that he had roamed Majipoor bereft of his mind and of his might. Lord Valentine shook his head. "No, the grand processional must be made. Must be extended, in fact. I had thought to travel only through Alhanroel, but I think we will need to visit both continents. The people of Zimroel also must see that there is a Coronal. And if Sleet is right that the Metamorphs are the ones we must fear, why, then Zimroel is the place we must go, for that is where the Metamorphs dwell."

Hissune had not expected that. A great surge of excitement arose in him. Zimroel too! That unimaginably distant place of forests and vast rivers and great cities, more than half legendary to him—magical cities with magical names—

"Ah, if that is the new plan, how splendid it sounds, my lord!" he said, smiling broadly. "I had thought never to see that land, except in dreams! Will we go to Ni-moya? And Pidruid, Til-omon, Narabal—"

"Quite likely I will," said the Coronal in an oddly flat voice that fell upon Hissune's ears like a cudgel.

"*I*, my lord?" said Hissune with sudden alarm.

Softly Lord Valentine said, "Another of the changes of plan. You will not be accompanying me on the grand processional."

A terrible chill swept through Hissune then, as if the wind that blows between the stars had descended and was scouring out the deepest chambers of the Labyrinth. He trembled, and his soul shriveled under that cold blast, and he felt himself withering away to a husk.

"Am I then dismissed from your service, lordship?"

"Dismissed? Not at all! Surely you understand that I have important plans for you!"

"So you have said, several times, my lord. But the processional—"

"Is not the right preparation for the tasks you someday will be called upon to perform. No, Hissune, I can't afford to let you spend the next year or two bounding around from province to province at my side. You're to leave for Castle Mount as soon as possible."

"Castle Mount, my lord?"

"To begin the training appropriate to a knight-initiate."

"My lord?" said Hissune in amazement.

"You are—what, eighteen? So you're years behind the others. But you're quick: you'll make up for the lost time, you'll rise to your true level soon enough. You must, Hissune. We have no idea what evil is about to come upon our world, but I know now that I must expect the worst, and prepare for it by preparing others to stand beside me when the worst arrives. So there will be no grand processional for you, Hissune."

"I understand, my lord."

"Do you? Yes, I think you do. There'll be time later for you to see Piliplok and Ni-moya and Pidruid, won't there? But now—now—"

Hissune nodded, though in truth he hardly dared to

think that he comprehended what Lord Valentine appeared to be telling him. For a long moment the Coronal stared at him; and Hissune met the gaze of those weary blue eyes steadily and evenly, though he was beginning to feel an exhaustion beyond anything he had ever known. The audience, he realized, had come to its end, though no word of dismissal had been uttered. In silence he made the starburst gesture and backed from the room.

He wanted nothing more than sleep now, a week of it, a month. This bewildering night had drained him of all his strength. Only two days ago this same Lord Valentine had summoned him to this very room, and told him to make ready at once to leave the Labyrinth, for he was to set forth as part of the royal entourage that was making the grand processional through Alhanroel; and yesterday he had been named one of the Coronal's aides, and given a seat at the high table of tonight's banquet; and now the banquet had come and gone in mysterious chaos, and he had beheld the Coronal haggard and all too human in his confusion, and the gift of the grand processional had been snatched back, and now—Castle Mount? A knight-initiate? Making up for lost time? Making up what? Life has become a dream, Hissune thought. And there is no one who can speak it for me.

In the hallway outside the Coronal's suite, Sleet caught him suddenly by the wrist and pulled him close. Hissune sensed the strange power of the man, the taut energies coiled within him.

"Just to tell you, boy—I meant no personal enmity, when I spoke so harshly to you in there."

"I never took it that way."

"Good. Good. I want no enmity with you."

"Nor I with you, Sleet."

"I think we'll have much work to do together, you and I, when the war comes."

"*If* the war comes."

Sleet smiled bleakly. "There's no doubt of it. But I won't fight that battle with you all over again just now. You'll come over to my way of thinking soon enough. Valentine can't see trouble until trouble's biting at his boots—it's his nature, he's too sweet, has too much faith in the good will of others, I think—but you're different, eh, boy? You walk with your eyes open. I think that's what the Coronal prizes the most in you. Do you follow what I say?"

"It's been a long night, Sleet."

"So it has. Get some sleep, boy. If you can."

9

The first rays of morning sun touched the ragged gray muddy shore of southeastern Zimroel and lit that somber coast with a pale green glow. The coming of dawn brought instant wakefulness to the five Liimen camped in a torn, many-times-patched tent on the flank of a dune a few hundred yards from the sea. Without a word they rose, scooped handfuls of damp sand, rubbed it over the rough, pockmarked gray-black skin of their chests and arms to make the morning ablution. When they left the tent, they turned toward the west, where a few faint stars still glowed in the dark sky, and offered their salute.

One of those stars, perhaps, was the one from which their ancestors had come. They had no idea which star that might be. No one did. Seven thousand years had passed since the first Liiman migrants had come to Majipoor, and in that time much knowledge had been lost. During their wanderings over this giant planet, going wherever there might be simple menial jobs to perform, the Liimen had long since forgotten the place that was their starting point. But someday they would know it again.

The eldest male lit the fire. The youngest brought forth the skewers and arranged the meat on them. The two women silently took the skewers and held them in the flames until they could hear the song of the dripping fat. In silence then they handed the chunks of meat around, and in silence the Liimen ate what would be their only meal of the day.

Silent still, they filed from the tent, eldest male, then the women, then the other two males: five slender, wide-shouldered beings with flat broad heads and fierce bright eyes arrayed in a triple set across their expressionless faces. Down to the edge of the sea they walked, and took up positions on a narrow snub of a headland, just out of reach of the surf, as they had done every morning for weeks.

There they waited, in silence, each hoping that this day would bring the coming of the dragons.

*   *   *

The southeastern coast of Zimroel—the huge province known as Gihorna—is one of Majipoor's most obscure regions: a land without cities, a forgotten place of thin gray sandy soil and moist blustery breezes, subject at unpredictable intervals to colossal, vastly destructive sandstorms. There is no natural harbor for hundreds of miles along that unhappy coast, only an endless ridge of low shabby hills sloping down to a sodden strand against which the surf of the Inner Sea crashes with a sad dull sound. In the early years of the settlement of Majipoor, explorers who ventured into that forlorn quarter of the western continent reported that there was nothing there worth a second look, and on a planet otherwise so full of miracles and wonders that was the most damning dismissal imaginable.

So Gihorna was bypassed as the development of the new continent got under way. Settlement after settlement was established—Piliplok first, midway up the eastern coast at the mouth of the broad River Zimr, and then Pidruid in the distant northwest, and Ni-moya on the great bend of the Zimr far inland, and Til-omon, and Narabal, and Velathys, and the shining Ghayrog city of Dulorn, and many more. Outposts turned into towns, and towns into cities, and cities into great cities that sent forth tendrils of expansion creeping outward across the astonishing immensities of Zimroel; but still there was no reason to go into Gihorna, and no one did. Not even the Shapeshifters, when Lord Stiamot had finally subjugated them and dumped them down into a forest reservation just across the River Steiche from the western reaches of Gihorna, had cared to cross the river into the dismal lands beyond.

Much later—thousands of years later, when most of Zimroel had begun to seem as tame as Alhanroel—a few settlers at last did filter into Gihorna. Nearly all were Liimen, simple and undemanding people who had never woven themselves deeply into the fabric of Majipoori life. By choice, it seemed they held themselves apart, earning a few weights here and there as sellers of grilled sausages, as fishermen, as itinerant laborers. It was easy for these drifting folk, whose lives seemed bleak and colorless to the other races of Majipoor, to drift on into bleak and colorless Gihorna. There they settled in tiny villages, and strung nets just beyond the surf to catch the swarming silvery-gray fishes, and dug pits in which to trap the big glossy octagonal-shelled black crabs that scuttled along the beaches in packs numbering many hundreds, and for a feast went out to hunt the sluggish tenderfleshed dhumkars that lived half-buried in the dunes.

Most of the year the Liimen had Gihorna to themselves. But not in summer, for summer was dragon time.

In early summer, the tents of curiosity-seekers began to sprout like yellow calimbots after a warm rain, all along the coast of Zimroel from a point just south of Piliplok to the edge of the impassable Zimr Marsh. This was the season when the sea-dragon herds made their annual journey up the eastern side of the continent, heading out into the waters between Piliplok and the Isle of Sleep, where they would bear their young.

The coast below Piliplok was the only place on Majipoor where it was possible to get a good view of the dragons without going to sea, for here the pregnant cows liked to come close to shore, and feed on the small creatures that lived in the dense thatches of golden seaweed so widespread in those waters. So each year at dragon-passage time the dragon watchers arrived by the thousands, from all over the world, and set up their tents. Some were magnificent airy structures, virtual palaces of soaring slender poles and shimmering fabric, that were occupied by touring members of the nobility. Some were the sturdy and efficient tents of prosperous merchants and their families. And some were the simple lean-to's of ordinary folk who had saved for years to make this journey.

The aristocrats came to Gihorna in dragon time because they found it entertaining to watch the enormous sea dragons gliding through the water, and because it was agreeably unusual to spend a holiday in such a hideously ugly place. The rich merchants came because the undertaking of such a costly trip would surely enhance their position in their communities, and because their children would learn something useful about the natural history of Majipoor that might do them some good in school. The ordinary people came because they believed that it brought a lifetime of good luck to observe the passage of the dragons, though nobody was quite sure why that should be the case.

And then there were the Liimen, to whom the time of the dragons was a matter neither of amusement nor of prestige nor of the hope of fortune's kindness, but of the most profound significance: a matter of redemption, a matter of salvation.

No one could predict exactly when the dragons would turn up along the Gihorna coast. Though they always came in summer, sometimes they came early and sometimes they came late; and this year they were late. The five Liimen, taking up their positions on the little headland each morning, saw nothing day after day but gray sea, white foam, dark masses of seaweed. But they were not impatient people. Sooner or later the dragons would arrive.

The day when they finally came into view was warm and close, with a hot humid wind blowing out of the west. All that morning crabs in platoons and phalanxes and regiments marched restlessly up and down the beach, as though they were drilling to repel invaders. That was always a sign.

Toward noon came a second sign: up from the heaving surf tumbled a great fat pudding of a rip-toad, all belly and mouth and saw-edged teeth. It staggered a few yards ashore and hunkered down in the sand, panting, shivering, blinking its vast milky-hued eyes. A second toad emerged a moment later not far away and sat staring malevolently at the first. Then came a little procession of big-leg lobsters, a dozen or more gaudy blue and purple creatures with swollen orange haunches, that marched from the water with great determination and quickly began to dig themselves into the mud. They were followed by red-eyed scallops dancing on wiry little yellow legs, and little angular white-faced hatchet-eels, and even some fish, that lay helplessly flopping about as the crabs of the shore fell upon them.

The Liimen nodded to each other in rising excitement. Only one thing could cause the creatures of the offshore shallows to stray up onto the land this way. The musky smell of the sea dragons, preceding the dragons themselves by a little while, must have begun to pervade the water.

"Look now," the eldest male said shortly.

Out of the south came the vanguard of the dragons, two or three dozen immense beasts holding their black leathery wings spread high and wide and their long massive necks curving upward and out like great bows. Serenely they moved into the groves of seaweed and began to harvest them: slapping their wings against the surface of the water, stirring turmoil among the creatures of the seaweed, striking with sudden ferocity, gulping weed and lobsters and rip-toads and everything else, indiscriminately. These giants were males. Behind them swam a little group of females, rolling from side to side in the manner of pregnant cows to display their bulging flanks; and after them, by himself, the king of the herd, a dragon so big he looked like the upturned hull of some great capsized vessel, and that was only the half of him, for he let his haunches and tail dangle out of sight below the surface.

"Down and give praise," said the eldest male, and fell to his knees.

With the seven long bony fingers of his outstretched left hand he made the sign of the sea dragon again and again: the fluttering wings, the swooping neck. He bent forward and rubbed his cheek against the cool moist sand. He lifted his head and looked toward the sea-dragon king, who now was no more than two hundred yards off shore, and tried by sheer force of will to urge the great beast toward the land.

—*Come to us . . . come . . . come. . . .*

—*Now is the time. We have waited so long. Come . . . save us . . . lead us . . . save us. . . .*

—*Come!*

10

With a mechanical flourish he signed his name to what seemed like the ten thousandth official document of the day: *Elidath of Morvole, High Counsellor and Regent*. He scribbled the date next to his name, and one of Valentine's secretaries selected another sheaf of papers and put it down in front of him.

This was Elidath's day for signing things. It seemed to be a necessary weekly ordeal. Every Twoday afternoon since Lord Valentine's departure he left his own headquarters in the Pinitor Court and came over to the Coronal's official suite here in the inner Castle, and sat himself down at Lord Valentine's magnificent desk, a great polished slab of deep red palisander with a vivid grain that resembled the starburst emblem, and for hours the secretaries took their turns handing him papers that had come up from the various branches of the government for final approval. Even with the Coronal off on his grand processional, the wheels continued to turn, the unending spew of decrees and revisions of decrees and abrogations of decrees poured forth. And everything had to be signed by the Coronal or his designated regent, the Divine only knew why. One more: *Elidath of Morvole, High Counsellor and Regent.* And the date. There.

"Give me the next," Elidath said.

In the beginning he had conscientiously tried to read, or at least to skim, every document before affixing his signature. Then he had settled for reading the little summary, eight or ten lines long, that each document bore clipped to its cover. But he had given up even that, long ago. Did Valentine read them all? he wondered. Impossible. Even if he read only the summaries, he would spend all his days and nights at it, with no time left to eat or sleep, let alone to carry out the real responsibilities of his office. By now Elidath signed most without even glancing at them. For all he knew or cared, he might be signing a proclamation forbidding the eating of sausages on Winterday, or one that made rainfall illegal in Stoienzar Province, or even a decree confiscating all his own lands and turning them over to the retirement fund for administrative secretaries. He signed anyway. A king—or a king's understudy—must have faith in the competence of his staff, or the job becomes not merely overwhelming but downright unthinkable.

He signed. *Elidath of Morvole, High Counsellor and—*

"Next!"

He still felt a little guilty not reading them anymore. But did the Coronal really need to know that a treaty had been reached between the cities of Muldemar and Tidias, concerning the joint management of certain vineyards the title to which had been in dispute since the seventh year of the Pontifex Thimin and the Coronal Lord Kinniken? No. No. Sign and move on to other things, Elidath thought, and let Muldemar and Tidias rejoice in their new amity without troubling the king about it.

Elidath of Morvole—

As he reached for the next and began to search for the place to sign, a secretary said, "Sir, the lords Mirigant and Divvis are here."

"Have them come in," he replied without looking up.

Elidath of Morvole, High Counsellor and Regent—

The lords Mirigant and Divvis, counsellors of the inner

circle, cousin and nephew respectively of Lord Valentine, met him every afternoon about this time, so that he could go running with them through the streets of the Castle, and thereby purge his taut-nerved body of some of the tension that this regency was engendering in him. He had scarcely any other opportunity for exercise these days: the daily jaunt with them was an invaluable safety valve for him.

He managed to sign two more documents during the time that they were entering the huge room, so splendidly paneled with strips of bannikop and semotan and other rare woods, and making their way toward him with a clatter of booted feet against the elaborately inlaid floor. He picked up a third, telling himself that it would be the last one he'd do this day. It was merely a single sheet, and somehow Elidath found himself idly scanning it as he signed: a patent of nobility, no less, raising some fortunate commoner to the rank of Initiate Knight of Castle Mount, in recognition of his high merit and greatly valued services and this and that—

"What are you signing now?" Divvis asked, leaning across the desk and penciling at the paper in front of Elidath. He was a big, heavy-shouldered, dark-bearded man, who as he came into his middle years was taking on an eerie resemblance to his father, the former Coronal. "Is Valentine lowering taxes again? Or has he decided to make Carabella's birthday a holiday?"

Accustomed though he was to Divvis's brand of wit, Elidath had no taste for it after a day of such dreary meaningless work. Sudden anger flared in him. "Do you mean the *Lady* Carabella?" he snapped.

Divvis seemed startled. "Oh, are we so formal today, High Counsellor Elidath?"

"If I happened to refer to your late father simply as *Voriax*, I can imagine what you—"

"My father was Coronal," said Divvis in a cold, tight voice, "and deserves the respect we give a departed king. Whereas the *Lady* Carabella is merely—"

"The Lady Carabella, cousin, is the consort of your present king," said Mirigant sharply, turning on Divvis with more anger than Elidath had ever seen that kindly man display. "And also, I remind you, she is the wife of your father's brother. For two reasons, then—"

"All right," Elidath said wearily. "Enough of this foolishness. Are we going to run this afternoon?"

Divvis laughed. "If you're not too tired from all this Coronaling you've been doing."

"I'd like nothing better," said Elidath, "to run down the Mount from here to Morvole, taking maybe five months of good easy striding to get there, and then to spend the next three years pruning my orchards and—ah! Yes, I'll come running with you. Let me finish just this one last paper—"

"The Lady Carabella's birthday holiday," said Divvis, smiling.

"A patent of nobility," Elidath said. "Which will, if you'll keep quiet long enough, give us a new Knight-Initiate, a certain Hissune son of Elsinome, it says here, resident of the Pontifical Labyrinth, in recognition of his high merit and—"

"Hissune son of Elsinome?" Divvis whooped. "Do you know who that is, Elidath?"

"Why should I be expected to know any such thing?"

"Think back to Valentine's restoration ceremony, when he insisted on having all those unlikely people with us in the Confalume throne room—his jugglers and the Skandar sea-captain with the missing arm and the Hjort with orange whiskers and the rest. Do you remember a boy there too?"

"Shanamir, you mean?"

"No, an even younger boy! A small skinny boy, ten or eleven years old, with no respect for anybody, a boy with the eyes of a thief, who went around asking embarrassing questions, and wheedling people into letting him have their medals and decorations, and pinning them all over his tunic and staring at himself endlessly in mirrors? That boy's name was Hissune!"

"The little Labyrinth boy," said Mirigant, "who made everyone promise to hire him as a guide if they ever came to the Labyrinth. I remember him, yes. A very clever rascal, I'd say."

"That rascal is now a Knight-Initiate," Divvis said. "Or will be, if Elidath doesn't tear up that sheet of paper that he's staring at so blankly. You aren't going to approve this, are you, Elidath?"

"Of course I am."

"A Knight-Initiate who comes from the *Labyrinth*?"

Elidath shrugged. "Wouldn't matter to me if he was a Shapeshifter out of Ilirivoyne. I'm not here to overrule the Coronal's decisions. If Valentine says Knight-Initiate, Knight-Initiate he is, whether he be rascal, fisherman, sausage peddler, Metamorph, dung sweeper—" Quickly he inscribed the date beside his signature. "There. Done! Now the boy's as noble as you are, Divvis."

Divvis drew himself up pompously. "My father was the Coronal Lord Voriax. My grandfather was the High Counsellor Damiandane. My great-grandfather was—"

"Yes. We know all that. And I say, the boy is just as noble as you are now, Divvis. This paper says so. As some similar paper said for some ancestor of yours, I know not how long ago and certainly not why. Or do you think being noble is something innate, like Skandars having four arms and dark fur?"

"Your temper is short today, Elidath."

"So it is. Therefore make allowances for me, and try not to be so tiresome."

"Forgive me, then," said Divvis, not very contritely.

Elidath stood and stretched and peered out the great curving window before the Coronal's desk. It afforded a stupendous view into the open abyss of air that dropped away from the summit of Castle Mount on this side of the royal complex. Two mighty black raptors, wholly at home in these dizzying altitudes, flew in great arrogant arcs about one another out there, sunlight rebounding dazzlingly from the crest of glassy feathers on their golden heads, and Elidath, watching the easy unfettered movements of the huge birds, found himself envying their freedom to soar in those infinite spaces. He shook his head slowly. The day's toil had left him groggy. *Elidath of Morvole, High Counsellor and Regent—*

Six months this week, he thought, since Valentine had set out on the processional. It felt like years already. Was it like this to be Coronal? Such drudgery, such captivity? For a decade, now, he had lived with the possibility of becoming Coronal in his own right, for he was the clear and obvious next in line. That had been plain almost from the day Lord Voriax had been killed in the forest and the crown had so unexpectedly passed to his younger brother. If anything were to happen to Lord Valentine, Elidath knew, they would come to him with the starburst crown. Or if the Pontifex Tyeveras ever actually died and Valentine had to enter the Labyrinth, that too could make Elidath Coronal. Unless he was too old for the job by the time that occurred, for the Coronal must be a man of vigorous years, and Elidath was already past forty, and it looked as though Tyeveras would live forever.

If it came to him, he would not, could not, consider refusing. Refusing was unimaginable. But each passing year he found himself praying more fervently for continued long life for the Pontifex Tyeveras and a long healthy reign for the Coronal Lord Valentine. And these months as regent had only deepened those feelings. When he was a boy and this had been Lord Malibor's Castle, it had seemed the most wondrous thing in the world to him to be Coronal, and his envy had been keen when Voriax, eight years his senior, was chosen upon Lord Malibor's death. Now he was not quite so sure how wondrous it might be. But he would not refuse, if the crown came to him. He remembered the old High Counsellor Damiandane, father to Voriax and Valentine, saying once that the best one to choose as Coronal was one who was qualified for the crown, but did not greatly want it. Well, then, Elidath told himself cheerlessly, perhaps I am a good choice. But maybe it will not come to that.

"Shall we run?" he said with forced heartiness. "Five miles, and then some good golden wine?"

"Indeed," said Mirigant.

As they made their way from the room, Divvis paused at the giant globe of bronze and silver, looming against the far wall, that bore the indicator of the Coronal's travels. "Look," he said putting his finger to the ruby sphere that glowed upon the surface of the globe like a rock-monkey's bloodshot eye. "He's well west of the Labyrinth already. What's this river he's sailing down? The Glayge, is it?"

"The Trey, I think," said Mirigant. "He's bound for Treymone, I imagine."

Elidath nodded. He walked toward the globe and ran his hand lightly over its silken-smooth metal skin. "Yes. And Stoien from there, and then I suppose he'll take ship across the Gulf to Perimor, and on up the coast as far as Alaisor."

He could not lift his hand from the globe. He caressed the curving continents as though Majipoor were a woman and her breasts were Alhanroel and Zimroel. How beautiful the world, how beautiful this depiction of it! It was only a half-globe, really, for there was no need of representing the far side of Majipoor, which was all ocean and scarcely even explored. But on its one vast hemisphere the three continents were displayed. Alhanroel with the great jagged spire of Castle Mount jutting out into the room, and many-forested Zimroel, and the desert wasteland that was Suvrael down below, and the blessed Lady's Isle of Sleep in the Inner Sea between them. Many of the cities were marked in detail, the mountain ranges, the larger lakes and rivers. Some mechanism Elidath did not understand tracked the Coronal at all times, and the glowing red sphere moved as the Coronal moved, so there could never be doubt of his whereabouts. As though in a trance Elidath traced out with his fingers the route of the grand processional, Stoien, Perimor, Alaisor, Sintalmond, Daniup, down through the Kinslain Gap into Santhiskion, and back by a winding course through the foothills to Castle Mount—

"You wish you were with him, don't you?" Divvis asked.

"Or that you were making the trip in his place, eh?" said Mirigant.

Elidath whirled on the older man. "What is that supposed to mean?"

Flustered, Mirigant said, "It should be obvious."

"You accuse me, I think, of an unlawful ambition."

"Unlawful? Tyeveras has outlived his time by twenty years. He's kept alive only by grace of some sort of magic—"

"By the finest of medical care, you mean," Elidath said.

With a shrug Mirigant said, "It's the same thing. In the natural order of things Tyeveras should long ago have been dead, and Valentine our Pontifex. And a new Coronal should be off undertaking his first grand processional."

"These are not decisions for us to make," Elidath grumbled.

Divvis said, "They are Valentine's decisions, yes. And he will not make them."

"He will, at the proper time."

"When? Five more years? Ten? Forty?"

"Would you coerce the Coronal, Divvis?"

"I would advise the Coronal. It is our duty—yours, mine, Mirigant's, Tunigorn's, all of us who were in the government before the overthrow. We must tell him: it is time for him to move on to the Labyrinth."

"I think it is time for us to have our run," said Elidath stiffly.

"Listen to me, Elidath! Am I an innocent? My father was a Coronal; my grandfather held the post you hold now; I have spent all my life close to the heart of power. I understand things as well as most. We have no Pontifex. For eight or ten years we've merely had a thing more dead than alive, floating in that glass cage in the Labyrinth. Hornkast speaks to him, or pretends to, and receives decrees from him, or pretends to, but in effect there's no Pontifex at all. How long can the government function that way? I think Valentine is trying to be Pontifex and Coronal both, which is impossible for any man to carry off, and so the whole structure is suffering, everything is paralyzed—"

"Enough," Mirigant said.

"—and he will not move along to his proper office, because he's young and hates the Labyrinth, and because he has come back from his exile with his new retinue of jugglers and herdboys, who are so captivated by the splendors of the Mount that they will not allow him to see that his true responsibility lies—"

"Enough!"

"One moment more," said Divvis earnestly. "Are you blind, Elidath? Only eight years back we experienced something altogether unique in our history, when a lawful Coronal was overthrown without our knowing it, and an unanointed king put in his place. And what kind of man was that? A Metamorph puppet, Elidath! And the King of Dreams himself an actual Metamorph! Two of the four Powers of the Realm usurped, and this very Castle filled with Metamorph impostors—"

"All of them discovered and destroyed. And the throne bravely regained by its rightful holder, Divvis."

"Indeed. Indeed. And do you think the Metamorphs have gone politely back to their jungles? I tell you, they are scheming right this instant to destroy Majipoor and take back for themselves whatever is left, which we have known since the moment of Valentine's restoration, and what has he done about it? What has he done about it, Elidath? Stretched out his arms to them in love. Promised them that he will right ancient wrongs and remedy old injustices. Yes, and still they scheme against us!"

"I will run without you," said Elidath. "Stay here, sit at the Coronal's desk, sign those mounds of decrees. That's what you want, isn't it, Divvis? To sit at that desk?" He swung about angrily and started from the room.

"Wait," Divvis said. "We're coming." He sprinted after Elidath, came up alongside him, caught him by the elbow. In a low intense tone quite different from his usual mocking drawl he declared, "I said nothing of the succession, except that it is necessary for Valentine to move on to the Pontificate. Do you think I would challenge you for the crown?"

"I am not a candidate for the crown," said Elidath.

"No one is ever a candidate for the crown," Divvis answered. "But even a child knows you are the heir presumptive. Elidath, Elidath—!"

"Let him be," said Mirigant. "We are here to run, I thought."

"Yes. Let us run, and no more of this talk for now," said Divvis.

"The Divine be praised," Elidath muttered.

He led the way down the flights of broad stone stairs, worn smooth by centuries of use, and out past the guardposts into Vildivar Close, the boulevard of pink granite blocks that linked the inner Castle, the Coronal's primary working quarters, to the all but incomprehensible maze of outer buildings that surrounded it at the summit of the Mount. He felt as though a band of hot steel had been wrapped about his forehead. First to be signing a myriad foolish documents, then to have to listen to Divvis's treasonous harangue—

Yet he knew Divvis to be right. The world could not much longer continue this way. When great actions needed to be undertaken, Pontifex and Coronal must consult with one another, and let their shared wisdom check all folly. But there was no Pontifex, in any real sense. And Valentine, attempting to operate alone, was failing. Not even the greatest of Coronals, not Confalume, not Prestimion, not Dekkeret, had presumed to try to rule Majipoor alone. And the challenges they had faced were as nothing compared with the one confronting Valentine. Who could have imagined, in Lord Confalume's day, that the humble subjugated Metamorphs would ever rise again to seek redress for the loss of their world? Yet that uprising was well under way in secret places. Elidath was not likely ever to forget the last hours of the war of restoration, when he had fought his way into the vaults where the machines that controlled the climate of Castle Mount were kept, and to save those machines had had to slay troops clad in the uniform of the Coronal's own guard—who as they died changed form and became slit-mouthed, noseless, slope-eyed Shapeshifters. That was eight years ago: and Valentine still hoped to reach that nation of malcontents with his love, and find some honorable peaceful way of healing their anger. But after eight years there were no concrete achievements to show; and who knew what new infiltration the Metamorphs had effected by now?

Elidath pulled breath deep into his lungs and broke into a furious pounding gallop, that left Mirigant and Divvis far behind within moments.

"Hoy!" Divvis called. "Is that your idea of jogging?"

He paid no attention. The pain within him could be burned away only by another kind of pain; and so he ran, in a frenzy, pushing himself to the limits of his strength. On, on, on, past the delicate five-peaked tower of Lord Arioc, past Lord Kinniken's chapel, past the Pontifical guest-house. Down the Guadeloom Cascade, and around the squat black mass of Lord Prankipin's treasury, and up the Ninety-Nine Steps, heart beginning to thunder in his breast, toward the vestibule of the Pinitor Court—on, on, through precincts he had traversed every day for thirty years, since as a child he had come here from Morvole at the foot of the Mount to be taught the arts of government. How many times he and Valentine had run like this, or Stasilaine or Tunigorn—they were close as brothers, the four of them, four wild boys roaring through Lord Malibor's Castle, as it was known in those days—ah, how joyous life had been for them then! They had assumed they would be counsellors under Voriax when he became Coronal, as everyone knew would happen, but not for many years; and then Lord Malibor died much too early, and also Voriax who followed him, and to Valentine went the crown and nothing had ever been the same for any of them again.

And now? *It is time for Valentine to move on to the Labyrinth,* Divvis had said. Yes. Yes. Somewhat young to be Pontifex, yes, but that was the hard luck of coming to the throne in Tyeveras's dotage. The old emperor deserved the sleep of the grave, and Valentine must go to the Labyrinth, and the starburst crown must descend—

To me? Lord Elidath? Is this to be Lord Elidath's Castle?

The thought filled him with awe and wonder: and also with fear. He had seen, these past six months, what it was to be Coronal.

"Elidath! You'll kill yourself! You're running like a madman!" That was Mirigant's voice, from far below, like something blown by the wind out of a distant city. Elidath was nearly at the top of the Ninety-Nine Steps now. There was a booming in his chest, and his vision was beginning to blur, but he forced himself onward, to the last of the steps, and into the narrow vestibule of dark green royal-stone that led to the administrative offices of the Pinitor Court. Blindly he careened around a corner, and felt a numbing impact and heard a heavy grunt; and then he fell and sprawled and lay breathing hard, more than half stunned.

He sat up and opened his eyes and saw someone—a youngish man, slender, dark of complexion, with fine black hair elaborately decked out in some fancy new style—getting shakily to his feet and coming toward him.

"Sir? Sir, are you all right?"

"Crashed into you, did I? Should have—looked where I was going—"

"I saw you, but there was no time. You came running so fast—here, let me help you up—"

"I'll be fine, boy. Just need to—catch my breath—"

Disdaining the young man's help, he pulled himself up, dusted off his doublet—there was a great rip up one knee, and bloody skin was showing through—and straightened his cloak. His heart was still thumping frighteningly, and he felt wholly absurd. Divvis and Mirigant were coming up the stairs, now. Turning to the young man, Elidath began to frame an apology, but the strange expression on the other's face halted him.

"Is something wrong?" Elidath asked.

"Do you happen to be Elidath of Morvole, sir?"

"I do, yes."

The boy laughed. "So I thought, when I took a close look. Why, you're the one I was looking for, then! They said I might find you in the Pinitor Court. I bring a message for you."

Mirigant and Divvis had entered the vestibule now. They came alongside Elidath, and from their look he knew he must be a frightful sight, flushed, sweating, half crazed from his lunatic run. He tried to make light of it, gesturing at the young man and saying, "It seems I ran down this messenger in my haste, and he's bearing something for me. Who's it from, boy?"

"Lord Valentine, sir."

Elidath stared. "Is this a joke? The Coronal is on the grand processional, somewhere west of the Labyrinth."

"So he is. I was with him in the Labyrinth, and when he sent me to the Mount he asked me to find you as the first thing I did, and tell you—"

"Well?"

He looked uneasily at Divvis and Mirigant. "I believe the message is for you alone, my lord."

"These are the lords Mirigant and Divvis, of the Coronal's own blood. You can speak in front of them."

"Very well, sir. Lord Valentine instructs me to tell Elidath of Morvole—I should say, sir, that I am the Knight-Initiate Hissune, son of Elsinome—instructs me to tell Elidath of Morvole that he has changed his plan, that he is extending the grand processional to the continent of Zimroel as well, and also will visit his mother the Lady of the Isle before he returns, and that therefore you are requested to serve as regent throughout the full time of his absence. Which he estimates to be—"

"The Divine spare me!" Elidath whispered hoarsely.

"—a year or perhaps a year and a half beyond the time already planned," said Hissune.

11

The second sign of trouble that Etowan Elacca noticed was the drooping leaves on the niyk trees, five days after the falling of the purple rain.

The purple rain itself was not the first sign of trouble. There was nothing uncommon about such a thing over on the eastern slope of the Dulorn Rift, where there were significant outcroppings of fluffy light skuvva-sand of a pale reddish-blue color. At certain seasons the wind from the north that was called the Chafer scoured the stuff free and hurled it high overhead, where it stained the clouds for days, and tinted the rainfall a fine lavender hue. It happened that the lands of Etowan Elacca were a thousand miles west of that district, on the other slope of the Rift entirely, just a short distance inland of Falkynkip; and winds laden with skuvva-sand were not known to blow that far west. But winds, Etowan Elacca knew, had a way of changing their courses, and perhaps the Chafer had chosen to visit a different side of the Rift this year. And in any event a purple rain was nothing to worry about: it merely left a fine coating of sand on everything, that was all, and the next normal rain washed it all away. No, the first sign of trouble was not the purple rain but the shriveling of the

sensitivos in Etowan Elacca's garden; and *that* happened two
or three days before the rain.

Which was puzzling, but not really extraordinary. It was
no great task to make sensitivos shrivel. They were small
golden-leaved psychosensitive plants with insignificant green
flowers, native to the forests west of Mazadone, and any sort
of psychic discordance within the range of their receptors—
angry shouting, or the growling of forest beasts in combat, or
even, so it was said, the mere proximity of someone who had
committed a serious crime—was sufficient to make their
leaflets fold together like praying hands and turn black. It was
not a response that seemed to have any particular biological
benefit, Etowan Elacca had often thought; but doubtless it
was a mystery that would unfold itself upon close examination, and someday he meant to make that examination.
Meanwhile he grew the sensitivos in his garden because he
liked the cheerful yellow glint of their leaves. And, because
Etowan Elacca's domain was a place of order and concord,
never once in the time he had been growing them had his
sensitivos undergone a withering—until now. That was the
puzzle. Who could have exchanged unkind words at the
border of his garden? What snarling animals, in this province
of bland domesticated creatures, might have put the equilibrium of his estate into disarray?

Equilibrium was what Etowan Elacca prized above all
else. He was a gentleman farmer, sixty years old, tall and
straight-backed, with a full head of dazzling white hair. His
father was the third son of the Duke of Massissa, and two of
his brothers had served in succession as Mayor of Falkynkip,
but government had never interested him: as soon as he
came into his inheritance, he had purchased a lordly span of
land in the placid rolling green countryside on the western
rim of the Dulorn Rift, and there he had built a Majipoor in
miniature, a little world, distinguished by its great beauty
and its calm, level, harmonious spirit.

He raised the usual crops of the district: niyk and glein,
hingamorts, stajja. Stajja was his mainstay, for there was
never any wavering of demand for the sweet, buoyant bread
that was made from stajja tubers, and the farms of the Rift
were hard pressed to produce enough to meet the needs of
Dulorn and Falkynkip and Pidruid, with close on thirty
million people among them, and millions more in the outlying towns. Slightly upslope from the stajja fields was the glein

plantation, row after row of dense, dome-shaped bushes ten
feet high, between whose blade-shaped silvery leaves nestled
great clusters of the plump, delicious little blue fruits. Stajja
and glein were everywhere grown side by side: it had been
discovered long ago that the roots of glein bushes seeped a
nitrogenous fluid into the soil, which, when washed downslope
by the rains, spurred the growth of stajja tubers.

Beyond the glein was the hingamort grove, where succu-
lent, fungoid-looking yellow fingers, swollen with sugary
juice, pushed up weirdly through the soil: light-seeking or-
gans, they were, that carried energy to the plants buried far
below. And all along the borders of the estate was Etowan
Elacca's glorious orchard of niyk trees, in groups of five laid
out, as was the custom, in intricate geometrical patterns. He
loved to walk among them and slide his hands lovingly over
their slim black trunks, no thicker than a man's arm and
smoother than fine satin. A niyk tree lived only ten years: in
the first three it grew with astonishing swiftness to its forty-
foot height, in the fourth it bore for the first time its stunning
cup-shaped golden flowers, blood-red at the center, and from
then on it yielded an abundance of translucent, crescent-
shaped, tart-flavored white fruits, until the moment of its
death came suddenly upon it and within hours the graceful
tree became a dried husk that a child could snap in half. The
fruit, though poisonous when raw, was indispensable in the
sharp, harsh stews and porridges favored in the Ghayrog
cuisine. Only in the Rift did niyk grow really well, and
Etowan Elacca enjoyed a steady market for his crop.

Farming provided Etowan Elacca with a sense of usefulness;
but it did not fully satisfy his love of beauty. For that he had
created on his property a private botanical garden where he
had assembled a wondrous ornamental display, taking from all
parts of the world every fascinating plant that could thrive in
the warm, moist climate of the Rift.

Here were alabandinas both of Zimroel and Alhanroel, in
all the natural colors and most of the hybrids as well. Here
were tanigales and thwales, and nightflower trees from the
Metamorph forests, that at midnight on Winterday alone
produced their brief, stupefying display of brilliance. Here
were pinninas and androdragmas, bubblebush and rubbermoss,
halatingas grown from cuttings obtained on Castle Mount,
and caramangs, muornas, sihornish vines, sefitongals, eldirons.
He experimented also with such difficult things as fireshower

palms from Pidruid, which sometimes lived six or seven seasons for him, but would never flower this far from the sea, and needle trees of the high country, which waned quickly without the chill they required, and the strange ghostly moon-cactus of the Velalisier Desert, which he tried in vain to shelter from the too-frequent rains. Nor did Etowan Elacca ignore the plants native to his own region of Zimroel, merely because they were less exotic: he grew the odd bloated bladdertrees that swayed, buoyant as balloons, on their swollen stems, and the sinister carnivorous mouthplants of the Mazadone forests, and singing ferns, cabbage trees, a couple of enormous dwikkas, half a dozen prehistoric-looking fern trees. By way of ground cover he used little clumps of sensitivos wherever it seemed appropriate, for their shy and delicate nature seemed a suitable contrast to the gaudier and more assertive plants that were the core of his collection.

The day he discovered the withering of the sensitivos had begun in more than ordinary splendor. Last night there had been light rain; but the showers had moved on, Etowan Elacca perceived, as he set forth on his customary stroll through his garden at dawn, and the air was cloudless and unusually clear, so that the rising sun struck startling green fire from the shining granite hills to the west. The alabandina blossoms glistened; the mouthplants, awakening and hungry, restlessly clashed the blades and grinders that lay half-submerged in the deep cups at the hearts of their huge rosettes; tiny crimson-winged longbeaks fluttered like sparks of dazzling light through the branches of the androdragmas. But for all that he had an odd sense of foreboding—he had dreamed badly the night before, of scorpions and dhiims and other vermin burrowing in his fields—and it was almost without surprise that he came upon the poor sensitivos, charred and crumpled from some torment of the dark hours.

For an hour before breakfast he worked alone, grimly ripping out the damaged plants. They were still alive below the injured branches, but there was no saving them, for the withered foliage would never regenerate, and if he were to cut it away the shock of the pruning would kill the lower parts. So he pulled them out by the dozens, shuddering to feel the plants writhing at his touch, and built a bonfire of them. Afterward he called his head gardener and his foremen together in the sensitivo grove and asked if anyone knew what had happened to upset the plants so. But no one had any idea.

The incident left him gloomy all morning, but it was not Etowan Elacca's nature to remain downcast for long, and by afternoon he had obtained a hundred packets of sensitivo seeds from the local nursery: he could not buy the plants themselves, of course, since they would never survive a transplanting. He spent the next day planting the seeds himself. In six or eight weeks there would be no sign of what had occurred. He regarded the event as no more than a minor mystery, which perhaps he would someday solve, more likely not; and he put the matter from his mind.

A day or two later came another oddity: the purple rain. A strange event, but harmless. Everyone said the same thing: "Winds must be changing, to blow the skuvva this far west!" The stain lasted less than a day, and then another rainshower, of a more usual kind, rinsed everything clean. That event, too, Etowan Elacca put quickly from his mind.

The niyk trees, though—

He was supervising the plucking of the glein fruit, some days after the purple rain, when the senior foreman, a leathery-looking, unexcitable Ghayrog named Simoost, came to him in what was, for Simoost, amazing agitation—serpentine hair madly tangling, forked tongue flickering as though trying to escape from his mouth—and cried, "The niyk! The niyk!"

The grayish-white leaves of niyk trees are pencil-shaped, and stand erect in sparse clumps at the ends of black two-inch stems, as though they had been turned upright by some sudden electric shock. Since the tree is so slender and its branches are so few and angular, this upturning of the leaves gives it a curious thorny look that makes a niyk tree unmistakable even at a great distance. Now, as Etowan Elacca ran with Simoost toward the grove, he saw while still hundreds of yards away that something had occurred that he would not have thought possible: every leaf on every niyk tree had turned downward, as though they were not niyks but some sort of weeping tanigale or halatinga!

"Yesterday they were fine," Simoost said. "This *morning* they were fine! But now—now—"

Etowan Elacca reached the first group of five niyks and put his hand to the nearest trunk. It felt strangely light; he pushed and the tree gave way, dry roots ripping easily from the ground. He pushed a second, a third.

"Dead," he said.

"The leaves—" said Simoost. "Even a dead niyk still keeps its leaves facing up. Yet these—I've never seen anything like this—"

"Not a natural death," Etowan Elacca murmured. "Something new, Simoost."

He ran from group to group, shoving the trees over; and by the third group he was no longer running, and by the fifth he was walking very slowly indeed, with his head bowed.

"Dead—all dead—my beautiful niyks—"

The whole grove was gone. They had died as niyks die, swiftly, all moisture fleeing their spongy stems; but an entire grove of niyks planted in staggered fashion over a ten-year cycle should not die all at once, and the strange behavior of the leaves was inexplicable.

"We'll have to report this to the agricultural agent," Etowan Elacca said. "And send messengers too, Simoost, to Hagidawn's farm, and Nismayne's, and what's-his-name by the lake—find out if they've had trouble with their niyks too. Is it a plague, I wonder? But niyks have no diseases—a new plague, Simoost? Coming upon us like a sending of the King of Dreams?"

"The purple rain, sir—"

"A little colored sand? How could that harm anything? They have purple rain a dozen times a year on the other side of the Rift, and it doesn't bother *their* crops. Oh, Simoost, my niyks, my niyks—!"

"It was the purple rain," said Simoost firmly. "That was not the rain of the eastern lands. It was something new, sir: it was poison rain, and it killed the niyks!"

"And killed the sensitivos too, three days before it actually fell?"

"They are very delicate, sir. Perhaps they felt the poison in the air, as the rain was coming toward us."

Etowan Elacca shrugged. Perhaps. Perhaps. And perhaps the Shapeshifters have been flying up from Piurifayne on broomsticks or magical flying machines in the night, and scattering some baleful enchantment on the land. Perhaps. In the world of perhaps anything at all was possible.

"What good is speculating?" he asked bitterly. "We know nothing. Except that the sensitivos have died, and the niyk trees have died. What will be next, Simoost? *What will be next?*"

12

Carabella, who had been staring all day out of the window of the floater car as though she hoped somehow to speed the journey through this bleak wasteland by the force of her eyes, called out in sudden glee, "Look, Valentine! I think we're actually coming out of the desert!"

"Surely not yet," he said. "Surely not for three or four more days. Or five, or six, or seven—"

"Will you *look*?"

He put down the packet of dispatches through which he had been leafing, and sat up and peered past her. Yes! By the Divine, it was green out there! And not the grayish green of twisted scruffy stubborn pathetic desert plants, but the rich, vibrant green of real Majipoori vegetation, throbbing with the energies of growth and fertility. So at last he was beyond the malign spell of the Labyrinth, now that the royal caravan was emerging from the parched tableland in which the subterranean capital was situated. Duke Nascimonte's territory must be coming near—Lake Ivory, Mount Ebersinul, the fields of thuyol and milaile, the great manor-house of which Valentine had heard so much—

Lightly he rested his hand on Carabella's slender shoulder and drew his fingers along her back, digging gently into the firm bands of muscle in what was in part a massage, in part a caress. How good it was to have her with him again! She had joined him on the processional a week ago, at the Velalisier ruins, where together they had inspected the progress the archaeologists were making at uncovering the enormous stone city that the Metamorphs had abandoned fifteen or twenty thousand years ago. Her arrival had done much to lift him from his bleak and cheerless mood.

"Ah, lady, it was a lonely business without you in the Labyrinth," he said softly.

"I wish I could have been there. I know how you hate that place. And when they told me you'd been ill—oh, I felt such guilt and shame, knowing I was far away when you—when you—" Carabella shook her head. "I would have been with you, if it had been possible. You know that, Valentine.

But I had promised the people in Stee that I would attend the dedication of their new museum, and—"

"Yes. Of course. The consort of the Coronal has her own responsibilities."

"It seems so strange to me, still. 'The consort of the Coronal'—! The little juggler girl from Til-omon, running around Castle Mount making speeches and dedicating museums—"

"'The little juggler girl from Til-omon,' still, after so many years, Carabella?"

She shrugged and ran her hands through her fine, close-cropped dark hair. "My life has been only a chain of strange accidents, and how can I ever forget that? If I hadn't been staying at that inn with Zalzan Kavol's juggling troupe when you came wandering in—and if you hadn't been robbed of your memory and dumped down in Pidruid with no more guile to you than a black-nosed blave—"

"Or if you had been born in Lord Havilbove's time, or on some other world—"

"Don't tease me, Valentine."

"Sorry, love." He took her small cool hand between both of his. "But how long will you go on looking backward at what you once were? When will you let yourself truly accept the life you lead now?"

"I think I never will truly accept it," she said distantly.

"Lady of my life, how can you say—"

"You know why, Valentine."

He closed his eyes a moment. "I tell you again, Carabella, you are beloved on the Mount by every knight, every prince, every lord—you have their devotion, their admiration, their respect, their—"

"I have Elidath's, yes. And Tunigorn's, and Stasilaine's, and others of that kind. Those who truly love you love me also. But to many of the others I remain an upstart, a commoner, an intruder, an accident—a concubine—"

"Which others?"

"You know them, Valentine."

"Which others?"

"Divvis," she said, after some hesitation. "And the little lords and knights in Divvis's faction. And others. The Duke of Halanx spoke mockingly of me to one of my own ladies-in-waiting—Halanx, Valentine, your native city! Prince Manganot of Banglecode. And there are more." She turned to him, and he saw the anguish in her dark eyes. "Am I imagining these things? Am I hearing whispers where it's only the rustling of the leaves? Oh, Valentine, sometimes I think that they're right, that a Coronal should not have married a commoner. I'm not one of them. I never will be. My lord, I must be so much grief for you—"

"You are joy to me, and nothing other than joy. Ask Sleet what my mood was like last week when I was in the Labyrinth, and how I've been since you joined me on this journey. Ask Shanamir—Tunigorn—anyone, anyone at all—"

"I know, love. You looked so dark, so grim the day I arrived. I barely recognized you, with that frown, with those glowering eyes."

"A few days with you heals me of anything."

"And yet I think you are still not yourself entirely. Is it that you still have the Labyrinth too much with you? Or perhaps it's the desert that's depressing you. Or the ruins."

"No, I think not."

"What is it, then?"

He studied the landscape beyond the floater window, noting its increasing greenness, the gradual encroachment of trees and grass as the terrain grew more hilly. That should have cheered him more than it did. But there was a weight on his soul that he could not shed.

After a moment he said, "The dream, Carabella—that vision, that omen—there's no way I can rid my mind of that. Ah, what a page I'll have in history! The Coronal who lost his throne and became a juggler, and got back his throne, and afterward governed foolishly, and allowed the world to collapse into chaos and madness—ah, Carabella, Carabella, is that what I'm doing? After fourteen thousand years, am I to be the last Coronal? Will there be anyone even to *write* my history, do you think?"

"You have never governed foolishly, Valentine."

"Am I not too gentle, too even-tempered, too eager to see both sides of an issue?"

"Those are not faults."

"Sleet thinks they are. Sleet feels that my dread of warfare, of any sort of violence, leads me on the wrong path. He's told me so in almost so many words."

"But there'll be no warfare, my lord."

"That dream—"

"I think you take that dream too literally."

"No," he said. "Such talk gives me only idle comfort. Tisana and Deliamber agree with me that we stand on the brink of some great calamity, perhaps a war. And Sleet: he's convinced of it. He's made up his mind that it's the Metamorphs who are about to rise against us, the holy war that they've been planning, he says, for seven thousand years."

"Sleet is too bloodthirsty. And he has had an irrational fear of Shapeshifters since he was a young man. You know that."

"When we recaptured the Castle eight years ago and found it full of disguised Metamorphs, was that just a delusion?"

"What they tried to do back then ultimately failed, did it not?"

"And will they never try again?"

"If your policies succeed, Valentine—"

"My policies! What policies? I reach toward the Metamorphs and they slide beyond my grasp! You know that I hoped to have half a dozen Metamorph chieftains by my side when we toured Velalisier last week. So that they could observe how we've restored their sacred city, and see the treasures we've found, and perhaps take the holiest objects with them back to Piurifayne. But I had no response from them, not even a refusal, Carabella."

"You were aware that the Velalisier excavations might create complications. Perhaps they resent our even entering the place, let alone trying to put it back together. Isn't there a legend that they plan to rebuild it themselves some day?"

"Yes," said Valentine somberly. "After they've regained control of Majipoor and driven us all from their world. So Ermanar once told me. All right: maybe inviting them to Velalisier was a mistake. But they've ignored all my other overtures, too. I write to their queen the Danipiur in Ilirivoyne, and if she replies at all, it's in letters of three sentences, cold, formal, empty—" He drew in his breath deeply. "Enough of all this misery, Carabella! There'll be no war. I'll find a way to break through the hatred the Shapeshifters feel for us, and win them to my side. And as for the lords of the Mount who've been snubbing you, if indeed they have—I beg you, ignore them. Snub them back! What is a Divvis to you, or a Duke of Halanx? Fools, is all they are." Valentine smiled. "I'll soon give them worse things to worry about, love, than my consort's pedigree!"

"What do you mean?"

"If they object to having a commoner for the Coronal's consort," said Valentine, "how will they feel when they have a commoner for their Coronal?"

Carabella looked at him in bewilderment. "I understand none of this, Valentine."

"You will. In time, you'll understand all. I mean to work such changes in the world—oh, love, when they write the history of my reign, if Majipoor survives long enough for that history to be written, they'll need more than one volume for it, I promise you! I will do such things—such earthshaking things—" He laughed. "What do you think, Carabella? Listen to me ranting! The good Lord Valentine of the gentle soul turns the world upside down! Can he do it? Can he actually bring it off?"

"My lord, you mystify me. You speak in riddles."

"Perhaps so."

"You give me no clue to the answer."

He said, after a moment's pause, "The answer to the riddle, Carabella, is Hissune."

"Hissune? Your little Labyrinth urchin?"

"An urchin no longer. A weapon, now, which I have hurled toward the Castle."

She sighed. "Riddles and still more riddles!"

"It's a royal privilege to speak in mysteries." Valentine winked and pulled her toward him, and brushed his lips lightly against hers. "Allow me this little indulgence. And—"

The floater came suddenly to a halt.

"Hoy, look! We've arrived!" he cried. "There's Nascimonte! And—by the Lady, I think he's got half his province out here to greet us!"

The caravan had pulled up in a broad meadow of short dense grass so dazzlingly green it seemed some other color altogether, some unworldly hue from the far end of the spectrum. Under the brilliant midday sun a great celebration was already in progress that might have stretched for miles, tens of thousands of people holding carnival as far as the eye could see. To the booming sound of cannons and the shrill jangling melodies of sistirons and double-chorded galistanes, volley after volley of day-fireworks rose overhead, sketching stunning hard-edged patterns in black and violet against the clear bright sky. Stilt walkers twenty feet tall, wearing huge clown-masks with swollen red foreheads and gigantic noses, frolicked through the crowd. Great posts had been erected from which starburst banners rippled joyously in the light summer breeze; half a dozen orchestras at once, on half a dozen different bandstands, burst loose with anthems and marches and chorales; and a veritable army of jugglers had been assembled, probably anyone in six hundred leagues who had the slightest skill, so that the air was thick with clubs and knives and hatchets and blazing torches and gaily colored balls and a hundred other sorts of objects, flying back and forth in tribute to Lord Valentine's beloved pastime. After the gloom and murk of the Labyrinth, this was the most splendid imaginable recommencement of the grand processional: frantic, overwhelming, a trifle ridiculous, altogether delightful.

In the midst of it all, waiting calmly near the place where the caravan of floaters had come to rest, was a tall, gaunt man of late middle years, whose eyes were bright with a strange intensity and whose hard-featured face was set in the most benevolent of smiles. This was Nascimonte, landowner turned bandit turned landowner again, once self-styled Duke of Vornek Crag and Overlord of the Western Marches, now by proclamation of Lord Valentine more properly ennobled with the title of Duke of Ebersinul.

"Oh, will you look!" Carabella cried, struggling to get the words out through her laughter. "He's wearing his bandit costume for us!"

Valentine nodded, grinning.

When first he had encountered Nascimonte, in the forlorn nameless ruins of some Metamorph city in the desert southwest of the Labyrinth, the highwayman duke was decked out in a bizarre jacket and leggings fashioned from the thick red fur of some ratty little desert creature, and a preposterous yellow fur cap. That was when, bankrupted and driven from his estates by the callous destructiveness of the followers of the false Lord Valentine as they passed through this region while the usurper was making his grand processional, Nascimonte had taken up the practice of robbing wayfarers in the desert. Now his lands were his own again, and he could dress, if he chose, in silks and velvets, and array himself with amulets and feather-masks and eye-jewels, but there he was in the same scruffy absurd garb he had favored during his time of exile. Nascimonte had always been a man of great style: and, Valentine thought, such a nostalgic choice of raiment on such a day as this was nothing if not a show of style.

It was years since last Valentine and Nascimonte had met. Unlike most of those who had fought beside Valentine in the final days of the war of restoration, Nascimonte had not cared to accept an appointment to the Coronal's councils on Castle Mount, but had wanted only to return to his ancestral land in the foothills of Mount Ebersinul, just above Lake Ivory. Which had been difficult to achieve, since title to the land had passed legitimately to others since Nascimonte's illegitimate losing of it; but the government of Lord Valentine had devoted much time in the early years of the restoration to such puzzles, and eventually Nascimonte had regained all that had been his.

Valentine wanted nothing more than to rush from his floater and embrace his old comrade-at-arms. But of course protocol forbade that: he could not simply plunge into this wild crowd as though he were just an ordinary free citizen.

Instead he had to wait while the ponderous ceremony of the arraying of the Coronal's guard took place: the great burly shaggy Skandar, Zalzan Kavol, who was the chief of his guards, shouting and waving his four arms officiously about, and the men and women in their impressive green-and-gold uniforms emerging from their floaters and forming a living enfilade to hold back the gaping populace, and the royal musicians setting up the royal anthem, and much more like that, until at last Sleet and Tunigorn came to the royal floater and opened its royal doors to allow the Coronal and his consort to step forth into the golden warmth of the day.

And then at last, to walk between the double rows of guards with Carabella on his arm to a point halfway toward Nascimonte, and there to wait while the Duke advanced, and bowed and made the starburst gesture, and most solemnly bowed again to Carabella—

And Valentine laughed and came forward and took the gaunt old bandit into his arms, and held him tight, and then they marched together through the parting crowd toward the reviewing stand that surmounted the festival.

Now began a grand parade of the kind customary to a visit of the Coronal, with musicians and jugglers and acrobats and tandy-prancers and clowns and wild animals of the most terrifying aspect, which were not in fact wild at all, but carefully bred for tameness; and along with these performers came all the general citizenry, marching in a kind of glorious random way, crying out as they passed the stand, "Valentine! Valentine! Lord Valentine!"

And the Coronal smiled, and waved, and applauded, and otherwise did what a Coronal on processional must do, which is to radiate joy and cheer and a sense of the wholeness of the world. This he found now to be unexpectedly difficult work, for all the innate sunniness of his nature: the dark cloud that had passed across his soul in the Labyrinth still shadowed him with inexplicable despond. But his training prevailed, and he smiled, and waved, and applauded for hours.

The afternoon passed and the festive mood ebbed, for even in the presence of the Coronal how can people cheer and salute with the same intensity for hour after hour? After the rush of excitement came the part Valentine liked least, when he saw in the eyes of those about him that intense probing curiosity, and he was reminded that a king is a freak, a sacred monster, incomprehensible and even terrifying to those who know him only as a title, a crown, an ermine robe, a place in history. That part, too, had to be endured, until at last all the parade had gone by, and the din of merrymaking had given way to the quieter sound of a wearying crowd, and the bronze shadows lengthened, and the air grew cool.

"Shall we go now to my home, lordship?" Nascimonte asked.

"I think it is time," said Valentine.

Nascimonte's manor-house proved to be a bizarre and wonderful structure that lay against an outcropping of pink granite like some vast featherless flying creature briefly halting to rest. In truth it was nothing more than a tent, but a tent of such size and strangeness as Valentine had never imagined. Some thirty or forty lofty poles upheld great outswooping wings of taut dark cloth that rose to startling steep peaks, then subsided almost to ground level, and went climbing again at sharp angles to form the chamber adjoining. It seemed as though the house could be disassembled in an hour and moved to some other hillside; and yet there was great strength and majesty to it, a paradoxical look of permanence and solidity within its airiness and lightness.

Inside, that look of permanence and solidity was manifest, for thick carpeting in the Milimorn style, dark green shot through with scarlet, had been woven to the underside of the roof canvas to give it a rich, vivid texture, and the heavy tentpoles were banded with glittering metal, and the flooring was of pale violet slate, cut thin and buffed to a keen polish. The furnishings were simple—divans, long massive tables, some old-fashioned armoires and chests, and not much else, but everything sturdy and in its way regal.

"Is this house anything like the one the usurper's men torched?" Valentine asked, when he was alone with Nascimonte a short while after they had entered.

"In construction, identical in all respects, my lord. The original, you know, was designed by the first and greatest Nascimonte, six hundred years ago. When we rebuilt, we used the old plans, and altered nothing. I reclaimed some of the furnishings from the creditors and duplicated the others. The plantation too—everything is just as it was before they came and carried out their drunken wrecking. The dam has been rebuilt, the fields have been drained, the fruit trees replanted: five years of constant toil, and now at last the havoc of that awful week is undone. All of which I owe to you, my lord. You have made me whole again—you have made all the world whole again—"

"And so may it remain, I pray."

"And so it shall, my lord."

"Ah, do you think so, Nascimonte? Do you think we are out of our troubles yet?"

"My lord, what troubles?" Nascimonte lightly touched the Coronal's arm, and led him to a broad porch from which there was a magnificent prospect of all his property. By the twilight glow and the soft radiance of drifting yellow glowfloats tethered in the trees, Valentine saw a long sweep of lawn leading down to elegantly maintained fields and gardens, and beyond it the serene crescent of Lake Ivory, on whose bright surface the many peaks and crags of Mount Ebersinul, dominating the scene, were indistinctly mirrored. There was the faint sound of distant music, the twanging of gardolans, perhaps, and some voices raised in the last gentle songs of the long festal afternoon. All was peace and prosperity out there. "When you look upon this, my lord, can you believe that trouble exists in the world?"

"I take your point, old friend. But there is more to the world than what we can see from your porch."

"It is the most peaceful of worlds, my lord."

"So it has been, for thousands of years. But how much longer will that long peace endure?"

Nascimonte stared, as though seeing Valentine for the first time that day.

"My lord?"

"Do I sound gloomy, Nascimonte?"

"I've never seen you so somber, my lord. I could almost believe that the trick has been played again, that a false Valentine has been substituted for the one I knew."

With a thin smile Valentine said, "I am the true Valentine. But a very tired one, I think."

"Come, I'll show you to your chamber, and there will be dinner when you're ready, a quiet one, only my family and a few guests from town, no more than twenty at the most, and thirty more of your people—"

"That sounds almost intimate, after the Labyrinth," said Valentine lightly.

He followed Nascimonte through the dark and mysterious windings of the manor-house to a wing set apart on the high eastern arm of the cliff. Here, behind a formidable barricade of Skandar guards that included Zalzan Kavol himself, was the royal suite. Valentine, bidding his host farewell, entered and found Carabella alone within, stretched languidly in a sunken tub of delicate blue and gold Ni-moyan tile, her slender body dimly visible beneath a curious crackling haze at the surface of the water.

"This is astonishing!" she said. "You ought to come in with me, Valentine."

"Most gladly I will, lady!"

He kicked off his boots, peeled away his doublet, tossed his tunic aside, and with a grateful sigh slipped into the tub beside her. The water was effervescent, almost electrical, and now that he was in it he saw a faint glow playing over its surface. Closing his eyes, he stretched back and put his head against the smooth tiled rim, and curled his arm around Carabella to draw her against him. Lightly he kissed her forehead, and then, as she turned toward him, the briefly exposed tip of one small round breast.

"What have they put in the water?" he asked.

"It comes from a natural spring. The chamberlain called it 'radioactivity.'"

"I doubt that," said Valentine. "Radioactivity is something else, something very powerful and dangerous. I've studied it, so I believe."

"What is it like, if not like this?"

"I can't say. The Divine be blessed, we have none of it on Majipoor, whatever it may be. But if we did, I think we'd not be taking baths in it. This must be some lively kind of mineral water."

"Very likely," Carabella said.

They bathed together in silence awhile. Valentine felt the vitality returning to his spirit. The tingling water? The comforting presence of Carabella close by, and the freedom at last from the press of courtiers and followers and admirers and petitioners and cheering citizens? Yes, and yes, those things could only help to bring him back from his brooding, and also his innate resilience must be manifesting itself at last, drawing him forth from that strange and un-Valentine-like darkness that had oppressed him since entering the Labyrinth. He smiled. Carabella lifted her lips to his; and his hands slipped down the sleekness of her lithe body, to her lean muscular midsection, to the strong supple muscles of her thighs.

"In the bath?" she asked dreamily.

"Why not? This water is magical."

"Yes. Yes."

She floated above him. Her legs straddled him; her eyes, half open, met his for a moment, then closed. Valentine caught her taut little buttocks and guided her against him. Was it ten years, he wondered, since that first night in Pidruid, in that moonlit glade, under the high gray-green bushes, after the festival for that other Lord Valentine? Hard to imagine: ten years. And the excitement of her had never waned for him. He locked his arms about her, and they moved in rhythms that had grown familiar but never routine, and he ceased to think of that first time or of all the times since, or of anything, indeed, but warmth and love and happiness.

Afterward, as they dressed for Nascimonte's intimate dinner for fifty guests, she said, "Are you serious about making Hissune Coronal?"

"What?"

"I think that that surely was the meaning of what you were saying earlier—those riddles of yours, just as we arrived at the festival, do you recall?"

"I recall," Valentine said.

"If you prefer not to discuss—"

"No. No. I see no reason to hide this matter from you any longer."

"So you *are* serious!"

Valentine frowned. "I think he could be Coronal, yes. It's a thought that first crossed my mind when he was just a dirty little boy hustling for crowns and royals in the Labyrinth."

"But can an ordinary person become Coronal?"

"You, Carabella, who were a street-juggler, and are now consort to the Coronal, can ask that?"

"You fell in love with me and made a rash and unusual choice. Which has not been accepted, as you know, by everyone."

"Only by a few foolish lordlings! You're hailed by all the rest of the world as my true lady."

"Perhaps. But in my case the consort is not the Coronal. And the common people will never accept one of their own as Coronal. To them the Coronal is royal, sacred, almost divine. So I felt, when I was down there among them, in my former life."

"You are accepted. He will be accepted too."

"It seems so arbitrary—picking a boy out of nowhere, raising him to such a height. Why not Sleet? Zalzan Kavol? Anyone at random?"

"Hissune has the capacity. That I know."

"I am no judge of that. But the idea that that ragged little boy will wear the crown seems terribly strange to me, too strange even to be something out of a dream."

"Does the Coronal always have to come from the same narrow clique on Castle Mount? That's how it's been; yes, for hundreds of years—thousands, perhaps. The Coronal always selected from one of the great families of the Mount: or even when he is not of one of those, and I could not just now tell you when we last went outside the Mount for the choice, he has been highborn, invariably, the son of princes and dukes. I think that was not how our system was originally designed, or else why are we forbidden to have hereditary monarchs? And now such vast problems are coming to the surface, Carabella, that we must turn away from the Mount for answers. We are too isolated up there. We understand less than nothing, I often think. The world is in peril: it's time now for us to be reborn, to give the crown to someone truly from the outside world, someone not part of our little self-perpetuating aristocracy—someone with another perspective, who has seen the view from below—"

"He's so young, though!"

"Time will take care of that," said Valentine. "I know there are many who think I should already have become Pontifex, but I will go on disappointing them as long as I can. The boy must have his full training first. Nor will I pretend, as you know, any eagerness to hurry onward to the Labyrinth."

"No," Carabella said. "And we talk as though the present Pontifex is already dead, or at death's door. But Tyeveras still lives."

"He does, yes," said Valentine. "At least in certain senses of the word. Let him continue to live some while longer, I pray."

"And when Hissune is ready—?"

"Then I'll let Tyeveras rest at last."

"I find it hard to imagine you as Pontifex, Valentine."

"I find it even harder, love. But I will do it, because I must. Only not soon: not soon, is what I ask!"

After a pause Carabella said, "You will unsettle Castle Mount for certain, if you do this thing. Isn't Elidath supposed to be the next Coronal!"

"He is very dear to me."

"You've called him the heir presumptive yourself, many times."

"So I have," Valentine said. "But Elidath has changed, since we first had our training together. You know, love, anyone who desperately wants to be Coronal is plainly unfit for the throne. But one must at least be willing. One must have a sense of calling, an inner fire of a sort. I think that fire has gone out, in Elidath."

"You thought it had gone out in yourself, when you were juggling and first were told you had a higher destiny."

"But it returned, Carabella, as my old self reentered my mind! And it remains. I often weary of my crown—but I think I've never regretted having it."

"And Elidath would?"

"So I suspect. He's playing at being Coronal now, while I'm away. My guess is that he doesn't like it much. Besides, he's past forty. The Coronal should be a young man."

"Forty is still young, Valentine," said Carabella with a grin.

He shrugged. "I hope it is, love. But I remind you that if

I have my way, there'll be no cause to name a new Coronal
for a long time. And by then, I think, Hissune will be
prepared and Elidath will step gracefully aside."

"Will the other lords of the Mount be as graceful,
though?"

"They will have to be," said Valentine. He offered her
his arm. "Come: Nascimonte is waiting for us."

13

Because it was the fifth day of the fifth week of the fifth
month, which was the holy day that commemorated the
exodus from the ancient capital beyond the sea, there was an
important obeisance to perform before Faraataa could begin
the task of making contact with his agents in the outlying
provinces.

It was the time of the year in Piurifayne when the rains
came twice daily, once at the hour before dawn, once at
twilight. It was necessary to make the Velalisier ritual in
darkness but also in dryness, and so Faraataa had instructed
himself to awaken at the hour of the night that is known as
the Hour of the Jackal, when the sun still rests upon Alhanroel
in the east.

Without disturbing those who slept near him, he made
his way out of the flimsy wicker cottage that they had
constructed the day before—Faraataa and his followers kept
constantly on the move; it was safest that way—and slipped
into the forest. The air was moist and thick, as always, but
there was no scent yet of the morning rains.

He saw, by the glitter of starlight coming through rifts in
the clouds, other figures moving also toward the jungle
depths. But he did not acknowledge them, nor they him. The
Velalisier obeisance was performed alone: a private ritual for a
public grief. One never spoke of it; one simply did it, on the
fifth day of the fifth week of the fifth month, and when one's
children were of age one instructed them in the manner of
doing it, but always with shame, always with sorrow. That was
the Way.

He walked into the forest for the prescribed three hundred strides. That brought him to a grove of slender towering
gibaroons; but he could not pray properly here, because

aerial clumps of gleam-bells dangled from every crotch and pucker of their trunks, casting a sharp orange glow. Not far away he spied a majestic old dwikka tree, standing by itself, that had been gouged by lightning some ages ago: a great cavernous charred scar, covered along its edges by regrown red bark, offered itself to him as a temple. The light of the gleam-bells would not penetrate there.

Standing naked in the shelter of the dwikka's huge scar, he performed first the Five Changes.

His bones and muscles flowed, his skin cells modified themselves, and he became the Red Woman; and after her, the Blind Giant; and then the Flayed Man; and in the fourth of the Changes he took on the form of the Final King; and then, drawing breath deeply and calling upon all his power, he became the Prince To Come. For Faraataa, the Fifth Change was the deepest struggle: it required him to alter not only the outer lineaments of his body but the contours of the soul itself, from which he had to purge all hatred, all hunger for vengeance, all lust for destruction. The Prince To Come had transcended those things. Faraataa had no hope of achieving that. He knew that in his soul there dwelled nothing but hatred, hunger for vengeance, lust for destruction; to become the Prince To Come, he must empty himself to a husk, and that he could not do. But there were ways of approaching the desired state. He dreamed of a time when all that he had been working for was accomplished: the enemy destroyed, the forsaken lands reclaimed, the rites reestablished, the world born anew. He journeyed forth into that era and let its joy possess him. He forced from his soul all recollection of defeat, exile, loss. He saw the tabernacles of the dead city come alive. In the grip of such a vision, what need for vengeance? What enemy was there to hate and destroy? A strange and wondrous peace spread through his spirit. The day of rebirth had arrived; all was well in the world; his pain was gone forever, and he was at rest.

In that moment he took on the form of the Prince To Come.

Maintaining that form with a discipline that grew less effortful by the moment, he knelt and arranged the stones and feathers to make the altar. He captured two lizards and a night-crawling bruul and used them for the offering. He passed the Three Waters, spittle, urine, and tears. He gathered pebbles and laid them out in the shape of the Velalisier rampart. He uttered the Four Sorrows and the Five Griefs. He knelt and ate earth. A vision of the lost city entered his mind: the blue stone rampart, the dwelling of the king, the Place of Unchangingness, the Tables of the Gods, the six high temples, the seventh that was defiled, the Shrine of the Downfall, the Road of the Departure. Still maintaining, with an effort, the form of the Prince To Come, he told himself the tale of the downfall of Velalisier, experiencing that dark tragedy while feeling the grace and aura of the Prince upon him, so that he could comprehend the loss of the great capital not with pain but with actual love, seeing it as a necessary stage in the journey of his people, unavoidable, inevitable. When he knew he had come to accept the truth of that he allowed himself to shift form, reverting to the shapes of the Final King, the Flayed Man, the Blind Giant, the Red Woman, and then at last to that of Faraataa of Avendroyne.

It was done.

He lay sprawled face down on the soft mossy soil as the first rains of morning began to fall.

After a time he rose, gathered the stones and feathers of the little altar, and walked back toward the cottage. The peace of the Prince To Come still lay upon his soul, but he strived now to put that benign aura from him: the time had come to commence the work of the day. Such things as hatred, destruction, and vengeance might be alien to the spirit of the Prince To Come, but they were necessary tools in the task of bringing the kingdom of the Prince into being.

He waited outside the cottage until enough of the others had returned from their own obeisances to allow him to enter upon the calling of the water-kings. One by one, they took up their positions about him, Aarisiim with his hand to Faraataa's right shoulder, Benuuiab to the left, Siimii touching his forehead, Miisiim his loins, and the rest arranged in concentric circles about those four, linked arm to arm.

"Now," Faraataa said. And their minds joined and thrust outward.

—*Brother in the sea!*

The effort was so great that Faraataa felt his shape flowing and shifting of its own accord, like that of a child just learning how to bring the power into play. He sprouted feathers, talons, six terrible beaks; he became a bilantoon, a sigimoin, a snorting raging bidlak. Those about him gripped him all the more tightly, although the intensity of his signal

held such force that some of them too fluttered as he did from
form to form.

—*Brother! Hear me! Help me!*

And from the vastness of the depths came the image of
huge dark wings slowly opening and closing over titanic
bodies. And then a voice like a hundred bells tolling at once:

—*I hear, little land-brother.*

It was the water-king Maazmoorn who spoke. Faraataa
knew them all by the music of their minds: Maazmoorn the
bells, Girouz the singing thunder, Sheitoon the slow sad
drums. There were dozens of the great kings, and the voice
of each was unmistakable.

—*Carry me, O King Maazmoorn!*

—*Come upon me, O land-brother.*

Faraataa felt the pull, and yielded himself to it, and was
lifted upward and out, leaving his body behind. In an instant
he was at the sea, an instant more and he entered it; and then
he and Maazmoorn were one. Ecstasy overwhelmed him:
that joining, that communion, was so potent that it could
easily be an end in itself, a delight that fulfilled all yearnings,
if he would allow it. But he never would allow it.

The seat of the water-king's towering intelligence was
itself like an ocean—limitless, all-enfolding, infinitely deep.
Faraataa, sinking down and down and down, lost himself in it.
But never did he lose awareness of his task. Through the
strength of the water-king he would achieve what he never
could have done unaided. Gathering himself, he brought his
powerful mind to its finest focus and from his place at the
core of that warm cradling vastness he sent forth the messages he had come here to transmit:

—*Saarekkin?*

—*I am here.*

—*What is the report?*

—*The lusavender is altogether destroyed throughout the
eastern Rift. We have established the fungus beyond hope of
eradication, and it is spreading on its own.*

—*What action is the government taking?*

—*The burning of infected crops. It will be futile.*

—*Victory is ours, Saarekkin!*

—*Victory is ours, Faraataa!*

—*Tii-haanimak?*

—*I hear you, Faraataa.*

—*What news?*

*—The poison traveled upon the rain, and the niyk-trees
are destroyed in all Dulorn. It leaches now through the soil,
and will ruin the glein and the stajja. We are preparing the
next attack. Victory is ours, Faraataa!*

—Victory is ours! Iniriis?

*—I am Iniriis. The root-weevils thrive and spread in the
fields of Zimroel. They will devour the ricca and the milaile.*

—When will the effects be visible?

—They are visible now. Victory is ours, Faraataa!

*—We have won Zimroel. The battle now must shift to
Alhanroel, Iniriis. Begin shipping your weevils across the
Inner Sea.*

—It will be done.

—Victory is ours, Iniriis! Y-Uulisaan?

—This is Y-Uulisaan, Faraataa.

—You follow the Coronal still?

—I do. He has left Ebersinul and makes for Treymone.

—Does he know what is happening in Zimroel?

*—He knows nothing. The grand processional absorbs his
energies completely.*

*—Bring him the report, then. Tell him of weevils in the
valley of the Zimr, of lusavender blight in the Rift, of the
death of niyk and glein and stajja west of Dulorn.*

—I, Faraataa?

*—We must get even closer to him. The news must reach
him sooner or later through legitimate channels. Let it come
from us first, and let that be our way of approach to him. You
will be his adviser on the diseases of plants, Y-Uulisaan. Tell
him the news; and aid him in the struggle against these
blights. We should know what counterattacks are planned.
Victory is ours, Y-Uulisaan.*

—Victory is ours, Faraataa!

14

The message was more than an hour old when it finally
reached the high spokesman Hornkast in his private lair far
uplevel, just outside the Sphere of Triple Shadows:

> *Meet me in the throne room right away.*
> *—Sepulthrove*

The high spokesman glared at the messengers. They knew he was never to be disturbed in this chamber except for a matter of the greatest urgency.

"What is it? Is he dying? Dead already?"

"We were not told, sir."

"Did Sepulthrove seem unusually disturbed?"

"He seemed uneasy, sir, but I have no idea—"

"All right. Never mind. I'll be with you in a moment."

Hastily Hornkast cleansed himself and dressed. If it has truly come, he thought sourly, it comes at a most inconvenient moment. Tyeveras has waited at least a dozen decades for his dying; could he not have held off another hour or two? If it has truly come.

The golden-haired woman who had been visiting him said, "Shall I stay here until you come back?"

He shook his head. "There's no telling how long this will take. If the Pontifex has died—"

The woman made the Labyrinth sign. "The Divine forbid!"

"Indeed," said Hornkast drily.

He went out. The Sphere of Triple Shadows, rising high above the gleaming obsidian walls of the plaza, was in its brightest phase, casting an eerie blue-white light that obliterated all sensations of dimensionality or depth: the passersby looked like mere paper dolls, floating on a gentle breeze. With the messengers beside him and hard pressed to keep up with his pace, Hornkast hastened across the plaza to the private lift, moving, as always, with a vigor that belied his eighty years.

The descent to the imperial zone was interminable.

Dead? Dying? Inconceivable. Hornkast realized that he had never taken into account the contingency of an unexpected natural death for Tyeveras. Sepulthrove had assured him that the machinery would not fail, that the Pontifex could be kept alive, if need be, another twenty or thirty years, perhaps as much as fifty. And the high spokesman had assumed that his death, when it came, would be the outcome of a carefully arrived at political decision, not something awkwardly happening without warning in the middle of an otherwise ordinary morning.

And if it had? Lord Valentine must be summoned at once from the westlands. Ah, how he would hate that, dragged into the Labyrinth before he had fairly begun his processional! I will have to resign, of course, Hornkast told himself.

Valentine will want his own high spokesman: that little scar-faced man Sleet, no doubt, or even the Vroon. Hornkast considered what it would be like to train one of them in the duties of the office he had held so long. Sleet full of contempt and condescension, or the wizardy little Vroon, those huge glittering eyes, that beak, those tentacles—

That would be his last responsibility, to instruct the new high spokesman. And then I will go away, he thought, and I suspect I will not long survive the loss of my office. Elidath, I suppose, will become Coronal. They say he is a good man, very dear to Lord Valentine, almost like a brother. How strange it will be, after all these years, to have a real Pontifex again, actively working with his Coronal! But I will not see it, Hornkast told himself. I will not be here.

In that mood of foreboding and resignation he arrived at the ornately embellished door to the imperial throne room. He slipped his hand into the recognition glove and squeezed the cool yielding sphere within; and at his touch the door slid back to reveal the great globe of the imperial chamber, the lofty throne upon the three broad steps, the elaborate mechanisms of the Pontifex's life-support systems, and, within the bubble of pale blue glass that had held him for so many years, the long-limbed figure of the Pontifex himself, fleshless and parched like his own mummy, upright in his seat, jaws clenched, eyes bright, bright, bright still with inextinguishable life.

A familiar crew of grotesques stood beside the throne: ancient Dilifon, the withered and trembling private secretary; the Pontifical dream-speaker, the witch Narrameer; and Sepulthrove the physician, hawk-nosed, skin the color of dried mud. From then, even from Narrameer, who kept herself young and implausibly beautiful by her sorceries, came a pulsing aura of age, decay, death. Hornkast, who had seen these people every day for forty years, had never before perceived with such intensity how frightful they were: and, he knew, he must be just as frightful himself. Perhaps the time has come, he thought, to clear us all away.

"I came as soon as the messengers could reach me," he said. He glanced toward the Pontifex. "Well? He's dying, is he? He looks just the same to me."

"He is very far from dying," said Sepulthrove.

"Then what's going on?"

"Listen," the physician said. "He's starting again."

The creature in the life-support globe stirred and swayed from side to side in minute oscillations. A low whining sound came from the Pontifex, and then a kind of half-whistled snore, and a thick bubbling gurgle that went on and on.

Hornkast had heard all these sounds many times before. They were the private language the Pontifex in his terrible senility had invented, and which the high spokesman alone had mastered. Some were almost words, or the ghosts of words, and within their blurred outlines the original meanings were still apparent. Others had evolved from words over the years into mere noise, but Hornkast, because he had observed those evolutions in their various stages, knew what meanings were intended. Some were nothing but moans and sighs and weepings without a verbal content. And some seemed to have a certain complexity of form that might represent concepts that had been perceived by Tyeveras in his long mad sleepless isolation, and were known to him alone.

"I hear the usual," said Hornkast.

"Wait."

He listened. He heard the string of syllables that meant Lord Malibor—the Pontifex had forgotten Malibor's two successors, and thought Malibor was Coronal still—and then a skein of other royal names, Prestimion, Confalume, Dekkeret. Malibor again. The word for sleep. The name of Ossier, who had been Pontifex before Tyeveras. The name of Kinniken, who had preceded Ossier.

"He rambles in the remote past, as he often does. For this you called me down here with such urgent—"

"Wait."

In growing irritation Hornkast turned his attention again to the inchoate monolog of the Pontifex, and was stunned to hear, for the first time in many years, a perfectly enunciated, completely recognizable word:

"Life."

"You heard?" Sepulthrove asked.

Hornkast nodded. "When did this start?"

"Two hours ago, two and a half."

"Majesty."

"We have made a record of all of this," said Dilifon.

"What else has he said that you can understand?"

"Seven or eight words," Sepulthrove replied. "Perhaps there are others that only you can recognize."

Hornkast looked toward Narrameer. "Is he awake or dreaming?"

"I think it is wrong to use either of those terms in connection with the Pontifex," she said. "He lives in both states at once."

"Come. Rise. Walk."

"He's said those before, several times," Dilifon murmured.

There was silence. The Pontifex seemed to have lapsed into sleep, though his eyes were still open. Hornkast stared grimly. When Tyeveras first had become ill, early in the reign of Lord Valentine, it had seemed only logical to sustain the old Pontifex's life in this way, and Hornkast had been one of the most enthusiastic supporters of the scheme that Sepulthrove had proposed. It had never happened before that a Pontifex had outlived two Coronals, so that the third Coronal of the reign came into power when the Pontifex was already in extreme old age. That had distorted the dynamics of the imperial system. Hornkast himself had pointed out at that time that Lord Valentine, young and untried, barely in command of the duties of the Coronal, could not be sent on to the Labyrinth so soon. By general agreement it was essential that the Pontifex remain on his throne a few more years, if he could be kept alive. Sepulthrove had found the means to keep him alive, though quickly it was apparent that Tyeveras had lapsed into senility and dwelled in hopeless lunatic death-in-life.

But then had come the episode of the usurpation, and then the difficult years of restoration, when all the Coronal's energies were needed to repair the chaos of the upheaval. Tyeveras had had to remain in his cage year after year. Though the continued life of the Pontifex meant Hornkast's own continuance in power, and the power he had amassed by default of the Pontifex by now was extraordinary, nevertheless it was a repellent thing to watch, this cruel suspension of a life long since deserving of a termination. Yet Lord Valentine asked for time, and more time, and yet more time still, to finish his work as Coronal. Eight years, now: was that not time enough? With surprise Hornkast found himself almost ready now to pray for Tyeveras's deliverance from this captivity. If only it were possible to let him sleep!

"Va—Va—"

"What's that?" Sepulthrove asked.

"Something new!" whispered Dilifon.

Hornkast gestured to them to be quiet.

"*Va—Valentine—*"

"This is new indeed!" said Narrameer.

"*Valentine Pontifex—Valentine Pontifex of Majipoor—*"

Followed by silence. Those words, plainly enunciated, free of all ambiguities, hovered in the air like exploding suns.

"I thought he had forgotten Valentine's name," Hornkast said. "He thinks Lord Malibor is Coronal."

"Evidently he does not," said Dilifon.

"Sometimes toward the end," Sepulthrove said quietly, "the mind repairs itself. I think his sanity is returning."

"He is as mad as ever!" cried Dilifon. "The Divine forbid that he should regain his understanding, and know what we have done to him!"

"I think," said Hornkast, "that he has always known what we have done to him, and that he is regaining not his understanding but his ability to communicate with us in words. You heard him: *Valentine Pontifex*. He is hailing his successor, and he knows who his successor ought to be. Sepulthrove, is he dying?"

"The instruments indicate no physical change in him. I think he could continue this way for some long while."

"We must not allow it," said Dilifon.

"What are you suggesting?" Hornkast asked.

"That this has gone on long enough. I know what it is to be old, Hornkast—and perhaps you do also, though you show little outer sign of it. This man is half again as old as any of us. He suffers things we can scarcely imagine. I say make an end. Now. This very day."

"We have no right," said Hornkast. "I tell you, I feel for his sufferings even as you. But it is not our decision."

"Make an end, nevertheless."

"Lord Valentine must take responsibility for that."

"Lord Valentine never will," Dilifon muttered. "He'll keep this farce running for fifty more years!"

"It is his choice," said Hornkast firmly.

"Are we his servants, or the servants of the Pontifex?" asked Dilifon.

"It is one government, with two monarchs, and only one of them now is competent. We serve the Pontifex by serving the Coronal. And—"

From the life-support cage came a bellow of rage, and then an eerie indrawn whistling sound, and then three harsh growls. And then the words, even more clearly than before:

"*Valentine—Pontifex of Majipoor—hail!*"

"He hears what we say, and it angers him. He begs for death," said Dilifon.

"Or perhaps he thinks he has already reached it," Narrameer suggested.

"No. No. Dilifon is right," said Hornkast. "He's over-heard us. He knows we won't give him what he wants."

"*Come. Rise. Walk.*" Howlings. Babblings. "*Death! Death! Death!*"

In a despair deeper than anything he had felt in decades, the high spokesman rushed toward the life-support globe, half intending to rip the cables and tubes from their mountings and bring an end to this now. But of course that would be insanity. Hornkast halted; he peered in; his eyes met those of Tyeveras, and he compelled himself not to flinch as that great sadness poured out upon him. The Pontifex was sane again. That was unarguable. The Pontifex understood that death was being withheld from him for reasons of state.

"Your majesty?" Hornkast asked, speaking in his richest, fullest tone. "Your majesty, do you hear me? Close one eye if you hear me."

There was no response.

"I think, nevertheless, that you hear me, majesty. And I tell you this: we know what you suffer. We will not allow you much longer to endure it. That we pledge to you, majesty."

Silence. Stillness. Then:

"*Life! Pain! Death!*"

And then a moaning and a babbling and a whistling and a shrieking that was like a song from beyond the grave.

15

"—and that is the temple of the Lady," said Lord Mayor Sambigel, pointing far up the face of the astonishing vertical cliff that rose just east of his city. "The holiest of her shrines in the world, saving only the Isle itself, of course."

Valentine stared. The temple gleamed like a solitary white eye set in the dark forehead of the cliff.

It was the fourth month of the grand processional now, or the fifth, or perhaps the sixth: days and weeks, cities and provinces, everything had begun to blur and merge. This day he had arrived at the great port of Alaisor, far up the northwestern coast of Alhanroel. Behind him lay Treymone, Stoienzar, Vilimong, Estotilaup, Kimoise: city upon city, all flowing together in his mind into one vast metropolis that spread like some sluggish many-armed monster across the face of Majipoor.

Sambigel, a short swarthy man with a fringe of dense black beard around the edge of his face, droned on and on, bidding the Coronal welcome with his most sonorous platitudes. Valentine's eyes felt glazed; his mind wandered. He had heard all this before, in Kikil, in Steenorp, in Klai: never-to-be-forgotten occasion, love and gratitude of all the people, proud of this, honored by that. Yes. Yes. He found himself wondering which city it was that had shown him its famous vanishing lake. Was it Simbilfant? And the aerial ballet, that was Montepulsiane, or had it been Ghrav? The golden bees were surely Beilemoona, but the sky-chain? Arkilon? Sennamole?

Once more he looked toward the temple on the cliff. It beckoned powerfully to him. He yearned to be there at this very moment: to be caught on the fingertip of a gale; and swept like a dry leaf to that lofty summit.

—*Mother, let me rest with you awhile!*

There came a pause in the lord mayor's speech, or perhaps he was done. Valentine turned to Tunigorn and said, "Make arrangements for me to sleep at that temple tonight."

Sambigel seemed nonplussed. "It was my understanding, my lord, that you were to see the Tomb of Lord Stiamot this afternoon, and then to go to the Hall of Topaz for a reception, followed by a dinner at—"

"Lord Stiamot has waited eight thousand years for me to pay homage to him. He can wait one day more."

"Of course, my lord. So be it, my lord." Sambigel made a hasty flurry of starbursts. "I will notify the hierarch Ambargarde that you will be her guest tonight. And now, if you will permit, my lord, we have an entertainment to offer you—"

An orchestra struck up some jubilant anthem. From hundreds of thousands of throats came what he did not doubt were stirring verses, though he could not make out a syllable of them. He stood impassively, gazing out over that vast throng, nodding occasionally, smiling, making contact now and then with the eyes of some awed citizen who would never forget this day. A sense of his own unreality came over him. He did not need to be a living man, he thought, to be playing this part. A statue would do just as well, some cunning marionette, or even one of those waxworks things that he had once seen in Pidruid on a festival night long ago. How useful it would be to send an imitation Coronal of some such sort out to these events, capable of listening gravely and smiling appreciatively and waving heartily and perhaps even of delivering a few heartfelt words of gratitude—

Out of the coener of his eye he saw Carabella watching him worriedly. He made a little gesture with two fingers of his right hand, a private sign they had between them, to tell her he was all right. But the troubled look did not leave her face. And it seemed to him that Tunigorn and Lisamon Hultin had edged forward until they stood oddly close to him. To catch him if he fell? Confalume's whiskers, did they think he was going to collapse the way he had in the Labyrinth?

He held himself all the more erect: wave, smile, nod, wave, smile, nod. Nothing was going to go wrong. Nothing. Nothing. But would this ceremony ever end?

There was half an hour more. But at last it was over, and the royal party, leaving by way of an underground passage, quickly made its way toward the quarters set aside for the Coronal in the lord mayor's palace on the far side of the square. When they were alone Carabella said, "It seemed to me you were growing ill up there, Valentine."

He said as lightly as he could, "If boredom is a malady, then I was growing ill, yes."

She was silent a moment. Then she said, "Is it absolutely essential to continue with this processional?"

"You know I have no choice."

"I fear for you."

"Why, Carabella?"

"There are times I scarcely know you any longer. Who is this brooding fretful person who shares my bed? What has become of the man called Valentine I knew once in Pidruid"

"He is still here."

"So I would believe. But hidden, as the sun is hidden when the shadow of a moon falls upon it. What shadow is on you, Valentine? What shadow is on the world? Something strange befell you in the Labyrinth. What was it? Why?"

"The Labyrinth is a place of no joy for me, Carabella. Perhaps I felt enclosed there, buried, smothered—" He shook his head. "It was strange, yes. But the Labyrinth is far behind me. Once we began to travel in happier lands I felt my old self returning, I knew joy again, love, I—"

"You deceive yourself, perhaps, but not me. There's no joy in it for you, not now. At the beginning you drank in everything as if you couldn't possibly get enough of it—you wanted to go everywhere, behold everything, taste all that is to be tasted—but not anymore. I see it in your eyes, I see it on your face. You move about like a sleepwalker. Do you deny it?"

"I do grow weary, yes. I admit that."

"Then abandon the processional! Return to the Mount, which you love, where you always have been truly happy!"

"I am the Coronal. The Coronal has a sacred duty to present himself to the people he governs. I owe them that."

"And what do you owe to yourself, then?"

He shrugged. "I beg you, sweet lady! Even if I grow bored, and I do—I won't deny it, I hear speeches in my sleep now, I see endless parades of jugglers and acrobats—nevertheless, no one has ever died of boredom. The processional is my obligation. I must continue."

"At least cancel the Zimroel part of it, then. One continent is more than enough. It'll take you months simply to return to Castle Mount from here, if you stop at every major city along the way. And then Zimroel? Piliplok, Ni-moya, Til-omon, Narabal, Pidruid—it'll take years, Valentine!"

He shook his head slowly. "I have an obligation to all the people, not only the ones who live in Alhanroel, Carabella."

Taking his hand, she said, "That much I understand. But you may be demanding too much of yourself. I ask you again: consider eliminating Zimroel from the tour. Will you do that? Will you at least give it some thought?"

"I'd return to Castle Mount this very evening, if I could. But I must go on. I must."

"Tonight at the temple you hope to speak in dreams with your mother the Lady, is that not so?"

"Yes," he said. "But—"

"Promise me this, then. If you reach her mind with yours, ask her if you should go to Zimroel. Let her advice guide you in this, as it has so well in so many other things. Will you?"

"Carabella—"

"Will you ask her? Only ask!"

"Very well," he said. "I will ask. That much do I promise."

She looked at him mischievously. "Do I seem a shrewish wife, Valentine? Chivvying and pressing you this way? I do this out of love, you know."

"That I know," said he, and drew her close and held her.

They said no more, for it was time then to make ready for the journey up Alaisor Heights to the temple of the Lady. Twilight was descending as they set out up the narrow winding road, and the lights of Alaisor sparkled behind them like millions of bright gems scattered carelessly over the plain.

The hierarch Ambargarde, a tall, regal-looking woman with keen eyes and lustrous white hair, waited at the gateway of the temple to receive the Coronal. While awed acolytes looked on gaping, she offered him a brief and warm welcome— he was, she said, the first Coronal to visit the temple since Lord Tyeveras had come, on his second processional—and led him through the lovely grounds until the temple itself came into view: a long building a single story in height, built of white stone, unornamented, even stark, situated in a spacious and open garden of great simplicity and beauty. Its western face curved in a crescent arc along the edge of the cliff, looking outward to the sea; and, on its inner side, wings set apart from one another at narrow angles radiated toward the east.

Valentine passed through an airy loggia to a small portico beyond that seemed to be suspended in space on the cliff's outermost rim. There he stood a long while in silence, with Carabella and the hierarch beside him, and Sleet and Tunigorn close by. It was wondrously quiet here: he heard nothing but the rush of the cool clear wind that blew without pause from the northwest, and the faint fluttering of Carabella's scarlet cloak. He looked down toward Alaisor. The great seaport lay like a giant outspread fan at the base of the cliff, ranging so far to the north and south that he could not see its limits. The dark spokes of colossal avenues ran its entire length, converging on a distant, barely visible circle of grand boulevards where six giant obelisks rose skyward: the tomb of Lord Stiamot, conqueror of the Metamorphs. Beyond lay only the sea, dark green, shrouded in the low-lying haze.

"Come, my lord," said Ambargarde. "The last light of the day is going. May I show you to your chamber?"

He would sleep alone that night, in an austere little room close by the tabernacle. Nor would he eat, or drink anything except the wine of the dream-speakers that would open his mind and make it accessible to the Lady. When Ambargarde had gone, he turned to Carabella and said, "I have not forgotten my promise, love."

"That I know. Oh, Valentine, I pray she tells you to turn back to the Mount!"

"Will you abide by it if she does not?"

"How can I not abide by whatever you decide? You are the Coronal. But I pray she tells you turn back. Dream well, Valentine."

"Dream well, Carabella."

She left him. He stood for some time at the window, watching as night engulfed the shoreline and the sea. Somewhere due west of here, he knew, lay the Isle of Sleep that was his mother's domain, far below the horizon, the home of that sweet and blessed Lady who brought wisdom to the world as it dreamed. Valentine stared intently seaward, searching in the mists and the gathering darkness as if he could see, if only he peered hard enough, the brilliant white ramparts of chalk on which the Isle rested.

Then he undressed and lay down on the simple cot that was the room's only furniture, and lifted the goblet that held the dark red dream-wine. He took a deep draft of the sweet thick stuff, and then another, and lay back and put himself into the trance state that opened his mind to impulses from afar, and waited for sleep.

—*Come to me, mother. This is Valentine.*

Drowsiness came over him, and he slipped downward into slumber.

—*Mother*—

—*Lady*—

—*Mother*—

Phantoms danced through his brain. Tenuous elongated figures burst like bubbles from vents in the ground, and spiraled upward to the roof of the sky. Disembodied hands sprouted from the trunks of trees, and boulders opened yellow eyes, and rivers grew hair. He watched and waited, letting himself glide downward and yet deeper downward into the realm of dreams, and all the while sending forth his soul to the Lady.

Then he had a glimpse of her seated by the eight-sided pool in her chamber of fine white stone at Inner Temple on the Isle. She was bending forward, as though studying her reflection. He floated toward her and hovered just behind her, and looked down and saw the familiar face glimmering in the pool, the dark shining hair, the full lips and warm loving eyes, the flower as always behind one ear, the silver band about her forehead. He said softly, "Mother? It's Valentine."

She turned to face him. But the face he saw was the face of a stranger: a pale, haggard, frowning, puzzled face.

"Who are you?" he whispered.

"Why, you know me! I am the Lady of the Isle!"

"No—no—"

"Most certainly I am."

"No."

"Why have you come to me here? You should not have done that, for you are Pontifex, and it is more fitting for me to journey toward you than you toward me."

"Pontifex? Coronal, you mean."

"Ah, did I say that? Then I was mistaken."

"And my mother? Where is she?"

"I am she, Valentine."

And indeed the haggard pale face was but a mask, which grew thin and peeled away like a sheath of old skin, to reveal his mother's wondrous smile, his mother's comforting eyes. And that in turn peeled away to show the other face once more, and then the true Lady's beneath that, but this time she was weeping. He reached for her and his hands passed through her, and he found himself alone. She did not return to him that night, though he pursued her through vision after vision, into realms of such strangeness that he would gladly have retreated if he could; and at last he abandoned the quest and gave himself over to the deepest and most dreamless of sleeps.

When he awakened it was midmorning. He bathed and stepped from his chamber and found Carabella outside, face drawn and tense, eyes reddened as though she had not slept at all.

"How is my lord?" she asked at once.

"I learned nothing last night. My dreams were hollow, and the Lady did not speak with me."

"Oh, love, how sorry I am!"

"I'll attempt it again tonight. Perhaps I had too little dream-wine, or too much. The hierarch will advise me. Have you eaten, Carabella?"

"Long since. But I'll breakfast again with you now, if you wish. And Sleet wants to see you. Some urgent message arrived in the night, and he would have gone right in to you, but I forbade it."

"What message is that?"

"He said nothing to me. Shall I send for him now?"

Valentine nodded. "I'll wait out there," he said, indicating with a wave of his arm the little portico overlooking the outer face of the cliff.

Sleet had a stranger with him when he appeared: a slender smooth-skinned man with a wide-browed triangular face and large somber eyes, who made a quick starburst gesture and stood staring at Valentine as though the Coronal were a creature from some other world. "Lordship, this is Y-Uulisaan, who came last night from Zimroel."

"An unusual name," Valentine said.

"It has been in our family many generations, my lord. I am associated with the office of agricultural affairs in Nimoya, and it is my mission to carry unhappy tidings to you from Zimroel."

Valentine felt a tightening in his chest.

Y-Uulisaan held forth a sheaf of folders. "It is all described in here—the full details of each of the plagues, the area it affects, the extent of the damage—"

"Plagues? What plagues?"

"In the agricultural zones, my lord. In Dulorn the lusavender smut has reappeared, and also there has been a dying of niyk trees to the west of the Rift, and also the stajja and glein are affected, and root weevils have attacked the ricca and milaile in—"

"My lord!" Carabella cried suddenly. "Look, look there!"

He whirled to face her. She was pointing skyward.

"What are *those*?"

Startled, Valentine looked up. On the bosom of the brisk breeze there journeyed a strange army of large glossy transparent floating creatures, unlike anything he had ever seen, appearing suddenly out of the west. They had bodies perhaps a man's length in diameter, shaped like shining cups upcurved to give them buoyancy, and long hairy legs that they held straight out on all sides. Their eyes, running in double rows across their heads, were like black beads the size of a man's fists, shining dazzlingly in the sunlight. Hundreds, even thousands, of the spiders were passing overhead, a migratory procession, a river of weird wraiths in the sky.

Carabella said, shuddering, "What monstrous-looking things! Like something out of the worst sending of the King of Dreams."

Valentine watched in astonishment and horror as they drifted past, dipping and soaring on the wind. Shouts of alarm now came from the courtyard of the temple. Valentine, beckoning Sleet to follow him, ran inward, and saw the old hierarch standing in the center of the lawn, waving an energy-thrower about. The air was thick with the floating things, some of which were drifting toward the ground, and she and half a dozen acolytes were attempting to destroy them before they landed, but several score had already reached ground. Wherever they touched down they remained motionless; but the rich green lawn was instantly burned yellow over an area perhaps twice the creatures' size.

Within minutes the onslaught was over. The floating things had passed by and were disappearing to the east, but the grounds and garden of the temple looked as if they had been attacked with blowtorches. The hierarch Ambargarde, seeing Valentine, put down her energy-thrower and walked slowly toward him.

"What were those things?" he asked.

"Wind-spiders, my lord."

"I've not heard of them. Are they native to this region?"

"The Divine be thanked, my lord, they are not! They come from Zimroel, from the mountains beyond Khyntor. Every year, when it is their mating season, they cast themselves into the stream of the high winds, and while they are aloft they couple, and let loose their fertile eggs, which are blown eastward by the contrary lower winds of the mountains until they land in the hatching-places. But the adults are caught by the currents of the air and carried out to sea, and sometimes they are swept all the way to the coast of Alhanroel."

Sleet, with a grimace of disgust, walked toward one last wind-spider that had fallen nearby. It lay quietly, making only the faintest movements, feeble twitchings of its thick shaggy legs.

"Keep back from it!" called Ambargarde. "Every part of it is poisonous!" She summoned an acolyte, who destroyed it with a burst from her energy-thrower. To Valentine the hierarch said, "Before they mate they are harmless enough things, eaters of leaves and soft twigs, and such. But once they have let loose their eggs they change, and become dangerous. You see what they have done to the grass. We will have to dig that all out, or nothing will ever grow there again."

"And this happens every year?" Valentine asked.

"Oh, no, no, thanks be to the Divine! Most of them perish out at sea. Only once in many years do they get this far. But when they do—ah, my lord, it is always a year of evil omen!"

"When did they last come?" the Coronal asked.

Ambargarde seemed to hesitate. At length she said, "In the year of the death of your brother Lord Voriax, my lord."

"And before that?"

Her lips trembled. "I cannot remember. Perhaps ten years before, perhaps fifteen."

"Not in the year of the death of Lord Malibor, by any chance?"

"My lord—forgive me—"

"There is nothing that needs forgiveness," Valentine said quietly. He walked away from the group and stood staring at the burned places in the devastated lawn. In the Labyrinth, he thought, the Coronal is smitten with dark visions at the feasting table. In Zimroel there are plagues upon the crops. In Alhanroel the wind-spiders come, bearing evil omens. And when I call upon my mother in my dreams I see a stranger's face. The message is very clear, is it not? Yes. The message is very clear.

"Sleet!" he called.

"Lordship?"

"Find Asenhart, and have him make ready the fleet. We sail as soon as possible."

"For Zimroel, my lord?"

"For the Isle, first, so I may confer with the Lady. And then to Zimroel, yes."

"Valentine?" a small voice said.

It was Carabella. Her eyes were fixed and strange and her face was pale. She looked almost like a child now—a small frightened child whose soul has been brushed in the night by the King of Dreams.

"What evil is loose in our land, my lord?" she asked in a voice he could scarcely hear. "What will happen to us, my lord? Tell me: what will happen to us?"

TWO

The Book
of the
Water-Kings

1

"Your task is to reach Ertsud Grand," the instructor had said. "Your route is the open country south of the Pinitor Highway. Your weapons are cudgel and dagger. Your obstacles are seven tracker beasts: vourhain, malorn, zeil, kassai, min-mollitor, weyhant, and zytoon. They are dangerous and will injure you if you allow them to take you by surprise."

Hissune concealed himself behind a thick-trunked ghazan tree so gnarled and twisted that it could well have been ten thousand years old, and peered cautiously down the long narrow valley ahead of him. All was still. He saw none of his fellow trainees, nor any of the tracker beasts.

This was his third day on the trail and he still had twelve miles to go. But what lay immediately before him was dismaying: a bleak slope of loose broken granite that probably would begin to slide the moment he stepped out onto it, sending him crashing onto the rocks of the distant valley floor. Even if this was only a training exercise, he knew that he could get quite authentically killed out here if he blundered.

But going back the way he had come and trying some other route of descent was even less appealing. Once more to risk that narrow ledge of a trail winding in miserable switch-backs over the face of the cliff, the thousand-foot drop that a single false step would bring, those ghastly overhangs that had forced him to crawl forward with his nose to the ground and barely half a foot's clearance above the back of his head—no. Better to trust himself to that field of rubble in front of him than to try to turn back. Besides, there was that creature prowling still up there, the vourhain, one of the seven trackers. Having come past those sickle tusks and great curving claws once, he had no appetite for confronting them a second time.

Using his cudgel as a walking-stick, he edged warily out onto the gravel field.

The sun was bright and penetrating, this far down Castle Mount, well below the perpetual band of clouds that sheathed the great mountain in its upper middle reaches. Its brilliant light struck fragments of mica embedded in the shattered sharp-edged granite of the slope and rebounded into his eyes, dazzling him.

He put one foot carefully forward, leaned into his step, found the rubble firm beneath his weight. He took another step. Another. A few small chunks of rock came loose and went skittering down the slope, flashing like little mirrors as they turned over and over in their fall.

There seemed no danger yet that the entire slope would give way. He continued downward. His ankles and knees, sore from yesterday's difficult crossing of a high windswept pass, protested the steep downhill angle. The straps of his backpack sliced into him. He was thirsty and his head ached slightly: the air was thin in this stretch of Castle Mount. There were moments when he found himself wishing he was safely back at the Castle, poring over the texts on constitutional law and ancient history that he had been condemned to study for the past six months. He had to smile at that, remembering how in the weariest days of his tutoring he had been desperately counting the days until he was released from his books and could move on to the excitement of the survival test. Just now, though, his days in the library of the Castle did not seem nearly so burdensome, nor this journey anything but a grueling ordeal.

He looked up. The sun seemed to fill half the sky. He raised his hand before his eyes as a shield.

It was almost a year, now, since Hissune had left the Labyrinth, and he still was not wholly used to the sight of that fiery thing in the sky, or to the touch of its rays on his skin. There were times when he reveled in its unfamiliar warmth—he had long since exchanged the Labyrinth pallor for a deep golden tan—and yet at other times it kindled fear in him, and he wanted to turn from it and bury himself a thousand feet below the surface of the earth, where it could not reach him.

Idiot. Simpleton. The sun's not your enemy! Keep moving. Keep moving.

On the distant horizon he saw the black towers of Ertsud

Grand to the west. That pool of gray shadow off to the other way was the city of Hoikmar, from which he had set forth. By his best calculation he had come twenty miles—through heat and thirst, across lakes of dust and ancient seas of ash, down spiraling fumaroles and over fields of clinking metallic lava. He had eluded the kassai, that thing of twitching antennae and eyes like white platters which had stalked him half a day. He had fooled the vourhain with the old trick of the double scent, letting the animal go chasing off after his discarded tunic while he went down a trail too narrow for the beast to follow. Five trackers left. Malorn, zeil, weyhant, min-mollitor, zytoon.

Strange names. Strange beasts, native to nowhere. Perhaps they were synthetics, created as mounts had been by the forgotten witchcraft-sciences of the old days. But why create monsters? Why set them loose on Castle Mount? Simply for the testing and annealing of the young nobility? Hissune wondered what would happen if the weyhant or the zytoon rose suddenly out of all this rocky rubble and sprang upon him unawares. *They will injure you if you allow them to take you by surprise*. Injure, yes. But kill? What was the purpose of this test? To hone the survival skills of young Knight-Initiates, or to eliminate the unfit? At this time, Hissune knew, some three dozen initiates like himself were scattered along the thirty miles of the testing grounds. How many would live to reach Ertsud Grand?

He would, at least. Of that he was certain.

Slowly, poking with his cudgel to test the stability of the rocks, he made his way down the granite chute. Halfway down came the first mishap: a huge, secure-looking triangular slab turned out to be only precariously balanced, and gave way to the first light touch of his left foot. For an instant he wavered in a wild lurching way, desperately trying to steady himself, and then he plunged forward. The cudgel flew from his hands and as he stumbled, dislodging a small avalanche of rocks, his right leg slipped thigh-deep between two great slabs keen as knifeblades.

He grabbed whatever he could and held on. But the rocks below him did not begin to slide. Fiery sensations were running the length of his leg. Broken? Torn ligaments, strained muscles? He began slowly to pull it free. His legging was slit from thigh to calf, and blood was flowing freely from a deep cut. But that seemed to be the worst of it, that and a throbbing in his groin that would probably cause him some bothersome lameness tomorrow. Recovering his cudgel, he went cautiously onward.

Then the character of the slope changed: the big cracked slabs gave way to a fine gravel, even more treacherous underfoot. Hissune adopted a slow sliding gait, turning his feet sideways and pushing the surface of the gravel ahead of him as he descended. It was hard on his sore leg but afforded some degree of control. The bottom of the slope was coming into view now.

He slipped twice on the gravel. The first time he skidded only a few feet; the second carried him a dozen yards downslope, and he saved himself from tumbling all the way only by jamming his feet against the gravel and burrowing under for six or seven inches while hanging on fiercely with his hands.

When he picked himself up he could not find his dagger. He searched some while in the gravel, with no success, and finally he shrugged and went on. The dagger would be of no use against a weyhant or a min-mollitor anyway, he told himself. But he would miss it in small ways when he foraged for his food along the trail: digging for edible tubers, peeling the skins from fruits.

At the bottom of the slope the valley opened into a broad rocky plateau, dry, forbidding, dotted here and there by ancient-looking ghazan trees, all but leafless, bent in the usual grotesque convoluted shapes. But he saw, a short way off toward the east, trees of another sort, slender and tall and leafy, clumped close together. They were a good indication of water, and he headed for them.

But that clump of greenery proved to be farther away than he thought. An hour of plodding toward it did not seem to bring it much closer. Hissune's injured leg was stiffening rapidly. His canteen was all but empty. And when he came across the crest of a low ridge he found the malorn waiting for him on the other side.

It was a strikingly hideous creature: a baggy oval body set within ten enormously long legs that made a huge V-bend to hold its thorax three feet off the ground. Eight of the legs ended in broad flat walking-pads. The two front ones were equipped with pincers and claws. A row of gleaming red eyes ran completely around the rim of its body. A long curved tail bristled with stingers.

"I could kill you with a mirror!" Hissune told it. "Just let you see your reflection and you'd ugly yourself to death!"

The malorn made a soft hissing sound and began to move slowly toward him, jaws working, pincers twitching. Hissune hefted his cudgel and waited. There was nothing to fear, he told himself, if he kept calm: the idea of this test was not to kill the trainees but only to toughen them, and perhaps to observe their behavior under stress.

He let the malorn get within ten yards. Then he picked up a rock and flipped it toward the creature's face. The malorn batted it aside easily and kept advancing. Gingerly Hissune edged around to the left, into a saddle of the ridge, keeping to the high ground and gripping his cudgel with both hands. The malorn looked neither agile nor swift, but if it tried to charge him Hissune intended that it would have to run uphill.

"Hissune?"

The voice came from behind him. "Who is it?" Hissune called, without looking around.

"Alsimir." A knight-initiate from Peritole, a year or two older than he was.

"Are you all right?" Hissune asked.

"I'm hurt. Malorn stung me."

"Hurt bad?"

"My arm's puffing up. Venomous."

"I'll be there right away. But first—"

"Watch out. It jumps."

And indeed the malorn seemed to be flexing its legs for a leap. Hissune waited, balancing on the balls of his feet, rocking lightly. For an infinitely long moment nothing happened. Time itself seemed frozen: and Hissune stared patiently at the malorn. He was perfectly calm. He left no room in his mind for fear, for uncertainty, for speculation on what might happen next.

Then the strange stasis broke and suddenly the creature was aloft, kicking itself into the air with a great thrust of all its legs; and in the same moment Hissune rushed forward, scrambling down the ridge toward the soaring malorn, so that the beast in its mighty leap would overshoot him.

As the malorn coursed through the air just above Hissune's head he threw himself to the ground to avoid the stabbing swipes of the deadly tail. Holding the cudgel in both his hands, he jabbed fiercely upward, ramming it as hard as he could into the creature's underbelly. There was a whooshing sound of expelled air and the malorn's legs flailed in anguish in all directions. Its claws came close to grazing Hissune as it fell.

The malorn landed on its back a few feet away. Hissune went to it and danced forward between the thrashing legs to bring the cudgel down into the malorn's belly twice more. Then he stepped back. The malorn was still moving feebly. Hissune found the biggest boulder he could lift, held it high above the malorn, let it fall. The thrashing legs grew still. Hissune turned away, trembling now, sweating, and leaned on his cudgel. His stomach churned wildly and heaved; and then, after a moment, he was calm again.

Alsimir lay some fifty feet up the ridge, with his right hand clasped to his left shoulder, which seemed swollen to twice its normal size. His face was flushed, his eyes glassy.

Hissune knelt beside him. "Give me your dagger. I've lost mine."

"It's over there."

Swiftly Hissune cut away Alsimir's sleeve, revealing a star-shaped wound just above the biceps. With the tip of the dagger he cut a cross over the star, squeezed, drew blood, sucked it, spat, squeezed again. Alsimir trembled, whimpered, cried out once or twice. After a time Hissune wiped the wound clean and rummaged in his pack for a bandage.

"That might do it," he said. "With luck you'll be in Ertsud Grand by this time tomorrow and you can get proper treatment."

Alsimir stared in horror at the fallen malorn. "I was trying to edge around it, same as you—and suddenly it jumped at me and bit me. I think it was waiting for me to die before it ate me—but then you came along."

Hissune shivered. "Ugly beast. It didn't look half so repulsive in the training manual pictures."

"Did you kill it?"

"Probably. I wonder if we're supposed to kill the trackers. Maybe they need them for next year's tests."

"That's their problem," said Alsimir. "If they're going to send us out here to face those things, they shouldn't be annoyed if we kill one occasionally. Ah, by the Lady, this hurts!"

"Come. We'll finish the trek together."

"We aren't supposed to do that, Hissune."

"What of it? You think I'm going to leave you alone like this? Come on. Let them flunk us, if they like. I kill their malorn, I rescue a wounded man—all right, so I fail the test. But I'll be alive tomorrow. And so will you."

Hissune helped Alsimir to his feet and they moved slowly toward the distant green trees. He found himself trembling again, suddenly, in a delayed reaction. That ghastly creature floating over his head, the ring of red staring eyes, the clacking jaws, the soft exposed underbelly—it would be a long time before he forgot any of that.

As they walked onward, a measure of calmness returned.

He tried to imagine Lord Valentine contending with malorns and zeils and zytoons in this forlorn valley, or Elidath, or Divvis, or Mirigant. Surely they all had had to go through the same testing in their knight-initiate days, and perhaps it was this same malorn that had hissed and clacked its jaws at the young Valentine twenty years ago. It all felt faintly absurd to Hissune: what did escaping from monsters have to do with learning the arts of government? No doubt he would see the connection sooner or later, he thought. Meanwhile he had Alsimir to worry about, and also the zeil, the weyhant, the min-mollitor, the zytoon. With any luck he'd only have to contend with one or two more of the trackers: it went against probability that he'd run into all seven during the trek. But it was still a dozen miles to Ertsud Grand, and the road ahead looked barren and harsh. So this was the jolly life on Castle Mount? Eight hours a day studying the decrees of every Coronal and Pontifex from Dvorn to Tyeveras, interrupted by little trips out into the scrub country to contend with malorns and zytoons? What about the feasting and the gaming? What about the merry jaunts through the parklands and forest preserves? He was beginning to think that people of the lowlands held an unduly romantic view of life among the highborn of the Mount.

Hissune glanced toward Alsimir. "How are you doing?"

"I feel pretty weak. But the swelling seems to be going down some."

"We'll wash the wound out when we reach those trees. There's bound to be water there."

"I'd have died if you hadn't come along just then, Hissune."

Hissune shrugged. "If I hadn't come, someone else would. It's the logical path across that valley."

After a moment Alsimir said, "I don't understand why they're making you take this training."

"What do you mean?"

"Sending you out to face all these risks."

"Why not? All initiates have to do it."

"Lord Valentine has special plans for you. That's what I heard Divvis saying to Stasilaine last week."

"I'm destined for great things, yes. Master of the stables. Keeper of the hounds."

"I'm serious. Divvis is jealous of you, you know. And afraid of you, because you're the Coronal's favorite. Divvis wants to be Coronal—everybody knows that. And he thinks you're getting in the way."

"I think the venom is making you delirious."

"Believe me. Divvis sees you as a threat, Hissune."

"He shouldn't. I'm no more likely to become Coronal than—than Divvis is. Elidath's the heir presumptive. And Lord Valentine, I happen to know, is going to stay Coronal himself as long as he possibly can."

"I tell you—"

"Don't tell me anything. Just conserve your energy for the march. It's a dozen miles to Ertsud Grand. And four more tracker beasts waiting for us along the way."

2

This is the dream of the Piurivar Faraataa:

It is the Hour of the Scorpion and soon the sun will rise over Velalisier. Outside the gate of the city, along the road that was known as the Road of the Departure but will be known from this day forward as the Road of the Return, an immense procession is assembled, stretching far toward the horizon. The Prince To Come, wrapped in an emerald aura, stands at the head of the line. Behind him are four who wear the guise of the Red Woman, the Blind Giant, the Flayed Man, and the Final King. Then come the four prisoners, bound with loose withes; and then come the multitudes of the Piurivar folk: Those Who Return.

Faraataa floats high above the city, drifting easily, moving at will over all its vastness, taking in the immensity of it at a glance. It is perfect: everything has been made new, the rampart restored, the shrines set up once more, the fallen columns replaced. The aqueduct carries water again, and the gardens thrive, and the weeds and shrubs that had invaded every crevice have been hacked down, and the sand drifts swept away.

Only the Seventh Temple has been left as it was at the time of the Downfall: a flat stump, a mere foundation, surrounded by rubble. Faaraataa hovers above it, and in the eye of his mind he journeys backward through the dark ocean of time, so that he sees the Seventh Temple as it had been before its destruction, and he is granted a vision of the Defilement.

Ah! There, see! Upon the Tables of the Gods the unholy sacrifice is being readied. On each of the Tables lies a great water-king, still living, helpless under its own weight, wings moving feebly, neck arched, eyes glowering with rage or fear. Tiny figures move about the two huge beings, preparing to enact the forbidden rites. Faaraataa shivers. Faaraataa weeps, and his tears fall like crystal globes to the distant ground. He sees the long knives flashing; he hears the water-kings roaring and snorting; he sees the flesh peeled away. He wants to cry out to the people, *No, no, this is monstrous, we will be punished terribly,* but what good, what good? All this has happened thousands of years ago. And so he floats, and so he watches. Like ants they stream across the city, the sinful ones, each with his fragment of the water-king held on high, and they carry the sacrifice meat to the Seventh Temple, they hurl it on the pyre, they sing the Song of the Burning. *What are you doing?* Faaraataa cries, unheard. *You burn our brothers!* And the smoke rises, black and greasy, stinging Faaraataa's eyes, and he can remain aloft no more, and falls, and falls, and falls, and the Defilement is performed, and the doom of the city is assured, and all the world is lose with it.

Now the first light of day gleams in the east. It crosses the city and strikes the moon-crescent mounted on its high pole atop the stump of the Seventh Temple. The Prince To Come lifts his arm and gives the signal. The procession advances. As they march, Those Who Return shift form from moment to moment, in accordance with the teachings of the Book of the Water-Kings. They take on in turn the guises known as the Flame, the Flow, the Falling Leaf, the Blade, the Sands, the Wind. And as they pass the Place of

Unchangingness they return themselves to the true Piurivar form, and maintain it thenceforth.

The Prince To Come embraces each of the four prisoners. Then they are led to the altars atop the Tables of the Gods. The Red Woman and the Flayed Man take the younger king and his mother to the east Table, where long ago the water-king Niznorn perished on the night of blasphemy. The Blind Giant and the Final King conduct the older king and the one who comes by night in dreams to the west Table, where the water-king Domsitor was given into death by the Defilers.

The Prince To Come stands alone atop the Seventh Temple. His aura now is scarlet. Faraataa descends and joins him and becomes him: they are one.

"In the beginning was the Defilement, when a madness came over us and we sinned against our brothers of the sea," he cries. "And when we awakened and beheld what we had done, for that sin did we destroy our great city and go forth across the land. But even that was not sufficient, and enemies from afar were sent down upon us, and took from us all that we had, and drove us into the wilderness, which was our penance, for we had sinned against our brothers of the sea. And our ways were lost and our suffering was great and the face of the Most High was averted from us, until the time of the end of the penance came, and we found the strength to drive our oppressors from us and reclaim that which we had lost through our ancient sin. And so it was prophesied, that a prince would come among us and lead us out of exile at the time of the end of penance."

"This is the time of the end of penance!" the people reply. "This is the time of the Prince To Come!"

"The Prince To Come has arrived!"

"And you are the Prince To Come!"

"I am the Prince To Come," he cries. "Now all is forgiven. Now all debts have been paid. We have done our penance and are cleansed. The instruments of the penance have been driven from our land. The water-kings have had their recompense. Velalisier is rebuilt. Our life begins anew."

"Our life begins anew! This is the time of the Prince To Come!"

Faraataa lifts his staff, which flashes like fire in the morning light, and signals to those who wait upon the two Tables of the Gods. The four prisoners are thrust forward.

The long knives flash. The dead kings fall, and crowns roll in the dust. In the blood of the invaders are the Tables washed clean. The last act has been played. Faraataa holds high his hands.

"Come, now, and rebuild with me the Seventh Temple!"

The Piurivar folk rush forward. They gather the fallen blocks of the temple and at Faraataa's direction they place them where they once had been.

When it is complete, Faraataa stands at its highest point, and looks out across hundreds of miles to the sea, where the water-kings have gathered. He sees them beating the surface of the water with their great wings. He sees them lift their huge heads high and snort.

"Brothers! Brothers!" Faraataa calls to them.

"We hear you, land-brother."

"The enemy is destroyed. The city is reconsecrated. The Seventh Temple has risen again. Is our penance done, O brothers?"

And they reply: "It is done. The world is cleansed and a new age begins."

"Are we forgiven?"

"You are forgiven, O land-brothers."

"We are forgiven," cries the Prince To Come.

And the people hold up their hands to him, and change their shapes, and become in turn the Star, the Mist, the Darkness, the Gleam, the Cavern.

And only one thing remains, which is to forgive those who committed the first sin, and who have remained in bondage here amidst the ruins ever since. The Prince To Come stretches forth his hands, and reaches out to them, and tells them that the curse that was upon them is lifted and they are free.

And the stones of fallen Velalisier give up their dead, and the spirits emerge, pale and transparent; and they take on life and color; and they dance and shift their shapes, and cry out in joy.

And what they cry is:

"All hail the Prince To Come, who is the King That Is!"

That was the dream of the Piurivar Faraataa, as he lay on a couch of bubblebush leaves under a great dwikka-tree in the province of Piurifayne, with a light rain falling.

3

The Coronal said, "Ask Y-Uulisaan to come in here."

Maps and charts of the blighted zones of Zimroel, heavily marked and annotated, were spread out all over the desk in Lord Valentine's cabin aboard his flagship, the *Lady Thiin*. This was the third day of the voyage. He had departed from Alaisor with a fleet of five vessels under the command of the Grand Admiral Asenhart, bound for the port of Numinor on the Isle of Sleep's northeastern coast. The crossing would be a journey of many weeks, even under the most favorable of winds, and just now the winds were contrary.

While he waited for the agricultural expert to arrive, Valentine scanned once more the documents Y-Uulisaan had prepared for him and those that he had called up out of the historical archives. It was perhaps the fiftieth time he had looked them over since leaving Alaisor, and the story they told grew no less melancholy with repetition.

Blights and pestilences, he knew, were as old as agriculture itself. There was no reason why Majipoor, fortunate world though it was, should be entirely exempt from such ills, and indeed the archives showed ample precedent for the present troubles. There had been serious disruptions of crops through disease or drought or insect attack in a dozen reigns or more, and major ones in at least five: that of Setiphon and Lord Stanidor, that of Thraym and Lord Vildivar, that of Struin and Lord Guadeloom, that of Kanaba and Lord Sirruth, and in the time of Signor and Lord Melikand, deep in the misty recesses of the past.

But what was happening now seemed far more threatening than any of those, Valentine thought, and not merely because it was a present crisis rather than something safely entombed in the archives. The population of Majipoor was immensely greater than it had been during any of the earlier pestilences: twenty billion, where in Struin's time, say, it had been scarcely a sixth as much, and in Signor's only a relative handful. A population so huge could fall easily into famine if its agricultural base were disrupted. The structure of society itself might collapse. Valentine was well aware that the stabil-

120

ity of the Majipoori way over so many thousands of years—so
contrary to the experience of most civilizations—was founded
on the extraordinarily benign nature of life on the giant
planet. Because no one was ever in real need, there was
nearly universal acquiescence in the order of things and even
in the inequalities of the social order. But take away the
certainty of a full belly and all the rest might fall apart
overnight.

And these dark dreams of his, these visions of chaos, and
the strange omens—wind-spiders drifting over Alhanroel,
and other such things—all of that instilled in him a sense of
grim danger, of unique peril.

"My lord, Y-Uulisaan is here," said Sleet.

The agricultural expert entered, looking hesitant and ill
at ease. In an awkward way he began to make the starburst
gesture that etiquette demanded. Valentine shook his head
impatiently and beckoned Y-Uulisaan to take a seat. He
pointed to the zone marked in red along the Dulorn Rift.

"How important a crop is lusavender?"

Y-Uulisaan said, "Essential, my lord. It forms the basis
for carbohydrate assimilation in all of northern and western
Zimroel."

"And if severe shortages develop?"

"It might be possible to create diet supplements using
such foods as stajja."

"But there's a stajja blight too!"

"Indeed, my lord. And milaile, which fulfills similar
nutritional needs, is suffering from root weevils, as I have
shown you. Therefore we can project general hardship in this
entire sector of Zimroel within six to nine months—"

With the tip of a finger Y-Uulisaan drew a broad circle
over the map covering a territory that ran almost from
Ni-moya in the east to Pidruid on the western coast, and
southward as far as Velathys. What was the population of that
territory, Valentine wondered? Two and a half billion, perhaps? He tried to imagine two and a half billion hungry
people, accustomed all their lives to a plentitude of food,
crowding into the cities of Til-omon, Narabal, Pidruid—

Valentine said, "The imperial granaries will be able to
meet the need in the short run. Meanwhile we'll endeavor to
get these blights under control. Lusavender smut was a
problem a century or so ago, so I understand, and it was
beaten then."

"Through extreme measures, my lord. Whole provinces were quarantined. Entire farms were put to the torch, and afterward scraped bare of topsoil. The cost ran into the many millions of royals."

"What does money matter when people are starving? We'll do it again. If we begin an immediate program in the lusavender-growing regions, how long do you estimate it'll take to return things to normal?"

Y-Uulisaan was silent a moment, rubbing his thumbs reflectively against his strangely broad and sharp cheekbones. At length he said:

"Five years, minimum. More likely ten."

"Impossible!"

"The smut spreads swiftly. Probably a thousand acres have been infested during the time we have been talking this afternoon, my lord. The problem will be to contain it, before we can eradicate it."

"And the niyk-tree disease? Is that spreading as fast?"

"Faster, my lord. And it appears to be linked to the decline of the stajja plants that are usually grown in conjunction with niyk."

Valentine stared toward the cabin wall, and saw only a gray nothingness.

He said after a time, "Whatever this costs, we'll defeat it. Y-Uulisaan, I want you to draw up a plan for countering each of these blights, and I want estimates of expense. Can you do that?"

"Yes, my lord,"

To Sleet the Coronal said, "We'll have to coordinate our efforts with those of the Pontificate. Tell Ermanar to open contact at once with the minister of agricultural affairs at the Labyrinth—find out what if anything he knows of what's going on in Zimroel, what steps are proposed, and so forth."

Tunigorn said, "My lord, I've just spoken with Ermanar. He's already been in touch with the Pontificate."

"And?"

"The ministry of agricultural affairs knows nothing. In fact the post of minister of agricultural affairs itself is currently vacant."

"Vacant? How?"

Quietly Tunigorn said, "I understand that with the incapacitation of the Pontifex Tyeveras, many high posts have been left unfilled in recent years, my lord, and therefore a certain slowing of Pontifical functions has developed. But you can learn much more on this point from Ermanar himself, since he is our chief liaison with the Labyrinth. Shall I send for him?"

"Not at the moment," said Valentine bleakly. He turned back to Y-Uulisaan's maps. Running his finger up and down the length of the Dulorn Rift, he said, "The two worst problems seem to be concentrated in this area. But according to the charts, there are significant lusavender-growing zones elsewhere, in the flatlands between Thagobar and the northern boundaries of Piurifayne, and over here south of Ni-moya stretching down to the outskirts of Gihorna. Am I correct?"

"You are, my lord," Y-Uulisaan said.

"Therefore our first line of priority must be to keep the lusavender smut out of those regions." He looked up, at Sleet, Tunigorn, Deliamber. "Notify the dukes of the affected provinces at once that all traffic between the smut-infested zones and the healthy lusavender districts is halted at once: a complete closing of the borders. If they don't like it, let them send a delegation to the Mount to complain to Elidath. Oh, and notify Elidath of what's going on, too. Settlement of unpaid trade balances can be routed through Pontifical channels for the time being. Hornkast had better be told to be prepared for a lot of screaming, I suppose. Next: in the stajja-growing districts—"

For close to an hour a stream of instructions flowed from the Coronal, until every immediate aspect of the crisis appeared to be covered. He turned often to Y-Uulisaan for advice, and always the agricultural expert had something useful to offer. There was something curiously unlikable about the man, Valentine thought, something remote and chilly and overly self-contained, but he was plainly well versed in the minutiae of Zimroel agriculture, and it was a tremendous stroke of good luck that he had turned up in Alaisor just in time to sail for Zimroel with the royal flagship.

All the same, Valentine was left with an odd feeling of futility when the meeting broke up. He had given dozens of orders, had sent messages far and wide, had taken firm and decisive action to contain and eradicate these pestilences. And yet, and yet—he was only one mortal man, in a small cabin aboard a tiny ship tossing in the midst of an immense sea that was itself only a puddle on this gigantic world, and at this moment invisible organisms were spreading blight and death over thousands of acres of fertile farmland, and what could all his bold orders do against the inexorable march of those forces of doom? Yet again he felt himself slipping into a mood of hopeless depression, so alien to his true nature. Perhaps *I* have some pestilence in me, he thought. Perhaps I am infested with some blight that robs me of my hope and cheer and buoyancy, and I am condemned now to live out my days in sullen misery.

He closed his eyes. Once more came that image out of his dream in the Labyrinth, an image that haunted him endlessly: great crevasses appearing in the solid foundations of the world, and huge slabs of land rearing up at steep angles to crash against their neighbors, and he in the midst of it all, desperately trying to hold the world together. And failing, failing, failing.

Is there a curse on me? he wondered. Why am I chosen, out of all the hundreds of Coronals that have been, to preside over the destruction of our world?

He looked into his soul and found no dark sin there that might be bringing the vengeance of the Divine upon him and upon Majipoor. He had not coveted the throne; he had not schemed to overthrow his brother; he had not made wrongful use of the power he had never expected to gain; he had not—

He had not—

He had not—

Valentine shook his head angrily. This was foolishness and a waste of spirit. A few coincidental troubles among the farmers were occurring, and he had had a few bad dreams; it was preposterous to exaggerate that into some kind of dread cosmic calamity. All would be well in time. The pestilences would be contained. His reign would be known in history for unusual troubles, yes, but also for harmony, balance, happiness. You are a good king, he told himself. You are a good man. You have no reason to doubt yourself.

The Coronal rose, left his cabin, went out on deck. It was late afternoon; the swollen bronze sun hung low in the west, and one of the moons was just rising to the north. The sky was stained with colors: auburn, turquoise, violet, amber, gold. A band of clouds lay thick on the horizon. He stood alone by the rail for a time, drawing the salt air deep into his lungs. All would be well in time, Valentine told himself once again. But imperceptibly he felt himself slipping back into uneasiness and distress. There seemed no escaping that mood for long. Never in his life had he been plunged so often into gloom and despair. He did not recognize the Valentine that he had become, that morbid man forever on the edge of sadness. He was a stranger to himself.

"Valentine?"

It was Carabella. He forced himself to thrust aside his forebodings, and smiled, and offered her his hand.

"What a beautiful sunset," she said.

"Magnificent. One of the best in history. Although they say there was a better one in the reign of Lord Confalume, on the fourteenth day of—"

"This is the best one, Valentine. Because this is the one we have tonight." She slipped her arm through his, and stood beside him in silence. He found it hard, just then, to understand why he had been so profoundly grim-spirited such a short while ago. All would be well. All would be well.

Then Carbella said, "Is that a sea dragon out there?"

"Sea dragons never enter these waters, love."

"Then I'm hallucinating. But it's a very convincing one. You don't see it?"

"Where am I supposed to look?"

"There. Do you see over there, where there's a track of color reflected on the ocean, all purple and gold? Now go just to the left. There. *There.*"

Valentine narrowed his eyes and peered intently out to sea. At first he saw nothing; then he thought it might be some huge log, drifting on the waves; and then a last shaft of sunlight cutting through the clouds lit up the sea, and he saw it clearly: a sea dragon, yes, unquestionably a dragon, swimming slowly northward by itself.

He felt a chill, and huddled his arms against his breast.

Sea dragons, he knew, moved only in herds; and they traveled a predictable path about the world, always in southern waters, going from west to east along the bottom of Zimroel, up the Gihorna coast to Piliplok, then eastward below the Isle of Sleep and along the torrid southern coast of Alhanroel until they were safely out into the uncharted reaches of the Great Sea. Yet here was a dragon, by itself, heading north. And as Valentine stared, the great creature brought its black enormous wings up into the air, and beat them against the water in a slow, determined way, slap and slap and slap and slap, as though it meant to do the impossible and lift itself from the sea, and fly off like some titanic bird toward the mist-shrouded polar reaches.

"How strange," Carabella murmured. "Have you ever seen one do anything like that?"

"Never. Never." Valentine shivered. "Omen upon omen, Carabella. What am I being told by all this?"

"Come. Let's go in, and have a warm mug of wine."

"No. Not yet."

He stood as if chained to the deck, straining his eyes to make out that dark figure against the darkness of the sea in the gathering dimness of the evening. Again and again the huge wings flailed the sea, until at last the dragon furled them in, and raised its long neck high and threw back its heavy three-cornered head and let out a booming mournful cry that resounded like a foghorn cutting through the dusk. Then it slipped below the surface and was lost entirely to his sight.

4

Whenever it rained, and at this time of the year in Prestimion Vale it rained all the time, the sour odor of charred vegetation rose from the burned fields and infiltrated everything. As Aximaan Threysz shuffled into the municipal meeting-hall in the center of town, her daughter Heynok guiding her carefully with a hand to her elbow, she could smell the scent of it even here, miles from the nearest of the torched plantations.

There was no escaping it. It lay upon the land like floodwaters. The acrid reek found its way through every door and every window. It penetrated to the cellars where the wine was stored, and tainted the sealed flasks. The meat on the table stank of it. It clung to one's clothes and could not be rinsed away. It seeped through every pore and into one's body, and fouled one's flesh. It even entered the soul, Aximaan Threysz was beginning to believe. When the time came for her to return to the Source, if ever she was permitted to quit this interminable life, Aximaan Threysz was sure that the guardians of the bridge would halt her and coldly turn her back, saying with disdain, "We want no smell of vile ashes here, old woman. Take up your body again and go away."

"Would you like to sit here, mother?" Heyrok asked.

"I don't care. Anywhere."

"These are good seats. You'll be able to hear well from here."

There was a little commotion in the row as people shifted about, making room for her. Everyone treated her like a doddering old woman now. Well, of course she was old, monstrously old, a survivor out of Ossier's time, so old that she remembered when Lord Tyeveras had been young, but there was nothing new about her being old, so why were they all suddenly so patronizing? She had no need of special treatment. She still could walk; she still could see well enough; she still could go out into the fields at harvest time and gather the pods—and gather—go out into—the fields—and—gather—

Aximaan Threysz, faltering just a little, fumbling about, took her seat. She heard murmurs of greeting, and acknowledged them in a remote way, for she was having trouble now in matching names and faces. When the Vale folk spoke with her these days it was always with condolence in their voices, as though there had been a death in her family. In a way, that was so. But not the death she was looking for, the death that was denied her, which was her own.

Perhaps that day would never come. It seemed to her that she was condemned to go on and on forever in this world of ruination and despair, tasting that pungent stench with every breath she drew.

She sat quietly, staring at nothing in particular.

Heynok said, "He's very courageous, I think."

"Who is?"

"Sempeturn. The man who's going to speak tonight. They tried to stop him in Mazadone, saying that he preaches treason. But he spoke anyway, and now he's traveling through all the farming provinces, trying to explain to us why the crops have been ruined. Everyone in the Vale is here tonight. It's a very important event."

"A very important event, yes," said Aximaan Threysz, nodding. "Yes. A very important event."

She felt a certain discomfort over the presence of so many people around her. It was months since she had last been in town. She rarely left the house any longer, but spent nearly all her days sitting in her bedroom with her back to the window, never once looking toward the plantation. But tonight Heynok had insisted. A very important event, she kept saying.

"Look! There he is, mother!"

Aximaan Threysz was vaguely aware that a human had stepped out on the platform, a short red-faced one with thick ugly black hair like the fur of an animal. That was strange, she thought, the way she had come in recent months to despise the look of humans, their soft flabby bodies, their pasty sweaty skins, their repellent hair, their weak watery eyes. He waved his arms about and began to speak in an ugly rasping voice.

"People of Prestimion Vale—my heart goes out to you in this moment of your trial—this darkest hour, this unexpected travail—this tragedy, this grief—"

So this was the important event, Aximaan Threysz thought. This noise, this wailing. Yes, undoubtedly important. Within moments she had lost the thread of what he was saying, but it was plainly important, because the words that wandered up from the platform to her had an important sound: "Doom . . . destiny . . . punishment . . . transgression . . . innocence . . . shame . . . deceit. . . ." But the words, important though they might be, floated past her like little transparent winged creatures.

For Aximaan Threysz the last important event had already happened, and there would be no others in her life. After the discovery of the lusavender smut her fields had been the first to be burned. The agricultural agent Yerewain Noor, looking deeply grieved, making endless fluttery apologies, had posted a notice of labor levy in the town, tacking up the sign on the door of this same municipal hall where Aximaan Threysz sat now, and one Starday morning every able-bodied worker in Prestimion Vale had come to her plantation to carry out the torching. Spreading the fuel carefully on the perimeter, making long crosses of it down the center of the fields, casting the firebrands—

And then Mikhyain's land, and Sobor Simithot's, and Palver's, and Nitikkimal's—

All gone, the whole Vale, black and charred, the lusavender and the rice. There would be no harvest next season. The silos would stand empty, the weighing bins would rust, the summer sun would shed its warmth on a universe of ashes. It was very much like a sending of the King of Dreams, Aximaan Threysz thought. You settled down for your two months of winter rest, and then into your mind came terrifying visions of the destruction of everything you had labored to create, and as you lay there you felt the full weight of the

King's spirit on your soul, squeezing you, crushing you, telling you, *This is your punishment, for you are guilty of wrongdoing*.

"How do we know," the man on the platform said, "that the person we call Lord Valentine is indeed the anointed Coronal, blessed by the Divine? How can we be certain of this?"

Aximaan Threysz sat suddenly forward, her attention caught.

"I ask you to consider the facts. We knew the Coronal Lord Voriax, and he was a dark-complected man, was he not? Eight years he ruled us, and he was wise, and we loved him. Did we not? And then the Divine in its inifinite unknowable mercy took him from us too soon, and word came forth from the Mount that his brother Valentine was to be our Coronal, and he too was a dark-complected man. We know that. He came amongst us on the grand processional—oh, no, not here, not to this province, but he was seen in Piliplok, he was seen in Ni-moya, he was seen in Narabal, in Til-omon, in Pidruid, and he was dark-complected, with shining black eyes and a black beard, and no doubt of it that he was brother to his brother, and our legitimate Coronal.

"But then what did we hear? A man with golden hair and blue eyes arose, and said to the people of Alhanroel, I am the true Coronal, driven from my body by witchery, and the dark one is an impostor. And the people of Alhanroel made the starburst before him and bowed themselves down and cried hail. And when we in Zimroel were told that the man we thought was Coronal was not Coronal, we too accepted him, and accepted his tale of witchery-changes, and these eight years he has had the Castle and held the government. Is that not so, that we took the golden-haired Lord Valentine in the place of the dark-haired Lord Valentine?"

"Why, this is treason pure and simple," shouted the planter Nitikkimal, sitting close by Aximaan Threysz. "His own mother the Lady accepted him as true!"

The man on the platform glanced up into the audience. "Aye, the Lady herself accepted him, and the Pontifex as well, and all the high lords and princes of Castle Mount. I do not deny that. And who am I to say they are wrong? They bow their knees to the golden-haired king. He is acceptable to them. He is acceptable to you. But is he acceptable to the

Divine, my friends? I ask you, look about yourselves! This day I journeyed through Prestimion Vale. Where are the crops? Why are the fields not green with rich growth? I saw ashes! I saw death! Look you, the blight is on your land, and it spreads through the Rift each day, faster than you can burn your fields and purge the soil of the deadly spores. There will be no lusavender next season. There will be empty bellies in Zimroel. Who can remember such a time? There is a woman here whose life has spanned many reigns, and who is replete with the wisdom of years, and has she ever seen such a time? I speak to you, Aximaan Threysz, whose name is respected throughout the province—your fields were put to the torch, your crops were spoiled, your life is blighted in its glorious closing years—"

"Mother, he's talking about you," Heynok whispered sharply.

Aximaan Threysz shook her head uncomprehendingly. She had lost herself in the torrent of words. "Why are we here? What is he saying?"

"What do you say, Aximaan Threysz? Has the blessing of the Divine been withdrawn from Prestimion Vale? You know it has! But not by your sin, or the sin of anyone here! I say to you that it is the wrath of the Divine, falling impartially upon the world, taking the lusavender from Prestimion Vale and the milaile from Ni-moya and the stajja from Falkynkip and who knows what crop will be next, what plague will be loosed upon us, and all because a false Coronal—"

"Treason! Treason!"

"A false Coronal, I tell you, sits upon the Mount and falsely rules—a golden-haired usurper who—"

"Ah, has the throne been usurped again?" Aximaan Threysz murmured. "It was just the other year, when we heard tales of it, that someone had taken the throne wrongfully—"

"I say, let him prove to us that he is the chosen of the Divine! Let him come amongst us on his grand processional and stand before us and show us that he is the true Coronal! I think he will not do it. I think he cannot do it. And I think that so long as we suffer him to hold the Castle, the wrath of the Divine will fall upon us in ever more dreadful ways, until—"

"Treason!"

"Let him speak!"

Heynok touched Aximaan Threysz's arm. "Mother, are you all right?"

"Why are they so angry? What are they shouting?"

"Perhaps I should take you home, mother."

"I say, down with the usurper!"

"And I say, call the proctors, arraign this man for treason."

Aximaan Threysz looked about her in confusion. It seemed that everyone was on his feet now, shouting. Such noise! Such uproar! And that strange smell in the air—that smell of damp burned things, what was that? It stung her nostrils. Why were they shouting so much?

"Mother?"

"We'll begin putting in the new crop tomorrow, won't we? And so we should go home now. Isn't that so, Heynok?"

"Oh, mother, mother—"

"The new crop—"

"Yes," Heynok said. "We'll be planting in the morning. We should go now."

"Down with all usurpers! Long life to the true Coronal!"

"Long life to the true Coronal!" Aximaan Threysz cried suddenly, rising to her feet. Her eyes flashed; her tongue flickered. She felt young again, full of life and vigor. Into the fields at dawn tomorrow, spread the seeds and lovingly cover them, and offer the prayers, and—

No. No. No.

The mist cleared from her mind. She remembered everything. The fields were charred. They must lie fallow, the agricultural agent had said, for three more years, while the smut spores were being purged. That was the strange smell: the burned stems and leaves. Fires had raged for days. The rain stirred the odor and made it rise into the air. There would be no harvest this year, or the next, or the next.

"Fools," she said.

"Who do you mean, mother?"

Aximaan Threysz waved her hand in a wide circle. "All of them. To cry out against the Coronal. To think that this is the vengeance of the Divine. Do you think the Divine wants to punish us that badly? We will all starve, Heynok, because the smut has killed the crop, and it makes no difference who is Coronal. It makes no difference at all. Take me home."

"Down with the usurper!" came the cry again, and it

rang in her ears like the tolling of a funeral bell as she strode from the hall.

5

Elidath said, looking carefully around the council room at the assembled princes and dukes, "The orders are in Valentine's hand and signed with Valentine's seal, and they are unmistakably genuine. The boy is to be raised to the principate at the earliest possible appropriate time."

"And you think that time has come?" asked Divvis coldly.

The High Counsellor met Divvis's angry gaze evenly. "I do."

"By what do you judge?"

"His instructors tell me that he has mastered the essence of all the teachings."

"So then he can name all the Coronals from Stiamot to Malibor in the correct order! What does that prove?"

"The teachings are more than merely lists of kings, Divvis, as I hope you have not forgotten. He has had the full training and he comprehends it. The Synods and Decretals, the Balances, the Code of Provinces, and all the rest: I trust you recall those things? He has been examined, and he is flawless. His understanding is deep and wise. And he has shown courage, too. In the crossing of the ghazan-tree plain he slew the malorn. Did you know that, Divvis? Not merely eluded it, but slew it. He is extraordinary."

"I think that word is the right one," said Duke Elzandir of Chorg. "I have ridden with him on the hunt, in the forests above Ghiseldorn. He moves quickly, and with a natural grace. His mind is alert. His wit is agile. He knows what gaps exist in his knowledge, and he takes pains to fill them. He should be elevated at once."

"This is madness!" cried Divvis, slapping the flat of his hand several times angrily against the council-hall table. "Absolute raving madness!"

"Calmly, calmly," Mirigant said. "Such shouting as this is unseemly, Divvis."

"The boy is too young to be a prince!"

"And let us not forget," the Duke of Halanx added, "that he is of low birth."

Quietly Stasilaine said, "How old is he, Elidath?"

The High Counsellor shrugged. "Twenty. Twenty-one, perhaps. Young, I agree. But hardly a child."

"You called him 'the boy' yourself a moment ago," the Duke of Halanx pointed out.

Elidath turned his hands palm upward. "A figure of speech and nothing more. He has a youthful appearance, I grant you. But that's only because he's so slight of build, and short of stature. Boyish, perhaps: but not a boy."

"Not yet a man, either," observed Prince Manganot of Banglecode.

"By what definition?" Stasilaine asked.

"Look about you in this room," Prince Manganot said. "Here you see the definition of manhood. You, Stasilaine: anyone can see the strength of you. Walk as a stranger through the streets of any city, Stee, Normork, Bibiroon, simply walk through the streets, and people will automatically defer to you, having no notion of your rank or name. Elidath the same. Divvis. Mirigant. My royal brother of Dundilmir. We are *men*. He is not."

"We are princes," said Stasilaine, "and have been for many years. A certain bearing comes to us in time, from long awareness of our station. But were we like this twenty years ago?"

"I think so," Manganot said.

Mirigant laughed. "I remember some of you when you were at Hissune's age. Loud and braggartly, yes, and if that makes one a man, then you surely were men. But otherwise—ah, I think it is all a circular thing, that princely bearing comes of feeling princely, and we put it on ourselves as a cloak. Look at us in our finery, and then cover us in farmer's clothes and set us down in some seaport of Zimroel, and who will bow to us then? Who will give deference?"

"He is not princely now and never will be," said Divvis sullenly. "He is a ragged boy out of the Labyrinth, and nothing more than that."

"I still maintain that we can't elevate a stripling like that to our rank," said Prince Manganot of Banglecode.

"They say that Prestimion was short of stature," the Duke of Chorg remarked. "I think his reign is generally deemed to have been successful, nevertheless."

The venerable Cantalis, nephew of Tyeveras, looked up suddenly out of an hour's silence and said in amazement, "You compare him with Prestimion, Elzandir? What precisely is it that we are doing, then? Are we creating a prince or choosing a Coronal?"

"Any prince is a potential Coronal," Divvis said. "Let us not forget that."

"And the choosing of the next Coronal must soon occur, no doubt of that," the Duke of Halanx said. "It's utterly scandalous that Valentine has kept the old Pontifex alive this long, but sooner or later—"

"This is altogether out of order," Elidath said sharply.

"I think not," said Manganot. "If we make him a prince, there's nothing stopping Valentine from putting him eventually on the Confalume Throne itself."

"These speculations are absurd," Mirigant said.

"Are they, Mirigant? What absurdities have we not already seen from Valentine? To take a juggler-girl as his wife, and a Vroon wizard as one of his chief ministers, and the rest of his raggle-taggle band of wanderers surrounding him as a court within the court, while we are pushed to the outer rim—"

"Be cautious, Manganot," Stasilaine said. "There are those in this room that love Lord Valentine."

"There is no one here who does not," Manganot retorted. "You may be aware, and Mirigant can surely confirm it, that upon the death of Voriax I was one of the strongest advocates of letting the crown pass to Valentine. I yield to no one in my love of him. But we need not love him uncritically. He is capable of folly, as are we all. And I say it is folly to take a twenty-year-old boy from the back alleys of the Labyrinth and make him a prince of the realm."

Stasilaine said, "How old were you, Manganot, when you had your princehood? Sixteen? Eighteen? And you, Divvis? Seventeen, I think? Elidath, you?"

"It is different with us," said Divvis. "We were born to rank. I am the son of a Coronal. Manganot is of the high family of Banglecode. Elidath—"

"The point remains," Stasilaine said, "that when we were much younger than Hissune we were already at this rank. As was Valentine himself. It is a question of qualification, not of age. And Elidath assures us that he is qualified."

"Have we ever had a prince created out of commoner stock?" the Duke of Halanx asked. "Think, I beg you: what is this new prince of Valentine's? A child of the Labyrinth streets, a beggar-boy, or perhaps a pickpocket—"

"You have no true knowledge of that," said Stasilaine. "You give us mere slander, I think."

"Is it not the case that he was a beggar in the Labyrinth when Valentine first found him?"

"He was only a child then," said Elzandir. "And the story is that he hired himself out as a guide, and gave good value for the money, though he was only ten years old. But all of that is beside the point. We need not care about what he was. It is what he is that concerns us, and what he is to be. The Coronal Lord has asked us to make him a prince when, in Elidath's judgment, the time is right. Elidath tells us that the time is right. Therefore this debate is pointless."

"No," Divvis said. "Valentine is not absolute. He requires our consent to this thing."

"Ah, and would you overrule the will of the Coronal?" asked the Duke of Chorg.

Divvis, after a pause, said, "If my conscience bade me do so, I would, yes. Valentine is not infallible. There are times when I disagree greatly with him. This is one."

"Ever since the changing of his body," said Prince Manganot of Banglecode, "I have noted a change also in his personality, an inclination toward the romantic, toward the fantastic, that perhaps was present in him before the usurpation but which never was evident in any significant way, and which now manifests itself in a whole host of—"

"Enough!" said Elidath in exasperation. "We are required to debate this nomination, and we have done so, and I make an end to it now. The Coronal Lord offers us the knight-initiate Hissune son of Elsinome, for elevation to the principate with full privileges of rank. As High Counsellor and Regent I place the nomination before you with my seconding vote. If there is no opposition, I propose it to be recorded that he is elevated by acclamation."

"Opposed," said Divvis.

"Opposed," said Prince Manganot of Banglecode.

"Opposed," said the Duke of Halanx.

"Are there any others here," asked Elidath slowly, "who wish to be placed on record in opposition to the will of the Coronal Lord?"

Prince Nimian of Dundilmir, who had not previously spoken, now declared, "There is an implied threat in those words to which I take exception, Elidath."

"Your exception is duly noted, although no threat is intended. How do you vote, Nimian?"

"Opposed."

"So be it. Four stand in opposition, which falls well short of a carrying number. Stasilaine, will you ask Prince Hissune to enter the council-chamber?" Glancing about the room, Elidath added, "If any who cast opposing votes wish now to withdraw them, this is the moment."

"Let my vote stand," the Duke of Halanx said at once.

"And mine," said the Prince of Banglecode, and Nimian of Dundilmir also.

"And what says the son of Lord Voriax?" Elidath asked.

Divvis smiled. "I change my vote. The thing is done: let it have my support as well."

At that Manganot rose halfway from his seat, gaping in astonishment, face coloring. He began to say something, but Divvis cut short his words with an upraised hand and a sharp sudden glare. Frowning, shaking his head in bewilderment, Manganot subsided. The Duke of Halanx whispered something to Prince Nimian, who shrugged and made no reply.

Stasilaine returned, with Hissune beside him, clad in a simple white robe with a golden splash on the left shoulder. His face was lightly flushed, his eyes were unnaturally bright, but he was otherwise calm and contained.

Elidath said, "By nomination of the Coronal Lord Valentine and the acclamation of these high lords, we name you to the principate of Majipoor, with full rank and privilege."

Hissune bowed his head. "I am moved beyond words, my lords. I can barely express my gratitude to you all for bestowing this unimaginable honor upon me."

Then he looked up, and his gaze traveled through the room, resting for a moment on Nimian, and on Manganot, and on the Duke of Halanx, and then, for a long while, on Divvis, who returned his stare coolly and with a faint smile.

6

That lone sea dragon, so strangely beating its wings against the water at twilight, was a harbinger of stranger things to come. In the third week of the voyage from Alaisor to the Isle of Sleep an entire herd of the huge creatures suddenly manifested itself off the starboard side of the *Lady Thiin*.

Pandelume, the pilot, a Skandar with deep blue fur who

once had hunted sea dragons for her livelihood, was the first
to sight them, just after dawn, as she was taking her sightings
from the observation deck. She carried the news to Asenhart
the Grand Admiral, who conferred with Autifon Deliamber,
who took it upon himself to awaken the Coronal.

Valentine went quickly to the deck. By now the sun had
come up out of Alhanroel and cast long shadows upon the
waters. The pilot handed him her seeing-tube and he put it
to his eye, and she trained it for him on the shapes that
moved through the sea far in the distance.

He stared, seeing little at first except the gentle swells of
the open sea, then shifting his gaze slightly to the north and
refining his focus to bring the sea dragons into view: dark
humped shapes thronging the water, moving in close formation, swimming with strange purposefulness. Now and again
a long neck rose high above the surface, or vast wings were
fanned and fluttered and spread out on the bosom of the sea.

"There must be a hundred of them," cried Valentine,
amazed.

"More than that, my lord," said Pandelume. "Never
while I was hunting them did I encounter a herd so big. Can
you see the kings? Five of them, at least. And half a dozen
more, nearly as large. And dozens of cows, and young ones,
too many to count—"

"I see them," Valentine said. In the center of the group
was a small phalanx of animals of monstrous size, all but
submerged, but their spine-ridges cleaving the surface. "Six
big ones, I'd say. Monsters—bigger even than the one that
shipwrecked me when I sailed on the *Brangalyn*! And in the
wrong waters. What are they doing here? Asenhart, have you
ever heard of sea-dragon herds coming up this side of the
Isle?"

"Never, my lord," the Hjort said somberly. "For thirty
years I have sailed between Numinor and Alaisor and never
once seen a dragon. Never once! And now an entire herd—"

"The Lady be thanked they're moving away from us,"
said Sleet.

"But why are they here at all?" Valentine asked.

No one had an answer to that. It seemed unreasonable
that the movements of sea dragons through the inhabited
parts of Majipoor should so suddenly undergo drastic change,
when for thousands of years the marine herds had with
extraordinary loyalty followed well-worn roads in the sea.

Placidly did each herd take the same route on each of its lengthy migrations around the world, to the dragons' great loss, for the dragon hunters out of Piliplok, knowing where to find them, fell upon them each year in the proper season and worked a fearful slaughter on them so that dragon meat and dragon oil and dragon milk and dragon bones and many another dragon-derived product might be sold at high profit in the marketplaces of the world. Still the dragons traveled as they always had traveled. The vagaries of winds and currents and temperatures sometimes might induce them to shift some hundreds of miles north or south of their customary paths, probably because the sea creatures on which they fed had shifted, but nothing like this departure had ever been seen before—a whole herd of dragons curving up the eastern side of the Isle of Sleep and apparently making for the polar regions, instead of passing south of the Isle and the coast of Alhanroel to enter the waters of the Great Sea.

Nor was this the only such herd. Five days later another was sighted: a smaller group, no more than thirty, with no giants among them, that passed within a mile or two of the fleet. Uncomfortably close, said Admiral Asenhart: for the ships bearing the Coronal and his party to the Isle carried no weaponry of any significant sort, and sea dragons were creatures of uncertain temper and formidable power, much given to shattering such hapless vessels as might stumble across their paths at the wrong moment.

Six weeks remained to the voyage. In dragon-infested seas that would seem like a very long while.

"Perhaps we should turn back, and make this crossing at another season," suggested Tunigorn, who had never been to sea before and had not been finding the experience much to his liking even before this.

Sleet also seemed more than uneasy about the journey; Asenhart appeared troubled; Carabella spent much time peering moodily to sea, as if expecting a dragon to breach the water just beneath the *Lady Thiin*'s hull. But Valentine, although he had known the fury of the sea dragon at first hand himself, having been not merely shipwrecked by one but indeed swept into its cavernous gut in the most bizarre of the adventures of his years of exile, would not hear of it. It was essential to continue, he insisted. He must confer with the Lady; he must inspect blight-stricken Zimroel; to return to Alhanroel, he felt, was to abdicate all responsibility. And what reason was there, anyway, to think that these strayed sea dragons meant any harm to the fleet? They seemed bound with great swiftness and intentness upon their mysterious route, and paid no heed to any of the ships that passed by them.

Yet a third group of dragons appeared, a week after the second. These were some fifty in number, with three giants among them. "It seems the entire year's migration must be going north," Pandelume said. There were, she explained, about a dozen separate dragon populations, that traveled at widely separated intervals about the world. No one knew exactly how long it took for each herd to complete the circumnavigation, but it could perhaps be decades. Each of these populations broke up, as it went, into smaller herds, but all moved in the same general way; and this entire population, evidently, had diverted itself to the new northward path.

Drawing Deliamber aside, Valentine asked the Vroon whether his perceptions brought him any understanding of these movements of the sea dragons. The little being's many tentacles coiled intricately in the gesture that Valentine had long since come to interpret as a sign of distress; but all he would say was, "I feel the strength of them, and it is a very strong strength indeed. You know that they are not stupid animals."

"I understand that a body of such size might well have a brain to match."

"Such is the case. I reach forth and I feel their presence, and I sense great determination, great discipline. But what course it is that they are bound upon, my lord, I cannot tell you this day."

Valentine attempted to make light of the danger. "Sing me the ballad of Lord Malibor," he told Carabella one evening as they all sat at table. She looked at him oddly, but he smiled and persisted, and at last she took up her pocket harp and struck up the roistering old tune:

> *Lord Malibor was fine and bold*
> *And loved the heaving sea,*
> *Lord Malibor came off the Mount,*
> *A hunter for to be.*
>
> *Lord Malibor prepared his ship,*
> *A gallant sight was she,*

> *With sails all of beaten gold,*
> *And masts of ivory.*

And Valentine, recalling the words now, joined in:

> *Lord Malibor stood at the helm*
> *And faced the heaving wave,*
> *And sailed in quest of the dragon free,*
> *The dragon fierce and brave.*

> *Lord Malibor a challenge called,*
> *His voice did boom and ring,*
> *"I wish to meet, I wish to fight,"*
> *Quoth he, "the dragon king."*

Tunigorn shifted about uncomfortably and swirled the wine in his bowl. "This song, I think, is unlucky, my lord," he muttered.

"Fear nothing," said Valentine. "Come, sing with us!"

> *"I hear, my lord," the dragon cried,*
> *And came across the sea*
> *Twelve miles long and three miles wide*
> *And two miles deep was he.*

> *Lord Malibor stood on the deck*
> *And fought both hard and well.*
> *Thick was the blood that flowed that day*
> *And great the blows that fell.*

The pilot Pandelume entered the mess-hall now, and approached the Coronal's table, halting with a look of some bewilderment on her thick-furred face as she heard the song. Valentine signaled her to join in, but her expression grew more gloomy, and she stood apart, scowling.

> *But dragon kings are old and sly,*
> *And rarely are they beaten.*
> *Lord Malibor, for all his strength*
> *Eventually was eaten.*

> *All sailors bold, who dragons hunt,*
> *Of this grim tale take heed!*
> *Despite all luck and skill, you may*
> *End up as dragon feed.*

"What is it, Pandelume?" Valentine asked, as the last raucous verse died away.

"Dragons, my lord, approaching out of the south."

"Many?"

"A great many, my lord."

"You see?" Tunigorn burst out. "We have summoned them, with this foolish song!"

"Then we will sing them on their way," said Valentine, "with another round of it." And he began again:

> *Lord Malibor was fine and bold*
> *And loved the heaving sea—*

The new herd was several hundred strong—a vast assemblage of sea dragons, a swarm so huge it passed all belief, with nine great kings at the center of the herd. Valentine, remaining outwardly calm, nevertheless felt a powerful sense of menace and danger, so strong it was almost tangible, emanating from the creatures. But they went by, none coming within three miles of the fleet, and disappeared rapidly to the north, swimming with a weird intensity of purpose.

In the depths of the night, as Valentine lay sleeping with his mind as ever open to the guidance that only dreams can bring, a strange vision imposed itself upon his soul. In the midst of a broad plain studded with angular rocks and odd pockmarked stiff-armed leafless plants a great multitude of people moves with an easy floating gait toward a distant sea. He finds himself among them, clad as they are in flowing robes of some gauzy white fabric that billows of its own accord, there being no breeze whatsoever. None of the faces about him is a familiar one, and yet he does not think of himself as being among strangers: he knows he is closely bound to these people, that they have been his fellow pilgrims on some trek that had lasted for many months, possibly even for years. And now the trek is arriving at its destination.

There lies the sea, many-hued, sparkling, its surface shifting as if roiled by the movements of titanic creatures far below, or perhaps in response to the tug of the swollen amber moon that rests heavily upon the sky. At the shore mighty waves rise up like bright curving crystalline claws, and fall back in utter silence, flailing the shining beaches weightlessly, as though they are not waves but merely the ghosts of waves.

And farther out, beyond all turbulence, a dark ponderous shape looms in the water.

It is a sea dragon; it is the dragon called Lord Kinniken's dragon, that is said to be the largest of all its kind, the king of the sea dragons, which no hunter's harpoon has ever touched. From its great humped bony-ridged back there streams an irresistible radiance, a mysterious shimmering amethystine glow that fills the sky and stains the water a deep violet. And there is the sound of bells, huge and deep, ringing out a steady solemn peal, a dark clangor that threatens to split the world in two at the core.

The dragon swims inexorably shoreward, and its huge mouth gapes like the mouth of a cavern.

—*My hour at last has come*, says the king of dragons, *and you are mine*.

The pilgrims, caught, drawn, mesmerized by the rich pulsating light that streams from the dragon, float onward toward the rim of the sea, toward that gaping mouth.

—*Yes. Yes. Come to me. I am the water-king Maazmoorn, and you are mine!*

Now the dragon king has reached the shallows, and the waves part for him, and he moves with ease onto the beach. The pealing of the bells grows louder still: insistently that terrible sound conquers the atmosphere and presses down upon it, so that with each new tolling the air grows thicker, slower, warmer. The dragon-king has unfurled the pair of colossal winglike fins that sprout from thick fleshy bases behind his head, and the wings thrust him onward over the wet sand. As he pulls his ponderous form to land, the first pilgrims reach him and without hesitation float on into the titanic maw and disappear; and behind them come others, an unending procession of willing sacrifices, racing forward to meet the dragon-king as he lurches landward to take them in.

And they enter the great mouth, and are engulfed into it, and Valentine is among them, and he goes down deep into the pit of the dragon's stomach. He enters a vaulted chamber of infinite size, and finds it already occupied by the legion of the swallowed, millions, billions—humans and Skandars and Vroons and Hjorts and Liimen and Su-Suheris and Ghayrogs, all the many peoples of Majipoor, impartially caught up in the gullet of the dragon-king.

And still Maazmoorn goes forward, deeper upon the land, and still the dragon-king feeds. He swallows all the world, gulping and gulping and still more ravenously gulping, devouring cities and mountains, the continents and the seas, taking within himself the totality of Majipoor, until at last he has taken it all, and lies coiled around the planet like a swollen serpent that has eaten some enormous globular creature.

The bells ring out a paean of triumph.

—Now at last has my kingdom come!

After the dream had left him Valentine did not return to full wakefulness, but allowed himself to drift into middlesleep, the place of sensitive receptivity, and there he lay, calm, quiet, reliving the dream, entering again that all-devouring mouth, analyzing, attempting to interpret.

Then the first light of morning fell upon him, and he came up to consciousness. Carabella lay beside him, awake, watching him. He slipped his arm about her shoulder and let his hand rest fondly, playfully, on her breast.

"Was it a sending?" she asked.

"No, I felt no presence of the Lady, nor of the King." He smiled. "You know always when I dream, don't you?"

"I could see the dream come upon you. Your eyes moved beneath the lids; your lip twitched; your nostrils moved like those of some hunting animal."

"Did I look troubled?"

"No, not at all. Perhaps at first you frowned; but then you smiled in your sleep, and a great calmness came over you, as if you were going forth toward some preordained fate and you accepted it entirely."

He laughed. "Ah, then I'll be gulped again by a sea dragon!"

"Is that what you dreamed?"

"More or less. Not the way it actually happened, though. This was the Kinniken dragon coming up on shore, and I marched right down its gullet. As did everyone else in the world, I think. And then it ate the world as well."

"And can you speak your dream?" she asked.

"In patches and fragments only," he said. "The wholeness of it still eludes me."

It was too simple, he knew, to call the dream merely a replaying of an event of his past, as though he had plugged in an entertainment cube and seen a reenactment of that strange event of his exile years, when he had indeed been swallowed by a sea dragon, after being shipwrecked off the Rodamaunt

Archipelago, and Lisamon Hultin, swallowed up in that same gulp, had cut a path to freedom through the monster's blubber-walled gut. Even a child knew better than to take a dream at its most literal autobiographical level.

But nothing yielded itself to him on the deeper level, either, except an interpretation so obvious as to be trivial: that these movements of sea-dragon herds he had lately observed were yet another warning that the world was in danger, that some potent force threatened the stability of society. That much he knew already, and it needed no reinforcement. Why sea dragons, though? What metaphor was churning in his mind that had transformed those vast marine mammals into a world-swallowing menace?

Carabella said, "Perhaps you look too hard. Let it pass, and the meaning will come to you when your mind is turned to something else. What do you say? Shall we go on deck?"

They saw no more herds of dragons in the days that followed, only a few solitary stragglers, and then none at all, nor were Valentine's dreams invaded again by threatening images. The sea was calm, the sky was bright and fair, the wind stood them well from the east. Valentine spent much of his time alone on the foredeck, looking off to sea; and at last came the day when out of the emptiness there suddenly came into view, like a bright white shield springing out of the dark horizon, the dazzling chalk cliffs of the Isle of Sleep, the holiest and most peaceful place of Majipoor, the sanctuary of the compassionate Lady.

7

The estate was virtually deserted now. All of Etowan Elacca's field hands were gone, and most of the house staff. Not one of them had bothered to make a formal leavetaking, even for the sake of collecting the pay he owed them: they simply slipped stealthily away, as though they dreaded remaining in the blighted zone a single hour more, and feared that he would somehow find a way to compel them to stay if he knew they wished to leave.

Simoost, the Ghayrog foreman, was still loyal, as was his wife Xhama, Etowan Elacca's head cook. Two or three of the housekeepers had stayed, and a couple of the gardeners. Etowan Elacca did not greatly mind that the rest had fled— there was, after all, no work for most of them to do any longer, nor could he afford to pay them properly, with no crop going to market. And sooner or later it would have become a problem simply to feed them all, if what he had heard about a growing food shortage in the entire province was true. Nevertheless, he took their departures as a rebuke. He was their master; he was responsible for their welfare; he was willing to provide for them as long as his resources lasted. Why were they so eager to go? What hope did they have, these farm workers and gardeners, of finding work in the ranching center of Falkynkip, which was where he assumed they had gone? And it was odd to see the place so quiet, where once there had been such bustling activity all through the day. Etowan Elacca often felt like a king whose subjects had renounced their citizenship and gone to some other land, leaving him to prowl an empty palace and issue orders to the unheeding air.

Yet he attempted to live as he had always lived. Certain habits remain unbroken even in the most dire time of calamity.

In the days before the falling of the purple rain, Etowan Elacca had risen each morning well ahead of the sun, and at the dawn hour went out into the garden to make his little tour of inspection. He took always the same route, through the alabandina grove to the tanigales, then a left turn into the shady little nook where the caramangs clustered, and onward under the fountaining profusion of the thagimole tree, which from its short stubby trunk sent graceful branches perpetually laden with fragrant blue-green flowers arching upward sixty feet or more. Then he saluted the mouthplants, he nodded to the glistening bladdertrees, he paused to hear the song of the singing ferns; and eventually he would come to the border of brilliant yellow mangahone bushes that marked the boundary between the garden and the farm, and he would look up the slight slope toward the plantings of stajja and glein and hingamorts and niyk.

There was nothing at all left of the farm and very little of the garden, but Etowan Elacca maintained his morning rounds all the same, pausing by each dead and blackened plant just as if it still thrived and grew and was making ready to burst into bloom. He knew that it was an absurd and pathetic thing to do, that anyone who discovered him at it would surely say,

"Ah, there is a poor crazed old man, whose grief has driven him mad." Let them say it, Etowan Elacca thought. It had never mattered much to him what other people said about him, and it mattered even less now. Perhaps he *had* gone mad, though he did not think so. He meant to continue his morning strolls all the same; for what else was there to do?

During the first weeks after the lethal rain his gardeners had wanted to clear each plant away as it died, but he had ordered them to let everything be, because he hoped that many of them were merely injured, not dead, and would spring back after a time, as they threw off the effects of whatever poisonous substance the purple rain had brought. After a while it became apparent even to Etowan Elacca that most of them had perished, that there would be no new life arising from the roots. But by that time the gardeners had begun to disappear, and soon only a handful remained, barely enough to carry out the necessary maintenance in the sectors of the garden that survived, let alone to cut down and haul away the dead plants. He thought at first that he would handle that melancholy task himself, little by little as time permitted; but the scope of the project so overwhelmed him that he decided shortly to leave everything as it was, letting the ruined garden remain as a kind of funereal monument to its former beauty.

As he moved slowly through his garden at dawn one morning many months after the time of the purple rain, Etowan Elacca found a curious object jutting from the soil in the pinnina bed: the polished tooth of some large animal. It was five or six inches long and sharp as a dagger. He plucked it out, stared at it puzzledly, and pocketed it. Farther on, among the muornas, he found two more teeth, of the same size, thrust into the ground at a distance of about ten feet from one another; and he looked up the slope toward the fields of dead stajja plants and saw three more, still farther apart. Beyond were another two, and then a single one, so that the whole group of teeth marked out a diamond-shaped pattern covering a large area of his land.

He returned quickly to the house, where Xhama was preparing the morning meal.

"Where is Simoost?" he asked.

The Ghayrog woman replied, without looking up, "He is in the niyk orchard, sir."

"The niyks are long dead, Xhama."

"Yes, sir. But he is in the niyk orchard. He has been there all night, sir."

"Go to him. Tell him I want to see him."

"He will not come, sir. And the food will burn if I leave."

Etowan Elacca, astounded by her refusal, could not for the moment find words. Then, realizing that in this time of changes some new and bewildering further change must be in the process of occurring, he nodded curtly and turned without a word and went outside once more.

As quickly as he could he ascended the sloping terrain, past the dismal fields of stajja, a sea of yellowed shriveled shoots, and up through the stark leafless glein bushes and the dried pasty stuff that was all that was left of the hingamorts, until in time he entered the niyk orchard. The dead trees were so light that they were easily uprooted by strong winds, and most had fallen, with the others standing at precarious angles as though a giant had slapped them playfully with the back of his hand. At first Etowan Elacca did not see Simoost; and then he caught sight of the foreman wandering in a peculiarly haphazard way along the outer edge of the grove, threading a path between the leaning trees, pausing now and then to push one over. Was this the way he had spent the night? Since Ghayrogs did all their year's sleeping in a few months of hibernation, it had never surprised Etowan Elacca to learn that Simoost had been at work during the night, but this sort of aimlessness was not at all like him.

"Simoost?"

"Ah, sir. Good morning, sir."

"Xhama said you were up here. Are you all right, Simoost?"

"Yes, sir. I am very well, sir."

"Are you sure?"

"Very well, sir. Very well indeed." But Simoost's tone lacked conviction.

Etowan Elacca said, "Will you come down? I have something to show you."

The Ghayrog appeared to be considering the request with care. Then he slowly descended until he reached the level where Etowan Elacca waited. The snaky coils of his hair, which were never entirely still, moved now in nervous jerky writhings, and from his powerful scaly body came a scent which Etowan Elacca, long familiar with the varying odors of Ghayrogs, knew to signify great distress and appre-

hension. Simoost had been with him for twenty years: Etowan
Elacca had never before detected that scent coming from
him.

"Sir?" Simoost said.

"What's troubling you, Simoost?"

"Nothing, sir. I am very well, sir. You wished to show me
something?"

"This," said Etowan Elacca, taking from his pocket the
long tapering tooth he had found in the pinnina bed. He held
it forth and said, "I came upon this while I was making the
garden tour half an hour ago. I wondered if you had any idea
what it was."

Simoost's lidless green eyes flickered uneasily. "The
tooth of a young sea dragon, sir. So I believe."

"Is that what it is?"

"I am quite sure, sir. Were there others?"

"Quite a few. Eight more, I think."

Simoost traced a diamond shape in the air. "Arranged in
a pattern like this?"

"Yes," said Etowan Elacca, frowning. "How did you
know that?"

"It is the usual pattern. Ah, there is danger, sir, great
danger!"

In exasperation Etowan Elacca said, "You're being deliberately mysterious, aren't you? *What* usual pattern? Danger
from whom? By the Lady, Simoost, tell me in plain words
what you know about all this!"

The Ghayrog's odor grew more pungent: it spoke of
intense dismay, fear, embarrassment. Simoost appeared to
struggle for words. At length he said, "Sir, do you know
where everyone who used to work for you has gone?"

"To Falkynkip, I assume, to look for work on the ranches.
But what does that—"

"No, not to Falkynkip, sir. Farther west. Pidruid is
where they have gone. To wait for the coming of the dragons."

"What?"

"As in the revelation, sir."

"Simoost—!"

"You know nothing about the revelation, then?"

Etowan Elacca felt a surge of anger such as he had rarely
known in his tranquil and well-fulfilled life. "I know nothing
whatever about the revelation, no," he said with barely
controllable fury.

"I will tell you, sir. I will tell you everything."

The Ghayrog was silent an instant, as though arranging his thoughts with some precision.

Then he took a deep breath and said, "There is an old belief, sir, that at a certain time great trouble will come upon the world, and all Majipoor will be thrust into confusion. And at that time, so it is said, the sea dragons will leave the sea, they will go forth onto the land and proclaim a new kingdom, and they will work an immense transformation in our world. And that time will be known as the time of the revelation."

"Whose fantasy is this?"

"Yes, fantasy is a good word for it, sir. Or fable, or, if you like, fairy-tale. It is not scientific. We understand that the sea-dragons are unable to emerge from the water. But the belief is quite widespread among some people, and they take much comfort from it."

"Which ones are those?"

"The poor people, chiefly. Mainly the Liimen, though some of the other races subscribe to it also, sir. I have heard it is prevalent among some Hjorts, and certain Skandars. It is not widely known among humans, and particularly not by such gentry as you, sir. But I tell you there are many now who say that the time of the revelation has come, that the blight upon the land and the shortage of food is the first sign of it, that the Coronal and Pontifex will soon be swept away and the reign of the water-kings will begin. And those who believe such a thing, sir, are going now toward the cities of the coast, toward Pidruid and Narabal and Til-omon, so that they can see the water-kings come ashore and be among the first to worship them. I know this to be the truth, sir. It is happening all through the province, and for all I know, it is happening everywhere in the world. Millions have begun to march toward the sea."

"How astonishing," said Etowan Elacca. "How ignorant I am, here in my little world within the world!" He ran his finger down the length of the dragon-tooth, to the sharp tip, and pressed it tightly until he felt the pain. "And these? What do they signify?"

"As I understand it, sir, they place them here and there, as signs of the revelation and as trail markers showing the route to the coast. A few scouts move ahead of the great multitude of pilgrims heading west, and place the teeth, and soon afterward the others follow in their path."

"How do they know where the teeth have been placed?"

"They know, sir. I do not know how they know. Perhaps the knowledge comes in dreams. Perhaps the water-kings issue sendings, like those of the Lady and of the King of Dreams."

"So we will shortly be overrun by a horde of wanderers?"

"I think so, sir."

Etowan Elacca tapped the tooth against the palm of his hand. "Simoost, why have you spent the night in the niyk orchard?"

"Trying to find the courage to tell you these things, sir."

"Why did it require courage?"

"Because I think we must flee, sir, and I know you will not want to flee, and I do not wish to abandon you, but I do not wish to die, either. And I think we will die if we stay here longer."

"You knew about the dragon-teeth in the garden?"

"I saw them placed, sir. I spoke with the scouts."

"Ah. When?"

"At midnight, sir. There were three of them, two Liimen and a Hjort. They say that four hundred thousand people are heading this way out of the eastern Rift country."

"Four hundred thousand people will march across my land?"

"I think so, sir."

"There won't be anything left once they've passed through, will there? They'll come through like a plague of locusts. They'll clean out such food supplies as we have, and I imagine they'll plunder the house, and they'll kill anyone who gets in their way, so I would suppose. Not out of malice, but merely in the general hysteria. Is that how you see it also, Simoost?"

"Yes, sir."

"And when will they be here?"

"Two days, perhaps three, so they told me."

"Then you and Xhama should leave this morning, should you not? All the staff should go right away. To Falkynkip, I would say. You ought to be able to reach Falkynkip before the mob gets there, and then you should be safe."

"You will not leave, sir?"

"No."

"Sir, I beg you—"

"No, Simoost."

"You will surely perish!"

"I have perished already, Simoost. Why should I flee to Falkynkip? What would I do there? I have perished already, Simoost, can't you perceive that? I am my own ghost."

"Sir—sir—"

"There's no more time to waste," said Etowan Elacca. "You should have taken your wife and gone at midnight, when you saw the teeth being placed. Go. Go. Now."

He swung about and descended the slope, and as he passed back through the garden he replaced the dragon-tooth where he had found it, in the pinnina bed.

In midmorning the Ghayrog and his wife came to him and implored him to leave with them—they were as close to tears as Etowan Elacca had ever seen a Ghayrog come, for Ghayrog eyes have no tear ducts—but he stood firm, and in the end they departed without him. He called the others who had remained loyal together, and dismissed them, giving them such money as he happened to have on hand, and much of the food from the larder.

That night he prepared his own dinner for the first time in his life. He thought he showed respectable skill, for a novice. He opened the last of the fireshower wine, and drank rather more than he would normally have allowed himself. What was happening to the world was very strange to him, and difficult to accept, but the wine made it a little easier. How many thousands of years of peace there had been! What a pleasant world, what a smoothly functioning world! Pontifex and Coronal, Pontifex and Coronal, a serene progression moving from Castle Mount to the Labyrinth, governing always with the consent of the many for the benefit of all; though of course some benefited more than others, yet no one went hungry, no one lived in need. And now it was ending. Poisonous rain comes from the sky, gardens wither, crops are destroyed, famines begin, new religions take hold, ravenous crazy mobs swarm toward the sea. Does the Coronal know? Does the Lady of the Isle? The King of Dreams? What is being done to repair these things? What *can* be done? Will kindly dreams from the Lady help to fill empty bellies? Will threatening dreams from the King turn the mobs back? Will the Pontifex, if indeed there is a Pontifex, come forth from the Labyrinth and make lofty proclamations? Will the Coronal ride from province to province, urging patience? No. No. No. No. It is over, Etowan Elacca thought. What a pity that this could not have waited another twenty years, or thirty perhaps, so that I could have died quietly in my garden, and the garden still in bloom.

He kept watch through the night, and all was still.

In the morning he imagined he could hear the first rumblings of the oncoming horde to the east. He went through the house, opening every door that was locked, so they would do as little damage as possible to the building as they ransacked it for his food and his wines. It was a beautiful house, and he loved it and hoped it would come to no harm.

Then he went out into the garden, among the shriveled and blackened plants. Much of it, he realized, had actually survived the deadly rain: rather more than he thought, since he had had eyes all these dark months only for the destruction, but indeed the mouthplants were still flourishing and the nightflower trees and some of the androdragmas, the dwikkas, the sihornish vines, even the fragile bladdertrees. For hours he walked among them. He thought of giving himself to one of the mouthplants, but that would be an ugly death, he thought, slow and bloody and inelegant, and he wanted it said of him, even if there might be no one to say it, that he had been elegant to the last. Instead he went to the sihornish vines, which were festooned with unripened fruits, still yellow. The ripe sihornish was one of the finest of delicacies, but the fruit when yellow brims with deadly alkaloids. For a long while Etowan Elacca stood by the vine, utterly without fear, simply not yet quite ready. Then came the sound of voices, not imagined this time, the harsh voices of city folk, many of them, borne on the fragrant air from the east. Now he was ready. He knew it would be more gentlemanly to wait until they were here, and bid them be welcome to his estate, and offer them his best wines and such dinner as he could provide; but without his staff he could not provide much in the way of hospitality, after all; and, besides, he had never really liked city folk, particularly when they came as uninvited guests. He looked about one last time at the dwikkas and the bladdertrees and the one sickly halatinga that somehow had survived, and commended his soul to the Lady, and felt the beginnings of tears. He did not think weeping was seemly. And so he put the yellow sihornish to his lips, and bit eagerly into its hard unripe flesh.

8

Though she had merely intended to rest her eyes a moment or two before she began preparing dinner, a deep and powerful sleep came quickly over Elsinome when she lay down, drawing her into a cloudy realm of yellow shadows and rubbery pink hills; and though she had scarcely expected a sending to come to her during a casual before-dinner nap, she felt a gentle pressure at the gateways of her soul as she descended into the fullness of her slumber, and knew it to be the presence of the Lady coming upon her.

Elsinome was tired all the time, lately. She had never worked so hard as in the last few days, since news of the crisis in western Zimroel had reached the Labyrinth. Now the café was full all day long with tense officials of the Pontificate, exchanging the latest information over a few bowls of fine Muldemar or good golden Dulornese wine—they wanted only the best, when they were this worried. And so she was constantly running back and forth, juggling her inventories, calling in extra supplies from the wine merchants. It had been exciting, in a way, at first: she felt almost as though she were participating herself in this critical moment of history. But now it was merely exhausting.

Her last thought before falling asleep was of Hissune: *Prince* Hissune, as she was still trying to learn to regard him. She had not heard from him in months, not since that astonishing letter, so dreamlike itself, telling her that they had called him to the highest circle of the Castle. He had begun to seem unreal to her after that, no longer the small sharp-eyed clever boy who once had amused and comforted and supported her, but a stranger in fine robes who spent his days among the councils of the great, holding unimaginable discourse on the ultimate destinies of the world. An image came to her of Hissune at a vast table polished to mirror brightness, sitting among older men whose features were unclearly limned but from whom there radiated great presence and authority, and they were all looking toward Hissune as he spoke. Then the scene vanished and she saw yellow clouds and pink hills, and the Lady entered her mind.

It was the briefest of sendings. She was on the Isle—that much she knew from the white cliffs and the steeply rising terraces, though she had never actually been there, never in fact been outside the Labyrinth—and in a dreamlike drifting way she was moving through a garden that was at first immaculate and airy and then imperceptibly became dark and overgrown. The Lady was by her side, a black-haired woman in white robes who seemed sad and weary, not at all the strong, warm, comforting person Elsinome had met in earlier sendings: she was bowed with care, her eyes were hooded and downcast, her movements uncertain. "Give me your strength," the Lady murmured. This is all wrong, thought Elsinome. The Lady comes to us to offer strength, not to receive it. But the dream-Elsinome did not hesitate. She was vigorous and tall, with a nimbus of light flickering about her head and shoulders. She drew the Lady to her, and took her against her breast and held her in a close strong embrace, and the Lady sighed and it seemed that some of the pain went from her. Then the two women drew apart and the Lady, glowing now as Elsinome was, touched her fingers to her lips and threw a kiss to Elsinome, and vanished.

That was all. With startling suddenness Elsinome woke and saw the familiar dreary walls of her flat in Guadeloom Court. The afterglow of a sending was on her beyond any doubt, but the sendings of other years had left her always with a strong sense of new purpose, of directions redirected, and this one had brought only mystification. She could not understand the purpose of such a sending; but perhaps it would manifest itself to her, she thought, in a day or two.

She heard sounds in her daughters' room.

"Ailimoor? Maraune?"

Neither girl answered. Elsinome peered in and saw them huddling close over some small object, which Maraune put quickly behind her back.

"What's that you have there?"

"It's nothing, mother. Just a little thing."

"What kind of thing?"

"A trinket. Sort of."

Something in Maraune's tone made Elsinome suspicious. "Let me see it."

"It really isn't *anything*."

"Let me see."

Maraune shot a quick look toward her older sister. Ailimoor, looking uneasy and awkward, simply shrugged.

"It's personal, mother. Doesn't a girl get to have any *privacy?*" Maraune said.

Elsinome held out her hand. Sighing, Maraune brought forth and reluctantly surrendered a small sea-dragon tooth, finely carved over much of its surface with unfamiliar and peculiarly disturbing symbols of an odd, narrow-angled sort. Elsinome, still in part enveloped in the strange aura of the sending, found the little amulet sinister and menacing.

"Where'd you get this?"

"Eveeryone's got them, mother."

"I asked you where it came from."

"Vanimoon. Actually Vanimoon's sister Shulaire. But she got it from him. Can I please have it back?"

"Do you know what this thing means?" Elsinome asked.

"Means?"

"That's what I said. What it means."

Shrugging, Maraune said, "It doesn't mean anything. It's just a trinket. I'm going to drill a hole in it and wear it on a string."

"Do you expect me to believe that?"

Maraune was silent. Ailimoor said, "Mother, I—" She faltered.

"Go on."

"It's just a fad, mother. Everyone's got them. There's some crazy new Liiman idea going around that the sea dragons are gods, that they're going to take over the world, that all the trouble that's been happening lately is a sign of what's to come. And people say that if we carry the sea-dragon teeth, we'll be saved when the dragons come ashore."

Coldly Elsinome said, "There's nothing new about it. Nonsense like that has been going around for hundreds of years. But always hidden, always in whispers, because it's crazy and dangerous and sick. Sea dragons are oversized fish and nothing more. The One who looks over us is the Divine, protecting us through the Coronal and the Pontifex and the Lady. Do you understand? Do you understand?"

She snapped the tapering tooth in half with a quick angry motion and tossed the pieces to Maraune, who glared at her with a fury that Elsinome had never seen in the eyes of one of her daughters before. Hastily she turned away, toward the kitchen. Her hands were shaking, and she felt chilled;

and if the peace of the Lady had descended upon her at all in the sending—that sending which now seemed to have come to her weeks ago—it was entirely gone from her now.

9

The entry to Numinor harbor took all the skill the most skillful pilot could muster, for the channel was narrow and the currents were swift, and sandy reefs sometimes were born overnight in the volatile underbeds. But Pandelume was a calm and confident figure on the wheel deck, giving her signals with clear decisive gestures, and the royal flagship came in jauntily, past the neck of the channel and into the broad sweet safe anchorage, the only possible one on the Alhanroel side of the Isle of Sleep, the one place where a breach existed in the tremendous chalk wall of First Cliff.

"I can feel my mother's presence from here," said Valentine as they made ready to go ashore. "She comes to me like the fragrance of alabandina blossoms on the wind."

"Will the Lady be here to greet us today?" Carabella asked.

"I much doubt it," Valentine said. "Custom calls for son to go to mother, not mother to son. She'll remain at Inner Temple, and send her hierarchs, I suppose, to fetch us."

A group of hierarchs indeed was waiting when the royal party disembarked. Among these women, in golden robes trimmed with red, was one already well known to Valentine, the austere white-haired Lorivade, who had accompanied him during the war of restoration on his journey from the Isle to Castle Mount, training him in the techniques of trance and mental projection that were practiced on the Isle. A second figure in the group seemed familiar to Valentine but he could not place her until the very instant when she spoke her name: and simultaneous with that came the flash of recognition, that this was Talinot Esulde, the slender, enigmatic person who had been his first guide on his pilgrimage to the Isle long ago. Then she had had a shaven skull, and Valentine had been unable to guess her sex, suspecting her to be male from her height or female from the delicacy of her features and the lightness of her frame; but since her advancement to the inner hierarchy she had allowed her hair to grow, and those long silken locks, as golden as Valentine's own but far finer of texture, left no doubt that she was a woman.

"We carry dispatches for you, my lord," said the hierarch Lorivade. "There is much news, and none of it good, I fear. But first we should conduct you to the royal lodging-place."

There was a house in Numinor port known as the Seven Walls, which was a name that no one understood, because it was so ancient that its origins had been forgotten. It stood on the rampart of the city overlooking the sea, with its face toward Alhanroel and its back to the steep triple tiers of the Isle, and it was built of massive blocks of dark granite hewn from the quarries of the Stoienzar Peninsula, fitted together in a perfect joining with no trace of mortar. Its sole function was to serve as a place of refreshment for a visiting Coronal newly arrived on the Isle, and so it went unused for years at a time; yet it was scrupulously maintained by a large staff, as though a Coronal might arrive without warning at any moment and must needs have his house in order at the hour of his landing.

It was very old, as old as the Castle itself, and older, so far as archaeologists could determine, than any of the temples and holy terraces now in existence elsewhere on the Isle. According to legend it had been built for the reception of Lord Stiamot by his mother, the fabled Lady Thiin, upon his visit to the Isle of Sleep at the conclusion of the Metamorph wars of eight thousand years ago. Some said that the name Seven Walls was a reference to the entombing in the foundations of the building, as it was being constructed, of the bodies of seven Shapeshifter warriors slain by Lady Thiin's own hand during the defense of the Isle against Metamorph invasion. But no such remains had ever come to light in the periodic reconstructions of the old building; and also it was thought unlikely by most modern historians that Lady Thiin, heroic woman that she was, had actually wielded weapons herself in the Battle of the Isle. By another tradition, a seven-sided chapel erected by Lord Stiamot in honor of his mother once had stood in the central courtyard, giving its name to the entire structure. That chapel, so the story went, had been dismantled on the day of Lord Stiamot's death and shipped to Alaisor to become the pediment of his tomb. But that too was unproven, for no trace of an early seven-sided structure could be detected in the courtyard now, and there was little likelihood that anyone today would excavate Lord Stiamot's tomb to see what could be learned from its paving-blocks. Valentine himself preferred a different version of the origin of the name, which held that Seven Walls was merely a corruption into the Majipoori tongue of certain ancient Metamorph words that meant "The place where the fish scales are scraped off," and referred to the prehistoric use of the shore of the Isle by Shapeshifter fishermen sailing from Alhanroel. But it was unlikely that the truth would ever be determined.

There were rituals of arrival that a Coronal was supposed to perform upon reaching the Seven Walls, by way of aiding his transition from the world of action that was his usual sphere to the world of the spirit in which the Lady was supreme. While Valentine carried these things out—a matter of ceremonial bathing, of the burning of aromatic herbs, of meditation in a private chamber whose walls were airy damasks of pierced marble—he left Carabella to read through the dispatches that had accumulated for him during the weeks he was at sea; and when he returned, cleansed and calm, he saw at once from the stark expression of her eyes that he had gone about his rituals too soon, that he would be drawn back instantly into the realm of events.

"How bad is the news?" he asked.

"It could scarcely be worse, my lord."

She handed him the sheaf of documents, which she had winnowed so that the uppermost sheets gave him the gist of the most important documents. Failure of crops in seven provinces—severe shortage of food in many parts of Zimroel—the beginnings of a mass migration out of the heartland of the continent toward the western coastal cities—sudden prominence of a formerly obscure religious cult, apocalyptic and millennial in nature, centering around the belief that sea dragons were supernatural beings that would soon come ashore to announce the birth of a new epoch—

He looked up, aghast.

"All this in so short a time?"

"And these are only fragmentary reports, Valentine. No one really knows what's going on out there right now—the distances are so vast, the communications channels so disturbed—"

His hand sought hers. "Everything foretold in my dreams and visions is coming to pass. The darkness is coming, Carabella, and I am all that stands in its path."

"There are some who stand beside you, love."

"That I know. And for that am I grateful. But at the last

moment I will be alone, and then what will I do?" He smiled ruefully. "There was a time when we were juggling at the Perpetual Circus in Dulorn, do you recall, and the knowledge of my true identity was only then beginning to break through to my awareness. And I was speaking with Deliamber, and telling him that perhaps it was the will of the Divine that I had been overthrown, and that perhaps it was just as well for Majipoor that the usurper keep my name and my throne, for I had no real desire to be king and the other might indeed prove to be a capable ruler. Which Deliamber denied completely, and said there could be only one lawfully conse-crated king and I was that one, and must return to my place. You ask a great deal of me, I said. 'History asks a great deal,' he replied. 'History has demanded, on a thousand worlds across many thousands of years, that intelligent beings choose between order and anarchy, between creation and destruc-tion, between reason and unreason.' And also: 'It matters, my lord, it matters very much,' said he, 'who is to be Coronal and who is not to be Coronal.' I have never forgotten those words of his, and I never will."

"And how did you answer him?"

"I answered 'yes' and then I added 'perhaps,' and he said, 'You'll go on wavering from *yes* to *perhaps* a long while, but *yes* will govern in the end.' And so it did, and therefore I recaptured my throne—and nevertheless we move farther every day from order and creation and reason, and closer to anarchy, destruction, unreason." Valentine stared at her in anguish. "Was Deliamber wrong, then? *Does* it matter who is to be Coronal and who is not to be Coronal? I think I am a good man, and sometimes I think even that I am a wise ruler; and yet even so the world falls apart, Carabella, despite my best efforts or because of them, I know not which. It might have been better for everyone if I had stayed a wandering juggler."

"Oh, Valentine, what foolish talk this is!"

"Is it?"

"Are you saying that if you'd left Dominin Barjazid to rule, there would have been a fine lusavender harvest this year? How are you to blame for crop failures in Zimroel? These are natural calamities, with natural causes, and you'll find a wise way to deal with them, because wisdom is your way, and you are the chosen of the Divine."

"I am chosen of the princes of Catle Mount," he said. "They are human and fallible."

"The Divine speaks through them when a Coronal is chosen. And the Divine did not mean you to be the instrument of Majipoor's destruction. These reports are serious but not terrifying. You will speak with your mother in a few days, and she'll fortify you where weariness makes you weaken; and then we'll proceed on to Zimroel and you will set all to rights."

"So I hope, Carabella. But—"

"So you know, Valentine! I say once more, my lord, I hardly recognize in you the man I know, when you speak this gloomy way." She tapped the sheaf of dispatches. "I would not minimize these things. But I think there is much we can do to turn back the darkness, and that it will be done."

He nodded slowly. "So I think myself, much of the time. But at other times—"

"At other times it's best not to think at all." A knock sounded at the door. "Good," she said. "We are interrupted, and I give thanks for that, for I tire of hearing you make all these downcast noises, my love."

She admitted Talinot Esulde to the room. The hierarch said, "My lord, your mother the Lady has arrived, and wishes to see you in the Emerald Room."

"My mother here? But I expected to go to her tomorrow, at Inner Temple!"

"She has come to you," said Talinot Esulde imperturbably.

The Emerald Room was a study in green: walls of green serpentine, floors of green onyx, translucent panes of green jade in place of windows. The Lady stood in the center of the room, between the two huge potted tanigales, covered with dazzling blossoms of metallic green, that were virtually all that the chamber contained. Valentine went quickly toward her. She stretched her hands to him, and as their fingertips met he felt the familiar throbbing of the current that radiated from her, the sacred force that, like spring water draining into a well, had accumulated in her through all her years of intimate contact with the billions of souls of Majipoor.

He had spoken with her in dreams many times, but he had not seen her in years, and he was unprepared for the changes time had worked upon her. She was still beautiful: the passing of the years could not affect that. But age now had cast the faintest of veils over her, and the sheen was gone from her black hair, the warmth of her gaze was ever so slightly diminished, her skin seemed somehow to have loosened its grasp on her flesh. Yet she carried herself as splendidly as ever, and she was, as always, magnificently robed in white, with a flower behind one ear, and the silver circlet of her power on her brow: a figure of grace and majesty, of force and of infinite compassion.

"Mother. At last."

"Such a long while, Valentine! So many years!"

She touched his face gently, his shoulders, his arms. The brush of her fingers over him was feather-light, but it left him tingling, so great was the power within this woman. He had to remind himself that she was no goddess, but only mortal flesh and daughter of mortal flesh, that upon a time long ago she had been wife to the High Counsellor Damiandane, that two sons had sprung from her and he was one of them, that once he had nestled at her breast and listened happily to her soft song, that it was she who had wiped the mud from his cheeks when he came home from play, that in the tempests of childhood he had wept in her arms and drawn comfort and wisdom from her. Long ago, all that: it seemed almost to be in another life. When the sceptor of the Divine had descended upon the family of the High Counsellor Damiandane and raised Voriax to the Confalume Throne it had by the same stroke transformed the mother of Voriax into the Lady of the Isle, and neither one could ever again be regarded even within the family as merely mortal. Valentine found himself then and always after unable to think of her simply as his mother, for she had donned the silver circlet and had gone to the Isle, and dwelled there in majesty as Lady, and the comfort and wisdom that formerly she had dispensed to him she shared now with the entire world, who looked to her with reverence and need. Even when another stroke of that same scepter had elevated Valentine to Voriax's place, and he too passed in some way beyond the realm of the ordinary and became larger than life, virtually a figure of myth, he had retained his awe of her, for he had no awe of himself, Coronal or no, and could not through his own inner vision see himself with the awe that others held for him, or he for this Lady.

Yet they talked of family things before they turned to higher questions. He told her such details as he knew of the doings of her sister Galiara and her brother Sait of Stee, and of Divvis and Mirigant and the daughters of Voriax. She asked

him whether he returned often to the old family lands at
Halanx, and if he found the Castle a happy place, and
whether he and Carabella were still so loving and close. The
tensions within him eased, and he felt almost as though he
were a real person, some minor lordling of the Mount,
visiting amiably with his mother, who had settled in a different clime but still was avid for news of home. But it was
impossible to escape the truths of their position for long, and
when the conversation began to grow forced and strained he
said, in somewhat another tone, "You should have let me
come to you in the proper way, mother. This is not right, the
Lady descending from Inner Temple to visit the Seven Walls."

"Such formality is unwise now. Events crowd us: the
actions must be taken."

"Then you've had the news from Zimroel?"

"Of course." She touched her circlet. "This brings me
news from everywhere, with the swiftness of the speed of
thought. Oh, Valentine, such an unhappy time for our reunion! I had imagined that when you made your processional
you would come here in joy, and now you are here and I feel
only pain in you, and doubt, and fear of what is to come."

"What do you see, mother? What is to come?"

"Do you think I have some way of knowing the future?"

"You see the present with great clarity. As you say, you
receive news from everywhere."

"What I see is dark and clouded. Things stir in the world
that are beyond my understanding. Once again the order of
society is threatened. And the Coronal is in despair. That is
what I see. Why do you despair, Valentine? Why is there so
much fear in you? You are the son of Damiandane and the
brother of Voriax, and they were not men who knew despair,
and despair is not native to my soul either, or to yours, so I
thought."

"There is great trouble in the world, as I have learned
since my arrival here, and that trouble increases."

"And is that cause for despair? It should only increase
your desire to set things right, as once you did before."

"For the second time, though, I see Majipoor overtaken
by calamity during my reign. What I see," said Valentine, "is
that my reign has been an unlucky one, and will be unluckier
yet, if these plagues and famines and panicky migrations grow
more severe. I fear that some curse lies on me."

He saw anger briefly flare in her eyes, and he was

reminded again of the formidable strength of her soul, of the icy discipline and devotion to duty that lay below her warm and gentle appearance. In her way she was as fierce a warrior as the famed Lady Thiin of ancient times, who had gone out upon the barricades to drive back the invading Metamorphs. This Lady too might be capable of such valor, if there were need. She had no tolerance, he knew, for weakness in her sons, or self-pity, or despondency, because she had none for those things in herself. And, remembering that, he felt some of the bleakness of his mood begin to go from him.

She said tenderly, "You take blame on yourself without proper cause. If a curse hangs over this world, and I think that that is the case, it lies not on the noble and virtuous Coronal, but upon us all. You have no reason for guilt: you least of all, Valentine. You are not the bearer of the curse, but rather the one who is most capable of lifting it from us. But to do that you must act, and act quickly."

"And what curse is this, then?"

Putting her hand to her brow, she said, "You have a silver circlet that is the mate to mine. Did you carry it with you on this journey?"

"It goes everywhere with me."

"Fetch it here, then."

Valentine went from the room and spoke with Sleet, who waited outside; and shortly an attendant came, bearing the jeweled case in which the circlet resided. The Lady had given it to him when first he went to the Isle as a pilgrim, during his years of exile. Through it, in communion with his mother's mind, he had received the final confirmation that the simple juggler of Pidruid and Lord Valentine of Majipoor were one and the same person, for with its aid and hers his lost memories had come flooding back. And afterward the hierarch Lorivade had taught him how, by virtue of the circlet, he could enter the trance by which he might have access to the minds of others. He had used it little since his restoration to the throne, for the circlet was an adjunct of the Lady, not of the Coronal, and it was unfitting for one Power of Majipoor to transgress on the domain of another. Now he donned the fine metal band again, while the Lady poured for him, as she had done long ago on this Isle, a flask of the dark, sweet, spicy dream-wine that was used in the opening of mind to mind.

He drank it off in a single draught, and she drank down a

flask of her own, and they waited a moment for the wine to take effect. He put himself into the state of trance that gave him the fullest receptivity. Then she took his hands and slipped her fingers tightly between his to complete the contact, and into his mind came such a rush of images and sensations as to daze and stun him, though he had known what sort of impact there would be.

This now was what the Lady had for many years experienced each day as she and her acolytes sent their spirits roving through the world to those in need of aid.

He saw no individual minds: the world was far too huge and crowded to permit precision of that sort except with the most strenuous of concentration. What he detected, as he soared like a gust of hot wind riding the thermal waves of the sky, were pockets of sensation: apprehension here, fear, shame, guilt, a sudden sharp stabbing zone of madness, a gray sprawling blanket of despair. He dipped low and saw the textures of souls, the black ridges shot through with ribbons of scarlet, the harsh jagged spikes, the roiling turbulent roadways of bristling tight-woven fabric. He soared high into tranquil realms of nonbeing; he swooped across dismal deserts that emanated a numbing throb of isolation; he whirled over glittering snowfields of the spirit, and meadows whose every blade of glass glistened with an unbearable beauty. And he saw the places of blight, and the places of hunger, and the places where chaos was king. And he felt terrors rising like hot dry winds from the great cities; and he felt some force beating in the seas like an irresistible booming drum; and he felt a powerful sense of gathering menace, of oncoming disaster. An intolerable weight had fallen upon the world, Valentine saw, and was crushing it by slow increments of intensity, like a gradually closing fist.

Through all of this his guide was the blessed Lady his mother, without whom he might well have sizzled and charred in the intensity of the passion that radiated from the well of the world-mind. But she stayed at his side, lifting him easily through the darker places, and carrying him on toward the threshold of understanding, which loomed before him the way the immense Dekkeret Gate of Normork, that greatest of gates, which is closed only at times when the world is in peril, looms and dwarfs all those who approach it. But when he came to that threshold he was alone, and he passed through unaided.

On the far side there was only music, music made visible, a tremulous quavering tone that stretched across the abyss like the weakest of woven bridges, and he stepped out upon that bridge and saw the splashes of bright sound that stained the flow of substance below, and the dagger-keen spurts of rhythmic pulsation overhead, and the line of infinitely regressing red and purple and green arcs that sang to him from the horizon. Then all of these gave way to a single formidable sound, of a weight beyond any bearing, a black juggernaut of sound that embraced all tones into itself, and rolled forward upon the universe and pressed upon it mercilessly. And Valentine understood.

He opened his eyes. The Lady his mother stood calmly between the potted tanigales, watching him, smiling as she might have smiled down on him when he was a sleeping babe. She took the circlet from his brow and returned it to the jeweled case.

"You saw?" she asked.

"It is as I have long believed," said Valentine. "What is happening in Zimroel is no random event. There is a curse, yes, and it is on us all, and has been for thousands of years. My Vroon wizard Deliamber said to me once that we have gone a long way, here on Majipoor, without paying any sort of price for the original sin of the conquerors. The account, he said, accumulates interest. And now the note is being presented for collection. What has begun is our punishment, our humbling, the settling of the reckoning."

"So it is," said the Lady.

"Was what we saw the Divine Itself, mother? Holding the world in a tight grasp, and making the grasp tighter? And that sound I heard, of such terrible weight: was that the Divine also?"

"The images you saw were your own, Valentine. I saw other things. Nor can the Divine be reduced to anything so concrete as an image. But I think you saw the essence of the matter, yes."

"I saw that the grace of the Divine has been withdrawn from us."

"Yes. But not irredeemably."

"Are you sure it isn't already too late?"

"I am sure of it, Valentine."

He was silent a moment. Then he said, "So be it. I see what must be done, and I will do it. How appropriate that I should have come to the understanding of these things in the Seven Walls, which the Lady Thiin built to honor her son after he had crushed the Metamorphs! Ah, mother, mother, will you build a building like this for me, when I succeed in undoing Lord Stiamot's work?"

10

"Again," Hissune said, swinging about to face Alsimir and the other knight-initiate. "Come at me again. Both of you at once this time."

"Both?" said Alsimir.

"Both. And if I catch you going easy on me, I promise you I'll have you assigned to sweep the stables for a month."

"How can you withstand us both, Hissune?"

"I don't know that I can. That's what I need to learn. Come at me, and we'll see."

He was slick with sweat and his heart was hammering, but his body felt loose and well tuned. He came here, to the cavernous gymnasium in the Castle's east wing, for at least an hour every day, no matter how pressing his other responsibilities.

It was essential, Hissune believed, that he strengthen and develop his body, build up his physical endurance, increase his already considerable agility. Otherwise, so it plainly seemed, he would be under a heavy handicap pursuing his ambitions here. The princes of Castle Mount tended to be athletes and to make a cult of athleticism, constantly testing themselves: riding, jousting, racing, wrestling, hunting, all those ancient simpleminded pastimes that Hissune, in his Labyrinth days, had never had the opportunity or the inclination to pursue. Now Lord Valentine had thrust him among these burly, energetic men, and he knew he must meet them on their own ground if he meant to win a lasting place in their company.

Of course there was no way he could transform his slight, slender frame into something to equal the robust muscularity of a Stasilaine, an Elidath, a Divvis. They were big men, and he would never be that. But he could excel in his own way. This game of baton, for example: a year ago he had not even heard of it, and now, after many hours of practice, he was coming close to mastery. It called for quickness of eye and foot, not for overwhelming physical power, and so in a sense it served as a metaphor for his entire approach to the problem of life.

"Ready," he called.

He stood in a balanced partial crouch, alert, pliant, with his arms partly extended and his baton, a light, slender wand of nightflower wood with a cup-shaped hilt of basketwork at one end, resting across them. His eyes flickered from one opponent to the other. They both were taller than he was, Alsimir by two or three inches, and his friend Stimion even more. But he was quicker. Neither of them had come close to putting a baton on him all morning. Two at once, though— that might be a different matter—

"Challenge!" Alsimir called. "Post! Entry!"

They came toward him, and as they moved in they raised their batons into attack position.

Hissune drew a deep breath and concentrated on constructing a spherical zone of defense about himself, impermeable, impenetrable, a volume of space enclosed in armor. It was purely imaginary, but that made no difference. Thani, his baton-master, had shown him that: maintain your defensive zone as though it is a wall of steel, and nothing would get through it. The secret lay in the intensity of your concentration.

Alsimir reached him a fraction of a second ahead of Stimion, as Hissune had expected. Alsimir's baton went high, probed the northwest quadrant of Hissune's defense, then feinted for a lower entry. As it neared the perimeter of Hissune's defended area Hissune brought his baton up with a whip-like action of his wrist, parried Alsimir's thrust solidly, and in the same motion—for he had already calculated it, though in no conscious way—he continued around to his right, meeting the thrust from Stimion that was coming in a shade late out of the northeast.

There was the whickering sound of wood sliding against wood as Hissune let his baton ride halfway up the length of Stimion's; then he pivoted, leaving Stimion only empty space to plunge through as the force of his thrust carried him forward. All that took only a moment. Stimion, grunting in surprise, lurched through the place where Hissune had been. Hissune tapped him lightly on the back with his baton and swung around again on Alsimir. Up came Alsimir's baton; inward came the second thrust. Hissune blocked it easily and answered with one of his own that Alsimir handled well, parrying so firmly that the shock of the impact went rattling up Hissune's arm to the elbow. But Hissune recovered quickly, sidestepped Alsimir's next attempt, and danced off to one side to elude Stimion's baton.

Now they found themselves in a new configuration, Stimion and Alsimir standing to either side of Hissune rather than facing him. They surely would attempt simultaneous thrusts, Hissune thought. He could not allow that.

Thani had taught him: *Time must always be your servant, never your master. If there is not enough time for you to make your move, divide each moment into smaller moments, and then you will have enough time for anything.*

Yes. Nothing is truly simultaneous, Hissune knew.

As he had for many months been training himself to do, he shifted into the time-splitting mode of perception that Thani had instilled in him: viewing each second as the sum of ten tenths of itself, he allowed himself to dwell in each of those tenths in turn, the way one might dwell in each of ten caves on successive nights during the crossing of a desert. His perspective now was profoundly altered. He saw Stimion moving in jerky discontinuous bursts, struggling like some sort of crude automaton to bring his baton up and jab it toward him. With the greatest simplicity of effort Hissune slipped himself into the interval between two slices of a moment and knocked Stimion's baton aside. The thrust from Alsimir was already on its way, but Hissune had ample time to withdraw himself from Alsimir's reach, and as Alsimir's arm came to full extension Hissune gave it a light touch with his own weapon, just above the elbow.

Returning now to the normal perception mode, Hissune confronted Stimion, who was coming round for another thrust. Instead of making ready to parry, Hissune chose to move forward, stepping inside the startled Stimion's guard. From that position he brought his baton upward, touching Alsimir again and swinging round to catch Stimion with the tip as he whirled in confusion.

"Touch and double touch," Hissune called. "Match."

"How did you do that?" asked Alsimir, tossing down his baton.

Hissune laughed. "I have no idea. But I wish Thani had been here to see it!" He dropped to a kneeling position and let sweat drip freely from his forehead onto the mats. It had been, he knew, an amazing display of skill. Never had he fought that well before. An accident, a moment of luck? Or had he truly reached a new level of accomplishment? He recalled Lord Valentine speaking of his juggling, which he had taken up in the most casual of ways, merely to earn a livelihood, when he was wandering lost and bewildered in Zimroel. Juggling, the Coronal had said, had shown him the key to the proper focusing of his mental abilities. Lord Valentine had gone so far as to suggest that he might not have been able to regain his throne, but for the disciplines of spirit that his mastery of juggling had imposed on him. Hissune knew he could hardly take up juggling himself—it would be too blatant a flattery of the Coronal, too open a gesture of imitation—but he was beginning to see that he might attain much of the same discipline through wielding the baton. Certainly his performance just now had carried him into extraordinary realms of perception and achievement. He wondered if he was capable of repeating it. He looked up and said, "Well, shall we go another, one on two?"

"Don't you ever get tired?" Stimion said.

"Of course I do. But why stop just because you're tired?"

He took his stance again, waiting for them. Another fifteen minutes of this, he thought. Then a swim, and then to the Pinitor Court to get some work done, and then—

"Well? Come at me," he said.

Alsimir shook his head. "There's no sense in it. You're getting too good for us."

"Come," Hissune said again. "Ready!"

Somewhat reluctantly Alsimir moved into dueling position, and gestured Stimion to do the same. But as the three men stood poised, bringing their minds and bodies to the degree of balance the match required, a gymnasium attendant stepped out on the balcony above them and called Hissune's name. A message for the prince, he said, from the Regent Elidath: Prince Hissune is asked to report at once to the Regent at the office of the Coronal.

"Another day, then?" Hissune said to Alsimir and Stimion.

He dressed quickly and made his way upward and through the intricate coils and tangles of the Castle, cutting across courtyards and avenues, past Lord Ossier's parapet and its amazing view of Castle Mount's vast slope, on beyond the Kinniken Observatory and the music room of Lord Prankipin and Lord Confalume's garden-house and the dozens of other structures and outbuildings that clung like barnacles to the core of the Castle. At last he reached the central sector, where the offices of government were, and had himself admitted to the spacious suite in which the Coronal worked, now occupied during Lord Valentine's prolonged absence by the High Counsellor Elidath.

He found the Regent pacing back and forth like a restless bear in front of the relief map of the world opposite Lord Valentine's desk. Stasilaine was with him, seated at the council table. He looked grim, and acknowledged Hissune's arrival only with the merest of nods. In an offhand, preoccupied way Elidath gestured to Hissune to take a seat beside him. A moment later Divvis arrived, formally dressed in eye-jewels and feather-mask, as though the summons had interrupted him on his way to a high state ceremony.

Hissune felt a great uneasiness growing in him. What reason could Elidath possibly have for calling a meeting like this so suddenly, in such an irregular way? And why just these few of us, out of all the princes? Elidath, Stasilaine, Divvis—surely those were the three prime candidates to succeed Lord Valentine, the innermost of the inner circle. Something major has happened, Hissune thought. The old Pontifex has died at last, perhaps. Or perhaps the Coronal—

Let it be Tyeveras, Hissune prayed. *Oh, please, let it be Tyeveras!*

Elidath said, "All right. Everyone's here: we can begin."

With a sour grin Divvis said, "What is it, Elidath? Has someone seen a two-headed milufta flying north?"

"If you mean, Is this a time of evil omen, then the answer is that it is," said Elidath somberly.

"What has happened?" Stasilaine asked.

Elidath tapped a sheaf of papers on the desk. "Two important developments. First, fresh reports have come in from western Zimroel, and the situation is far more serious than we've realized. The entire Rift sector of the continent is disrupted, apparently, from Mazadone or thereabouts to a point somewhere west of Dulorn, and the trouble is spreading. Crops continue to die of mysterious blights, there's a tremendous shortage of basic foods, and hundreds of thousands of people, perhaps millions, have begun migrating toward the coast. Local officials are doing their best to requisition emergency food supplies from regions still unaffected—apparently there's been no trouble yet around

Tilomon or Narabal, and Ni-moya and Khyntor are still relatively untouched by the farming troubles—but the distances are so great and the situation so sudden that very little's been accomplished so far. There is also the question of some peculiar new religious cult that has sprung up out there, something involving sea-dragon worship—"

"*What?*" said Stasilaine, astonishment bringing color to his face.

"It sounds insane, I know," Elidath said. "But the report is that the word is spreading that the dragons are gods of some sort, and that they've decreed that the world is going to end, or some such idiocy, and—"

"It's not a new cult," said Hissune quietly.

The other three all turned to face him. "You know something about this?" Divvis asked.

Hissune nodded. "I used to hear of it sometimes when I lived in the Labyrinth. It's always been a secret shadowy sort of thing, very vague, never taken too seriously so far as I ever knew. And strictly lower class, something to whisper behind the backs of the gentry. Some of my friends knew a little about it, or maybe more than a little, though I was never mixed up in it. I remember mentioning it once to my mother long ago, and she told me it was dangerous nonsense and I should keep away from it, and I did. I think it got started among the Liimen, a long time ago, and has gradually been spreading across the bottom levels of society in an underground sort of way, and I suppose now is surfacing because of all the troubles that have begun."

"And what's the main belief?" Stasilaine asked.

"More or less as Elidath said: that the dragons will come ashore some day and take command of the government and end all misery and suffering."

"*What* misery and suffering?" Divvis said. "I know of no great misery and suffering anywhere in the world, unless you refer to the whining and muttering of the Shapeshifters, and they—"

"You think everyone lives as we do on Castle Mount?" Hissune demanded.

"I think no one is left in need, that all are provided for, that we are happy and prosperous, that—"

"All this is true, Divvis. Nevertheless there are some who live in castles and some who sweep the dung of mounts from the highways. There are those who own great estates and those who beg for coins in the streets. There are—"

"Spare me. I need no lectures from you on social injustice."

"Forgive me then for boring you," Hissune snapped. "I thought you wanted to know why there were people who wait for water-kings to deliver them from hardship and pain."

"Water-kings?" Elidath said.

"Sea dragons. So they are called by those who worship them."

"Very well," said Stasilaine. "There's famine in Zimroel, and a troublesome cult is spreading among the lower classes. You said there were two important new developments. Are those the two you meant?"

Elidath shook his head. "Those are both parts of the same thing. The other important matter concerns Lord Valentine. I have heard from Tunigorn, who is greatly distressed. The Coronal, he says, has had some sort of revelation during his visit with his mother on the Isle, and has entered a mood of high elevation, a very strange mood indeed, in which he appears almost totally unpredictable."

"What sort of revelation?" Stasilaine asked. "Do you know?"

"While in a trance guided by the Lady," said Elidath, "he had a vision that showed him that the agricultural troubles in Zimroel indicate the displeasure of the Divine."

"Who could possibly think otherwise?" Stasilaine cried. "But what does that have to—"

"According to Tunigorn, Valentine thinks now that the blights and the food shortages—which as we now know are much more serious than our own first reports made them seem—have a specifically supernatural origin—"

Divvis, shaking his head slowly, let out his breath in a derisive snort.

"—a specifically supernatural origin," Elidath continued, "and are, in fact, a punishment imposed upon us by the Divine for our mistreatment of the Metamorphs down through the centuries."

"But this is nothing new," said Stasilaine. "He's been talking that way for years."

"Evidently it *is* something new," Elidath replied. "Tunigorn says that since the day of the revelation, he's been keeping mainly to himself, seeing only the Lady and Carabella, and sometimes Deliamber or the dream-speaker Tisana. Both

Sleet and Tunigorn have had difficulty gaining access to him, and when they do it's to discuss only the most routine matters. He seems inflamed, Tunigorn says, with some grandiose new idea, some really startling project, which he will not discuss with them."

"This does not sound like the Valentine I know," said Stasilaine darkly. "Whatever else he may be, irrational he is not. It sounds almost as though some fever has come over him."

"Or that he's been made a changeling again," Divvis said.

"What does Tunigorn fear?" Hissune asked.

Elidath shrugged. "He doesn't know. He thinks Valentine may be hatching some very bizarre idea indeed, one that he and Sleet would be likely to oppose. But he's giving no clues." Elidath went to the world globe, and tapped the bright red sphere that marked the Coronal's whereabouts. "Valentine is still on the Isle, but he'll sail shortly for the mainland. He'll land in Piliplok, and he's scheduled to head up the Zimr to Ni-moya and then keep going into the famine-stricken regions out west. But Tunigorn suspects that he's changed his mind about that, that he's obsessed with this notion that we're suffering the vengeance of the Divine and might be planning some spiritual event, a fast, a pilgrimage, a restructuring of society in a direction away from purely secular values—"

"What if he's involved with this sea-dragon cult?" Stasilaine said.

"I don't know," said Elidath. "It could be anything. I tell you only that Tunigorn seemed deeply troubled, and urged me to join the Coronal on the processional as quickly as I could, in the hope that I'll be able to prevent him from doing something rash. I think I could succeed where others, even Tunigorn, would fail."

"What?" Divvis cried. "He's thousands of miles from here! How can you possibly—"

"I leave in two hours," Elidath answered. "A relay of fast floaters will carry me westward through the Glayge Valley to Treymone, where I've requisitioned a cruiser to take me to Zimroel via the southern route and the Rodamaunt Archipelago. Tunigorn, meanwhile, will attempt to delay Valentine's departure from the Isle as long as he can, and if he can get any cooperation from Admiral Asenhart he'll see to it that the

voyage from the Isle to Piliplok is a slow one. With any luck,
I might reach Piliplok only a week or so after Valentine does,
and perhaps it won't be too late to bring him back to his
senses."

"You'll never make it in time," said Divvis. "He'll be
halfway to Ni-moya before you can cross the Inner Sea."

"I must attempt it," Elidath said. "I have no choice. If
you knew how concerned Tunigorn is, how fearful that Valentine is about to commit himself to some mad and perilous
course of action—"

"And the government?" Stasilaine said softly. "What of
that? You are the regent, Elidath. We have no Pontifex, you
tell us that the Coronal has become some sort of visionary
madman, and now you propose to leave the Castle leaderless?"

"In the event that a regent is called away from the
Castle," said Elidath, "it's within his powers to appoint a
Council of Regency to deal with all business that would fall
within the Coronal's jurisdiction. This is what I intend."

"And the members of this council?" Divvis asked.

"There will be three. You are one, Divvis. Stasilaine,
you also. And you, Hissune."

Hissune, astounded, sat bolt upright. "*I?*"

Elidath smiled. "I confess I couldn't understand, at first,
why Lord Valentine had chosen to advance someone of the
Labyrinth, and such a young man at that, so quickly toward
the center of power. But gradually his design has come clear
to me, as this crisis has fallen upon us. We've lost touch, here
on Castle Mount, with the realities of Majipoor. We've stayed
up here on our mountaintop and mysteries have sprung up
around us, without our knowing. I heard you say, Divvis, that
you think everyone in the world is happy except perhaps the
Metamorphs, and I confess I thought the same. And yet an
entire religion, it seems, has taken root out there among the
discontented, and we knew nothing of it, and now an army of
hungry people marches toward Pidruid to worship strange
gods." He looked toward Hissune. "There are things you
know, Hissune, that we need to learn. In the months of my
absence, you'll sit beside Divvis and Stasilaine in the place of
judgment—and I believe you'll offer valuable guidance. What
do you say, Stasilaine?"

"I think you've chosen wisely."

"And you, Divvis?"

Divvis's face was blazing with barely controlled fury.

"What can I say? The power's yours. You've made your appointment. I must abide by it, must I not?" He rose stiffly and held forth his hand to Hissune. "My congratulations, prince. You've done very well for yourself in a very short time."

Hissune met Divvis's cold gaze evenly. "I look forward to serving in the council with you, my lord Divvis," said Hissune with great formality. "Your wisdom will be an example for me." And he took Divvis's hand.

Whatever reply Divvis intended to make seemed to choke in his throat. Slowly he withdrew his hand from Hissune's grasp, glared, and stalked from the room.

11

The wind was out of the south, and hot and hard, the kind of wind that the dragon-hunting captains called "the Sending," because it blew up from the barren continent of Suvraël where the King of Dreams had his lair. It was a wind that parched the soul and withered the heart, but Valentine paid no heed to it: his spirit was elsewhere, dreaming of the tasks that lay before him, and these days he stood for hours at a time on the royal deck of the *Lady Thiin*, looking to the horizon for the first sign of the mainland and giving no thought to the torrid, sharp-edged gusts that whistled about him.

The voyage from the Isle to Zimroel was beginning to seem interminable. Asenhart had spoken of a sluggish sea and contrary winds, of the need to shorten sail and take a more southerly route, and other such problems. Valentine, who was no sailor, could not quarrel with these decisions, but he grew fiercely impatient as the days went by and the western continent grew no closer. More than once they were compelled to change course to avoid sea-dragon herds, for on this side of the Isle the waters were thick with them. Some of the Skandar crewmen claimed that this was the greatest migration in five thousand years. Whether or not that was true, certainly they were abundant, and terrifying: Valentine had seen nothing like this on his last crossing of these waters many years ago, in that ill-fated journey when the giant dragon stove in the hull of Captain Gorzval's *Brangalyn*.

Generally the dragons moved in groups of thirty to fifty, at several days' distance from one another. But occasionally a single huge dragon, a veritable dragon-king, was seen swimming steadfastly by itself, moving unhurriedly, as though deep in weighty meditations. Then after a time no more dragons, great or small, were seen, and the wind strengthened, and the fleet made haste toward the port of Piliplok.

And one morning came shouts from the top deck: "Piliplok ho! Piliplok!"

The great seaport loomed up suddenly, dazzling and splendid in its forbidding, intense way, on its high promontory overlooking the southern shore of the mouth of the Zimr. Here, where the river was enormously wide and stained the sea dark for hundreds of miles with the silt it had swept from the heart of the continent, stood a city of eleven million people, rigidly laid out according to a complex and unyielding master design, spread out along with precise arcs intersected by the spokes of grand boulevards that radiated from the waterfront. It was, Valentine thought, a difficult city to love, for all the beauty of its broad welcoming harbor. Yet as he stood staring at it he caught sight of his Skandar companion Zalzan Kavol, who was native to Piliplok, gazing out upon it with a tender expression of wonder and delight on his harsh, dour face.

"The dragon-ships are coming!" someone cried, when the *Lady Thiin* was somewhat nearer to the shore. "Look, there, it must be the whole fleet!"

"Oh, Valentine, how lovely!" Carabella said softly, close beside him.

Lovely indeed. Until this moment, Valentine had never thought that the vessels in which the seafarers of Piliplok went forth to hunt the dragons were beautiful in any way. They were sinister things, swollen of hull, grotesquely decorated with hideous figureheads and threatening spiky tails and gaudy, painted rows of white teeth and scarlet-and-yellow eyes along their flanks; and taken one by one they seemed merely barbaric, repellent. Yet somehow in a flotilla this huge—and it looked as though every dragon-ship in Piliplok was on its way out to sea to greet the arriving Coronal—they took on a bizarre kind of glory. Along the line of the horizon their sails, black striped with crimson, bellied out in the breeze like festive flags.

When they drew near, they spread out about the royal

fleet in what surely was a carefully planned formation, and hoisted great Coronal ensigns in green and gold into their riggings, and shouted raucously into the wind, "Valentine! Lord Valentine! Hail, Lord Valentine!" The music of drums and trumpets and sistirons and galistanes drifted across the water, blurred and muddled but nonetheless jubilant and touching.

A very different reception, thought Valentine wryly, from the one he had had on his last visit to Piliplok, when he and Zalzan Kavol and the rest of the jugglers had gone pitifully from one dragon-captain to the next, trying in vain to hire one to carry them toward the Isle of Sleep, until finally they had managed to buy passage aboard the smallest and shabbiest and unluckiest vessel of all. But many things had altered since then.

The grandest of the dragon-ships now approached the *Lady Thiin*, and put forth a boat bearing a Skandar and two humans. When they came alongside, a floater-basket was lowered to draw them up on deck, but the humans remained at their oars, and only the Skandar came aboard.

She was old and weatherbeaten and tough-looking, with two of her powerful incisor teeth missing and fur of a dull grayish color. "I am Guidrag," she said, and after a moment Valentine remembered her: the oldest and most revered of the dragon-captains, and one of those who had refused to take the jugglers on as passengers on her own ship; but she had refused in a kindly way, and had sent them on to Captain Gorzval and his *Brangalyn*. He wondered if she remembered him: very likely not. When one wears the Coronal's robes, Valentine had long ago discovered, the man within the robes tends to become invisible.

Guidrag made a rough but eloquent speech of welcome on behalf of all her shipmates and fellow dragon-hunters and presented Valentine with an elaborately carved necklace made from interlocking sea-dragon bones. Afterward he gave thanks for this grand naval display, and asked her why the dragon-ship fleet was idle here in Piliplok harbor and not out hunting on the high seas; to which she replied that this year's migration had brought the dragons past the coast in such astonishing and unprecedented numbers that all the dragon-ships had fulfilled their lawful quotas in the first few weeks of the hunt; their season had ended almost as soon as it had begun.

"This has been a strange year," said Guidrag. "And I fear more strangeness awaits us, my lord."

The escort of dragon-ships stayed close by, all the way to port. The royal party came ashore at Malibor Pier, in the center of the harbor, where a welcoming party waited: the duke of the province with a vast retinue, the mayor of the city and an equally vast swarm of officials, and a delegation of dragon-captains from the ships that had accompanied the Coronal to shore. Valentine entered into the ceremonies and rituals of greetings like one who dreams that he is awake: he responded gravely and courteously and at all the right times, he conducted himself with serenity and poise, and yet it was as though he moved through a throng of phantoms.

The highway from the harbor to the great hall of the city, where Valentine was to lodge, was lined with thick scarlet ropes to keep back the throngs, and guards were posted everywhere. Valentine, riding in an open-topped floater with Carabella at his side, thought that he had never heard such clamor, a constant incomprehensible roar of jubilant welcome so thunderous that it took his mind away, for the moment, from thoughts of crisis. But the respite lasted only a short while, for as soon as he was settled in his quarters he asked that the latest dispatches be brought him, and the news they contained was unrelievedly grim.

The lusavender blight, he learned, had spread somehow into the quarantined unaffected provinces. The stajja harvest was going to be half normal this year. A pest called the wireworm, long thought eradicated, had entered the regions where thuyol, an important forage crop, was grown: ultimately that would threaten the supply of meat. A fungus that attacked grapes had caused widespread dropping of unripe fruit in the wine country of Khyntor and Ni-moya. All of Zimroel now was affected by some sort of agricultural disturbance, except only the area of the remote southwest around the tropical city of Narabal.

Y-Uulisaan, when Valentine had showed him the reports, said gravely, "It will not be contained now. These are ecologically interlocking events: Zimroel's food supply will be totally disrupted, my lord."

"There are eight billion people in Zimroel!"

"Indeed. And when these blights spread to Alhanroel—?"

Valentine felt a chill. "You think they will?"

"Ah, my lord, I know they will! How many ships go back and forth between the continents each week? How many birds and even insects make the crossing? The Inner Sea is not that broad, and the Isle and the archipelagos make useful halfway houses." With a strangely serene smile the agricultural expert said, "I tell you, my lord, this cannot be resisted, this cannot be defeated. There will be starvation. There will be plague. Majipoor will be devoured."

"No. Not so."

"If I could give you comforting words, I would. I have no comfort for you, Lord Valentine."

The Coronal stared intently into Y-Uulisaan's strange eyes. "The Divine has brought this catastrophe upon us," he said. "The Divine will take it from us."

"Perhaps. But not before there has been great damage. My lord, I ask permission to withdraw. May I study these papers an hour or so?"

When Y-Uulisaan had gone, Valentine sat quietly for a time, thinking through one last time the thing that he was intending to do, and which now seemed more urgent than ever, in the face of these calamitous new reports. Then he summoned Sleet and Tunigorn and Deliamber.

"I mean to change the route of the processional," he said without preamble.

They looked warily toward one another, as though they had been expecting for weeks some such sort of troublesome surprise.

"We will not go on to Ni-moya at this time. Cancel all arrangements for Ni-moya and beyond." He saw them staring at him in a tense and somber way, and knew he would not win their support without a struggle. "On the Isle of Sleep," he continued, "it was made manifest to me that the blights that have come upon Zimroel, and which may before long come upon Alhanroel as well, are a direct demonstration of the displeasure of the Divine. You, Deliamber, raised that point with me long ago, when we were at the Velalisier ruins, and you suggested that the troubles of the realm that had grown from the usurpation of my throne might be the beginning of the retribution for the suppression of the Metamorphs. We have gone a long way here on Majipoor, you said, without paying the price for the original sin of the conquerors, and now chaos was upon us because the past was starting to send us its reckoning at last, with compound interest added."

"So I remember. Those were my words, almost exactly."

"And I said," Valentine went on, "that I would dedicate my reign to making reparations for the injustices we visited upon the Metamorphs. But I have not done that. I have been preoccupied with other problems, and have made only the most superficial of gestures toward entering into an understanding with the Shapeshifters. And while I delayed, our punishment has intensified. Now that I am on Zimroel, I intend to go at once to Piurifayne—"

"To *Piurifayne*, my lord?" said Sleet and Tunigorn in virtually the same instant.

"To Piurifayne, to the Shapeshifter capital at Ilirivoyne. I will meet with the Danipiur. I will hear her demands, and take cognizance of them. I—"

"No Coronal has ever gone into Metamorph territory before," Tunigorn cut in.

"One Coronal has," said Valentine. "In my time as a juggler I was there, and performed, in fact, before an audience of Metamorphs and the Danipiur herself."

"A different matter," Sleet said. "You could do anything you pleased, when you were a juggler. That time we went among the Shapeshifters, you scarce believed you were Coronal yourself. But now that you are undoubted Coronal—"

"I will go. As a pilgrimage of humility, as the beginning of an act of atonement."

"My lord—!" Sleet sputtered.

Valentine smiled. "Go ahead. Give me all the arguments against it. I've been expecting for weeks to have a long dreary debate with you three about this, and now I suppose the time has come. But let me tell you this first: when we are done speaking, I will go to Piurifayne."

"And nothing will shake you?" Tunigorn asked. "If we speak of the dangers, the breach of protocol, the possible adverse political consequences, the—"

"No. No. No. Nothing will shake me. Only by kneeling before the Danipiur can I bring an end to the disaster that is ravaging Zimroel."

"Are you so sure, my lord," said Deliamber, "that will be as simple as that?"

"It is something that must be tried. Of that I am convinced, and you will never shake me from my resolve."

"My lord," Sleet said, "it was the Shapeshifters that witched you off your throne, or so I do recall it, and I think you have some recollection of it also. Now the world stands at the edge of madness, and you propose to offer yourself up into their hands, in their own trackless forests. Does that seem—"

"Wise? No. Necessary? Yes, Sleet. Yes. One Coronal more or less doesn't matter. There are many others who can take my place and do as well, or better. But the destiny of Majipoor matters. I must go to Ilirivoyne."

"I beg you, my lord—"

"I beg *you*," said Valentine. "We have talked enough. My mind is set on this."

"You will go to Piurifayne," said Sleet in disbelief. "You will offer yourself to the Shapeshifters."

"Yes," Valentine said. "I will offer myself to the Shape-shifters."

THREE

The Book
of the
Broken Sky

1

Millilain would always remember the day when the first of
the new Coronals proclaimed himself, because that was the
day she paid five crowns for a couple of grilled sausages.

She was on her way at noon to meet her husband
Kristofon at his shop on the esplanade by Khyntor Bridge. It
was the beginning of the third month of the Shortage. That
was what everyone in Khyntor called it, the Shortage, but
inwardly Millilain had had a more realistic name for it: *the
famine*. No one was starving—yet—but no one was getting
enough to eat, either, and the situation seemed to be worsening
daily. The night before last, she and Kristofon had eaten
nothing but some porridge he had made out of dried calimbots
and a bit of ghumba root. Tonight's dinner would be stajja
pudding. And tomorrow—who knew? Kristofon was talking of
going hunting for small animals, mintuns, droles, things of
that sort, in Prestimion Park. Filet of mintun? Roast breast of
drole? Millilain shuddered. Lizard stew would be next, probably. With boiled cabbage-tree leaves on the side.

She came down Ossier Boulevard to the place where it
turned into Zimr Way, which led to the bridge esplanade.
And just as she passed the Proctorate office the unmistakable
and irresistible aroma of grilled sausages came to her.

I'm hallucinating, she thought. Or dreaming, maybe.

Once there had been dozens of sausage peddlers along
the esplanade. But not for weeks, now, had Millilain seen
one. Meat was hard to come by these days: something about
cattle starving in the western ranching country for lack of
forage, and livestock shipments from Suvrael, where things
still seemed to be all right, being disrupted by the sea-dragon
herds that were thronging the maritime lanes.

But the smell of those sausages was very authentic.
Millilain stared in all directions, seeking its source.

Yes! There!

185

No hallucination. No dream. Incredibly, astoundingly, a sausage peddler had emerged onto the esplanade, a little stoop-shouldered Liiman with a dented old cart in which long red sausages hung skewered over a charcoal fire. He was standing there just as if everything in the world were exactly as it had always been. As if there were no Shortage. As if the food shops had not gone on a three-hour-a-day schedule, because that was usually how long it took them to sell out everything they had in stock.

Millilain began to run.

Others were running too. From all sides of the esplanade they converged on the sausage peddler as though he were giving away ten-royal pieces. But in fact what he had to offer was far more precious than any shiny silver coin could be.

She ran as she had never run before, elbows flailing, knees coming up high, hair streaming out behind her. At least a hundred people were heading toward the Liiman and his cart. He couldn't possibly have enough sausages for everyone. But Millilain was closer than anyone else: she had seen the vendor first, she was running the hardest. A long-legged Hjort woman was coming up close behind her, and a Skandar in an absurd business suit was thundering in from the side, grunting as he ran. Who could ever have imagined a time, Millilain wondered, when you'd *run* to buy sausages from a street vendor?

The Shortage—the famine—had started somewhere out west, in the Rift country. At first it had seemed unimportant and almost unreal to Millilain, since it was happening so far away, in places that were themselves unreal to her. She had never been west of Thagobar. When the first reports came in, she had felt a certain abstract compassion for the people who were said to be going hungry in Mazadone and Dulorn and Falkynkip, but it was hard for her to believe that it was actually happening—nobody ever went hungry on Majipoor, after all—and whenever word came of some new crisis out west, a riot or a mass migration or an epidemic, it struck her as being remote not only in space but in time, not something taking place right this moment but more like something out of a history book, an event of Lord Stiamot's time, say, thousands of years ago.

But then Millilain began to find that there were days when things like niyk and hingamorts and glein were in short supply at the places where she shopped. It's because of the crop failures out west, the clerks told her: nothing much is coming out of the Rift farm belt any longer, and it's a slow and costly business to ship produce in from other areas. After that, such basic things as stajja and ricca suddenly were being rationed, even though they were grown locally and there had been no disruptions of agriculture in the Khyntor region. The explanation this time was that surplus food stocks were being shipped to the afflicted provinces; we must all make sacrifices in such a time of dire need, et cetera, et cetera, said the imperial decree. Then came the news that certain of the plant diseases had shown up around Khyntor also, and east of Khyntor as far downriver as Ni-moya. Allotments of thuyol and ricca and stajja were cut in half, lusavender disappeared entirely from sale, meat began to become scarce. There was talk of bringing in supplies from Alhanroel and Suvrael, where apparently everything was still normal. But that was only talk, Millilain knew. There weren't enough cargo ships in the whole world to carry produce from the other continents in quantities big enough to make a difference, and even if there were, the cost would be prohibitive. "We're all going to starve," she told Kristofon.

So the Shortage reached Khyntor at last.

The Shortage. *The famine*.

Kristofon didn't think anyone would really starve. He was always optimistic. Somehow things will get better, he said. Somehow. But here were a hundred people desperately converging on a sausage vendor.

The Hjort woman tried to pass her. Millilain hit her hard with her shoulder and knocked her sprawling. She had never hit anyone before. She felt a strange lightheaded sensation, and a tightness in her throat. The Hjort screamed curses at her, but Millilain ran on, heart pounding, eyes aching. She jostled someone else aside and elbowed her way into the line that was forming. Up ahead, the Liiman was handing out sausages in that strange impassive Liiman way, not at all bothered, it seemed, by the struggling mob in front of him.

Tensely Millilain watched the queue moving forward. Seven or eight in front of her—would there be enough sausages for her? It was hard to see what was going on up there, whether new skewers were going on the fire as the old ones were sold. Would there be any left for her? She felt like a greedy child worrying if there were enough party favors to go around. I am being very crazy, she told herself. Why should a sausage matter so much? But she knew the answer. She had had no meat at all for three days, unless the five strips of dried salted sea-dragon flesh she had found on Starday while prowling in her cupboard qualified as meat, and she doubted that. The aroma of those sizzling sausages was powerfully attractive. To be able to purchase them was suddenly the most important thing in the world for her, perhaps the *only* thing in the world.

She reached the head of the line.

"Two skewers," she said.

"One to a customer."

"Give me one, then!"

The Liiman nodded. His three intense, glowing eyes regarded her with minimal interest. "Five crowns," the Liiman said.

Millilain gasped. Five crowns was half a day's pay for her. Before the Shortage, she remembered, sausages had been ten weights the skewer. But that had been before the Shortage, after all.

"You aren't serious," she said. "You can't charge fifty times the old price. Even in times like these."

Someone behind her yelled, "Pay up or move out, lady!"

The Liiman said calmly, "Five crowns today. Next week, eight crowns. Week after that, a royal. Week after that, five royals. Next month, no sausages any price. You want sausages? Yes? No?"

"Yes," Millilain muttered. Her hands were trembling as she gave him the five crowns. Another crown bought her a mug of beer, flat and stale. Feeling drained and stunned, she drifted away from the line.

Five crowns! That was what she might have expected to pay for a complete meal in a fine restaurant, not very long ago. But most of the restaurants were closed now, and the ones that remained, so she had heard, had waiting lists weeks long for tables. And the Divine only knew what kind of prices they were charging now. But this was insane. A skewer of sausages, five crowns! Guilt assailed her. What would she tell Kristofon? The truth, she decided. I couldn't resist, she'd say. It was an impulse, a crazy impulse. I smelled them cooking on the grill, and I couldn't resist.

What if the Liiman had demanded eight crowns, though, or a royal? Five royals? She couldn't answer that. She suspected that she would have paid whatever she had to, so strong had the obsession been.

She bit into the sausage as though she feared someone would snatch it from her hand. It was astonishingly good: juicy, spicy. She found herself wondering what sort of meat had gone into it. Best not to consider that, she told herself. Kristofon might not be the only one who had had the idea of hunting for little animals in the park.

She took a sip of the beer and began to raise the skewer to her mouth again.

"Millilain?"

She looked up in surprise. "Kristofon!"

"I was hoping I'd find you here. I closed the shop and came out to see what that mob was all about."

"A sausage vendor appeared suddenly. As though a wizard had conjured him up."

"Ah. Yes, I see."

He was staring at the half-eaten sausage in her hand.

Millilain forced a smile. "I'm sorry, Kris. Do you want a bite?"

"Just a bite," he said. "I suppose it won't do to get back on the line."

"I think they'll all be sold in a little while." She handed him the skewer, working hard at concealing her reluctance, and watched tensely as he nibbled an inch or two of the sausage. She felt intense relief, and more than a little shame, as he gave the rest back to her.

"By the Lady, that was good!"

"It ought to have been. It cost five crowns."

"*Five*—"

"I couldn't help myself, Kris. Picking up the scent of them in the air—I was like a wild animal, getting on that line. I pushed, I shoved, I fought. I think I would have paid almost anything for one. Oh, Kris, I'm so sorry!"

"Don't apologize. What else is there to spend the money on, anyway? Besides, things will be changing soon. You've heard the news this morning?"

"What news?"

"About the new Coronal! He'll be here any minute. Right here, coming across Khyntor Bridge."

Bewildered, she said, "Has Lord Valentine become Pontifex, then?"

Kristofon shook his head. "Valentine no longer matters.

They say he's disappeared—carried off by the Metamorphs, or something. In any case it was proclaimed about an hour ago that Sempeturn is Coronal now."

"Sempeturn? The preacher?"

"That one, yes. He arrived in Khyntor last night. The mayor has backed him, and I hear the duke has fled to Ni-moya."

"This is impossible, Kris! A man can't just stand up and say he's Coronal! He has to be chosen, he has to be anointed, he has to come from Castle Mount—"

"We used to think so. But these are different times. Sempeturn's a true man of the people. That's the sort we need now. He'll know how to win back the favor of the Divine."

She stared in disbelief. The sausage dangled, forgotten, in her hand. "It can't be happening. It's craziness. Lord Valentine is our anointed Coronal. He—"

"Sempeturn says that he's a fraud, that the whole story of his having switched bodies is nonsense, that we're being punished with these plagues and famines because of his sins. That the only way we can save ourselves now is to depose the false Coronal and give the throne to someone who can lead us back to righteousness."

"And Sempeturn says he's the man, and therefore we're supposed to bow down and accept him and—"

"He's coming now!" Kristofon cried.

His face was flushed, his eyes were strange. Millilain could not remember ever having seen her husband in such a state of high excitement. He was almost feverish. She felt feverish herself, confused, dazed. A new Coronal? That little red-faced rabble-rouser Sempeturn sitting on the Confalume Throne? She couldn't grasp the idea. It was like being told that red was green, or that water henceforth would flow uphill.

There was the sudden sound of strident music. A marching band in green-and-gold costumes that bore the Coronal's starburst emblem came strutting across the bridge and down the esplanade. Then came the mayor and other city officials; and then, riding in a grand and ornately embellished open palanquin, smiling and accepting the plaudits of a vast crowd that was following him out of the town of Hot Khyntor on the far side of the bridge, a short florid-looking man with thick unruly dark hair. "Sempeturn!" the crowd roared. "Sempeturn! All hail Lord Sempeturn!"

"All hail Lord Sempeturn!" Kristofon bellowed.

This is a dream, Millilain thought. This is some dread sending that I do not understand.

"Sempeturn! Lord Sempeturn!"

Everyone on the esplanade was shouting it now. A kind of frenzy was spreading. Millilain numbly took the last bite of her sausage, swallowed it without tasting anything, let the skewer drop to the ground. The world seemed to be rippling beneath her feet. Kristofon still shouted, in a voice now growing hoarse, "Sempeturn! Lord Sempeturn!" The palanquin was going past them now: only twenty yards or so separated them from the new Coronal, if that was indeed what he was. He turned and looked straight into Millilain's eyes. And with amazement and steadily gathering terror she heard herself yell, "Sempeturn! All hail Lord Sempeturn!" along with all the others.

2

"He's going *where*?" Elidath said in astonishment.

"Ilirivoyne," said Tunigorn once more. "He set out three days ago."

Elidath shook his head. "I hear your words, and they make no sense to me. My mind will simply not accept them."

"By the Lady, neither will mine! But that doesn't make it any the less true. He means to go before the Danipiur, and beg her forgiveness for all our sins against her people, or some such madness."

It was only an hour since Elidath's ship had docked in Piliplok. He had sped at once to the great hall of the city hoping still to find Valentine there, or, at the worst, just embarking on his way toward Ni-Moya. But no one of the royal party was at the hall save Tunigorn, whom he found morosely shuffling papers in a small dusty office. And this tale that Tunigorn had to tell—the grand processional abandoned, the Coronal venturing into the wild jungles where the Shapeshifters lived—no, no, it was too much, it was beyond all reason!

Fatigue and despair pressed against Elidath's spirit like

monstrous boulders, and he felt himself succumbing to that crushing weight.

Hollowly he said, "I chased him halfway around the world to prevent something like this from happening. Do you know what my journey was like, Tunigorn? Night and day by floater to the coast, without ever halting a moment. And then racing across a sea full of angry dragons, that three times came so close to our cruiser I thought they were going to sink us. And finally to reach Piliplok half dead with exhaustion, only to hear that I've missed him by three days, that he's gone off on this absurd and perilous adventure, when perhaps if I had moved only a little more swiftly, if I had set out a few days sooner—"

"You couldn't have changed his mind, Elidath. No one could. Sleet couldn't, Deliamber couldn't, Carabella couldn't—"

"Not even Carabella?"

"Not even Carabella," said Tunigorn.

Elidath's despair deepened. He fought it fiercely, refusing to let himself be overwhelmed by fear and doubt. After a time he said, "Nevertheless, Valentine will listen to me, and I'll be able to sway him. Of that much I'm certain."

"I think you deceive yourself, old friend," Tunigorn said sadly.

"Why did you summon me, then, for a task you thought was impossible?"

"When I summoned you," Tunigorn said, "I had no idea what Valentine had in mind. I knew only that he was in an agitated state and was considering some rash and strange course of action. It seemed to me that if you were with him on the processional you might be able to calm him and divert him from whatever he planned. By the time he let us know his intentions, and made us see that nothing could swerve him from them, you were long since on your way west. Your journey has been wasted, and I have only my regrets to offer you."

"I'll go to him, all the same."

"You'll accomplish nothing, I'm afraid."

Elidath shrugged. "I've followed him this far: how can I abandon the quest now? Maybe there's some way I can bring him to his senses after all. You say you're planning to set out after him tomorrow?"

"At midday, yes. As soon as I've dealt with the last of the dispatches and decrees that I stayed behind to handle."

Elidath leaned forward eagerly. "Take them with you. We need to go tonight!"

"That wouldn't be wise. You told me yourself that your voyage had exhausted you, and I see the weariness in your face. Rest here in Piliplok this evening, eat well, sleep well, dream well, and tomorrow—"

"No!" Elidath cried. "Tonight, Tunigorn! Every hour we waste here brings him that much closer to Shapeshifter territory! Can't you see the risks?" He stared coolly at Tunigorn. "I'll leave without you, if I have to."

"I would not permit that."

Elidath lifted his eyebrows. "Is my travel subject to your permission, then?"

"You know what I'm saying. I can't let you head off into nowhere by yourself."

"Then come with me tonight."

"Wait only until tomorrow?"

"No!"

Tunigorn closed his eyes a moment. After a time he said quietly, "All right. So be it. Tonight."

Elidath nodded. "We'll hire a small, fast vessel, and with luck we'll overtake him before he gets to Ni-moya."

Tunigorn said bleakly, "He isn't traveling toward Ni-moya, Elidath."

"I don't understand. The only way from here to Ilirivoyne that I know is up the river past Ni-moya to Verf, is it not, and southward from Verf to Piurifayne Gate."

"I only wish he *had* gone that way."

"Why, what other route is there?" Elidath asked, surprised.

"None that makes any sense. But he devised it himself: southward into Gihorna, and then across the Steiche into Metamorph country."

Elidath stared. "How can that be? Gihorna's an empty wasteland. The Steiche is an impassable river. He knows that, and if he doesn't, his little Vroon certainly does."

"Deliamber did his best to discourage the idea. Valentine wouldn't listen. He pointed out that if he went by way of Ni-moya and Verf, he'd be obliged to halt at every city along the way for the usual ceremonies of the grand processional, and he doesn't want to delay his pilgrimage to the Metamorphs that long."

Elidath felt himself engulfed by dismay and alarm. "And so he means to wander through the sandstorms and miseries of Gihorna—and then find a way across a river that has already once nearly drowned him—"

"Yes, and all so he can pay a call on the people who successfully managed to push him off his throne ten years ago—"

"Madness!"

"Madness indeed," Tunigorn said.

"You agree? We set out tonight?"

"Tonight, yes."

Tunigorn put forth his hand, and Elidath took it and clasped it tight, and they stood in silence a moment.

Then Elidath said, "Answer me one question, will you, Tunigorn?"

"Ask it."

"You used the word 'madness' more than once, in speaking of this venture of Valentine's, and so did I. And so it is. But I have not seen him in a year or more, and you have been with him ever since he left the Mount. Tell me this: do you think he has truly gone mad?"

"Mad? No, I think not."

"Appointing young Hissune to the principate? Making pilgrimages to the Metamorphs?"

Tunigorn said, after a time, "Those are not things you or I would have done, Elidath. But I think they are signs not of Valentine's madness, but of something else in him, a goodness, a sweetness, a kind of holiness, that such as you and I are not fully able to understand. We have always known this about Valentine, that he is different from us in certain ways."

Frowning, Elidath said, "Better holy than mad, I suppose. But this goodness, this holiness: do you think those are the qualities that Majipoor most needs in its Coronal, as this time of strife and bewilderment unfolds?"

"I have no answer to that, old friend."

"Nor I. But I have certain fears."

"As do I," said Tunigorn. "As do I."

3

In the darkness Y-Uulisaan lay awake and tense, listening to the wind as it roared across the wastelands of Gihorna: a thin, cutting wind from the east that scoured up a swirl of damp sand and hurled it insistently against the sides of the tent.

The royal caravan with which he had been traveling so long was camped now many hundreds of miles southwest of Piliplok. The River Steiche lay no more than another few days' journey ahead, and beyond it was Piurifayne. Y-Uulisaan longed desperately to cross the river at last and breathe the air of his native province once more, and the closer the caravan came to it the more acute that longing grew. To be home again among his own, free of the strain of this unending masquerade—

Soon—soon—

But first he must warn Faraataa, somehow, of Lord Valentine's plans.

It was six days now since Faraataa last had made contact with Y-Uulisaan, and six days ago Y-Uulisaan had not known that the Coronal intended to undertake a pilgrimage into Piurivar country. Surely Faraataa had to have that information. But Y-Uulisaan had no reliable means of reaching him, whether through conventional channels, which were virtually nonexistent in this dreary and all but uninhabited place, or via the water-king communion. It took many minds to gain a water-king's attention, and Y-Uulisaan was alone on this mission.

All the same, he could try. As he had done on each of the last three nights he focused the energies of his mind and hurled them forth, straining to initiate some sort of contact across the thousand miles or so that separated him from the leader of the rebellion.

—*Faraataa? Faraataa?*

Hopeless. Without the aid of a water-king as an intermediary, transmission of this sort was all but impossible. Y-Uulisaan knew that. Yet he went on attempting to call. Perhaps—so he compelled himself to believe—there might be some slight chance that a passing water-king would pick up the transmission and amplify it. A slight chance, a negligible chance, but one he dared not fail to assay.

—*Faraataa?*

Y-Uulisaan's shape wavered slightly under the effort. His legs lengthened, his nose diminished in size. Grimly he checked the change before it could become perceptible to any of the others in the tent, and compelled himself back to the human form. Since first assuming it in Alhanroel he had not dared to relax his shape even for a moment, lest they discover him for the Piurivar spy he was. Which created a pressure within him that by this time had become well-nigh intolerable; but he held himself to his chosen form.

He continued to pump his soul's force outward into the night.

—*Faraataa? Faraataa?*

Nothing. Silence. Solitude. The usual.

After a while he abandoned the attempt and tried to sleep. Morning was still distant. He lay back and closed his throbbing eyes.

But sleep would not come for him. Sleep rarely did, in this journey. At best he could manage only a shallow fitful doze. There were too many distractions: the harshness of the wind, the sound of wind-driven sand pelting against canvas, the rough snuffling breathing of the members of the Coronal's entourage who shared this tent with him. And above all the ever-present numbing pain of his isolation among these hostile alien folk. Taut, strung tight, he waited for the coming of dawn.

Then somewhere between the Hour of the Jackal and the Hour of the Scorpion he felt the sound of a droning, insinuating music brush lightly against his mind. So taut was he that the startling intrusion robbed him for an instant of his shape-stability: he went fluttering uncontrollably through a range of forms, mimicking two of the sleeping humans nearby, then tumbling into the Piurivar form for a fraction of a second before regaining mastery of himself. He sat up, heart thundering, breath ragged, and searched for that music again.

Yes. There. A dry, whining tone, sliding strangely between the intervals of the scale. He recognized it now as the mind song of a water-king, unmistakable in its quality and timbre even though he had never heard the song of this particular water-king before. He opened his mind to contact, and an instant later, with enormous relief, he heard the mind-voice of Faraataa:

—*Y-Uulisaan?*

—*At last, Faraataa! How long I've waited for this call!*

—*It comes at the appointed time, Y-Uulisaan.*

—*Yes, that I know. But I have had urgent news for you. I've called out to you night after night, trying to make contact before this. You heard nothing?*

—*I heard nothing. This is the regular call.*

—*Ah.*

—*Where are you, Y-Uulisaan, and what is your news?*

—*I am somewhere in Gihorna, far down the coast from Piliplok and well inland, almost at the Steiche. I travel still with the Coronal's party.*

—*And can it be that the grand processional has taken him into Gihorna?*

—*He has given over the processional, Faraataa. He journeys now toward Ilirivoyne, to hold conference with the Danipiur.*

In response came silence, a silence so crisp and hard that it crackled like the lightning energies, with a sizzling hissing sound beneath it. Y-Uulisaan wondered after a time if contact had been lost altogether. But finally Faraataa said:

—*The Danipiur? What would he want from her?*

—*Forgiveness.*

—*Forgiveness for what, Y-Uulisaan?*

—*All of the crimes of his people against ours.*

—*He has gone mad, then?*

—*Some of his followers do think that. Others say that it is only Valentine's way, to meet hatred with love.*

There was another long silence.

—*He must not speak with her, Y-Uulisaan.*

—*So I believe also.*

—*This is not a time for forgiveness. This is a time for strife, or we will have no victory. I will keep him from her. He must not meet with her. He may attempt to arrive at a compromise with her, and there must be no compromises!*

—*I understand.*

—*Victory is almost ours. The government is collapsing. The rule of order is breaking up. Do you know, Y-Uulisaan, that three false Coronals have arisen? One has proclaimed himself in Khyntor, and another in Ni-moya, and one in Dulorn.*

—Is it true?

—Most certainly it is. You know nothing of it?

—Nothing. And I think Valentine knows nothing of it either. We are very far from civilization here. Three false Coronals! It is the beginning of the end for them, Faraataa!

—So we believe. All moves well for us. The plagues continue to spread. With your help, Y-Uulisaan, we have been able to find ways of countering the government's counter-measures, and making matters ever worse. Zimroel is in chaos. The first serious troubles have begun to arise in Alhanroel. Victory is ours!

—Victory is ours, Faraataa!

—But we must intercept the Coronal as he moves toward Ilirivoyne. Tell me your precise location, if you can.

—We have gone by floater southwest from Piliplok toward the Steiche for three days. I heard someone this evening say that the river is no more than two days' journey from us, perhaps less. Yesterday the Coronal himself and a few of his followers set out for it ahead of the main body of the caravan. They must be nearly there by this time.

—And how does he plan to cross it?

—That I do not know. But—

"Now! Grab him!"

At the sudden outcry all contact with Faraataa was lost. Two huge forms loomed in the darkness and pounced. Y-Uulisaan, astonished, unprepared, gasped in surprise.

He perceived that it was the vast warrior-woman Lisamon Hultin and the fierce shaggy Skandar Zalzan Kavol who gripped him. The Vroon Deliamber hovered somewhere at a safe distance, tentacles coiling in intricate patterns.

"What do you think you're doing?" Y-Uulisaan demanded. "This is an outrage!"

"Ah, that it is," replied the Amazon cheerfully. "Most certainly it is."

"Let go of me at once!"

"Very small chance of that, spy!" the Skandar rumbled.

Desperately Y-Uulisaan tried to free himself from the grasp of his assailants, but he was like a mere doll in their hands. Panic seized him, and he felt his form-control begin to break down. He could do nothing to reassert it, though the loss of it revealed him for what he truly was. They held him as he writhed and twisted and frantically ran through a host of shapechanges, becoming now this creature or that, this mass of spines and knobs or that length of sinuous serpent. Unable to free himself, his energies so depleted by the contact with Faraataa that he could not generate any of his defensive abilities, the electric shocks and the like, he screamed and roared in frustration until, abruptly, the Vroon slipped a tentacle against his forehead and administered a short stunning jolt. Y-Uulisaan went limp and lay half conscious.

"Take him to the Coronal," Deliamber said. "We will interrogate him in Lord Valentine's presence."

4

As he rode westward toward the Steiche all that day with the vanguard of the royal caravan, Valentine saw the landscape hourly undergoing dramatic change: drab Gihorna was giving way to the mysterious lushness of the Piurifayne rain forest. Behind him lay a scruffy seacoast of dunes and sand drifts, of sparse shaggy tufts of saw-edged grass and small stunted trees with limp yellow leaves. Now the soil was no longer so sandy, but grew ever darker, ever more rich, and supported a riotous lushness of growth; the air no longer carried the acrid flavor of the sea, but had taken on the sweet, musky aroma of a jungle. Yet this was mere transitional country, Valentine knew. The true jungle lay ahead, beyond the Steiche, a realm of mists and strangeness, dense dark greenery, fog-swept hills and mountains: the kingdom of the Shapeshifters.

An hour or so before twilight they reached the river. Valentine's floater was the first to arrive at it, the other two appearing a few minutes later. He signaled to their captains to pull the vehicles into parallel formation along the bank. Then he left his floater and walked to the water's edge.

Valentine had reason to remember this river well. He had come to it in his years of exile, that time when he and his fellow jugglers were fleeing the wrath of the Metamorphs of Ilirivoyne. Now, standing beside its swift waters, his mind journeyed back across time to glimpse again that wild ride across rain-soaked Piurifayne, and the bloody battle with Shapeshifter ambushers in the depths of the jungle, and the little apelike forest brethren who had saved them afterward by leading them to the Steiche. And then the terrifying and ill-fated raft ride down the turbulent river, among its menacing boulders and whirlpools and rapids, in the hope of reaching the safety of Ni-moya—

But here there were no rapids, no fanged rocks splitting the swirling surface, no high rocky walls flanking the channel. The river here was fast of flow, but broad and smooth and manageable.

"Can this really be the Steiche?" Carabella asked. "It hardly seems to be the same river that gave us such pain."

Valentine nodded. "All that lies north of here. This stretch of the river seems more civil."

"But hardly gentle. Can we get across?"

"We must," said Valentine, staring at the distant western bank and Piurifayne beyond it.

Dusk was beginning to descend now, and in the gathering darkness the Metamorph province seemed impenetrable, unfathomable, hermetic. The Coronal's mood began to turn somber once more. Was it folly, he wondered, this wild expedition into the jungle? Was this enterprise absurd, naive, foredoomed? Perhaps so. Perhaps the only outcome of his rash quest for the Shapeshifter queen's forgiveness would be mockery and shame. And perhaps then he would do well to resign this crown that he had never truly coveted, and turn the government into the hands of some more brutal and decisive man.

Perhaps. Perhaps.

He noticed that some strange sluggish creature had emerged from the water on the other shore and was moving slowly about over there at the river's edge—a long, baggy-bodied thing with pale blue skin and a single huge sad eye at the top of its blunt, bulbous head. As Valentine watched, bemused by the ugliness and clumsiness of the animal, it put its face to the muddy soil of the bank and began rocking from side to side, as though trying to excavate a pit with its chin.

Sleet approached. Valentine, entirely caught up in observing the odd beast across the way, allowed him to wait in silence a moment before turning to him.

It seemed to Valentine that Sleet's expression was pensive, even troubled. He said, "We're going to pitch camp here for the night, is that right, lordship? And wait until morning before we try to see if the floaters will travel over water that moves as fast as this?"

"So I intend, yes."

"With all respect, my lord, you might consider crossing the river tonight, if it's possible."

Valentine frowned. He felt curiously detached: Sleet's words appeared to be reaching him from a great distance. "As I recall, our plan was to spend tomorrow morning experimenting with the floaters, but to wait on this side of the river until the other half of the caravan had caught up with us before making the actual crossing into Piurifayne. Is that not so?"

"Yes, my lord, but—"

Valentine cut him off. "Then the order should be given to pitch camp before it's dark, eh, Sleet?" The Coronal put the issue from his mind and turned back toward the river. "Do you see that peculiar animal on the far bank?"

"The gromwark, you mean?"

"Is that what it is? What do you think it's up to, rubbing its face in the ground like that?"

"Digging a burrow, I'd say. To hunker down in when the storm strikes. They live in the water, you know, but I suppose it figures the river will be too badly stirred up, and—"

"Storm?" Valentine asked.

"Yes, my lord. I was trying to tell you, my lord. Look at the sky, my lord!"

"The sky darkens. Night's coming on."

"Look to the east, I mean," said Sleet.

Valentine swung around and stared into Gihorna. The sun should already be nearly down, back there; he would have expected the sky to have turned gray or even black by this time of day. But instead a weird kind of sunset seemed to be going on in the east, against all nature: a strange pastel glow streaked the sky, pink tinged with yellow, and pale green at the horizon. The colors had an odd throbbing intensity, as though the sky were pulsating. The world seemed extraordinarily still: Valentine heard the rushing of the river, but no other sound, not even the nightfall song of birds or the insistent high-pitched notes of the little scarlet tree-frogs that dwelled here by the thousands. And there was a desert dryness to the air, a combustible quality.

"Sandstorm, my lord," Sleet said quietly.

"Are you certain?"

"It must be blowing up just now, on the coast. The wind was out of the east all day, and that's where the Gihorna storms come from, off the ocean. A dry wind off the ocean, lordship, can you reckon that? I can't."

"I hate a dry wind," Carabella murmured. "Like the wind the dragon hunters call 'the sending.' It makes my nerves ache."

"You know of these storms, my lord?" Sleet asked.

Valentine nodded tensely. A Coronal's education is rich in the details of geography. The sandstorms of Gihorna occurred infrequently but were widely notorious: fierce winds that skinned the dunes like knives, and scooped up tons of sand and carried them with resistless ferocity toward the inland regions. They came but twice or thrice in a generation, but they were long remembered when they did.

"What will happen to our people back there?" Valentine asked.

Sleet said, "The storm's sure to pass right over them. It may be upon them already, or if not, it'll be there before long. Gihorna storms are swift. Listen, lordship: listen!"

A wind was rising.

Valentine heard it, still far away, a low hissing sound that had just now begun to intrude itself upon the unnatural silence. It was like the first quiet whisper of an awakening giant's slowly mounting fury that plainly was soon to give way to some awesome devastating roaring.

"And what of us?" Carabella said. "Will it reach this far, Sleet?"

"The gromwark thinks so, my lady. It seeks to wait things out underground." To Valentine Sleet said, "Shall I advise you, my lord?"

"If you will."

"We should cross the river now, while we still can. If the storm comes over us, it may destroy the floaters, or so badly disable them that they will be unable to travel on water."

"More than half my people are still in Gihorna!"

"If they still live, yes."

"Deliamber—Tisana—Shanamir—!"

"I know, my lord. But we can do nothing for them now. If we are to continue this expedition at all, we must cross the river, and later that may be impossible. On the far side we can hide in the jungle, and camp there until the others rejoin us, if ever they do. But if we stay here we may be pinned down forever, unable to go forward, unable to retreat."

A grim prospect, Valentine thought; and a plausible one. But nevertheless he hesitated, still reluctant to go on into Piurifayne while so many of his closest and dearest ones faced an uncertain fate under the lash of the wind-driven Gihorna sands. For an instant he felt the wild urge to order the floaters back toward the east, in order to search for the rest of the royal party. A moment's reflection told him of the folly of that. There was nothing he could achieve by going back at this moment except to put even more lives in jeopardy. The storm might yet not reach this far west; in that case it would be best to wait until its rage was spent, and then reenter Gihorna to pick up the survivors.

He stood still and silent, bleakly looking eastward into that realm of darkness now so strangely illuminated by the frightening glow of the sandstorm's destructive energies.

The wind continued to gain in force. The storm will reach us, Valentine realized. It will sweep over us and perhaps plunge on deep into the Piurifayne jungles as well, before its power is dissipated.

Then he narrowed his eyes and blinked in surprise and pointed. "Do you see lights approaching? Floater lights?"

"By the Lady!" Sleet muttered hoarsely.

"Are they here?" Carabella asked. "Do you think they've escaped the storm?"

"Only one floater, my lord," said Sleet quietly. "And not one from the royal caravan, I think."

Valentine had arrived at that conclusion at the same moment. The royal floaters were huge vehicles, capable of holding many people and much equipment. What was coming toward them now out of Gihorna appeared to be more like a small private floater, a two- or four-passenger model: it had only two lights in front, casting no very powerful beam, where the larger ones had three, of great brilliance.

The floater pulled to a halt no more than thirty feet from the Coronal. At once Lord Valentine's guards rushed forward to surround it, holding their energy-throwers at the ready. The doors of the floater swung open and two men, haggard, exhausted, came stumbling out.

Valentine gasped in astonishment. "Tunigorn? Elidath?"

It seemed impossible: a dream, a fantasy. Tunigorn at this moment should still have been in Piliplok, dealing with routine administrative chores. And Elidath? How could this be Elidath? Elidath belonged thousands of miles away, atop Castle Mount. Valentine no more expected to encounter him in this dark forest on Piurifayne's border than he would his own mother the Lady.

Yet that tall man with the heavy brows and the deep-cleft chin was surely Tunigorn; and that other, taller still, he of the piercing eyes and the strong, broad-boned face, was surely Elidath. Unless—unless—

The wind grew more powerful. It seemed to Valentine that thin gritty pennons of sand now rode upon it.

"Are you real?" he demanded of Elidath and Tunigorn. "Or just a pair of cunning Shapeshifter imitations?"

"Real, Valentine, real, altogether real!" cried Elidath, and held forth his arms toward the Coronal.

"By the Divine, it is the truth," Tunigorn said. "We are no counterfeits, and we have traveled day and night, my lord, to overtake you in this place."

"Yes," Valentine said, "I think you are real."

He would have gone toward Elidath's outstretched arms, but his own guards uncertainly interposed themselves. Angrily Valentine waved them aside and pulled Elidath into a close embrace. Then, releasing him, he stepped back to survey his oldest and closest friend. It was well over a year since last they had met; but Elidath seemed to have aged ten years for one. He looked frayed, worn, eroded. Was it the cares of the regency that had ground him down in this way, Valentine wondered, or the fatigue of his long journey to Zimroel? Once he had seemed to Valentine like a brother, for they were of an age with one another and of much the same cast of soul; and now Elidath was suddenly transformed into a weary old man.

"My lord, the storm—" Sleet began.

"A moment," Valentine said, brusquely gesturing him away. "There's much I must learn." To Elidath he said, "How can it be that you are here?"

"I came, my lord, to beg you not to go further into peril."

"What gave you to think I was in peril, or entering more deeply into it?"

"The word came to me that you were planning to cross into Piurifayne and speak with the Metamorphs," said Elidath.

"That decision was only lately taken. You must have left the Mount weeks or even months before the idea came into my mind." In some irritation Valentine said, "Is this your way of serving me, Elidath? To abandon your place at the Castle, and journey unbidden halfway round the world to interfere with my policies?"

"My place is with you, Valentine."

Valentine scowled. "Out of love for you I bid you greeting and offer my embrace. But I wish you were not here."

"And I the same," said Elidath.

"My lord," said Sleet insistently. "The storm is coming upon us now! I beg you—"

"Yes, the storm," Tunigorn said. "A Gihorna sandstorm, terrible to behold. We heard it raging along the coast as we set out after you, and it has followed us all the way. An hour, half an hour, perhaps less, and it will be here, my lord!"

Valentine felt a tight band of tension encase his chest. The storm, the storm, the storm! Yes, Sleet was right: they must take some action. But he had so many questions—there was so much he must know—

To Tunigorn he said, "You must have come by way of the other camp. Lisamon, Deliamber, Tisana—are they safe?"

"They will try to protect themselves as best they can. And we must do the same. Head west, try to take cover in the depths of the jungle before the worst of it reaches here—"

"My counsel exactly," Sleet said.

"Very well," said Valentine. He looked to Sleet and said, "Have our floaters made ready for the crossing."

"I will, my lord." He rushed away.

To Elidath Valentine said, "If you are here, who rules at the Castle?"

"I chose three to serve as a Council of Regency: Stasilaine, Divvis, and Hissune."

"Hissune?"

Color came to Elidath's cheeks. "It was my belief you wished him to move rapidly forward in the government."

"So I do. You did well, Elidath. But I suspect that there were some who were less than totally pleased with the choice."

"Indeed. Prince Manganot of Banglecode, and the Duke of Halanx, and—"

"Never mind the names. I know who they are," Valentine said. "They'll change their minds in time, I think."

"As do I. The boy is astonishing, Valentine. Nothing escapes his notice. He learns amazingly swiftly. He moves surely. And when he makes a mistake, he knows how to gain from an understanding of his error. He reminds me somewhat of you, when you were his age."

Valentine shook his head. "No, Elidath. He's not at all

like me. That's the thing I most value about him, I think. We see the same things, but we see them with very different eyes." He smiled and caught Elidath by the forearm, and held him a moment. Softly he said, "You understand what I intend for him?"

"I think I do."

"And are you troubled by it?"

Elidath's gaze was steady. "You know that I am not, Valentine."

"Yes. I do know that," the Coronal said.

He dug his fingers hard into Elidath's arm, and released him, and turned away before Elidath could see the sudden glistening in his eyes.

The wind, now thick with sand and howling eerily, came ripping through the grove of slender-stemmed trees that lay just to the east, cutting their broad leaves to tatters like a host of invisible knives. Valentine felt light showers of sand striking his face with stinging impact, and he turned from it, pulling his cloak up to protect himself. The others were doing the same. At the edge of the river, where Sleet was supervising the conversion of the floaters' ground-effect mechanisms for use on water, there was a great bustle of activity.

Tunigorn said, "There is much strange news, Valentine."

"Speak it, then!"

"The agricultural expert who has been traveling with us since Alaisor—"

"Y-Uulisaan? What of him? Has something happened to him?"

"He is a Shapeshifter spy, my lord."

The words reached Valentine like blows.

"*What?*"

"Deliamber detected it in the night: the Vroon felt a strangeness somewhere, and prowled about until he found Y-Uulisaan holding mind-speech with someone far away. He instructed your Skandar and the Amazon to seize him, and when they did, Y-Uulisaan began changing forms like a trapped demon."

Valentine spat in fury. "It goes beyond belief! All these weeks, carrying a spy with us, confiding in him all our plans for overcoming the blights and plagues of the farm provinces— no! No! What have they done with him?"

"They would have brought him to you this night for

interrogation," said Tunigorn. "But then the storm came, and Deliamber thought it wisest to wait it out at the camp."

"My lord!" Sleet called from the riverbank. "We are ready to attempt the crossing!"

"There is more," Tunigorn said.

"Come. Tell me about it as we ride across."

They hurried toward the floaters. The wind now was without mercy, and the trees leaned halfway to the ground under its brunt. Carabella, beside Valentine, stumbled and would have gone sprawling if he had not caught her. He wrapped one arm tightly about her: she was so slight, so buoyant, that any gust might carry her away.

Tunigorn said, "Word of new chaos reached Piliplok just as I set forth. In Khyntor a man named Sempeturn, an itinerant preacher, has proclaimed himself Coronal, and some of the people have acclaimed him."

"Ah," Valentine said softly, as though struck in the middle.

"That is not all. Another Coronal has arisen in Dulorn, they say: a Ghayrog named Ristimaar. And we have word of still another in Ni-moya, though his name did not come to me; and it is reported also that at least one false Pontifex has come forth in Velathys, or possibly Narabal. We are not sure, my lord, because the channels of communications have become so disturbed."

"It is as I thought," said Valentine in a tone of deadly quiet. "The Divine has in all truth turned against us. The commonwealth is shattered. The sky itself has broken and will fall upon us."

"Into the floater, my lord!" Sleet shouted.

"Too late," Valentine murmured. "There will be no forgiveness for us now."

As they scrambled into the vehicles the full fury of the storm broke upon them. First there was an odd moment of silence, as though the atmosphere itself had fled from this place in terror of the onrushing winds, taking with it all capacity for the transmission of sound; but in the next instant came something like a thunderclap, but dull and without resonance, like a short swift unechoing thud. And on the heels of that arrived the storm, screaming and snarling and turning the air opaque with churning whirlwinds of sand.

Valentine was in the floater by then, with Carabella close beside him and Elidath not far away. The vehicle, clumsily swaying and lumbering like some great amorfibot rousted

unwilling from the dune where it had been dozing, drifted
riverward and moved out over the water.

Darkness now had come, and within the darkness lay a
weird, glowing core of purplish-green light that seemed
almost to have been kindled by the force of air flowing over
air. The river had turned altogether black and its surface was
rippling and swelling alarmingly as sudden calamitous changes
in the air pressure above it tugged or thrust against it. Sand
pelted down in wild cyclonic sprays, etching pock-marked
craters on the heaving water. Carabella gagged and choked;
Valentine fought back an overwhelming dizziness; the floater
bucked and reared in a berserk, unruly way, nose rising and
slapping down against the water and rising again, and again
slapping down, *thwack thwack thwack*. The cascading sand
etched patterns of a curious loveliness in the windows, but
rapidly it became all but impossible to see through them,
though Valentine had the hazy impression that the floater just
to the left of his was standing on its tail, balanced immobile in
an impossible position for a frozen moment before starting to
slip down into the river.

Then everything outside the floater was invisible, and the
only sounds that could be heard were the booming of the
wind and the steady, abrasive drumbeat of the sand against
the floater's hull.

An odd tranquilizing giddiness began to possess Valentine. It seemed to him that the floater was pivoting rhythmi-
cally now along its longitudinal axis, jerking from side to side
in ever more abrupt yawing shrugs. Very likely, he realized,
the ground-effect rotors were losing whatever little purchase
they had had on the river's wildly unstable surface, and in
another few moments the vehicle would surely flip over.

"This river is accursed," said Carabella.

Yes, Valentine thought. So it did seem. The river was
under some dark spell, or else the Steiche was itself some
malevolent spirit that sought his doom. And now we will all
drown, he thought. But he was curiously calm.

The river, which nearly had me once but somehow
allowed me to be cast forth to safety, he told himself, has
waited all this while for a second chance. And now that
chance has come.

It did not matter. In the final analysis nothing really
mattered. Life, death, peace, war, joy, sadness: they were all
one and the same, words without meaning, mere noises,

empty husks. Valentine felt no regret for anything. They had asked him to serve, and he had served. Surely he had done his best. He had shirked no task, betrayed no trust, forsworn no oath. Now would he return to the source, for the winds had driven the river wild, and the river would devour them all, and so be it: it did not matter. It did not matter.

"Valentine!"

A face, inches from his own. Eyes looking into his. A voice, crying a name that he thought he knew, and crying it again.

"Valentine! Valentine!"

A hand gripping his arm. Shaking him, pushing him.

Whose face? Whose eyes? Whose voice? Whose hand?

"He seems in a trance, Elidath."

Another voice. Lighter, clearer, close by his side. Carabella? Yes. Carabella. Who was Carabella?

"There's not enough air in here. Vents choked by sand— we'll smother if we don't drown!"

"Can we get out?"

"Through the safety hatch. But we've got to snap him out of this. Valentine! *Valentine!*"

"Who is it?"

"Elidath. What's the matter with you?"

"Nothing. Nothing at all."

"You seem half asleep. Here, let me get that safety belt loose. Get up, Valentine! Get *up*. The floater's going to sink in another five minutes."

"Ah."

"Valentine, please, listen to him!" It was the other voice, the light one, the Carabella voice. "We're turning over and over. We have to get out of here and swim to shore. It's the only hope we have. One of the floaters has already gone down, and we can't see the other one, and—oh, Valentine, please! Stand up! Take a deep breath! That's it. Another. Another. Here, give me your hand—hold his other one, Elidath; we'll lead him to the hatch—there—there—just keep moving, Valentine—"

Yes. Just keep moving. Valentine became aware of tiny currents of air flowing past his face. He heard the faint spattering of sand as it fell from above. Yes. Yes. Crawl up here, wriggle past this, put your foot here, the other one here—step—step—hold this—pull—*pull*—

He clambered upward like an automaton, still only vaguely comprehending what was taking place, until he reached the top of the emergency ladder and poked his head out through the safety hatch.

A sudden blast of fresh air—hot, dry, thick with sand—swept brutally across his face. He gasped, breathed sand, swallowed sand, gagged, spat. But he was awake again. Clinging to the flange that rimmed the hatch, he stared out into the storm-riven night. The darkness was intense; the weird glow had greatly diminished; sprays of sand still whipped unrelentingly through the air, one howling vortex after another, battering against his eyes, his nostrils, his lips.

It was almost impossible to see. They were somewhere in midriver, but neither the eastern nor western bank was visible. The floater was tipped high on end, in an awkward and precarious way, rising half its length out of the savage chaos of the river. There was no sign of the other floaters. Valentine thought he saw heads bobbing about in the water, but it was hard to be sure: the sand veiled everything and merely to keep his eyes open was an agony.

"Down here! Jump, Valentine!" Elidath's voice.

"Wait," he called. He looked back. Carabella stood below him on the ladder, pale, frightened, almost dazed. He reached for her and she smiled when she saw that he had returned to himself; and he pulled her up beside him. She came in one quick bound and balanced beside him on the rim of the hatch, agile as an acrobat, no less trim and sturdy than she had been in her juggling days.

The sand choking the air was unendurable. They locked their arms together and jumped.

Hitting the water was like striking a solid surface. For a moment he clung to Carabella, but as they landed she was ripped from him. Valentine felt himself pushing down through the water until he was all but engulfed in it; then he kicked downward and recoiled and forced his way to the top. He called out for Carabella, Elidath, Sleet, but he saw no one, and even down here there was no place to hide from the sand, which fell like a burdensome rain and thickened the river to a diabolical turbidity.

I could almost walk to shore on this, Valentine thought.

He made out the dim hugeness of the floater to his left, sliding slowly downward into the water: there was still enough air in it to give it some buoyancy, and the bizarre, puddinglike consistency of the sand-glutted river provided some slight resistance to its entry, but yet the floater was plainly sinking, and Valentine knew that when it went under entirely it would kick up a perilous backlash nearby. He struggled to get away, looking about all the while for his companions.

The floater vanished. A great wave rose and struck him.

He was thrust under, came up briefly, went down again as a second wave hit him and then an eddying whirlpool sucked at his legs. He felt himself being swept downstream. His lungs were afire: full of water, full of sand? The apathy that had come over him aboard the doomed floater was altogether gone from him now; he kicked, wriggled, fought to stay afloat. He collided with someone in the darkness, clutched at him, lost hold, went under again. This time nausea overwhelmed him, and he thought he would never come up; but he felt strong arms seize him and begin to tow him, and he let himself go limp, for he understood that this frantic resistance to the river was an error. He breathed more easily, and drifted easily at the surface. His rescuer released him, disappearing into the night, but Valentine saw now that he was close to one of the river's banks, and in a stunned, weary way he pulled himself forward until he felt his waterlogged boots touching bottom. Slowly, as if he were marching through a river of syrup, he plodded shoreward, emerged on the muddy bank, and dropped down face first. He wished he could burrow like the gromwark into the wet earth and hide until the storm had passed by.

After a time, when he had caught his breath, he sat up and looked about. The air was still gritty with sand, but not so much so that he needed to cover his face, and the wind definitely seemed to be subsiding. A few dozen yards downstream from him lay one of the floaters, beached at the river's edge; he saw nothing of the other two. Three or four limp figures were sprawled nearby; alive or dead, he could not say. Voices, faint and dim, resounded in the distance. Valentine was unable to tell whether he was on the Piurifayne side of the river or the Gihorna, though he suspected he was in Piurifayne, for it seemed to him that a wall of all but impenetrable foliage rose just behind him.

He got to his feet.

"Lordship! Lordship!"

"Sleet? Here!"

The small, lithe figure of Sleet appeared out of the darkness. Carabella was with him, and Tunigorn not far

behind. Solemnly Valentine embraced each of them. Carabella
was shivering uncontrollably, though the night was warm,
and had grown humid now that the parched wind had blown
itself out. He drew her against him, and tried to brush away
the patches of wet sand that clung to her clothes, as to his,
like a thick constricting crust.

Sleet said, "My lord, two of the floaters are lost, and I
think a good many of their passengers with them."

Valentine nodded grimly. "So I fear. But surely not all!"

"There are some survivors, yes. As I came to you I heard
their voices. Some—I have no idea how many—scattered
along both banks. But you must prepare yourself, my lord,
for losses. Tunigorn and I saw several bodies along the shore,
and very likely there are others who were swept downstream
and drowned far away. When morning comes we'll know
more."

"Indeed," Valentine said, and fell silent a while. He sat
crosslegged on the ground, more like a tailor than a king, and
fell into a long silence, drawing his hand idly through the
sand that lay heaped as though it were some strange kind of
snow to a depth of some inches on the ground. There was one
question he dared not ask; but after a time he could no longer
keep it within himself. He glanced up at Sleet and Tunigorn
and said, "What news is there of Elidath?"

"None, my lord," said Sleet gently.

"None? None at all? Has he not been seen, or heard?"

Carabella said, "He was beside us in the water, Valentine, before our floater went down."

"Yes. I remember that. But since then?"

"Nothing," said Tunigorn.

Valentine gave him a quizzical look. "Has his body been
found, and are you not telling me?"

"By the Lady, Valentine, you know as much as I about
what has happened to Elidath!" Tunigorn blurted.

"Yes. Yes. I do believe you. This frightens me, not
knowing what has become of him. You know he means much
to me, Tunigorn."

"You think you need to inform me of that?"

Valentine smiled sadly. "Forgive me, old friend. This
night has unsettled my mind some, I do believe." Carabella
put her hand, cool and damp, over his; and he put his other
on hers. Quietly he said again, "Forgive me, Tunigorn. And
you, Sleet, and you, Carabella."

"Forgive you, my lord?" Carabella asked, amazed. "For what?"

He shook his head. "Let it pass, love."

"Do you blame yourself for what has happened tonight?"

"I blame myself for a great deal," said Valentine, "of which what has happened tonight is but a small part, though to me it is a vast catastrophe. The world was given into my stewardship, and I have led it to disaster."

"Valentine, no!" Carabella cried.

"My lord," said Sleet, "you are much too harsh on yourself!"

"Am I?" He laughed. "Famine in half of Zimroel, and three false Coronals proclaiming themselves, or is it four, and the Metamorphs coming around to collect their overdue reckoning, and here we sit at the edge of Piurifayne with sand in our craws and half our people drowned and who knows what dread fate overtaking the other half, and—and—" His voice was beginning to crack. With an effort he brought it under control, and himself, and said more calmly, "This has been a monstrous night, and I am very weary, and it worries me that Elidath has not appeared. But I will not find him by talking this way, will I? Will I? Come, let us rest, and wait for morning, and when morning comes we will begin to repair all that can yet be repaired. Eh?"

"Yes," said Carabella. "That sounds wise, Valentine."

There was no hope of sleep. He and Carabella and Sleet and Tunigorn lay close by one another, sprawled out in the sand, and the night passed in wakefulness amid a welter of forest sounds and the steady rumble of the river. Gradually dawn crept upon them out of Gihorna, and by that early gray light Valentine saw what horrendous destruction the storm had wrought. On the Gihorna side of the river, and for a short distance into Piurifayne, every tree had been stripped of its leaves, as if the wind had breathed fire, leaving only pitiful naked trunks. The ground was heaped with sand, strewn thinly in some places, piled high into miniature dunes in others. The floater in which Tunigorn and Elidath had arrived still sat upright on the far side of the river, but its metal skin had been scoured and pitted to a dull matte finish. The one floater that remained of Valentine's own caravan lay on its side like a dead sea dragon cast up by the waves.

One group of survivors, four or five of them, sat together on the opposite bank; half a dozen more, mainly Skandars of the Coronal's personal bodyguard, were camped just downslope from Valentine; some others could be seen walking about a hundred yards or so to the north, evidently searching for bodies. A few of the dead had been laid out neatly in parallel rows beside the overturned floater. Valentine did not see Elidath among them. But he had little hope for his old friend, and he felt no emotion, only a chill numb sensation beneath his breastbone, when shortly after dawn one of the Skandars appeared, carrying Elidath's burly body in his four arms as easily as though he held a child.

"Where was he?" Valentine asked.

"Half a mile downstream, my lord, or a little farther."

"Put him down, and begin seeing about graves. We will bury all our dead this morning, on that little rise overlooking the river."

"Yes, my lord."

Valentine peered down at Elidath. His eyes were closed, and his lips, slightly parted, seemed almost to turn upward in a smile, though it might just as easily be a grimace, Valentine thought. "He looked old last night," he said to Carabella. And to Tunigorn he said, "Did you not think also that he had aged greatly this past year? But now he seems young again. The lines are gone from his face: he might be no more than twenty-four. Does it not seem that way to you?"

"I blame myself for his death," Tunigorn said in a flat empty voice.

"How so?" Valentine asked sharply.

"It was I who called him down off Castle Mount. Come, I said, hurry to Zimroel: Valentine is contemplating strange deeds, though I know not what they are, and you alone can discourage him from them. And he came: and now see him. If he had stayed at the Castle—"

"No, Tunigorn. No more of this."

But in a stunned dreamlike way Tunigorn went on, apparently uncontrollably, "He would have been Coronal when you went on to the Labyrinth, and he would have lived long and happily at the Castle, and ruled wisely, and now—instead—instead—"

Gently Valentine said, "He would not have been Coronal, Tunigorn. He knew that, and he was content. Come, old friend, you make his death harder for me with this foolish talk. He is with the Source this morning, which with all my heart I would not have wished happen for another seventy years, but it has happened, and it cannot be undone, however much we talk of it and maybe and what might have been. And we who have lived through this night have much work to do. So let us begin it, Tunigorn. Eh? Eh? Shall we begin?"

"What work is that, my lord?"

"First, these burials. I will dig his grave myself, with my own hands, and let no one dare say me no to that. And when all that is done, you must find your way back across the river, and go in that little floater of yours eastward into Gihorna, and see what has become of Deliamber and Tisana and Lisamon and the rest of them, and if they live, you must bring them here, and lead them onward to me."

"And you, Valentine?" said Tunigorn.

"If we can right this other floater, I will continue on deeper into Piurifayne, for I still must go to the Danipiur, and say certain things to her that are long overdue to be said. You will find me in Ilirivoyne, as was my first intention."

"My lord—"

"I beg you. No more talk. Come, all of you! We have graves to dig, and tears to shed. And then we must complete our journeys." He looked once more to Elidath, thinking, I do not yet believe that he is dead, but I will believe it soon. And then there will be one more thing for which I will need forgiveness.

5

In early afternoon, before the regular daily Council meetings, Hissune made a practice of wandering by himself through the outlying reaches of the Castle, exploring its seemingly infinite complexities. He had lived atop the Mount long enough now so that the place no longer intimidated him, indeed was starting to feel very much like his true home: his Labyrinth life now seemed most distinctly a closed chapter of his past, encapsulated, sealed, stored away in the recesses of his memory. But yet he knew that even if he dwelled at the Castle fifty years, or ten times fifty, he would never come to be truly familiar with it all.

No one was. No one, Hissune suspected, ever had been. They said it had forty thousand rooms. Was that so? Had anyone made an accurate count? Every Coronal since Lord

Stiamot had lived here and had tried to leave his own imprint on the Castle, and the legend was that five rooms were added every year, and it was eight thousand years since Lord Stiamot first had taken up residence on the Mount. So there might well be forty thousand rooms here—or fifty thousand, or ninety thousand. Who could tell? One could tally a hundred rooms a day, and a year would not be enough to count them all, and by year's end a few new rooms would have been added somewhere anyway, so it would become necessary to search them out and add them to the list. Impossible. Impossible.

To Hissune the Castle was the most wondrous place in the world. Early in his stay here he had concentrated on coming to know the innermost zone, where the main court and the royal offices were, and the most famous buildings, Stiamot Keep and Lord Prestimion's Archive and Lord Arioc's Watchtower and Lord Kinniken's Chapel and the grand ceremonial chambers that surrounded the magnificent room the centerpiece of which was the Confalume Throne of the Coronal. Like any greenhorn tourist from the back woods of Zimroel, Hissune had gone over and over those places, including a good many that no greenhorn tourist would ever be allowed to see, until he knew every corner of them as well as any of the tour guides who had spent decades leading visitors through them.

The central reaches of the Castle, at least, were complete for all time: no one could build anything significant there any longer without first removing some structure erected by a past Coronal, and to do such a thing was unthinkable. Lord Malibor's trophy room had been the last building to go up in the inner zone, so far as Hissune had been able to discover. Lord Voriax in his short reign had constructed only some game courts far out on the eastern flank of the Castle, and Lord Valentine had not yet managed to add any rooms of consequence at all, though he did speak from time to time of building a great botanical garden to house all the marvelous and bizarre plants he had seen during his wanderings through Majipoor—as soon as the pressure of his royal responsibilities, he said, eased enough to allow him to give some serious thought to the project. Judging by the reports of devastation now coming in from Zimroel, Lord Valentine had perhaps waited too long to undertake it, Hissune thought: the blights on that continent were wiping out, so it appeared, not only the agricultural crops but also many of the unusual plants of the wilderness areas.

When he had mastered the inner zone to his own satisfaction Hissune began to extend his explorations to the baffling and almost endless sprawl that lay beyond it. He visited the subterranean vaults that housed the weather machines—designed in ancient times when such scientific matters were better understood on Majipoor—by which the eternal springtime of Castle Mount was maintained, even though the summit of the Mount thrust itself thirty miles above sea level into the chilly dark of space. He wandered through the great library that coiled from one side of the Castle to the other in vast serpentine loops, and was said to contain every book ever published anywhere in the civilized universe. He roamed the stables where the royal mounts, splendid high-spirited synthetic animals very little like their plodding cousins, the beasts of burden of every Majipoori town and farm, pranced and snorted and pawed the air as they waited for their next outing. He made the discovery of Lord Sangamor's tunnels, a series of linked chambers strung like a chain of sausages around an outjutting spire on the west face of the Mount, the walls and roof of which glowed with eerie radiance, one room a midnight blue, one a rich vermilion, one a subtle aquamarine, one a dazzling tawny yellow, one a somber throbbing russet, and on and on: no one knew why the tunnels had been built, or what was the source of the light that sprang of its own accord from the glistening paving-blocks.

Wherever he went he was admitted without question. He was, after all, one of the three regents of the realm: a surrogate Coronal, in a sense, or at least a significant fraction of one. But the aura of power had begun to settle about him long before Elidath had named him to the triumvirate. He felt eyes on him everywhere. He knew what those intent glances signified. *That is Lord Valentine's favorite. He came out of nowhere; he is already a prince; there will be no limits to his rise. Respect him. Obey him. Flatter him. Fear him.* At first he thought he could remain unchanged amidst all this attention, but that was impossible. *I am still only Hissune, who gulled tourists in the Labyrinth, who pushed papers about in the House of Records, who was jeered at by his own friends for putting on airs.* Yes, that would always be true; but it was also true that he was no longer ten years old, that he had been greatly deepened and transformed by what he had experienced peering into the lives of scores of other men and women in the Registry of Souls, and by the training he had had on Castle Mount, and by the honors and responsibilities—mainly the responsibilities—that had been conferred on him during Elidath's regency. He walked in a different way now: no longer the cocky but wary Labyrinth boy, always glancing in six directions for some bewildered stranger to exploit, nor the lowly, overworked clerk keeping to his proper place while nonetheless busily scrabbling for promotion to some senior desk, nor the apologetic neophyte bewilderingly thrust among the Powers of the realm and moving cautiously in their midst, but now the rising young lordling, striding with assurance and poise through the Castle, confident, secure, aware of his strengths, his purposes, his destiny. He hoped he had not become arrogant or overbearing or self-important; but he accepted himself calmly and without labored humility for what he had become and what he would be.

Today his route took him into a part of the Castle he had rarely visited, the north wing, which cascaded down a long rounded snout of the Mount's summit that pointed toward the distant cities of Huine and Gossif. The guards' residential quarters were here, and a series of beehive-shaped outbuildings that had been built in the reigns of Lord Dizimaule and Lord Arioc for purposes now forgotten, and a cluster of low weatherbeaten structures, roofless and crumbling, that no one understood at all. On his last visit to this zone, months ago, a team of archaeologists had been excavating there, two Ghayrogs and a Vroon overseeing a bunch of Skandar laborers sifting sand for potsherds, and the Vroon had told him then that she thought the buildings were the remnants of an old fort of the time of Lord Damlang, successor to Stiamot. Hissune had come by today to see if they were still at work and find out what they had learned; but the place was deserted, and the excavations had been filled. He stood for a time atop an ancient broken wall, looking toward the impossibly distant horizon, half concealed by the enormous shoulder of the Mount.

What cities lay down this way? Gossif, fifteen or twenty miles along, and below it Tentag, and then, he thought, either Minimool or Greel. And then, surely, Stee of the thirty million citizens, equalled only by Ni-moya in its grandeur.

He had never seen any of those cities, and perhaps he never would. Valentine himself often remarked that he had spent all his life on Castle Mount without finding the occasion to visit Stee. The world was too large for anyone to explore adequately in one lifetime: too large to comprehend, indeed.

And the thirty million folk of Stee, and the thirty million of Ni-moya, and Pidruid's eleven million, and the millions more of Alaisor, Treymone, Piliplok, Mazadone, Velathys, Narabal: how were they faring this very moment? Hissune wondered. Amid the famines, amid the panics, amid the cries of new prophets and self-appointed new kings and emperors? The situation now was critical, he knew. Zimroel had fallen into such confusion that it was all but impossible to find out what was going on there, though surely it was nothing good. And not long ago had come news of weevils and rusts and smuts and the Divine only knew what else beginning to make their sinister way through the farming belts of western Alhanroel, so in a little while the same madness would very likely be sweeping the senior continent. Already there were rumblings: tales of sea-dragon worship openly conducted in Treymone and Stoien, and mysterious new orders of chivalry, the Knights of Dekkeret and the Fellowship of the Mount and some others, springing up suddenly in cities like Amblemorn and Normork on Castle Mount itself. Ominous, troublesome signs of greater upheaval to come.

There were those who imagined that Majipoor had some inherent immunity to the universal inevitabilities of change, merely because its social system had undergone virtually no important evolution since it had taken its present form thousands of years ago. But Hissune had studied enough of history, both Majipoor's and that of the mother world Earth, to know that even so placid a population as Majipoor's, stable and content for millennia, lulled by the kindnesses of its climate and an agricultural fertility capable of supporting an almost unlimited number of people, would tumble with startling swiftness into anarchy and utter disintegration if those comforting props suddenly were knocked away. That had already begun, and it would grow worse.

Why had these plagues come? Hissune had no idea. What was being done to deal with them? Plainly, not enough. *Could* anything be done? What were rulers for, if not to maintain the welfare of their people? And here he was, a ruler of sorts, at least for the moment, in the grand isolation of Castle Mount, far above a crumbling civilization: badly informed, remote, helpless. But of course the ultimate responsibility for dealing with this crisis did not lie with him. What of Majipoor's true anointed rulers, then? Hissune had always thought of the Pontifex, buried down there at the bottom of the Labyrinth, as a blind mole who could not conceivably know what was happening in the world—even a Pontifex who, like Tyeveras, might be reasonably vigorous and sane. In fact the Pontifex did not need to keep close touch with events: he had a Coronal to do that, so the theory ran. But Hissune saw now that the Coronal too was cut off from reality, up here in the misty reaches of Castle Mount, just as thoroughly sequestered as the Pontifex was in his pit. At least the Coronal undertook the grand processional from time to time, and put himself back in touch with his subjects. Yet was that not precisely what Lord Valentine was doing now, and what help was that in healing the wound that widened in the heart of the world? Where was Valentine at this moment, anyway? What actions, if any, was he taking? Who in the government had heard so much as a word from him in months?

We are all wise and enlightened people, Hissune thought. *And with the best will in the world we are doing everything wrong.*

It was nearly time for the day's meeting of the Council of Regency. He turned and made his way at a quick lope toward the interior of the Castle.

As he began the ascent of the Ninety-Nine Steps he caught sight of Alsimir, whom he had lately named as the chief among his aides, waving wildly and shouting from far above. Taking the steps two and three at a time, Hissune raced upward while Alsimir came plunging down just as swiftly.

"We've been looking all over for you!" Alsimir blurted breathlessly, when he was still half a dozen steps away. He seemed amazingly agitated.

"Well, you've found me," Hissune snapped. "What's going on?"

Pausing to collect himself, Alsimir said, "There's been big excitement. A long message came in from Tunigorn an hour ago, in Gihorna—"

"Gihorna?" Hissune stared. "What in the name of the Divine is he doing *there*?"

"I couldn't tell you that. All I know is that that's where he sent the message from, and—"

"All right. All right." Catching Alsimir by the arm, Hissune said sharply, "Tell me what he said!"

"Do you think I know? Would they let someone like me in on great matters of state?"

"A great matter of state, is it, then?"

"Divvis and Stasilaine have been in session in the council room for the last forty-five minutes, and they've sent messengers to all corners of the Castle trying to find you, and half the high lords of the Castle have gone to the meeting and the others are on their way, and—"

Valentine must be dead, Hissune thought, chilled.

"Come with me," he said, and went sprinting furiously up the steps.

Outside the council chamber he found a madhouse scene, thirty or forty of the minor lords and princes and their aides milling about in confusion, and more arriving at every moment. As Hissune appeared they moved automatically aside for him, opening a path through which he moved like a sailing ship cutting its way imperiously through a sea thick with drifting dragon-grass. Leaving Alsimir by the door and instructing him to collect from the others whatever information they might have, he went in.

Stasilaine and Divvis sat at the high table: Divvis bleak-faced and grim, Stasilaine somber, pale, and uncharacteristically downcast, his shoulders slumped, his hand running nervously through his thick shock of hair. About them were most of the high lords: Mirigant, Elzandir, Manganot, Cantalis, the Duke of Halanx, Nimian of Dundilmir, and five or six others, including one that Hissune had seen only once before, the ancient and withered Prince Ghizmaile, grandson of the Pontifex Ossier who had preceded Tyeveras in the Labyrinth. All eyes turned upon Hissune as he entered, and he stood for a moment transfixed in the gaze of these men, the youngest of whom was ten or fifteen years his senior, and all of whom had spent their lives in the inner corridors of power. They were looking toward him as though he alone had the answer they required to some terrible and perplexing question.

"My lords," said Hissune.

Divvis, scowling, pushed a long sheet of paper across the

table toward him. "Read this," he muttered. "Unless you already know."

"I know only that there is a message from Tunigorn."

"Read it, then."

To Hissune's annoyance there was a tremor in his hand as he reached for the paper. He glowered at his fingers as though they were in rebellion against him, and forced them to grow steady.

Clusters of words leaped from the paper at him.

—Valentine gone off to Piurifayne to beg the forgiveness of the Danipiur—

—a Metamorph spy discovered traveling in the Coronal's own entourage—

—interrogation of the spy reveals that the Metamorphs themselves have created and spread the pestilences wracking the farmlands—

—a great sandstorm—Elidath dead, and many others—the Coronal has vanished into Piurifayne—

—Elidath dead—

—the Coronal has vanished—

—a spy in the Coronal's entourage—

—the Metamorphs have created the pestilences themselves—

—the Coronal has vanished—

—Elidath dead—

—the Coronal has vanished—

—the Coronal has vanished—

—the Coronal has vanished—

Hissune looked up, appalled. "How certain is it that this message is authentic?"

"There can be no doubt," said Stasilaine. "It came in over the secret transmission channels. The ciphers were the correct ones. The style of phrase is certainly Tunigorn's, that I will warrant myself. Put your faith on it, Hissune: this is altogether genuine."

"Then we have not one catastrophe to deal with, but three or four," Hissune said.

"So it would appear," said Divvis. "What are your thoughts on these matters, Hissune?"

Hissune gave the son of Lord Voriax a slow, careful look. There seemed to be no mockery in his question. It had appeared to Hissune that Divvis's jealousy of him and contempt for him had abated somewhat during these months of their working together on the Council of Regency, that Divvis had at last come to have some respect for his capabilities; but yet this was the first time Divvis had gone this far, actually showing what looked like a sincere desire to know Hissune's point of view—in front of the other high lords, even.

Carefully he said, "The first thing to recognize is that we are confronted not merely by a vast natural calamity, but by an insurrection. Tunigorn tells us that the Metamorph Y-Uulisaan has confessed, under interrogation by Deliamber and Tisana, that the responsibility for the plagues lies with the Metamorphs. I think we can have faith in Deliamber's methods, and we all know that Tisana can see into souls, even Metamorph souls. So the situation is precisely as I heard Sleet express it to the Coronal, when they were at the Labyrinth at the beginning of the grand processional—and which I heard the Coronal refuse to accept: that the Shapeshifters are making war upon us."

"And yet," said Divvis, "Tunigorn also tells us that the Coronal has responded by shuffling into Piurifayne to convey his royal apologies to the Danipiur for all our unkindnesses to her subjects down through the ages. We are all very much aware that Valentine regards himself as a man of peace: his gentle treatment of those who overthrew him long ago showed us that. It is a noble trait. But I have argued here this afternoon, Hissune, that what Valentine has done now goes beyond pacifism into madness. I say the Coronal, if he is still alive at all, is insane. Thus we have a lunatic Pontifex and a lunatic Coronal, and this while a deadly enemy is at our throats. What are your views, Hissune?"

"That you misinterpret the facts as Tunigorn provides them."

There was a flash of surprise and something like anger in Divvis's eyes; but his voice was under taut control as he said, "Ah, do you think so?"

Hissune tapped the sheet of paper. "Tunigorn says that the Coronal has gone into Piurifayne, *and* that a spy has been caught and made to confess. Nowhere can I find him saying that Lord Valentine went to Piurifayne after hearing of the spy's confession. I think it can be argued that the truth is quite the opposite: that Lord Valentine chose to undertake a mission of conciliation, the wisdom of which we clearly might wish to debate, but which is well within his character as we know it, and while he was away on that enterprise this other information came to light. Perhaps because of the storm, it became impossible for Tunigorn to communicate with the Coronal, although one would think Deliamber would be able to find some way." Glancing toward the great world-sphere of Majipoor against the far wall, Hissune said, "What information do we have of the Coronal's present location, anyway?"

"None," Stasilaine murmured.

Hissune's eyes widened.

The brilliant red light that indicated Lord Valentine's movements had gone out.

"The light is dark," said Hissune. "What does that mean? That he is dead?"

"It could mean that," Stasilaine said. "Or merely that he has lost or damaged the transmitter that he carries on him to broadcast his position."

Hissune nodded. "And there was a great storm, that caused many casualties. Although it's unclear from the message, I can easily believe that Lord Valentine himself was caught in the storm on his way into Piurifayne, which presumably he entered from Gihorna, leaving Tunigorn and some others behind—"

"And either he perished in the storm or the transmitter was lost; we have no way of knowing which," said Divvis.

"Let us hope the Divine has spared young Valentine's life," the aged Prince Ghizmaile declared suddenly in a voice so shriveled and sere it seemed barely to be that of a living creature. "But there is an issue we must deal with whether he is alive or dead, and that is the choice of a new Coronal."

Hissune felt himself swept with amazement at the words this most senior of Castle lords had just uttered.

He looked about the room. "Do I hear right? Are we discussing the overthrow of a king today?"

"You put it too strongly," Divvis answered smoothly. "All we discuss is whether it's appropriate for Valentine to continue to serve as Coronal, in view of what we now know of the hostile intentions of the Shapeshifters and in view of what we have long known of Valentine's methods of dealing with any sort of unpleasantness. If we are at war—and no one here any longer doubts that we are—then it's reasonable to argue that Valentine is not the right man to lead us at this time, if in fact he still lives. But to replace him is not to overthrow him. There is a legitimate constitutional means of removing Valentine from the Confalume Throne without in any way embroiling

Majipoor in conflict or manifesting a lack of love and respect for him."

"You mean, by allowing the Pontifex Tyeveras to die."

"Exactly. What say you to that, Hissune?"

Hissune did not at once reply. Like Divvis and Ghizmaile and, probably, most of the others here, he had been coming uneasily and reluctantly this afternoon to the conclusion that Lord Valentine must be replaced by someone more decisive, more aggressive, more belligerent, even. Nor was today the first time he had had those thoughts, though he had kept them to himself. And certainly there was an easy enough way of accomplishing a transfer of power, simply by bringing about Valentine's elevation, willing or not, to the Pontificate.

But Hissune's loyalty to Lord Valentine—his guide, his mentor, the architect of his career—was intense and deep-rooted. And he knew, perhaps better than any of these other men, the horror Valentine felt of being forced into the Labyrinth, which the Coronal saw not as an elevation but as a descent into the darkest depths. And to thrust that upon him behind his back, while he was in the midst of some valiant if misguided attempt to restore peace to the world without resorting to arms—why, it was cruelty, it was most monstrous cruelty indeed.

Yet reasons of state demanded it. Was there ever a time when reasons of state might countenance cruelty? Hissune knew what Lord Valentine would reply to such a question. But he was not wholly certain of his own answer.

He said after a time, "It may be so that Valentine is not the right Coronal for this time: I am of two minds on that score, and I would prefer to know more before I make an answer. I do tell you that I would not care to see him forcibly removed from office—has such a thing ever happened on Majipoor? I think not—but fortunately it would not be necessary to handle things that way, as we all recognize. However, I think we can leave the entire issue of Valentine's adequacy in this time of crisis to discuss another time. What we should be examining, regardless of all these other matters, is the line of succession."

There was a sudden tense stirring in the Council Room. Divvis's eyes sought Hissune's as though he were trying to penetrate the secrets of his soul. The Duke of Halanx reddened; the Prince of Banglecode sat stiffly upright; the Duke of Chorg leaned intently forward; only the two oldest men,

Cantalis and Ghizmaile, remained still, as if the actual matter of choosing a particular person to be Coronal was beyond the concern of those who knew they had only a short while to live.

Hissune went on, "In this discussion we have chosen to ignore one gigantic aspect of Tunigorn's message: that Elidath, who has so long been considered the heir to Lord Valentine, is dead."

"Elidath did not want to be Coronal," said Stasilaine in a voice almost too soft to be heard.

"That may be so," Hissune replied. "Certainly he gave no sign of hungering for the throne once he had a taste of the regency. But my point is only that the tragic loss of Elidath removes the man to whom the crown would surely have been offered if Lord Valentine were no longer Coronal. With him gone we have no clear plan of succession; and we may learn tomorrow that Lord Valentine is dead, or that Tyeveras himself is finally dead, or that events require us to engineer the removal of Valentine from his present office. We should be prepared for any of those eventualities. We are the ones who will choose the next Coronal: do we know who that will be?"

"Are you asking us to vote on an order of succession right now?" Prince Manganot of Banglecode demanded.

"It seems clear enough already," said Mirigant. "The Coronal appointed a Regent when he went off on the grand processional, and the Regent appointed three more—I assume with Lord Valentine's approval—when he too left the Castle. Those three have governed us for some months. If we must find a new Coronal, shall we not find it among those three?"

Stasilaine said, "You frighten me, Mirigant. Once I thought it would be a grand thing to be Coronal, as I suppose most of you also thought, when you were boys. I am a boy no longer, and I saw how Elidath changed, and not for the better, when the full weight of power descended upon him. Let me be the first to fall down in homage before the new Coronal. But let him be someone other than Stasilaine!"

"The Coronal," said the Duke of Chorg, "should never be a man who hungers too deeply for the crown. But I think he ought not to be one who dreads it, either."

"I thank you, Elzandir," said Stasilaine. "I am not a candidate, is it understood?"

"Divvis? Hissune?" Mirigant said.

Hissune felt a muscle leaping about in one of his cheeks, and a strange numbness in his arms and shoulders. He looked toward Divvis. The older man smiled and shrugged, and said nothing. There was a roaring in Hissune's ears, a throbbing at his temples. Should he speak? What was he to say? Now that it had come down to it at last, could he stand before these princes and blithely announce that he was willing to be Coronal? He felt that Divvis was engaged in some maneuver far beyond his comprehension; and for the first time since he had entered the Council Chamber this afternoon he had no idea of the direction to follow.

The silence seemed unending.

Then he heard his own voice—calm, even, measured— saying, "I think we need not carry the proceedings beyond this point. Two candidates have emerged: consideration of their qualifications seems now in order. Not here. Not today. For the moment we have done enough. What do you say, Divvis?"

"You speak wisely and with deep understanding, Hissune. As always."

"Then I call for adjournment," said Mirigant, "while we consider these matters and wait for the arrival of further news of the Coronal."

Hissune held up a hand. "One other thing, first."

He waited for their attention.

Then he said, "I have for some time wished to travel to the Labyrinth, to visit my family, to see certain friends. I believe also it would be useful for one of us to confer with the officials of the Pontifex, and get first-hand knowledge of the state of Tyeveras's health; for it may be that we will have to choose a Pontifex and a Coronal both, in the months just ahead, and we should be ready for such a unique event if it comes upon us. So I propose the designation of an official embassy from Castle Mount to the Labyrinth, and I offer myself as the ambassador."

"Seconded," said Divvis at once.

There was a business of discussing and voting, and once that was done there was a vote for adjournment, and then the meeting dissolved into a swirl of smaller groups. Hissune stood by himself, wondering when he would awaken from all this. He became aware after a moment of tall fair-haired Stasilaine looming over him, frowning and smiling both at the same time.

Quietly Stasilaine said, "Perhaps it is a mistake to leave the Castle at such a time, Hissune."

"Perhaps. It seemed the right thing for me to do, though. I'll risk it."

"Then proclaim yourself Coronal before you go!"

"Are you serious, Stasilaine? What if Valentine still lives?"

"If he lives, you know how to arrange for his becoming Pontifex. If he is dead, Hissune, you must seize his place while you can."

"I will do no such thing."

"You must! Otherwise you may find Divvis on the throne when you return!"

Hissune grinned. "Easily enough dealt with. If Valentine is dead and Divvis has replaced him, I will see to it that Tyeveras at last is allowed to rest. Divvis immediately becomes Pontifex and must go to the Labyrinth, and still another new Coronal is required, with only one candidate available."

"By the Lady, you are astonishing!"

"Am I? It seems an obvious enough move to me." Hissune took the older man's hand firmly in his. "I thank you for your support, Stasilaine. And I tell you that all will be well, at the end. If I must be Coronal to Divvis's Pontifex, so be it: we can work together, he and I, I do think. But for now let us pray for Lord Valentine's safety and success, and leave off all these speculations. Yes?"

"By all means," said Stasilaine.

They embraced briefly, and Hissune went from the council chamber. In the hallway outside, all was in the same confusion as before, though now perhaps a hundred or more of the lesser lords were gathered, and the looks that he received from them when he appeared were extraordinary. But Hissune said nothing to any of them, nor did he as much as let his eyes meet any of theirs as he moved through the throng. He found Alsimir at the edge of the crowd, gaping at him in a preposterous slack-jawed wide-eyed way. Hissune beckoned to him and told him to make ready for a journey to the Labyrinth.

The young knight looked at Hissune in total awe and said, "I should tell you, my lord, that a tale came through this crowd some minutes ago that you are to be made Coronal. Will you tell me if there is truth to that?"

"Lord Valentine is our Coronal," said Hissune brusquely.

"Now go and prepare yourself for departure. I mean to set out for the Labyrinth at dawn."

6

When she was still a dozen blocks from home, Millilain began to hear the rhythmic shouting in the streets ahead of her: "*Yah*-tah, *yah*-tah, *yah*-tah, *voom*," or something like that, nonsensical sounds, gibberish, pounded out at full-throated volume again and again and again by what sounded like a thousand madmen. She came to a halt and pressed herself fearfully against an old crumbling stone wall, feeling trapped. Behind her, in the square, a bunch of drunken March-men were roistering about, smashing windows and molesting passersby. Somewhere off to the east the Knights of Dekkeret were holding a rally in honor of Lord Sempeturn. And now this new craziness. *Yah*-tah, *yah*-tah, *yah*-tah, *voom*. There was no place to turn. There was no place to hide. All she wanted to do was to reach her house safely and bolt the door. The world had gone crazy. *Yah*-tah, *yah*-tah, *yah*-tah, *voom*.

It was like a sending of the King of Dreams, except that it went on hour after hour, day after day, month after month. Even the worst of sendings, though it might leave you shaken to the roots of your soul, lasted only a short while. But this never ended. And it grew worse and worse.

Riots and lootings all the time. No food but scraps and crusts, or occasionally a bit of meat that you might be able to buy from the March-men. They came down out of their mountains with animals they had killed, and sold you the meat for a ruinous price, if you had anything left to pay for it with, and then they drank up their profits and ran amok in the streets before they went home. And new troubles constantly springing up. The sea dragons, so it was said, were sinking any vessel that ventured out to sea, and commerce between the continents was virtually at an end. Lord Valentine was rumored to be dead. And not one new Coronal in Khyntor now but two, Sempeturn and that Hjort who called himself Lord Stiamot. And each with his own little army to march up and down shouting slogans and making trouble: Sempeturn with the Knights of Dekkeret, the other one with the Order of the Triple Sword, or some such name. Kristofon was a

Knight of Dekkeret now. She hadn't seen him in two weeks. Another Coronal in Ni-moya, and a couple of Pontifexes roaming around also. Now this. *Yah*-tah *yah*-tah *yah*-tah *voom*.

Whatever that was, she didn't want to get any closer to it. Most likely it was one more new Coronal with one more mob of hysterical followers. Millilain looked about warily, wondering if she dared go down Dizimaule Street and cut through the back alleyway to Malamola Road, which would run into her street a few blocks below the Voriax Causeway. The problem was that alleyway—she had heard some strange stories about what had been going on in there lately—

Night was coming on. A light rain, little more than a heavy mist, began to fall. She felt lightheaded and dizzy from hunger, though she was becoming accustomed to that. Out of the south, from the suburb of Hot Khyntor where all the geothermal formations were, came the sullen booming of Confalume Geyser, punctual as ever, marking the hour. Automatically Millilain looked toward it and saw its great column of steam rising heavenward, with a broad sulphurous mantle of yellow smoke surrounding it and seeming to fill half the sky. She had been looking at the geysers of Hot Khyntor all her life, taking them completely for granted, but somehow tonight the eruption frightened her as never before, and she made the sign of the Lady again and again until it began to subside.

The Lady. Did she still watch over Majipoor? What had become of her kindly sendings that gave such good counsel and warm comfort? For that matter, where was the King of Dreams? Once, in quieter times, those two Powers had kept everyone's life in balance, advising, admonishing, if necessary punishing. Perhaps they still reigned, Millilain thought: but the situation was so far out of hand that neither King nor Lady could possibly cope with it, though they might labor from dawn to dawn to bring matters back under control. It was a system designed to work beautifully in a world where most people gladly obeyed the law anyway. But now hardly anyone obeyed the law. There *was* no law.

Yah-tah *yah*-tah *yah*-tah *voom*.

And from the other side:

"Sempeturn! Lord Sempeturn! Hail, hail, hail, Lord Sempeturn!"

The rain was coming down harder, now. Get moving, she

told herself. March-men in the square, and the Divine only knows what madness ahead of you, and the Knights of Dekkeret cavorting behind you—trouble, any way at all. And even if Kristofon was among the Knights, she didn't want to see him, eyes glassy with devotion, hands upraised in the new form of the starburst salute. She began to run. Across Malibor to Dizimaule, down Dizimaule toward that little alleyway connecting with Malamola—did she dare?

Yah-tah *yah*-tah *yah*-tah *voom*.

A line of paraders coming up Dizimaule Street toward her, suddenly! Walking like some sort of soulless machines, nine or ten abreast, arms swinging stiffly up and down, right left right left, and that chant bursting from them in an endless insistent jabbing rhythm. They would parade right over her and never see her. She made a quick turn into the alleyway, only to find a horde of men and women with green-and-gold armbands clogging the far end and screaming in praise of the new Lord Stiamot.

Trapped! All the lunatics were out at once tonight!

Desperately glancing about, Millilain saw a door half ajar on the left-hand side of the alleyway and ducked quickly into it. She found herself in a dark corridor, with faint chanting and the sharp scent of a strange incense coming from a room at the far end of it. A shrine of some sort. One of the new cults, maybe. But at least they were unlikely to hurt her, here. She might be able to stay until all the various demented mobs outside had moved along to another part of town.

Cautiously she moved down the corridor and peered into the room at the end. Dark. Fragrant. A dais at one side and what looked like two small dried sea dragons mounted like flagpoles at either end of it. A Liiman standing between them, somber, silent, triple eyes burning like smouldering coals. Millilain thought she recognized him: the street vendor who once had sold her a skewer of sausages for five crowns. But maybe not. It was hard to tell one Liiman from the next, after all.

A hooded figure who smelled like a Ghayrog came up to her and whispered, "You are in time for communion, sister. Welcome and the peace of the water-kings be upon you."

The water-kings?

The Ghayrog took her gently by the elbow and just as gently propelled her into the room, so that she could take her place among the kneeling, murmuring congregation. No one looked at her; no one was looking at anyone else; all eyes were on the Liiman between the two little dried sea dragons. Millilain looked toward him too. She dared not glance about at those alongside her, for fear she might find friends of hers here.

"Take—drink—join—" the Liiman commanded.

They were passing wine-bowls from aisle to aisle. Out of the corner of her eye Millilain saw that each worshiper, when the bowl came to him, put it to his lips and drank deeply, so that the bowls had constantly to be refilled as they moved through the room. The closest one was four or five rows ahead of her just then.

The Liiman said, "We drink. We join. We go forth and embrace the water-king."

Water-kings were what the Liimen called the sea dragons. Millilain remembered. They worshipped the dragons, so it was reported. Well, she thought, maybe there's something to it. Everything else has failed: give the world to the sea dragons. The wine-bowl, she saw, was two rows ahead of her now, but moving slowly.

"We went among the water-kings and hunted them and took them from the sea," said the Liiman. "We ate their flesh and drank their milk. And this was their gift to us and their great willing sacrifice, for they are gods and it is right and proper for gods to give their flesh and their milk to lesser folk, to nurture them and make them like gods themselves. And now the time of the water-kings is coming. Take. Drink. Join."

The bowl was passing down Millilain's row.

"They are the great ones of the world," the Liiman intoned. "They are the masters. They are the monarchs. They are the true Powers, and we belong to them. We and all others who live on Majipoor. Take. Drink. Join."

The woman at Millilain's left was drinking from the wine-bowl now. A savage impatience came over her—she was so hungry, she was so thirsty!—and she was barely able to restrain herself from pulling the bowl from the woman's grasp, fearing none would be left for her. But she waited; and then the bowl was in her hands. She stared down into it: a dark wine, thick, glossy. It looked strange. Hesitantly she took a sip. It was sweet and spicy, and heavy on her tongue, and at first she thought it was like no wine she had ever

tasted, but then it seemed that there was something familiar
about it. She took another sip.

"Take. Drink. Join."

Why, it was the wine dream-speakers used, when they
made their communion with your mind and spoke the dream
that was troubling you! That was it, surely, dream-wine.
Though Millilain had been to a dream-speaker only five or six
times, and not for years, she recognized the unmistakable
flavor of the stuff. But how could that be? Only dream-
speakers were allowed to use it, or even to possess it. It was a
powerful drug. It was to be used only under a speaker's
supervision. But somehow in this backroom chapel they had
vats and vats of it, and the congregation was guzzling it as
though it were beer—

"Take. Drink. Join."

She realized she was holding up the passing of the bowl.
She turned to the man on her right with a silly grin and an
apology, but he was staring rigidly forward and paid no heed
to her; so with a shrug she put the bowl to her lips and took a
deep reckless gulp, and then another, and handed the bowl
onward.

Almost at once she felt the effect. She swayed, blinked,
had to struggle to keep her head from falling forward against
her knees. It's because I drank it on an empty stomach, she
told herself. She crouched down, leaned forward, began to
chant along with the congregation, a low wordless meaningless repetitious murmur, *oo wah vah mah, oo wah vah mah*,
just as absurd as what those others had been shouting in the
street, but somehow gentler, a tender crooning yearning cry,
oo wah vah mah, oo wah vah mah. And as she chanted it
seemed to her that she heard a distant music, weird, other-
worldly, the sound of many bells far away, ringing in patterns
of overlapping changes that were impossible to follow for
long, since one strand of melody quickly became lost inside
its successor, and that one in the next. *Oo wah vah mah*, she
sang, and back to her came the song of the bells, and then
she had a sense of something immense very close by, perhaps
even in this very room, something colossal and winged and
ancient and enormously intelligent, something whose intel-
lect was as far beyond her comprehension as hers would be
beyond a bird's. It was turning and turning and turning in
vast unhurried orbits, and each time it turned it unfolded its
giant wings and spread them to the ends of the world, and

when it folded them again they brushed against the gates of Millilain's mind—just a tickle, just the lightest of touches, a feather-whisk, and yet she felt herself transformed by it, lifted out of herself, made part of some organism of many minds, unimaginable, godlike. *Take. Drink. Join.* With each touch of those wings she joined more profoundly. *Oh wah vah mah. Oo wah vah mah.* She was lost. There was no more Millilain. There was only the water-king whose sound was the sound of bells, and the many-minded mind of which the former Millilain had become a part. *Oo. Wah. Vah. Mah.*

It frightened her. She was being drugged down to the bottom of the sea, and her lungs were filling with water, and the pain was terrible. She fought. She would not let the great wings touch her. She pulled back, and pounded with her fists, and forced her way upward, up toward the surface—

Opened her eyes. Sat up, dazed, terrified. All about her the chanting was going on. *Oo, wah, vah, mah.* Millilain shuddered. *Where am I? What have I done? I've got to get out of here,* she thought. In panic she struggled to her feet and went blundering down the row to the aisle. No one stopped her. The wine still muzzed her mind and she found herself lurching, staggering, clutching at the walls. She was out of the room, now. Stumbling down that long dark fragrant corridor. The wings were still beating about her, enfolding her, reaching toward her mind. *What have I done, what have I done?*

Out into the alleyway, the darkness, the rain. Were they still marching around out here, the Knights of Dekkeret and the Order of the Triple Sword and whoever those others were? She did not care. Let whatever come that may. She began to run, not knowing which way she ran. There was a dull heavy booming sound far away that she hoped was the Confalume Geyser. Other sounds pounded in her mind. *Yah-tah yah-tah yah-tah voom. Oo, wah, vah, mah.* She felt the wings closing about her. She ran, and tripped and fell, and rose and went on running.

7

The deeper they journeyed into the Shapeshifter province, the more familiar everything began to look to Valentine. And yet at the same time the conviction had come to grow in him that he was making some ghastly and terrible mistake.

He remembered the scent of the place: rich, musky, complex, the sweet heavy aroma of growth and decay going forward with equal intensities under the constant warm rainfall, an intricate mix of flavors that flooded the nostrils to dizzying effect at every intake of breath. He remembered the close, clinging, moist air, and the showers that fell almost hourly, pattering against the forest roof high overhead and trickling down from leaf to shiny leaf until just a little reached the ground. He remembered the fantastic profusion of plant life, everything sprouting and uncoiling almost while one watched, and yet somehow oddly disciplined, everything fitting into well-defined layers—the towering slender trees bare of branches for seven eighths of their height, then flaring out into great umbrellas of leaves tied together into a tight canopy by a tangle of vines and creepers and epiphytes, and under that a level of shorter, rounder, fuller, more shade-tolerant trees, and a stratum of clumping shrubbery below that, and then the forest floor, dark, mysterious, all but barren, a stark expanse of damp thin spongy soil that bounced jauntily underfoot. He remembered the sudden shafts of light, deep-hued and alien, that came spearing at unpredictable intervals through the canopy to provide quick startling moments of clarity in the dimness.

But the Piurifayne rain-forest spread over thousands of square miles of the heart of Zimroel, and one part of it very likely looked much like any other part. Somewhere in here was the Shapeshifter capital, Ilirivoyne: but what reason do I have, Valentine asked himself, to think that I am near it, merely because the smells and sounds and textures of this jungle are similar to the smells and sounds and textures I recall from years ago?

That other time—traveling with the wandering jugglers, when they had taken the mad notion that they might earn a few royals by going to perform at the Metamorphs' harvest festival—there had at least been Deliamber to cast a few Vroonish spells to sniff out the right fork in the road, and the valiant Lisamon Hultin, also wise in the ways of jungle lore. But on this second venture into Piurifayne Valentine was entirely on his own.

Deliamber and Lisamon, if they were still alive at all— and he was gloomy on that score, for in all these weeks he had had no contact with them even in dreams—were somewhere hundreds of miles behind him, on the far side of the Steiche. Nor had he had any sort of report from Tunigorn, whom he had sent back to look for them. He rode now only with Carabella and Sleet and a bodyguard of Skandars. Carabella had courage and endurance but little skill as a pathfinder, and the Skandars were strong and brave but not very bright, and Sleet, for all his shrewd, sober-minded ways, was in this region hampered greatly by the paralyzing dread of Shapeshifters that had been laid upon him in a dream while he was young, and which he had never fully been able to throw off. It was folly for a Coronal to be roaming the jungles of Piurifayne with so skimpy an entourage: but folly seemed to have become the hallmark of recent Coronals, Valentine thought, considering that his two predecessors, Malibor and Voriax, had met early and violent deaths while off doing foolish things. Perhaps it has become the custom, this rashness of kings.

And it seemed to him that from day to day he was neither getting closer to Ilirivoyne nor farther from it; that it was everywhere and nowhere, in these jungles; that perhaps the whole city had picked itself up and was moving onward just ahead of him, maintaining a constant distance from him, a gap he could never close. For the Shapeshifter capital, as he recalled it from that other time, was a place of flimsy wicker-work buildings, and only a few more substantial ones, and it had seemed to him then a makeshift phantom city that might well flit from one site to another at the whim of its inhabitants: a nomad-city, a dream city, a jungle will-o'-the-wisp.

"Look, there," Carabella said. "Is that a trail, Valentine?"

"Perhaps it is," he said.

"And perhaps not?"

"Perhaps not, yes."

They had seen hundreds of trails much like it: faint scars on the jungle floor, the unreadable imprints of some former presence, imprints made last month, possibly, or possibly in the time of Lord Dekkeret a thousand years before. An occasional stick planted in the ground, with a bit of feather fastened to it, maybe, or a scrap of ribbon; a row of grooves, as of something having been dragged this way once; or sometimes nothing in any way visible, just a psychic spoor, the mystifying vestigial trace of the passage of intelligent beings. But none of these things ever led them anywhere. Sooner or later the clues dwindled and became imperceptible and only virgin jungle lay ahead.

"Shall we make camp, my lord?" Sleet said.

Neither he nor Carabella had spoken a word yet against this expedition, foolhardy though it must seem to them. Did they understand, Valentine wondered, how urgently he felt the need to consummate his meeting with the Shapeshifter queen? Or was it out of fear of the wrath of king and husband that they kept this obliging silence through these weeks of aimless roaming, when surely they must think his time was better spent in the civilized provinces, coping with whatever awful crisis must be unfolding there? Or were they—worst of all—merely humoring him as he spun his mad way through these dense rain-swept glades? He dared not ask. He wondered only how long he would pursue the quest, despite his gathering conviction that he was never to find Ilirivoyne.

When they were settled for the night he donned the Lady's silver circlet and thrust himself once again into the trance state, the mind-casting state, and sent his spirit outward across the jungle, seeking Deliamber, seeking Tisana.

He thought it likely that he could reach their minds more easily than any of the others, sensitive as those two were to the witcheries of dreams. But he had tried, night after night, without ever once feeling a flicker of contact. Was distance the problem? Valentine had never attempted long-range mindcasting except with the aid of dream-wine, and he had none of that there. Or perhaps the Metamorphs had some way of intercepting or disrupting his transmissions. Or perhaps his messages were not getting through because those he was sending them to were dead. Or—

—*Tisana—Tisana*—

—*Deliamber*—

—*This is Valentine calling you—Valentine—Valentine—Valentine*—

—*Tisana*—

—*Deliamber*—

Nothing.

He tried reaching Tunigorn. Surely Tunigorn still lived, no matter what calamity had overtaken the others; and though his mind was stolid and well defended, nevertheless there was always the hope it might open to one of Valentine's probes. Or Lisamon's. Or Zalzan Kavol's. To touch any of them, to feel the familiar response of a familiar mind—

He went on for a time; and then, sadly, he removed the circlet and restored it to its case. Carabella gave him an inquiring glance. Valentine shook his head and shrugged. "It's very quiet out there," he said.

"Except for the rain."

"Yes. Except for the rain."

The rain was drumming delicately against the lofty forest canopy once more. Valentine peered gloomily into the jungle, but he saw nothing: the floater's beam was on, and would stay on all night, but beyond the golden sphere of light that that created lay only a wall of blackness. A thousand Metamorphs might be gathered in a ring around the camp, for all he knew. He wished it were so. Anything—even a surprise attack—would be preferable to these foolish weeks of wandering in an unknown and unknowable wilderness.

How long, he asked himself, am I going to keep this up?

And how are we ever going to find our way out of here, once I decide that this quest is absurd?

He listened somberly to the changing rhythms of the rain until he drifted finally into sleep.

Almost at once, he felt the onset of a dream.

By its intensity and by a certain vividness and warmth he knew it to be no ordinary dream but rather a sending of the Lady, the first he had had since leaving the coast of Gihorna; and yet as he waited for some tangible sign of the presence of his mother in his mind he grew perplexed, for she had not announced herself, and indeed the impulses penetrating his soul seemed to come from another source entirely. The King of Dreams? He too had the power to enter minds from afar, of course; but not even in such strange times as these would the King of Dreams presume to aim his instrument at the Coronal. Who, then? Valentine, watchful even in sleep, scanned the boundaries of his dream, seeking and not finding an answer.

The dream was almost entirely without narrative structure: it was a thing of shapeless forms and silent sounds, creating a sense of event by purely abstract means. But gradually the dream presented him with a cluster of moving images and slippery shifts of mood that became a metaphor for something quite concrete: the writhing, interlacing tentacles of a Vroon.

—*Deliamber?*

—*I am here, my lord.*

—*Where?*

—*Here. Close by you. Moving toward you.*

That much was communicated not in any kind of speech, mental or otherwise, but entirely through a grammar of shifting patterns of light and mind-state that carried unambiguous meaning. After a while the dream left him, and he lay still, neither awake nor asleep, reflecting on what had come to him; and for the first time in weeks he felt some sense of hope.

In the morning as Sleet was preparing to strike camp Valentine said, "No. I plan to remain here another few days. Or possibly even longer."

A look of doubt and confusion, instantly suppressed but briefly evident, passed across Sleet's face. But he merely nodded and went off to tell the Skandars to leave the tents as they were.

Carabella said, "This night has brought you news, my lord. I see that in your face."

"Deliamber lives. He and the others have been following us, trying to rejoin us. But we've been drifting about so much, traveling so quickly—they can't catch up with us. As soon as they have a fix on us, we head off in some new direction. If we remain in one place they'll be able to find us."

"You spoke with the Vroon, then?"

"With his image, with his shadow. But it was the true shadow, the authentic image. He'll be with us soon."

And indeed Valentine had no doubt of that. But a day passed, and another, and another. Each night he donned his circlet and sent forth a signal, and had no response. The Skandar guards took to prowling the jungle like restless beasts; Sleet grew tense and fidgety, and went off alone for hours at a time, despite the fear of Metamorphs he claimed to feel. Carabella, seeing matters growing so edgy, suggested that he and she and Valentine do a little juggling, for the sake of old times and to give themselves an amusement so demanding it would draw their minds away from other concerns; but Sleet said he had no heart for it and Valentine, when he agreed at her urging to try it, was so fumble-fingered from lack of practice that he would have abandoned the attempt in the first five minutes, but for Carabella's insistence. "Of *course* you're rusty!" she said. "Do you think the skill stays sharp without some honing? But it comes back, if you work at it. Here, Valentine: catch! Catch! Catch!"

Indeed she was right. A little effort, and he began to feel once more the old sense that the union of hand and eye could carry him to a place where time had no meaning and all of space became a single infinite point. The Skandars, though they must surely have known that juggling had once been Valentine's profession, were plainly astounded at seeing a Coronal do any such thing, and gaped in undisguised curiosity and awe as Valentine and Carabella tossed a motley galaxy of objects back and forth to one another.

"Hoy!" she cried, and "Hoy!" and "Hoy!" as she led him on to ever more complex feats. They were nothing compared with the tricks she had routinely performed in the old days, for her skill had been great indeed, and they were trivial even in comparison with the level of technique that Valentine, never Carabella's equal as a juggler, once had mastered. But it was fair going, he thought, for someone who had not juggled seriously in close to a decade. Within an hour, rain soaked and sweat soaked though he was, he felt better than he had in months.

Sleet appeared and, watching them, seemed to draw out of his anxiety and gloom; after a while he moved closer, and Carabella tossed a knife and a club and a hatchet to him, and he caught them casually and began to weave them into a lofty playful cascade to which he added three more things that Valentine sent his way. There was perhaps a shade of strain visible on Sleet's face that would not have been there a decade ago—except when he was doing his famous routine of juggling blindfolded, maybe—but in no other way did he betray any lessening of his great skill. "Hoy!" he cried, sending the club and the hatchet back toward Valentine, and remorselessly sending other things Valentine's way before the Coronal had caught the first. Then he and Valentine and Carabella went at it with very great seriousness indeed, as though they were wandering jugglers once more, and were rehearsing for a performance before the royal court.

Sleet's display of virtuosity inspired Carabella to some

intricate feats of her own, which led Sleet to call for some even more difficult maneuvers, and before long Valentine was totally out of his depth. All the same he attempted to keep up with them as long as he could, and did a creditable job at it, only dropping an occasional thing—until he found himself bombarded from both sides at once by a laughing Carabella and a cool, intense Sleet: and he found himself suddenly all elbows and no fingers, and allowed everything to go tumbling from his grasp.

"Ah, my lord, that's no way to do it!" boomed a harsh and wonderfully familiar voice.

"Zalzan Kavol?" Valentine cried in amazement and glee.

The huge Skandar came bounding toward him, quickly making the starburst salute and then scooping up all the things that Valentine had dropped; and with a manic delight he began to toss them at Sleet and Carabella in that wild four-armed way of his that could push any human juggler, no matter how skilled, to the limits of his ability.

Valentine looked deeper into the jungle and saw the others running through the rain: Lisamon Hultin, with the Vroon perched on her shoulder, Tunigorn, Tisana, Ermanar, Shanamir, and still more, erupting one after another from a battered and mud-splattered floater parked not far away. All of them had come, Valentine realized—everyone whom he had left behind in Gihorna, the entire party reunited at last. "Get out the wine!" he cried. "This calls for celebration!" He rushed among them, embracing this one and that, straining upward to throw his arms about the giantess, pummeling Shanamir joyfully, clasping hands solemnly with the dignified Ermanar, seizing Tunigorn in a hug that might have throttled a weaker man.

"My lord," shouted Lisamon, "you will never go off by yourself again, so long as I live! With all respects, my lord. Never again! Never!"

"If I had known, my lord," said Zalzan Kavol, "that when you said you would travel a day's journey ahead of us to the Steiche, that there was going to be a storm of such force, and that we would not see you again for this many weeks—ah, my lord, what kind of guardians do you think we are, to let you escape from us this way? When Tunigorn said you had survived the storm, but had gone chasing off into Piurifayne without waiting for us—ah, my lord, my lord, if you were not my lord I would have wanted to commit treason upon you when I caught up with you again, believe me, my lord!"

"And will you forgive me this escapade?" Valentine asked.

"My lord, my lord!"

"You know it was never my intention to separate myself from you this long. That was why I sent Tunigorn back, to find you and have you come after me. And each night I sent messages to you—I put the circlet on, I strived with all my mind's strength to reach out and touch you—you, Deliamber, and you, Tisana—"

"Those messages reached us, my lord," said Deliamber.

"They did?"

"Night after night. It gave us much joy, knowing that you were alive."

"And you made no reply?" Valentine asked.

"Ah, my lord, we replied every time," the Vroon said. "But we knew we were not getting through, that my power was not strong enough over such a distance. We longed to tell you to stay where you were, and let us come to you; but every day you were farther into the jungle, and there was no holding you back, and we were unable to overtake you, and I could not reach your mind, my lord. I could not reach your mind."

"But finally you did get through."

"With the help of your mother the Lady," said Deliamber. "Tisana went to her in sleep, and won from her a sending, and the Lady understood; and she made of her own mind the courier for mine, carrying me where I could not go myself. And that was how we spoke to you at last. My lord, there is so much to tell you, now!"

"Indeed," said Tunigorn. "You'll be astonished, Valentine. I pledge you that."

"Astonish me, then," Valentine said.

Deliamber said, "Tunigorn has told you, I think, that we discovered the agricultural expert Y-Uulisaan to be a Shapeshifter spy?"

"So he has told me, yes. But how was this discovered?"

"The day you set out for the Steiche, my lord, we came upon Y-Uulisaan deep in the communion of minds with some far-off person. I felt his mind reaching forth; I felt the force of the communion. And immediately I asked Zalzan Kavol and Lisamon to apprehend him."

Valentine blinked. "How could Y-Uulisaan possibly have had such a power?"

"Because he was a Shapeshifter, my lord," said Tisana, "and the Shapeshifters have a way of linking mind to mind using the great sea-dragon kings as their joining-place."

Like a man who has been attacked from two sides at once, Valentine glanced from Tisana to Deliamber, and back at the old dream-speaker again. He struggled to absorb the meaning of the things they had said, but there was so much in them that was strange, that was entirely bewildering, that he could at first grasp very little. "It baffles me," he said, "to hear of Metamorphs speaking to one another through sea dragons. Who could have supposed the dragons had any such power of mind?"

"Water-kings, my lord, is what they call them," Tisana said. "And it appears that the water-kings have very powerful minds indeed. Which enabled the spy to file his reports with great ease."

"Reports on what?" said Valentine uneasily. "And to whom?"

"When we found Y-Uulisaan in this communion," said Deliamber, "Lisamon and Zalzan Kavol seized him, and he at once began to change his shape. We would have brought him to you for interrogation, but you had gone ahead to the river, and then the storm began and we could not follow. So we interrogated him ourselves. He admitted that he was a spy, my lord, who would help you to formulate the government's response to the plagues and blights, and then immediately send word of what that response would be. Which was of great aid to the Metamorphs as they went about the business of causing and spreading those plagues."

Valentine gasped. "The Metamorphs—causing the plagues—spreading the plagues—?"

"Yes, my lord. Y-Uulisaan told us all. We were—ah—not gentle with him. In secret laboratories here in Piurifayne the Metamorphs have for years developed cultures of every enemy of our crops that has ever afflicted them. And when they were ready, they went forth in a thousand disguises—some of them, my lord, actually went to farmers masquerading as provincial agricultural agents, pretending to offer new ways of increasing farm yield, and secretly scattered their poisons over the fields while inspecting them. And also certain creatures were let loose by air, carried by birds that the Metamorphs released. Or things were sprayed, and became drifting clouds—"

Stunned, Valentine looked toward Sleet and said, "Then we have been at war, and did not know it!"

"We know it now, my lord," said Tunigorn.

"And I have been traveling through the kingdom of my enemy, thinking in my foolishness that all I needed to do was speak soft words, and open my arms in love, and the Danipiur would smile and the Divine would bless us once again. But in truth the Danipiur and her people have been waging a terrible war against us all the while, and—"

"No, my lord," Deliamber said. "Not the Danipiur. Not so far as we know."

"What do you say?"

"The one whom Y-Uulisaan served is named Faraataa, a being consumed with hate, a wild man, who could not get the Danipiur to give her backing to his program, and therefore went off with his followers to launch it himself. There are two factions among the Metamorphs, do you see, my lord? This Faraataa leads the radical ones, the war-hungry ones. It is their plan to starve us into chaos and compel us to leave Majipoor. Whereas the Danipiur appears to be more moderate, or at least less fierce."

"Then I must continue toward Ilirivoyne and speak with her."

"You will never find Ilirivoyne, my lord," said Deliamber.

"And why is that?"

"They have taken the city apart, and they carry it on their backs through the jungle. I feel its presence when I cast my spells—but it is a presence that moves. The Danipiur flees you, my lord. She does not want to meet with you. Perhaps it is too dangerous politically—perhaps she is unable to control her own people any longer, and fears they will all go over to the faction of Faraataa if she shows any favor toward you. I am only guessing, my lord. But I tell you, you will never find her, even if you search in this jungle a thousand years."

Valentine nodded. "Probably you are right, Deliamber. *Certainly* you are right." He closed his eyes and sought desperately to quell the turmoil in his mind. How badly he had misjudged things; how little he had understood! "This communication between Metamorphs through the minds of sea dragons—how long has that been going on?"

"Perhaps quite some time, my lord. The sea dragons appear to be more intelligent than we have thought—and there seems to be some kind of alliance between them and the Metamorphs, or at least with some Metamorphs. It is very unclear."

"And Y-Uulisaan? Where is he? We should question him further on these things."

"Dead, my lord," said Lisamon Hultin.

"How is that?"

"When the storm struck, all was confusion, and he attempted to escape. We recaptured him for a moment, but then the wind tore him from my grasp and it was impossible to find him again. We discovered his body the next day."

"A small loss, my lord," Deliamber said. "We could have extracted little else from him."

"I would have liked the chance to speak with him, all the same," Valentine replied. "Well, it will not happen. Nor will I speak with the Danipiur either, I suppose. But it is hard for me to abandon that idea. Is there utterly no hope of finding Ilirivoyne, Deliamber?"

"None, I think, my lord."

"I see her as an ally: does that sound strange to you? The Metamorph queen and the Coronal, joined in league against those who wage biological warfare against us. Folly, eh, Tunigorn? Come, speak openly: you think it's folly."

Tunigorn shrugged. "On that score I can say very little, Valentine. I know only that I believe Deliamber is right: the Danipiur wants no meeting with you, and will not allow herself to be found. And I think that to spend further time in quest of her now—"

"Would be foolish. Yes. Folly indeed, while there's so much for me to do elsewhere."

Valentine fell silent. Absentmindedly he took a couple of the juggling implements from Zalzan Kavol and began to toss them from hand to hand. Plagues, famines, false Coronals, he thought. Madness. Chaos. Biological warfare. The anger of the Divine made manifest. And the Coronal trekking endlessly through the Metamorph jungle on a fool's mission? No. No.

To Deliamber he said, "Do you have any idea where we are now?"

"As best I can calculate, some nineteen hundred miles southwest of Piliplok, my lord."

"How long, then, do you think it would take us to get there?"

Tunigorn said, "I wouldn't go to Piliplok at all just now, Valentine."

Frowning, Valentine said, "Why so?"

"The danger."

"Danger? For a Coronal? I was there just a month or two ago, Tunigorn, and I saw no danger!"

"Things have changed. Piliplok has proclaimed itself a free republic, so the word reaches us. The citizens of Piliplok, still having ample food supplies in storage, were fearful of having those supplies requisitioned for use in Khyntor and Ni-moya; and so Piliplok has seceded from the commonwealth."

Valentine stared as though into an infinite abyss. "Seceded? A free republic? These words have no meaning!"

"Nevertheless, they seem to have meaning for the citizens of Piliplok. We have no idea what sort of reception they would give you these days. I think it might be wise to go elsewhere until the situation becomes clearer," Tunigorn said.

Angrily Valentine responded, "How can I permit myself to fear entering one of my own cities? Piliplok would return to its allegiance the moment I arrived!"

Carabella said, "Can you be certain of that? Here is Piliplok, puffed up with pride and selfishness: and here comes the Coronal, arriving in a worn-out floater, wearing mildewed rags. And will they hail you, do you think? They have committed treason, and they know it. They might compound that treason rather than risk yielding themselves mildly up to your authority. Best not to enter Piliplok except at the head of an army, I say!"

"And I," Tunigorn added.

Valentine looked in dismay toward Deliamber, toward Sleet, toward Ermanar. They met his gaze silently, solemnly, sadly, bleakly.

"Then am I overthrown again?" Valentine asked, of no one in particular. "A ragged wanderer once more, am I? I dare not enter Piliplok? I *dare* not? And false Coronals in Khyntor and Ni-moya: they have armies, I suppose, and I have none, so I dare not go there either. What shall I do, become a juggler a second time?" He laughed. "No, I think not. Coronal is what I am: Coronal is what I shall remain. I thought I was done with this business of making repairs to my place in the world, but evidently not. Get me out of this

jungle, Deliamber. Find me my way to the coast, to some
port city that still gives me homage. And then we'll go forth
in search of allies, and set things to rights all over again, eh?"

"And where shall we find those allies, my lord?" Sleet
asked.

"Wherever we can," said Valentine with a shrug.

8

Throughout the journey down from Castle Mount through
the valley of the Glayge to the Labyrinth, Hissune had seen
signs, wherever he looked, of the turmoil that lay upon the
land. Although in this gentle and fertile region of Alhanroel
the situation had not yet grown as troubled as it was farther
west, or in Zimroel, there was nevertheless a visible and
virtually tangible tension everywhere: locked gates, frightened eyes, clenched faces. But in the Labyrinth itself, he
thought, nothing seemed greatly to have changed, perhaps
because the Labyrinth had always been a place of locked
gates, frightened eyes, clenched faces.

Though the Labyrinth might not have changed, Hissune
had; and the change was evident to him from the moment he
entered the Mouth of Waters, that grand and opulent ceremonial gateway traditionally used by the Powers of Majipoor
when coming into the city of the Pontifex. Behind him lay the
warm hazy afternoon of the Glayge Valley, fragrant breezes,
green hills, the joyous throbbing glow of rich sunlight. Ahead
lay the eternal night of the Labyrinth's secretive hermetic
coils, the hard glitter of artificial lighting, the strange lifelessness
of air that has never known the touch of wind or rain. And as
he passed from the one realm to the other, Hissune imagined
for just a flickering instant that a massive gate was clanging
shut behind him, that some horrific barrier now separated
him from all that was beautiful in the world; and he felt a chill
of fear.

It surprised him that a mere year or two on Castle
Mount could have worked such a transformation in him—that
the Labyrinth, which he doubted he had ever loved, but
where he had certainly felt at ease, should have become so
repellent to him. And it seemed to him that he had not really
understood, until this moment, the dread that Lord Valentine

felt for the place: but Hissune had had a taste of it now, the merest tincture of it, enough to let him see for the first time what kind of terror it was that invaded the Coronal's soul when he undertook this downward journey.

Hissune had changed in another way. When he had taken his leave of the Labyrinth he had been nobody in particular—a knight-initiate, to be sure, but that was no very important thing, especially to Labyrinth dwellers, not easily impressed by such matters of worldly pomp. Now he was returning just a few years later as Prince Hissune of the Council of Regency. Labyrinth dwellers might not be impressed by pomp, but they were by power, especially when it was one of their own that had attained it. Thousands of them lined the road that led from the Mouth of Blades to the Labyrinth's outer ring, and they jostled and shoved to get a better look at him as he came riding through the great gateway aboard a royal floater that bore the Coronal's own colors, and with a retinue of his own as if he were Coronal himself. They did not cheer or scream or call out his name. Labyrinth people were not known to do such things. But they stared. Silent, plainly awe-smitten, very likely envious, they watched him with a sullen fascination as he passed by. He imagined that he saw his old playmate Vanimoon in the crowd, and Vanimoon's pretty sister, and Ghisnet and Heulan and half a dozen others of the old Guadeloom Court bunch. Perhaps not: perhaps it was only a trick of his mind that put them there. He realized that he *wanted* them to be there, wanted them to see him in his princely robes and his grand floater, scrappy little Hissune of Guadeloom Court transformed now into the Regent Prince Hissune, with the aura of the Castle crackling about him like the light of another sun. It's all right to indulge in such petty pride once in a while, isn't it? he asked himself. And he replied, Yes, yes, why not? You can allow yourself a little bit of small-mindedness once in a while. Even saints sometimes must feel smug, and you've never been accused of saintliness. But allow it, and be done with it, and move along to your tasks. A steady diet of self-congratulation bloats the soul.

Pontifical officials in formal masks were waiting for him at the edge of the outer ring. With great solicitousness they greeted Hissune and took him at once to the liftshaft reserved for Powers and their emissaries, which carried him swiftly down to the deep imperial levels of the Labyrinth.

In short order he was installed in a suite nearly as

ostentatious as the one perpetually set aside for the Coronal's own use. Alsimir and Stimion and Hissune's other aides were given elegant rooms of their own adjoining his. When the Pontifical liaison officials were done bustling about seeing to Hissune's comfort, their chief announced to him, "The high spokesman Hornkast will be deeply pleased to dine with you this evening, my lord."

Despite himself, Hissune felt a little shiver of wonder. *Deeply pleased.* He still had enough of the Labyrinth in him to regard Hornkast with veneration bordering on fear: the real master of the Labyrinth, the puppeteer who pulled the Pontifex's strings. *Deeply pleased to dine with you this evening, my lord.* Really? Hornkast? It was hard to imagine old Hornkast deeply pleased about anything, Hissune thought. *My lord,* no less. Well, well, well.

But he could not allow himself to be awed by Hornkast, not a vestige, not a trace. He contrived to be unready when the high spokesman's envoys came calling for him, and was ten minutes late setting out. When he entered the high spokesman's private dining chamber—a hall of such glittering magnificence that even a Pontifex might have found its grandeur excessive—Hissune restrained himself from offering any sort of salute or obeisance, though the impulse fluttered quickly through him. This is *Hornkast*! he thought, and wanted to drop to his knees. But you are *Hissune*! he told himself angrily, and remained standing, dignified, faintly aloof. Hornkast was, Hissune compelled himself to keep in mind, merely a civil servant; whereas he himself was a person of rank, a prince of the Mount, and a member of the Council of Regency as well.

It was difficult, though, not to be swayed by Hornkast's formidable presence and power. He was old—ancient, even— yet he looked robust and energetic and alert, as though a witchery had stripped thirty or forty of his years from him. His eyes were shrewd and implacable, his smile was unsettlingly intricate, his voice deep and strong. With the greatest of courtesy he conducted Hissune to the table and offered him some rare glistening wine, a deep scarlet in hue, of which Hissune prudently took only the most shallow and widely spaced of sips. The conversation, amiable and general at first, then more serious, remained totally in Hornkast's control, and Hissune did not resist that. They spoke at first of the disturbances in Zimroel and western Alhanroel—Hissune had the impression that Hornkast, for all his sober mien as he talked of these things, was no more deeply troubled by anything that took place outside the Labyrinth than he would be by events on some other world—and then the high spokesman came round to the matter of Elidath's death, for which he hoped Hissune would convey full condolences when he returned to the Mount; and Hornkast stared keenly at Hissune as though to say, *I know that the passing of Elidath has worked great changes in the succession, and that you have emerged into a most powerful position, and therefore, O child of this Labyrinth, I am watching you very carefully.* Hissune expected that Hornkast, having heard enough of the news from overseas to be aware that Elidath was dead, would go on now to inquire after the safety of Lord Valentine; but to his amazement the high spokesman chose to speak next of other matters entirely, having to do with certain shortages now manifesting themselves in the granaries of the Labyrinth. No doubt that problem was much on Hornkast's mind, Hissune thought; but it was not primarily to discuss such things that he had undertaken this journey. When the high spokesman paused for a moment Hissune, seizing the initiative at last, said, "But perhaps it is time for us to consider what I think is the most critical event of all, which is the disappearance of Lord Valentine."

For once Hornkast's invincible serenity seemed shaken: his eyes flashed, his nostrils flared, his lips quirked quickly in surprise.

"Disappearance?"

"While Lord Valentine was traveling in Piurifayne we lost contact with him, and we have not been able to reestablish it."

"May I ask what the Coronal was doing in Piurifayne?"

Hissune offered a light shrug. "A mission of great delicacy, I am given to understand. He was separated from his party in the same storm that took Elidath's life. We have heard nothing since."

"And is the Coronal dead, do you think?"

"I have no idea, and guesses are without value. You can be sure we are making every effort to resume contact with him. But I think we must at least allow for the possibility that Lord Valentine is dead, yes. We have had discussions to that effect at the Castle. A plan of succession is emerging."

"Ah."

"And of course the health of the Pontifex is something that must figure prominently in our planning," said Hissune.

"Ah. Yes. I quite understand."

"The Pontifex, I take it, remains as he has been?"

Hornkast made no immediate reply, but stared at Hissune with mysterious and discomforting intensity a long while, as if engaged in the most intricate of political calculations.

Then at length he said, "Would you like to pay a call on his majesty?"

If not the last thing Hissune would have expected the high spokesman to say, it was close to it. A visit to the Pontifex? He had never dreamed of such a thing! It took him a moment to master his astonishment and regain his poise. Then he said, as coolly as he could manage it, "It would be a great privilege."

"Let us go, then."

"Now?"

"Now," said Hornkast.

The high spokesman signaled; servitors appeared and began clearing away the remnants of the meal; moments later Hissune found himself aboard a small snub-nosed floater, with Hornkast beside him, traveling down a narrow tunnel until they came to a place where they could go only on foot, and where one bronze door after another sealed the passageway at fifty-pace intervals. Hornkast opened each of these by sliding his hand into a hidden panel, and eventually one final door, inscribed with a gold-chased Labyrinth symbol and the imperial monogram over it, yielded to the high spokesman's touch and admitted them to the imperial throne-chamber.

Hissune's heart pounded with terrifying force. The Pontifex! Old mad Tyeveras! Throughout all his life he had scarcely believed that any such person truly existed. Child of the Labyrinth that he was, he had regarded the Pontifex always as some sort of supernatural being, hidden away here in the depths, the reclusive master of the world; and even now, for all Hissune's recent familiarity with princes and dukes and the household of the Coronal and the Coronal himself, he regarded the Pontifex as a being apart, dwelling in a realm of his own, invisible, unknowable, unreal, inconceivably remote from the world of ordinary beings.

But there he was.

It was exactly as the legend had it. The sphere of blue glass, the pipes and tubes and wires and clamps, the colored fluids bubbling in and out of their life-support chamber, and the old, old man within, sitting weirdly upright on the high-backed throne atop its three shallow steps. The eyes of the Pontifex were open. But did they see? Was he alive at all?

"He no longer speaks," Hornkast said. "It is the latest of the changes. But the physician Sepulthrove says that his mind is still active, that his body retains its vitality. Go forward another step or two. You may look closely at him. See? See? He breathes. He blinks. He is alive. He is most definitely alive."

Hissune felt as though he had stumbled into the presence of something of a former epoch, some prehistoric creature miraculously preserved. Tyeveras! Coronal to the Pontifex Ossier, how many generations ago? Survivor out of history. This man had seen Lord Kinniken with his own eyes. He had been old already when Lord Malibor came to the Castle. And here he still was: alive, yes, if this was in fact life.

Hornkast said, "You may greet him."

Hissune knew the convention: one pretended not to speak directly to the Pontifex, but addressed one's words to the high spokesman, pretending that the high spokesman would relay them to the monarch; but that was not actually done.

He said, "I pray you offer his majesty the greeting of his subject Prince Hissune son of Elsinome, who most humbly expresses his reverence and obedience."

The Pontifex made no reply. The Pontifex showed no sign of having heard anything.

"Once," said Hornkast, "he would make sounds that I learned to interpret, in response to what was said to him. No longer. He has not spoken in months. But we speak to him still, even so."

Hissune said, "Tell the Pontifex, then, that he is beloved by all the world, and his name is constantly in our prayers."

Silence. The Pontifex was motionless.

"Tell the Pontifex also," Hissune said, "that the world turns on its course, that troubles come and go, that the greatness of Majipoor will be preserved."

Silence. No response whatever.

"Are you done?" Hornkast asked.

Hissune stared across the room at the enigmatic figure within the glass cage. He longed to see Tyeveras stretch forth his hand in blessing, longed to hear him speak words of prophesy. But that would not happen, Hissune knew.

"Yes," he said. "I'm done."

"Come, then."

The high spokesman led Hissune from the throne chamber. Outside, Hissune realized that his fine robes were soaked with sweat, that his knees were quivering. Tyeveras! If I live to be as old as he is, Hissune thought, I will never forget that face, those eyes, that blue sphere of glass.

Hornkast said, "It is a new phase, this silence. Sepulthrove maintains that he is still strong, and perhaps so. But possibly this is the beginning of the end. There must be some limit, even with all this machinery."

"Do you think it will be soon?"

"I pray it is, but I have no way of knowing. We do nothing to hasten the end. That decision is in Lord Valentine's hands—or in the hands of his successor, if Valentine no longer lives."

"If Lord Valentine is dead," said Hissune, "then the new Coronal might immediately ascend to Pontifex. Unless he too chooses to sustain the life of Tyeveras."

"Indeed. And if Lord Valentine is dead, who then, do you think, will be that new Coronal?"

Hornkast's stare was overwhelming and merciless. Hissune felt himself sizzling in the fire of that stare, and all his hard-won shrewdness, all his sense of who he was and what he meant to achieve melted from him, leaving him vulnerable and muddled. He had a sudden wild dizzying image of himself catapulted upward through the Powers, becoming Coronal one morning, giving the orders to disconnect this tubing and machinery at noon, becoming Pontifex by nightfall. But of course that was absurd, he told himself in panic. *Pontifex? Me? Next month?* It was a joke. It was altogether preposterous. He struggled for balance and succeeded after a moment in drawing himself back to the strategy that had seemed so obvious to him at the Castle: if Lord Valentine is dead, Divvis must become Coronal, and then Tyeveras at last must die, and Divvis goes to the Labyrinth. It must be that way. It must.

Hissune said, "The succession cannot, of course, be voted upon until we are certain of the Coronal's death, and daily we offer our prayers for his safety. But if in fact some tragic fate has befallen Lord Valentine, I think it will be the pleasure of the Castle princes to invite the son of Lord Voriax to ascend the throne."

"Ah."

"And if that should come to pass, there are those of us who think it would be desirable then to allow the Pontifex Tyeveras at last to return to the Source."

"Ah," said Hornkast. "Ah, yes. You make your meaning quite clear, do you not?" His eyes met Hissune's one final time: cold, penetrating, all-seeing. Then they grew milder, as though a veil had been drawn over them, and suddenly the high spokesman seemed to be nothing more than a weary old man at the end of a long and fatiguing day. Hornkast turned away and walked slowly toward the waiting floater. "Come," he said. "It grows late, Prince Hissune."

Late it was indeed, but Hissune found it all but impossible to sleep. *I have seen the Pontifex,* he thought again and again. *I have seen the Pontifex.* He lay awake and tossing half the night, with the image of the ancient Tyeveras blazing in his mind; nor did that image relent when sleep did come, but burned even brighter, Pontifex on throne within sphere of glass. And was the Pontifex weeping? Hissune wondered. And if he wept, for whom did he weep?

At midday the next day Hissune, accompanied by an official escort, made the journey uplevel to the outer ring of the Labyrinth, to Guadeloom Court, to the drab little flat where he had lived so long.

Elsinome had insisted that it was wrong for him to come, that it was a grave breach of protocol for a Prince of the Castle to visit so shabby a place as Guadeloom Court even for the sake of seeing his own mother. But Hissune had brushed her objections aside. "I will come to you," he said. "You must not come to me, mother."

She seemed not greatly altered by the years since they last had met. If anything, she looked stronger, taller, more vigorous. But there was an unfamiliar wariness about her, he thought. He held out his arms to her and she held back, uneasy, almost as if she did not recognize him as her son.

"Mother?" he said. "You know me, don't you, mother?"

"I want to think I do."

"I am no different, mother."

"The way you hold yourself, now—the look in your eye—the robes you wear—"

"I am still Hissune."

"Prince Regent Hissune. And you say you are no different?"

"Everything is different now, mother. But some things remain the same." She appeared to soften a little at that, to relax, to accept him. He went to her and embraced her.

Then she stepped back. "What will happen to the world, Hissune? We hear such terrible things! They say whole provinces have starved. New Coronals have proclaimed themselves. And Lord Valentine—where is Lord Valentine? We know so little down here of what goes on outside. What will happen to the world, Hissune?"

Hissune shook his head. "It is all in the hands of the Divine, mother. But I tell you this: if there is a way to save the world from this disaster, we will save it."

"I feel myself beginning to shiver, when I hear you say *we*. Sometimes in dreams I see you on Castle Mount, among the great lords and princes—I see them looking to you, I see them asking your advice. But can it be true? I am coming to understand certain things—the Lady visits me often when I sleep, do you know that?—but even so, there is so much to understand—so much that I must absorb—"

"The Lady visits you often, you say?"

"Sometimes two or three times a week. I am greatly privileged by that. Although it troubles me, also: to see her so tired, to feel the weight that presses on her soul. She comes to me to help me, you know, but yet I feel sometimes that I should help her, that I should lend my strength to her and let her lean on me—"

"You will, mother."

"Do I understand you rightly, Hissune?"

For a long moment he did not reply. He glanced about the ugly little room at all the old familiar things of his childhood, the tattered curtains, the weary furniture, and he thought of the suite where he had passed the night, and of the apartments that were his on Castle Mount.

He said, "You will not remain in this place much longer, mother."

"Where am I to go, then?"

Again he hesitated.

Quietly he said, "I think they will make me Coronal,

mother. And when they do, you must go to the Isle, and take up a new and difficult task. Do you comprehend what I say?"

"Indeed."

"And are you prepared, mother?"

"I will do what I must," she told him, and she smiled, and shook her head as though in disbelief. And shook the disbelief away, and reached forth to take him into her arms.

9

"Now let the word go forth," Faraataa said.

It was the Hour of the Flame, the midday hour, and the sun stood high over Piurifayne. There would be no rain today: rain was impermissible today, for this was the day of the going forth of the word, and that was a thing that must be accomplished under a rainless sky.

He stood atop a towering wicker scaffold, looking out over the vast clearing in the jungle that his followers had made. Thousands of trees felled, a great slash upon the breast of the land; and in that huge open space his people stood, shoulder to shoulder, as far as he could see. To each side of him rose the steep pyramidal forms of the new temples, nearly as lofty as his scaffold. They were built of crossed logs, interwoven in the ancient patterns, and from their summits flew the two banners of redemption, the red and the yellow. This was New Velalisier, here in the jungle. Next year at this time, Faraataa was resolved, these rites would be celebrated at the true Velalisier across the sea, reconsecrated at last.

He performed now the Five Changes, easily and serenely journeying from form to form: the Red Woman, the Blind Giant, the Flayed Man, the Final King, each Change punctuated by a hissing outcry from those who looked on, and when he underwent the fifth of the Changes, and stood forth in the form of the Prince To Come, the sound was overwhelming. They were crying out his name now in mounting crescendos: "Faraataa! *Faraataa!* FARAATAA!"

"I am the Prince To Come and the King That Is," he cried, as he had so often cried in his dreams.

And they replied: "All hail the Prince To Come, who is the King That Is!"

And he said, "Join your hands together, and your spirits, and let us call the water-kings."

And they joined hands and spirits, and he felt the strength of them surging into him, and he sent out his call:

—Brothers in the sea!

He heard their music. He felt their great bodies stirring in the depths. All the kings responded: Maazmoorn, Girouz, Sheitoon, Diis, Narain, and more. And joined, and gave of their strength, and made from themselves a trumpet for his words.

And his words went forth, to every land, to all who had the capacity to hear.

—You who are our enemy, listen! Know that the war is proclaimed against you, and you are already defeated. The time of reckoning has come. You cannot withstand us. You cannot withstand us. You have begun to perish, and there is no saving you now.

And the voices of his people rose about him: "Faraataa! Faraataa! Faraataa!"

His skin began to gleam. His eyes emitted a radiance. He had become the Prince To Come; he had become the King That Is.

—For fourteen thousand years this world has been yours, and now we have regained it. Go from it, all you strangers! Get into your ships and take yourselves to the stars from which you came, for this world now is ours. Go!

"Faraataa! Faraataa!"

—Go, or feel our heavy wrath! Go, or be driven into the sea! Go, or we will spare none of you!

"Faraataa!"

He spread wide his arms. He opened himself to the surging energies of all those whose souls were linked before him, and of the water-kings who were his sustenance and his comfort. The time of exile and sorrow, he knew, was ending. The holy war was nearly won. Those who had stolen the world and spread themselves across it like a swarm of marauding insects now would be crushed.

—Hear me, O enemies. I am the King That Is!

And the silent voices cried in deafening tones:

—Hear him, O enemies. He is the King That Is!

—Your time has come! Your day is done! Your crimes will be punished, and none will survive! Go from our world!

—Go from our world!

"Faraataa!" they cried aloud. "Faraataa! Faraataa!"

"I am the Prince To Come. I am the King That Is!"

And they answered him, "All hail the Prince To Come, who is the King That Is!"

FOUR

The Book of the
Pontifex

1

"A strange day, my lord, when the Coronal must come as a beggar to the King of Dreams," Sleet said, holding his hand outspread before his face to shield himself against the torrid wind that blew unrelentingly toward them out of Suvrael. Just a few hours more and they would make landfall at Tolaghai, largest of the southern continent's ports.

"Not as a beggar, Sleet," said Valentine quietly. "As a brother-in-arms, seeking aid against a common enemy."

Carabella turned to him in surprise. "A brother-in-arms, Valentine? Never before have I heard you speak of yourself in such a warlike way."

"We are at war, are we not?"

"And will you fight, then? And will you take lives with your own hand?"

Valentine peered closely at her, wondering if she were somehow trying to goad him; but no, her face was gentle as ever, her eyes were loving. He said, "You know I will never shed blood. But there are other ways of waging war. I have fought one war already, with you beside me: did I take life then?"

"But who were the enemies then?" Sleet demanded impatiently. "Your own dearest friends, misled by Shapeshifter deception! Elidath—Tunigorn—Stasilaine—Mirigant—all of them took the field against you. Of course you were gentle with them! You had no wish to slay such as Elidath and Mirigant: only to win them to your side."

"Dominin Barjazid was no dear friend of mine. I spared him also: and I think we will be glad of that now."

"An act of great mercy, yes. But we have a different sort of enemy now—Shapeshifter filth, cruel vermin—"

"Sleet—!"

"That is what they are, my lord! Creatures that have vowed to destroy all that we have built on our world."

"On *their* world, Sleet," said Valentine. "Remember that: this is their world."

"*Was*, my lord. They lost it to us by default. A mere few million of them, on a planet large enough for—"

"And shall we have this tired dispute one more time, then?" Carabella burst out, making no effort to disguise her irritation. "Why? Is it not hard enough to breathe the blowtorch stuff that comes out of Suvrael, without straining our lungs in such futile talk as this?"

"I only mean to say, my lady, that the war of restoration was such a war as could be won by peaceful means, by open arms and a loving embrace. We have a different kind of enemy now. This Faraataa is consumed with hatred. He will not rest until we are all dead: and will he be won by love, do you think? Do you, my lord?"

Valentine looked away. "We will use whatever means are appropriate," he said, "to make Majipoor whole again."

"If you are sincere in what you say, then you must be prepared to destroy the enemy," replied Sleet darkly. "Not merely pen them up in the jungle as Lord Stiamot did, but to exterminate them, to eradicate them, to end forever the threat to our civilization that they—"

"Exterminate? Eradicate?" Valentine laughed. "You sound prehistoric, Sleet!"

"He does not mean it literally, my lord," Carabella said.

"Ah, he does, he does! Don't you, Sleet?"

With a shrug Sleet said, "You know that my loathing of Metamorphs is not entirely of my own making, but was laid upon me in a sending—a sending out of that very land that lies ahead of us. But apart from that: I think their lives are forfeit, yes, for the damage they have already done. I make no apology for believing that."

"And you would massacre millions of people for the crimes of our leaders? Sleet, Sleet, *you* are more than a threat to our civilization than ten thousand Metamorphs!"

Color surged to Sleet's pale fleshless cheeks, but he said nothing.

"You are offended by that," Valentine said. "I meant no offense."

In a low voice Sleet said, "The Coronal need not ask the

pardon of the bloodthirsty barbarian who serves him, my lord."

"I had no desire to mock you. Only to disagree with you."

"Then let us disagree," said Sleet. "If I were Coronal, I would kill them all."

"But I am Coronal—at least in some parts of this world. And so long as I am, I will search for ways of winning this war that fall short of exterminations and eradications. Is that acceptable to you, Sleet?"

"Whatever the Coronal wishes is acceptable to me, and you know it, my lord. I tell you only what I would do if I were Coronal."

"May the Divine spare you from that fate," said Valentine, with a faint smile.

"And you, my lord, from the need to meet violence with violence, for I know it is not in your nature," responded Sleet, smiling even more faintly. He offered a formal salute. "We will be arriving shortly in Tolaghai," he said, "and I must make a great many arrangements for our accommodations. May I have leave to withdraw, my lord?"

As Sleet moved off down the deck, Valentine stared after him a moment; then, shading his eyes against the harsh blaze of the sun, he stared into the wind at the southern continent, now a dark massive shape sprawling on the horizon.

Suvrael! The name alone evoked a shiver!

He had never expected to come here: the stepchild among Majipoor's continents, forgotten, neglected, a sparsely populated place of barren and forbidding wastelands, almost entirely bleak and arid, so little like the rest of Majipoor as to seem almost like a slice of some other planet. Though millions of people dwelled here, clustered in half a dozen cities scattered through the least uninhabitable regions of the place, Suvrael for centuries had maintained only the most perfunctory of ties with the two main continents. When officials of the central government were sent off for a tour of duty there, they regarded it virtually as a penal sentence. Few Coronals had ever visited it. Valentine had heard that Lord Tyeveras had been there, on one of his several grand processionals, and he thought that Lord Kinniken once had done the same. And of course there was the famous exploit of Dekkeret, roaming the Desert of Stolen Dreams in the company of the founder of the Barjazid

dynasty, but that had happened long before he had become
Coronal.

Out of Suvrael came only three things that impinged on
the life of Majipoor in any important way. One was wind: out
of Suvrael at all months of the year poured a torrent of
searing air that fell brutally upon the southern shores of
Alhanroel and Zimroel and rendered them nearly as disagreeable as Suvrael itself. Another was meat: on the western side
of the desert continent, mists rising from the sea drifted
inland to sustain a vast grassland where cattle were raised for
shipment to the other continents. And the third great export
of Suvrael was dreams. For a thousand years now the Barjazids
had held sway as Powers of the realm from their great domain
inland of Tolaghai: with the aid of thought-amplifying devices,
whose secret they jealously guarded, they filled the world
with their sendings, stern and troublesome infiltrations of the
soul that sought and found anyone who had done injury to a
fellow citizen, or even was merely contemplating it. In their
harsh and austere way the Barjazids were the consciences of
the world, and they long had been the rod and the scourge
by which the Coronal and the Pontifex and the Lady of the
Isle were able to sustain their more benign and gentle mode
of government.

The Metamorphs, when they made their first abortive
try at insurrection early in Valentine's reign, had understood
the power of the King of Dreams, and when the head of the
Barjazids, old Simonan, had fallen ill, they had cunningly
substituted one of their own in the place of the dying man.
Which had led then to the usurpation of Lord Valentine's
throne by Simonan's youngest son Dominin, though he had
never suspected that the one who had urged him into that
rash adventure was not his true father but a Metamorph
counterfeit.

And yes, Valentine thought, Sleet was right: how strange
indeed that the Coronal now should be turning to the Barjazids
almost as a suppliant, when his throne was once more in
jeopardy.

He had come almost accidentally to Suvrael. In making their retreat from Piurifayne, Valentine and his party
had taken a sharp southeasterly route toward the sea, for it
would clearly have been unwise to go northeast to rebellious Piliplok, and the central part of the Gihorna coast was
without cities or harbors. They emerged finally close by

the southern tip of eastern Zimroel, in the isolated province known as Bellatule, a humid tropical land of tall saw-edged grasses, spice-muck swamps, and feathered serpents.

The people of Bellatule were Hjorts, mainly: sober, glum-faced folk with bulging eyes and vast mouths filled with rows of rubbery chewing-cartilage. Most of them earned their livelihoods in the shipping trade, receiving manufactured goods from all over Majipoor and forwarding them to Suvrael in return for cattle. Since the recent worldwide upheavals had caused a sharp drop in manufacturing output and a nearly total breakdown in the traffic between provinces, the merchants of Bellatule were finding their trade greatly diminished; but at least there had been no famines, because the province was generally self-sufficient in its food supply, depending largely on its bountiful fisheries, and such little agriculture as was practiced there had been untouched by the blights afflicting other regions. Bellatule seemed calm and had remained loyal to the central government.

Valentine had hoped to take ship there for the Isle, in order to confer on matters of strategy with his mother. But the shipmasters of Bellatule warned him sternly against making the voyage to the Isle just now. "No ship's gone north from here in months," they told him. "It's the dragons: they're running crazy out there, smashing anything that sails up the coast or across toward the Archipelago. A voyage north or east while that's going on would be suicide and nothing else." It might be six or eight months more, they believed, before the last of the dragon swarms that lately had rounded the southeastern corner of Zimroel had completed their journey into northern waters and the maritime lanes were open again.

The prospect of being trapped in remote and obscure Bellatule appalled Valentine. Going back into Piurifayne seemed pointless, and making any sort of overland trek around the Metamorph province into the vast middle of the continent would be risky and slow. But there was one other option. "We can take you to Suvrael, my lord," the shipmasters said. "The dragons have not entered the southern waters at all and the route remains untroubled." *Suvrael?* At first consideration the idea was bizarre. But then Valentine thought, *Why not?* The aid of the Barjazids might be valuable; certainly it ought not be scorned out of hand. And perhaps there was some sea route out of the southern continent to the Isle, or to Alhanroel, that would take him beyond the zone infested by the unruly sea dragons. Yes. Yes.

So, then: Suvrael. The voyage was a swift one. And now the fleet of Bellatule merchantmen, gliding steadily south-ward against the scorching wind, began its entry into Tolaghai harbor.

The city baked in the late afternoon heat. It was a dismal place, a featureless clutter of mud-colored buildings a story or two high, stretching on and on along the shore and interminably back toward the ridge of low hills that marked the boundary between the coastal plain and the brutal interior desert. As the royal party was escorted ashore, Carabella glanced at Valentine in consternation. He offered her an encouraging smile, but without much conviction. Castle Mount seemed just then to be not ten thousand miles away, but ten million.

But five magnificent floaters ornamented with bold stripes of purple and yellow, the colors of the King of Dreams, waited in the courtyard of the customs house. Guards in livery of the same colors stood before them; and, as Valentine and Carabella approached, a tall, powerful-looking man with a thick black beard lightly flecked with gray emerged from one of the floaters and began to walk slowly toward them, limping slightly.

Valentine remembered that limp well, for it once had been his. As had the body that the black-bearded man once wore: for this was Dominin Barjazid, the former usurper, by whose orders Lord Valentine had been cast into the body of some unknown golden-haired man so that the Barjazid, taking Valentine's own body for his own, might rule in Valentine's guise on Castle Mount. And the limp was the doing of the young Valentine of long ago, when he had smashed his leg in a foolish accident while riding with Elidath in the pygmy forest by Amblemorn on the Mount.

"My lord, welcome," said Dominin Barjazid with great warmth. "You do us a high honor by this visit, for which we have hoped so many years."

Most submissively he offered Valentine the starburst gesture—with trembling hands, the Coronal observed. Valentine was far from unmoved himself. For it was a strange and disturbing experience once again to see his first body, now in the possession of another. He had not cared to undergo the risk of having that body back, after the defeat of Dominin, but all the same it stirred a mighty confusion in him to see another's soul looking outward through his eyes. And also it stirred him to see the onetime usurper now so wholly redeemed and cleansed of his treasons and so genuine in his hospitality.

There had been some who had wanted Dominin put to death for his crime. But Valentine had never been willing to countenance such talk. Perhaps some barbarian king on some remote prehistoric world might have had his enemies executed, but no crime—not even an attempt on a Coronal's life—had ever drawn so severe a penalty on Majipoor. Besides, the fallen Dominin had collapsed into madness, his mind wholly shattered by the revelation that his father, the supposed King of Dreams, was in truth a Metamorph impostor.

It would have been senseless to impose any sort of punishment on such a ruined creature. Valentine, upon resuming his throne, had pardoned Dominin and had had him handed over to emissaries of his family, so that he might be returned to Suvrael. There he slowly mended. Some years afterward he had begged leave to come to the Castle to ask the Coronal's forgiveness. "You have my pardon already," Valentine had replied; but Dominin came anyway, and knelt most humbly and sincerely before him on audience day in the Confalume throne-room, and cleared the burden of treason from his soul.

Now, thought Valentine, the circumstances are greatly altered once again: for this is Dominin's own domain, and I am little more than a fugitive in it.

Dominin said, "My royal brother Minax has sent me, my lord, to convey you to Palace Barjazid, where you are to be our guest. Will you ride with me in the lead floater?"

The palace lay well outside Tolaghai, in a cruel and doleful valley. Valentine had seen it now and then in dreams: an ominous, menacing structure of dark stone, topped with a fantastic array of sharp-tipped towers and angular parapets. Clearly it had been designed to intimidate the eye and inspire dread.

"How hideous!" Carabella whispered, as they neared it.

"Wait," said Valentine. "Only wait!"

They passed within the great gloomy portcullis and entered a place that on the inside displayed no kinship to its forbidding and repellent exterior. Airy courtyards resounded to the gentle music of splashing fountains, and cool, fragrant breezes replaced the bitter heat of the outer world. As Valentine dismounted from the floater with Carabella on his arm, he saw servitors waiting with iced wines and sherbets, and heard musicians strumming on delicate instruments. In the midst of all waited two figures clad in loose white robes, one soft-faced and pale and round-bellied, the other lean, hawk-faced, tanned almost black by the desert sun. About the forehead of the hawk-faced one rested the dazzling golden diadem that marked him as a Power of Majipoor. Valentine scarcely needed to be told that this was Minax Barjazid, now King of Dreams in his late father's place. The other and softer man was his brother Cristoph, in all likelihood. Both made the starburst gesture, and Minax came forward to offer Valentine a bowl of chilled blue wine with his own hands.

"My lord," he said, "these are stark times in which you come calling on us. But we greet you in all joy, no matter how somber the moment seems. We are mightily in your debt, my lord. All that is ours is yours. And all that we command is at your service." It was obviously a speech he had prepared with care, and the resonance and smoothness of his delivery showed careful rehearsal. But then the King of Dreams leaned forward until his hard and glittering eyes were only inches from the Coronal's own, and in a different voice, deeper, more private, he said, "You may have refuge here as long as you wish."

Quietly Valentine replied, "You misunderstand, your highness. I have not come here to take refuge, but to seek your aid in the struggle that lies ahead."

The King of Dreams seemed startled by that. "Such aid as I can give is yours, of course. But do you truly see any hope that we can fight our way free of the turmoil that assail us? For I must tell you, my lord, that I have looked at the world very closely through this"—he touched his diadem of power—"and I see no hope myself, my lord, none, none at all."

2

An hour before twilight the chanting started again down in Ni-moya: thousands or perhaps hundreds of thousands of voices crying out with tremendous force, "Thallimon! Thallimon! Lord Thallimon! *Thallimon! Thallimon!*" The sound of that fierce jubilant outcry came rolling up the slopes of the outlying Gimbeluc district and swept over the quiet precincts of the Park of Fabulous Beasts like a great unstoppable wave.

It was the third day since the demonstrations in honor of the newest of the new Coronals had begun, and tonight's uproar was the most frenzied so far. Very likely it was accompanied by rioting, looting, widespread destruction. But Yarmuz Khitain scarcely cared. This had already been one of the most terrifying days he had experienced in all his long tenure as curator of the park, an assault on everything that he considered proper and rational and sane: why should he now be perturbed over a little noise that some fools were making in the city?

At dawn that day Yarmuz Khitain had been awakened by a very young assistant curator who told him timidly, "Vingole Nayila has come back, sir. He is waiting at the east gate."

"Has he brought much back with him?"

"Oh, yes, sir! Three transport floaters full, sir!"

"I'll be right down," said Yarmuz Khitain.

Vingole Nayila, the park's chief field zoologist, had been exploring for the past five months in the disturbed areas of north central Zimroel. He was not a man of whom Yarmuz Khitain was greatly fond, for he tended to be cocky and overly self-satisfied, and whenever he exposed himself to deadly peril in the pursuit of some elusive beast he made sure that everyone knew just how deadly the peril had been. But professionally he was superb, an extraordinary collector of wild animals, indefatigable, fearless. When news had first begun to arrive that unfamiliar and grotesque creatures were causing havoc in the region between Khyntor and Dulorn, Nayila had lost no time mounting an expedition.

And a successful one, evidently. When Yarmuz Khitain reached the east gate he saw Nayila strutting busily about on the far side of the energy field that kept intruders out and the rare animals in. Beyond that zone of pink haze Nayila was supervising the unloading of a vast number of wooden containers, from which came all manner of hisses and growls and buzzes and drones and yelps. At the sight of Khitain, Nayila looked across and yelled:

"Khitain! You won't *believe* what I've brought back!"

"Will I want to?" asked Yarmuz Khitain.

The accessioning process, it seemed, had already begun: the entire staff, such as still remained, had turned out to transport Nayila's animals in their boxes through the gate and off toward the receiving building, where they could be installed in holding cages until enough was understood about them to allow their release into one of the open habitat ranges. "Careful!" Nayila bellowed, as two men struggling with a massive container nearly let it fall on its side. "If that animal gets loose, we're all going to be sorry—but you first of all!" Turning to Yarmuz Khitain, he said, "It's a real horror show. Predators—all predators—teeth like knives, claws like razors—I'm damned if I know how I got back here alive. Half a dozen times I thought I was done for, and me not having even recorded any of this for the Register of Souls. What a waste that would have been, what a waste! But here I am. Come—you've got to see these things—!"

A horror show, yes. All morning long, and on deep into the afternoon, Yarmuz Khitain found himself witness to a procession of the impossible and the hideous and the wholly unacceptable: freaks, monsters, ghastly anomalies.

"These were running around on the outskirts of Mazadone," said Nayila, indicating a pair of small furious snarling animals with fiery red eyes and three savagely sharp horns ten inches long rising from their foreheads. Yarmuz Khitain recognized them by their thick reddish fur as haiguses—but never had he seen a haigus with horns, nor any so determinedly vicious. "Nasty little killers," Nayila said. "I watched them run down a poor blave that had gone wild, and kill it in five minutes by leaping up and goring it in the belly. I bagged them while they were feeding, and then this thing came down to finish off the carcass." He pointed to a dark-winged canavong with a sinister black beak and a single glowering eye in the center of its distended forehead: an innocent scavenger mysteriously transformed into a thing out of a nightmare. "Have you ever seen anything so ugly?"

"I would never want to see anything uglier," said Yarmuz Khitain.

"But you will. You will. Uglier, meaner, nastier—just watch what comes out of these crates."

Yarmuz Khitain was not sure he wanted to. He had spent all his life with animals—studying them, learning their ways, caring for them. Loving them, in a real sense of the word. But these—these—

"And then look at this," Nayila went on. "A miniature dhumkar, maybe a tenth the size of the standard model, and fifty times as quick. It isn't content to sit there in the sand and poke around with its snout in search of its dinner. No, it's an evil little fast-moving thing that comes right after you, and would sooner chew your foot off at the ankle than breathe. Or this: a manculain, wouldn't you say?"

"Of course. But there are no manculains in Zimroel."

"That's what I thought, too, until I saw this fellow back of Velathys, along the mountain roads. Very similar to the manculains of Stoienzar, is it not? But with at least one difference." He knelt beside the cage that held the rotund many-legged creature and made a deep rumbling sound at it. The manculain at once rumbled back and began menacingly to stir the long stiletto-like needles that sprouted all over its body, as though it intended to hurl them through the wire mesh at him. Nayila said, "It isn't content with being covered with spines. The spines are *poisonous*. One scratch with them and your arm puffs up for a week. I know. I don't know what would have happened if the spine got in any deeper, and I don't want to find out. Do you?"

Yarmuz Khitain shivered. It sickened him to think of these horrendous creatures taking up residence in the Park of Fabulous Beasts, which had been founded long ago as a refuge for those animals, most of them gentle and inoffensive, that had been driven close to extinction by the spread of civilization on Majipoor. Of course the park had a good many predators in its collection, and Yarmuz Khitain had never felt like offering apologies for them: they were the work of the Divine, after all, and if they found it necessary to kill for their meals it was not out of any innate malevolence that they did so. But these—these—

These animals are evil, he thought. *They ought to be destroyed.*

The thought astounded him. Nothing like it had ever

crossed his mind before. Animals evil? How could animals be evil? He could say, *I think this animal is very ugly*, or, *I think this animal is very dangerous*, but evil? No. No. Animals are not capable of being evil, not even these. The evil has to reside elsewhere: in their creators. No, not even in them. They too have their reasons for setting these beasts loose upon the world, and the reason is not sheer malevolence for its own sake, unless I am greatly mistaken. Where then is the evil? The evil, Khitain told himself, is everywhere, a pervasive thing that slips and slides between the atoms of the air we breathe. It is a universal corruption in which we all participate. Except the animals.

Except the animals.

"How is it possible," Yarmuz Khitain asked, "that the Metamorphs have the skill to breed such things?"

"The Metamorphs have many skills we've never bothered to learn a thing about, it would appear. They've been sitting out there in Piurifayne concocting these animals quietly for years, building up their stock of them. Can you imagine what the place where they kept them all must have been like—a horror zoo, monsters only? And now they've been kind enough to share them with us."

"But can we be certain the animals come from Piurifayne?"

"I traced the distribution vectors very carefully. The lines radiate outward from the region southwest of Ilirivoyne. This is Metamorph work, no doubt about that. It simply can't happen that two or three dozen loathsome new kinds of animals would burst onto the scene in Zimroel all at the same time by spontaneous mutation. We know that we're at war: these are weapons, Khitain."

The older man nodded. "I think you're right."

"I've saved the worst for last. Come: look at these."

In a cage of closely woven metal mesh so fine that he was able to see through its walls, Khitain observed an agitated horde of small winged creatures fluttering angrily about, battering themselves against the sides of the cage, striking it furiously with their leathery black wings, falling back, rising again for another try. They were furry little things about eight inches long, with disproportionately large mouths and beady, glittering red eyes.

"Dhiims," said Nayila. "I captured them in a dwikka forest over by Borgax."

"Dhiims?" Khitain said hoarsely.

"Dhiims, yes. Found them feeding on a couple of little forest-brethren that I suppose they'd killed—so busy eating they didn't see me coming. I knocked them out with my collecting spray and gathered them up. A few of them woke up before I got them all in the box. I'm lucky still to have my fingers, Yarmuz."

"I know dhiims," said Khitain. "They're two inches long, half an inch wide. These are the size of rats."

"Yes. Rats that fly. Rats that eat flesh. Carnivorous giant dhiims, eh? Dhiims that don't just nibble and nip, dhiims that can strip a forest-brother down to its bones in ten minutes. Aren't they lovely? Imagine a swarm of them flying into Ni-moya. A million, two million—thick as mosquitos in the air. Sweeping down. Eating everything in their way. A new plague of locusts—flesh-eating locusts—"

Khitain felt himself growing very calm. He had seen too much today. His mind was overloaded with horror.

"They would make life very difficult," he said mildly.

"Yes. Very very difficult, eh? We'd need to dress in suits of armor." Nayila laughed. "The dhiims are their masterpiece, Khitain. You don't need bombs when you can launch deadly little flying rodents against your enemy. Eh? Eh?"

Yarmuz Khitain made no reply. He stared at the cage of frenzied angry dhiims as though he were looking into a pit that reached down to the core of the world.

From far away he heard the shouting begin: "Thallimon! Thallimon! Lord Thallimon!"

Nayila frowned, cocked an ear, strained to make out the words. "Thallimon? Is that what they're yelling?"

"Lord Thallimon," said Khitain. "The new Coronal. The *new* new Coronal. He surfaced three days ago, and every night they have a big rally for him outside Nissimorn Prospect."

"There was a Thallimon who used to work here. Is this some relative of his?"

"The same man," Khitain said.

Vingole Nayila looked stunned.

"What? Six months ago he was sweeping dung out of zoo cages, and now he's Coronal? Is it possible?"

"Anybody can be Coronal now," Yarmuz Khitain said placidly. "But only for a week or two, so it seems. Perhaps it will be your turn soon, Vingole." He chuckled. "Or mine."

"How did this happen, Yarmuz?"

Khitain shrugged. With a wide sweep of his hand he

indicated Nayila's newly collected animals, the snarling three-horned haigus, the dwarf dhumkar, the single-eyed canavong, the dhiims: everything bizarre and frightful, everything taut with dark hunger and rage. "How did any of this happen?" he asked. "If such strangenesses as these are loosed upon the world, why not make dung sweepers into Coronals? First jugglers, then dung sweepers, then zoologists, maybe. Well, why not? How does it sound to you? 'Vingole! Lord Vingole! All hail Lord Vingole!'"

"Stop it, Yarmuz."

"You've been off in the forest with your dhiims and your manculains. I've had to watch what's been happening here. I feel very tired, Vingole. I've seen too much."

"Lord Thallimon! Imagine!"

"Lord this, Lord that, Lord whoever—a plague of Coronals all month, and a couple of Pontifexes too. They don't last long. But let's hope Thallimon does. At least he's likely to protect the park," said Khitain.

"Against what?"

"Mob attack. There are hungry people down there, and up here we continue to feed the animals. They tell me that agitators in the city are stirring people up to break into the park and butcher everything for meat."

"Are you serious?"

"Apparently *they* are."

"But these animals are priceless—irreplaceable—!"

"Tell that to a starving man, Vingole," said Khitain quietly.

Nayila stared at him. "And do you really think this Lord Thallimon is going to hold back the mob, if they decide to attack the park?"

"He worked here once. He knows the importance of what we have here. He must have had some love for the animals, don't you think?"

"He swept out the cages, Yarmuz."

"Even so—"

"He may be hungry himself, Yarmuz."

"The situation is bad, but not that desperate. Not yet. And in any case what can be gained by eating a few scrawny sigimoins and dimilions and zampidoons? One meal, for a few hundred people, at such a cost to science?"

"Mobs aren't rational," Nayila said. "And you overestimate your dung-sweeper Coronal, I suspect. He may have hated this place—hated his job, hated you, hated the animals. Also he may decide that there are political points to be made by leading his supporters up the hill for dinner. He knows how to get through the gates, doesn't he?"

"Why—I suppose—"

"The whole staff does. Where the key-boxes are, how to neutralize the field so that you can pass through—"

"He wouldn't!"

"He may, Yarmuz. Take measures. Arm your people."

"*Arm* them? With what? Do you think I keep weapons here?"

"This place is unique. Once the animals perish, they'll never be restored. You have a responsibility, Yarmuz."

From the distance—but not, Khitain thought, so distant as before—came the cry: "Thallimon! Lord Thallimon!"

Nayila said, "Are they coming, do you think?"

"He wouldn't. He *wouldn't*."

"Thallimon! Lord Thallimon!"

"It sounds closer," Nayila said.

There was a commotion down at the far end of the room. One of the groundkeepers had come running in, breathless, wild-eyed, calling Khitain's name. "Hundreds of people!" he cried. "Thousands! Heading toward Gimbeluc!"

Khitain felt panic rising. He looked about at the members of his staff. "Check the gates. Make absolutely sure everything's shut tight. Then start closing the inner gates—whatever animals are out in the field should be pushed as far to the northern end of the park as possible. They'll have a better chance to hide in the woods back there. And—"

"This is not the way," Vingole Nayila said.

"What else can we do? I have no weapons, Vingole. *I have no weapons!*"

"I do."

"What do you mean?"

"I risked my life a thousand times to collect the animals in this park. Especially the ones I brought in today. I intend to defend them." He turned away from Yarmuz Khitain. "Here! Here, give me a hand with this cage!"

"What are you doing, Vingole?"

"Never mind. Go see after your gates." Without waiting for help, Nayila began to shove the cage of dhiims onto the little floater-dolly on which it had been rolled into the building. Khitain suddenly comprehended what weapon it was that Nayila meant to use. He rushed forward, tugging at the younger man's arm. Nayila easily pushed him aside, and, ignoring Khitain's hoarse protests, guided the dolly out of the building.

The invaders from the city, still roaring their leader's name, sounded closer and closer. The park will be destroyed, Khitain thought, aghast. And yet—if Nayila truly intends—

No. No. He rushed from the building, peered through the dusk, caught sight of Vingole Nayila far away, down by the east gate. The chanting was much louder now. "*Thall*imon! *Thall*imon!"

Khitain saw the mob, spilling into the broad plaza on the far side of the gate, where each morning the public waited until the hour of opening arrived. That fantastic figure in weird red robes with white trim—that was Thallimon, was it not? Standing atop some sort of palanquin, waving his arms madly, urging the crowd on. The energy field surrounding the park would hold back a few people, or an animal or two, but it was not designed to withstand the thrust of a vast frenzied mob. One did not ordinarily have to worry about vast frenzied mobs here. But now—

"Go back!" Nayila cried. "Stay away! I warn you!"

"*Thall*imon! *Thall*imon!"

"I warn you, keep out of here!"

They paid no attention. They thundered forward like a herd of maddened bidlaks, charging without heeding anything before them. As Khitain watched in dismay, Nayila signaled to one of the gatemen, who briefly deactivated the energy barrier, long enough for Nayila to shove the cage of dhiims forward into the plaza, yank open the bolt that fastened its door, and dart back behind the safety of the hazy pink glow.

"No," Khitain muttered. "Not even for the sake of defending the park—no—no—"

The dhiims streamed from their cage with such swiftness that one little animal blurred into the next, and they became an airborne river of golden fur and frantic black wings.

They sped upward, thirty, forty feet, and then turned and swooped down with terrible force and implacable voracity, plunging into the vanguard of the mob as though they had not eaten in months. Those under attack did not seem at first to realize what was happening to them; they tried to sweep the dhiims away with irritated backhand swipes, as one might try to sweep away annoying insects. But the dhiims would not be swept away so easily. They dived and struck and tore away strips of flesh, and flew upward to devour their meat in mid-air, and came swooping down again. The new Lord Thallimon, spurting blood from a dozen wounds, tumbled from his palanquin and went sprawling to the ground. The dhiims closed in, returning to those in the front line who had already been wounded, and slicing at them again and again, burrowing deep, twisting and tugging at strands of exposed muscle and the tenderer tissues beneath them. "No," said Khitain over and over, from his vantage point behind the gate. "No. No. No." The furious little creatures were merciless. The mob was in flight, people screaming, running in all directions, a chaos of colliding bodies as they sought to find the road back down to Ni-moya, and those who had fallen lay in scarlet pools as the dhiims dived and dived and dived again. Some had been laid bare to the bone—mere rags and scraps of flesh remaining, and that too being stripped away. Khitain heard sobbing; and only after a moment realized that it was his own.

Then it was all over. A strange silence settled over the plaza. The mob had fled; the victims on the pavement no longer moaned; the dhiims, sated, hovered briefly over the scene, wings whirring, and then rose one by one into the night and flew off, the Divine only knew where.

Yarmuz Khitain, trembling, shaken, walked slowly away from the gate. The park was saved. The park was saved. Turning, he looked toward Vingole Nayila, who stood like an avenging angel with his arms outspread and his eyes blazing.

"You should not have done that," Khitain said in a voice so choked with shock and loathing that he could barely get the words out.

"They would have destroyed the park."

"Yes, the park is saved. But look—look—"

Nayila shrugged. "I warned them. How could I let them destroy all we have built here, just to have a little fresh meat?"

"You should not have done it, all the same."

"You think so? I have no regrets, Yarmuz. Not one." He considered that a moment. "Ah: there is one. I wish I had had time to put a few of the dhiims aside, for our collection. But there was no time, and they are all far away by now, and I have no wish to go back to Borgax and look for others. I

regret nothing else, Yarmuz. And I had no choice but to turn
them loose. They have saved the park. How could we have
let those madmen destroy it? How, Yarmuz? How?"

3

Though it was barely past dawn, brilliant sunlight illuminated
the wide and gentle curves of the Glayge Valley when Hissune,
rising early, stepped out on the deck of the riverboat that was
carrying him back toward Castle Mount.

Of to the west, where the river made a fat bend into a
district of terraced canyons, all was misty and hidden, as
though this were time's first morning. But when he looked
toward the east Hissune saw the serene red-tiled roofs of the
great city of Pendiwane glowing in the early light, and far
upriver the sinuous low shadow of the Makroposopos waterfront was just coming into view. Beyond lay Apocrune, Stangard
Falls, Nimivan, and the rest of the valley cities, home to fifty
million people or more. Happy places where life was easy;
but now the menacing aura of imminent disruption hung over
these cities, and Hissune knew that all up and down the
Glayge people were waiting, wondering, fearing.

He wanted to stretch forth his arms to them from the
prow of the riverboat, to enfold them all in a warm embrace,
to cry out, "Fear nothing! The Divine is with us! All will be
well!"

But was it true?

No one knows the will of the Divine, Hissune thought.
But, lacking that knowledge, we must shape our destinies
according to our sense of what is fitting. Like sculptors we
carve our lives out of the raw stone of the future, hour by
hour by hour, following whatever design it is that we hold in
our minds; and if the design is sound and our carving is done
well, the result will seem pleasing when the last chisel-stroke
is made. But if our design is slapdash and our carving is hasty,
why, the proportions will be inelegant and the balance un-
true. And if the work thus be faulty, can we say it was the will
of the Divine that it is so? Or, rather, only that our plan was
poorly conceived?

My plan, he told himself, must not be poorly conceived.

And then all will be well; and then it will be said that the Divine was with us.

Throughout the swift river-journey northward he shaped and reshaped it, as he traveled past Jerrik and Ghiseldorn and Sattinor where the upper Glayge flowed from the foothills of Castle Mount. By the time he reached Amblemorn, southwesternmost of the Fifty Cities of the Mount, the design of what had to be done was clear and strong in his mind.

Here it was impossible to continue farther by the river, for Amblemorn was where the Glayge was born out of the host of tributaries that came tumbling down out of the Mount, and none of those lesser rivers was navigable. By floater, then, he proceeded up the flank of the Mount, through the ring of Slope Cities and that of Free Cities and that of Guardian Cities, past Morvole, where Elidath was born, and Normork of the great wall and the great gate, past Huyn, where the leaves of all the trees were scarlet or crimson or ruby or vermilion, past Greel of the crystal palisade and Sigla Higher of the five vertical lakes, and onward still, to the Inner Cities, Banglecode and Bombifale and Peritole and the rest, and on, on, the party of floaters racing up the enormous mountain.

"It is more than I can believe," said Elsinome, who was making this journey at her son's side. Never had she ventured from the Labyrinth at all, and to begin her travels in the world by the ascent of Castle Mount was no small assignment. Her eyes were as wide as a small child's, Hissune observed with pleasure, and there were days when she seemed so surfeited with miracles that she could scarcely speak.

"Wait," he said. "You have seen nothing."

Through Peritole Pass to Bombifale Plain, where the decisive battle of the war of restoration had been fought, and past the wondrous spires of Bombifale itself, and up another level to the zone of the High Cities—the mountain road of gleaming red flagstone led from Bombifale to High Morpin, then through fields of dazzling flowers along the Grand Calintane Highway, and up and up until Lord Valentine's Castle loomed overwhelmingly at the summit of all, sending its tentacles of brick and masonry wandering in a thousand directions over the crags and peaks.

As his floater entered the Dizimaule Plaza outside the

southern wing, Hissune was startled to see a delegation of welcomers waiting for him. Stasilaine was there, and Mirigant, and Elzandir, and a retinue of aides. But not Divvis.

"Have they come to hail you as Coronal?" Elsinome asked, and Hissune smiled and shook his head.

"I doubt that very much," he said.

As he strode toward them across the green porcelain cobblestones he wondered what changes had occurred here during his absence. Had Divvis proclaimed himself Coronal? Were his friends here to warn him to flee while he had the chance? No, no, they were smiling; they clustered round, they embraced him jubilantly.

"What news?" Hissune asked.

"Lord Valentine lives!" cried Stasilaine.

"The Divine be praised! Where is he now?"

"Suvrael," said Mirigant. "He is a guest at Palace Barjazid. So says the King of Dreams himself, and we have this very day had confirming word from the Coronal."

"Suvrael!" Hissune repeated in wonder, as though he had been told that Valentine had taken himself off to some unknown continent in the midst of the Great Sea, or to some other world entirely. "Why Suvrael? How did he get there?"

"He came forth from Piurifayne in the land of Bellatule," Stasilaine replied, "and the unruliness of the dragons kept him from sailing north; and also Piliplok, as I think you know, is in rebellion. So the Bellatule folk took him to the southland, and there he has forged an alliance with the Barjazids, who will use their powers to bring the world back to sanity."

"A bold move."

"Indeed. He sails shortly for the Isle to meet again with the Lady."

"And then?" Hissune asked.

"That is not yet determined." Stasilaine peered closely at Hissune. "The shape of the months ahead is not clear to us."

"I think it is to me," said Hissune. "Where is Divvis?"

"He has gone hunting today," Elzandir said. "In the forest by Frangior."

"Why, that is an unlucky place for his family!" Hissune said. "Is that not where his father Lord Voriax was slain?"

"So it is," said Stasilaine.

"I hope he is more careful," Hissune said. "There are great tasks ahead for him. And it surprises me that he is not here, if he knew that this was the day of my return from the

Labyrinth." To Alsimir he said, "Go, summon my lord Divvis: tell him there must be a session of the Council of Regency at once, and I await him." Then he turned to the others and said, "I have committed a grave discourtesy, my lords, in the first excitement of speaking here with you. For I have left this good woman to stand unintroduced, and that is not proper. This is the lady Elsinome, my mother, who for the first time in her life beholds the world that lies beyond the Labyrinth."

"My lords," she said, with color coming to her cheeks, but her face otherwise betraying no confusion, no embarrassment.

"The lord Stasilaine—Prince Mirigant—Duke Elzandir of Chorg—"

Each in turn saluted her with the highest respect, almost as though she were the Lady herself. And she received those salutes with a poise and presence that sent shivers of the most extreme delight through Hissune.

"Let my mother be taken," he said, "to the Pavilion of Lady Thiin, and given a suite worthy of some great hierarch of the Isle. I will join the rest of you in the council-chamber in an hour."

"An hour is not sufficient time for the lord Divvis to return from his hunt," said Mirigant mildly.

Hissune nodded. "So I comprehend. But it is not my fault that the Lord Divvis has chosen this day to go to the forest; and there is so much that needs to be said and done that I think we must begin before he arrives. My lord Stasilaine, will you concur with me in that?"

"Most surely."

"Then two of the three Regents are in agreement. It is sufficient to convene. My lords, the council-chamber in an hour?"

They were all there when Hissune, cleansed and in fresh robes, entered the hall fifty minutes later. Taking his seat at the high table beside Stasilaine, he glanced about at the assembled princes and said, "I have spoken with Hornkast, and I have beheld the Pontifex Tyeveras with my own eyes."

There was a stirring in the room, a gathering of tension.

Hissune said, "The Pontifex still lives. But it is not life as you or I understand it. He no longer speaks, even in such howls and shrieks as have been his recent language. He lives in another realm, far away, and I think it is the realm that lies just on this side of the Bridge of Farewells."

"And how soon, then, is he likely to die?" asked Nimian of Dundilmir.

"Oh, not soon, even now," replied Hissune. "They have their witcheries that can keep him for some years yet, I think, from making his crossing. But I believe that that crossing cannot now be much longer allowed to wait."

"It is Lord Valentine's decision to make," said the Duke of Halanx.

Hissune nodded. "Indeed. I will come to that in a little while." He rose and walked to the world-map, and laid his hand over the heart of Zimroel. "While traveling to and from the Labyrinth I received the regular dispatches. I know of the declaration of war against us made by the Piurivar Faraataa, whoever he may be; and I know that the Metamorphs now have begun to launch not only agricultural plagues into Zimroel but also a horde of ghastly new animals that create terrible havoc and fear. I am aware of the famine in the Khyntor district, the secession of Piliplok, the rioting in Ni-moya. I am not aware of what is taking place west of Dulorn, and I think no one is, this side of the Rift. I know also that western Alhanroel is rapidly approaching the chaotic condition of the other continent, and that the disruptions are heading swiftly eastward, even to the foothills of the Mount. In the face of all this we have done very little of a concrete nature so far. The central government appears to have vanished entirely, the provincial dukes are behaving as though they are altogether independent of one another, and we remain gathered on Castle Mount high above the clouds."

"And what do you propose?" Mirigant asked.

"Several things. First, the raising of an army to occupy the borders of Piurifayne, to seal the province off, and to penetrate the jungle in search of Faraataa and his followers, which I grant you will be no easy quest."

"And who will command this army?" said the Duke of Halanx.

"Permit me to return to that in a moment," Hissune said. "To continue: we must have a second army, also to be organized in Zimroel, to occupy Piliplok—peacefully, if possible, otherwise by force—and restore it to its allegiance to the central government. Third, we must call a general conclave of all provincial rulers to discuss a rational allocation of food supplies, with the provinces not yet afflicted sharing what they have with those suffering from famine—making it clear, of course, that we are calling for sacrifice but not an intolerable sacrifice. Those provinces unwilling to share, if there are any, will face military occupation."

"A great many armies," said Manganot, "for a society that has so little in the way of a military tradition."

"When armies have been needed," Hissune replied, "we have been able to raise them somehow. This was true in Lord Stiamot's time, and again during Lord Valentine's war of restoration, and it will be the case again now, since we have no choice. I point out, though, that several informal armies already exist, under the leadership of the various self-proclaimed new Coronals. We can make use of those armies, and of the new Coronals themselves."

"Make use of traitors?" the Duke of Halanx cried.

"Of anyone who can be of use," said Hissune. "We will invite them to join us; we will give them high rank, though not, I trust, the rank to which they have appointed themselves; and we will make it clear to them that if they do not cooperate, we will destroy them."

"Destroy?" Stasilaine said.

"It was the word I meant to use."

"Even Dominin Barjazid was pardoned and sent to his brothers. To take life, even the life of a traitor—"

"Is no trifling matter," said Hissune. "I mean to use these men, not to kill them. But I think we will have to kill them if they will not let themselves be used. I beg you, though, let us consider this point another time."

"*You* mean to use these men?" Prince Nimian of Dundilmir said. "You speak much like a Coronal!"

"No," Hissune said. "I speak like one of the two from whom the choice, by your own earlier agreement, is to be made. And in the unfortunate absence of my lord Divvis I speak perhaps too forcefully. But I tell you this, that I have given long thought to these plans, and I see no alternative to adopting them, no matter who is to rule."

"Lord Valentine rules," said the Duke of Halanx.

"As Coronal," said Hissune. "But I think we are agreed that in the present crisis we must have a true Pontifex to guide us, as well as a Coronal. Lord Valentine, so you tell me, is sailing to the Isle to meet with the Lady. I propose to make the same journey, and speak with the Coronal, and attempt to convince him of the importance of ascending to the Pontificate. If he sees the wisdom of my arguments, he will then convey his wishes in the matter of a successor. The new Coronal, I think, must take up the task of pacifying Piliplok and Ni-moya, and of winning over the allegiance of the false Coronals. The other of us, I suggest, should have command of the army that will invade the Metamorph lands. For my part it makes no difference to me which it is to wear the crown, Divvis or I, but it is essential that we take the field at once and begin the restoration of order, which is already long overdue."

"And shall we toss a royal-piece for it?" came a voice suddenly from the doorway.

Divvis, sweaty-looking and unshaven and still in his hunting clothes, stood facing Hissune.

Hissune smiled. "I am cheered to see you once again, my lord Divvis."

"I regret that I have missed so much of this meeting. Are we forming armies and choosing Coronals today, Prince Hissune?"

"Lord Valentine must choose the Coronal," Hissune replied calmly. "To you and me, after that, will fall the task of forming the armies and leading them. And it will be a while, I think, before either of us again has the leisure for such pastimes as hunting, my lord." He indicated the vacant chair beside him at the high table. "Will you sit, my lord Divvis? I have made some proposals before this meeting, which I will repeat to you, if you will grant me a few moments for it. And then we must come to some decisions. So will you sit and listen to me, my lord Divvis? Will you sit?"

4

Once more, then, to sea: through heat-haze and swelter, with the fiery wind out of Suvrael at his back and a swift unceasing current from the southwest pushing the ships swiftly toward northern lands. Valentine felt other currents, turbulent ones, sweeping through his soul. The words of the high spokesman Hornkast at the banquet in the Labyrinth still resounded in him, as though he had heard them only yesterday, and not what seemed like ten thousand years ago.

The Coronal is the embodiment of Majipoor. The Coro-

nal is Majipoor personified. He is the world; the world is the Coronal.

Yes. Yes.

And as he moved back and forth upon the face of the world, from Castle Mount to the Labyrinth, from the Labyrinth to the Isle, from the Isle to Piliplok to Piurifayne to Bellatule, from Bellatule to Suvrael—now from Suvrael again to the Isle—Valentine's spirit opened ever more widely to the anguish of Majipoor, his mind grew ever more receptive to the pain, the confusion, the madness, the horror, that now was ripping apart what had been the happiest and most peaceful of worlds. Night and day was he flooded with the outpourings of twenty billion tormented souls. And gladly did he receive it all; and eagerly did he accept and absorb all that Majipoor must pour into him; and willingly did he search for ways of easing that pain. But the strain was wearying him. Too much came flooding in; he could not process and integrate it all, and often it baffled and overwhelmed him; and there was no escaping from it, for he was a Power of the realm, and this was his task, which could not be refused.

All this afternoon he had stood by himself on the deck, staring straight ahead, and no one dared approach him, not even Carabella, so complete was the sphere of isolation in which he had enclosed himself. When after a time she did go to him, hesitantly, timidly, it was in silence. He smiled and drew her close, her hip against his thigh, her shoulder against the pit of his arm, but still he did not speak, for he had passed for the moment into a realm beyond words, where he was calm, where the eroded places of his spirit might begin to heal somewhat. He knew he could trust her not to intrude on that.

After a long while she glanced off to the west, and caught her breath sharply in surprise. But still she did not speak.

He said, as though from far away, "What is it you see, love?"

"A shape out there. A dragon shape, I think."

He made no reply.

She said, "Can it be possible, Valentine? They told us there wouldn't be any dragons in these waters at this time of year. But what is it I see, then?"

"You see a dragon."

"They said there wouldn't be any. But I'm sure of it. Something dark. Something large. Swimming in the same direction we're going. Valentine, how can there be a dragon here?"

"Dragons are everywhere, Carabella."

"Am I imagining it? Perhaps it's only a shadow on the water—a drifting mass of seaweed, maybe—"

He shook his head. "You see a dragon. A king-dragon, one of the great ones."

"You say that without even looking, Valentine."

"Yes. But the dragon is there."

"You sense it?"

"I sense it, yes. That great heavy dragon-presence. The strength of its mind. That powerful intelligence. I sensed it before you said anything."

"You sense so many things, now," she said.

"Too many," said Valentine.

He continued to look northward. The vast soul of the dragon lay like a weight upon his. His sensitivity had grown during these months of stress; he was able now to send his mind forth with scarcely an effort, indeed could scarcely keep himself from doing so. Awake or asleep, he roved deep into the soul of the world. Distance no longer seemed to be a barrier. He sensed everything, even the harsh bitter thoughts of the Shapeshifters, even the slow throbbing emanations of the sea dragons.

Carabella said, "What does the dragon want? Is it going to attack us, Valentine?"

"I doubt it."

"Can you be sure of that?"

"I'm not sure of anything, Carabella."

He reached toward the great beast in the sea. He strived to touch its mind with his. For an instant there was something like contact—a sense of opening, a sense of joining. Then he was brushed aside as though by a mighty hand, but not disdainfully, not contemptuously. It was as though the dragon were saying, *Not now, not here, not yet*.

"You look so strange," she said. "Will the dragon attack?"

"No. No."

"You seem frightened."

"Not frightened, no. I'm simply trying to understand. But I feel no danger. Only watchfulness—surveillance—that powerful mind, keeping watch over us—"

"Sending reports on us to the Shapeshifters, perhaps?"

"That may be, I suppose."

"If the dragons and the Shapeshifters are in alliance against us—"

"So Deliamber suspects, on the evidence of someone who is no longer available for questioning. I think it may be more complex than that. I think we will be a long time understanding what it is that links the Shapeshifters and the sea dragons. But I tell you, I feel no danger."

She was silent a moment, staring at him.

"You can actually read the dragon's mind?"

"No. No. I *feel* the dragon's mind. The presence of it. I can read nothing. The dragon is a mystery to me, Carabella. The harder I strive to reach it, the more easily it deflects me."

"It's turning. It's beginning to swim away from us."

"Yes. I can feel it closing its mind to me—pulling back, shutting me out."

"What did it want, Valentine? What did it learn?"

"I wish I knew," he said.

He clung tightly to the rail, drained, shaking. Carabella put her hand over his a moment, and squeezed it; and then she moved away and they were silent again.

He did not understand. He understood so very little. And he knew it was essential that he understand. He was the one through which this turmoil in the world might be resolved, and reunion accomplished: of that he was sure. He, only he, could bring the warring forces together into harmony. But how? How?

When, years ago, his brother's death had unexpectedly made him a king, he had taken on that burden without a murmur, giving himself over fully to it though often the kingship felt to him like a chariot that was pulling him mercilessly along behind it. But at least he had had the training a king must have. Now, so it was beginning to seem, Majipoor was demanding of him that he become a god; and he had had no training at all for that.

He sensed the dragon still there, somewhere not far away. But he could make no real contact; and after a time he abandoned the attempt. He stood until dusk, peering to the north as though he expected to see the Isle of the Lady shining like a beacon in the darkness.

But the Isle was still some days' journey away. They were only now passing the latitude of the great peninsula known as the Stoienzar. The sea-road from Tolaghai to the Isle cut sharply across the Inner Sea almost to Alhanroel—to the Stoienzar's tip, practically—and then angled up the back face of the Rodamaunt Archipelago to Numinor port. Such a route took fullest advantage of the prevailing wind from the south, and of the strong Rodamaunt Current: it was far quicker to sail from Suvrael to the Isle than from the Isle to Suvrael.

That evening there was much discussion of the dragon. In winter these waters normally abounded with them, for the dragons that had survived the autumn hunting season customarily proceeded past the Stoienzar coast on their eastward journey back to the Great Sea. But this was not winter; and, as Valentine and the others had already had the opportunity to observe, the dragons had taken a strange route this year, veering northward past the western coast of the Isle toward some mysterious rendezvous in the polar seas. But these days, though, there were dragons everywhere in the sea, or so it seemed, and who knew why? Not I, Valentine thought. Certainly not I.

He sat quietly among his friends, saying little, gathering his strength, replenishing himself.

In the night, lying awake with Carabella at his side, he listened to the voices of Majipoor. He heard them crying with hunger in Khyntor and whimpering with fear in Pidruid; he heard the angry shouts of vigilante forces running through the cobbled streets of Velathys, and the barking outbursts of street-corner orators in Alaisor. He heard his name called out, fifty million times. He heard the Metamorphs in their humid jungle savoring the triumph that was sure to come, and he heard the dragons calling to one another in great solemn tones on the floor of the sea.

And also he felt the cool touch of his mother's hand across his brow, and the Lady saying, "You will be with me soon, Valentine, and I will give you ease." And then the King of Dreams was with him to declare, "This night will I traverse the world seeking your enemies, friend Coronal, and if I can bring them to their knees, why, that I mean to do." Which gave him some repose, until the cries of dismay and pain began again, and then the singing of the sea-dragons, and then the whispering of the Shapeshifters; and so the night became morning, and he rose from his bed more weary than when he had entered it.

But once the ships had passed the tip of the Stoienzar and entered into the waters between Alhanroel and the Isle,

Valentine's malaise began to lift. The bombardment of anguish from every part of the world did not cease; but here the power of the Lady was paramount and grew daily stronger, and Valentine felt her beside him in his mind, aiding, guiding, comforting. In Suvrael, confronted with the pessimism of the King of Dreams, he had spoken eloquently of his conviction that the world could be restored. "There is no hope," said Minax Barjazid, to which Valentine replied, "There is, if only we reach out to seize it. I see the way." And the Barjazid said, "There is no way, and all is lost," to which Valentine replied, "Only follow me, and I will show the way." And eventually he had pulled Minax from his bleakness and won his grudging support. That shard of hope that Valentine had found in Suvrael had somehow slipped from his grasp during this voyage north; but again it seemed to be returning.

Now the Isle was very close. Now each day it stood higher above the horizon, and every morning, as the rising sun struck its eastern face, its chalky ramparts offered a brilliant display, pale pink in the first light, then a stunning scarlet that gave way imperceptibly to gold, and then at last, when the sun was fully aloft, the splendor of total whiteness, a whiteness that rang out across the waters like the clashing of giant cymbals and the upsurge of a vast sustained melody.

In Numinor port the Lady was waiting for him at the house known as the Seven Walls. Once more the hierarch Talinot Esulde conducted Valentine to her in the Emerald Room; once more he found her standing between the potted tanigale trees, smiling, her arms outstretched to him.

But startling and dismaying changes had occurred in her, he saw, since that other time, not a year ago, when they had met in this room. Her dark hair was shot through, now, with strands of white; the warm gleam of her eyes had turned dull and almost chilly; and time was making inroads now even on her regal bearing, rounding her shoulders, pulling her head down closer to them and thrusting it forward. She had seemed to him a goddess once; now she seemed a goddess being transformed gradually into an old woman, very much mortal.

They embraced. She seemed to have grown so light that the merest vagrant gust would carry her away. They drank a cool golden wine together, and he told her of his wanderings in Piurifayne, of his voyage to Suvrael, of his meeting with

Dominin Barjazid, and of the pleasure it had given him to see his old enemy restored to his right mind and proper allegiance.

"And the King of Dreams?" she asked. "Was he cordial?"

"To the utmost. There was great warmth between us, which surprised me."

"The Barjazids are rarely lovable. The nature of their life in that land, and of their dread responsibilities, prevents it, I suppose. But they are not the monsters that they are popularly thought to be. This Minax is a fierce man—I feel it in his soul, when our minds meet, which is not often—but a strong and virtuous one."

"He views the future bleakly, but he has pledged his fullest support to all that we must do. At this moment he lashes the world with his most potent sendings, in the hope of bringing the madness into check."

"So I am aware," said the Lady. "These weeks past I have felt the power of him flooding out of Suvrael, as it has never come before. He has launched a mighty effort. As have I, in my quieter way. But it will not be enough. The world has gone mad, Valentine. Our enemies' star ascends, and ours wanes, and hunger and fear rule the world now, not Pontifex and Coronal. You know that. You feel the madness pressing upon you, engulfing you, threatening to sweep everything away."

"Then we will fail, mother? Is that what you're saying? You, the fountain of hope, the bringer of comfort?"

Some of the old steely mettle returned to her eyes. "I said nothing of failure. I said only that the King of Dreams and Lady of the Isle are not of themselves able to stem the torrent of insanity."

"There is a third power, mother. Or do you think I am incapable of waging this war?"

"You are capable of anything you wish to achieve, Valentine. But even three Powers are not enough. A lame government cannot meet a crisis such as afflicts us now."

"Lame?"

"It stands on three legs. There should be four. It is time for old Tyeveras to sleep."

"Mother—"

"How long can you evade your responsibility?"

"I evade nothing, mother! But if I bottle myself up in the Labyrinth, what purpose will that achieve?"

"Do you think a Pontifex is useless? How strange a view of our commonwealth you must have, if you think that."

"I understand the value of the Pontifex."

"Yet you have ruled without one throughout your whole reign."

"It was not my fault that Tyeveras was senile when I came to the throne. What was I to do, go on to the Labyrinth immediately upon becoming Coronal? I had no Pontifex because I was not given one. And the time was not right for me to take Tyeveras's place. I had work of a more visible kind to do. I still have."

"You owe Majipoor a Pontifex, Valentine."

"Not yet. Not yet."

"How long will you say that?"

"I must remain in sight. I mean to make contact with the Danipiur somehow, mother, and bring her into a league with me against this Faraataa, our enemy, who will wreck all the world in the name of regaining it for his people. If I am in the Labyrinth, how can I—"

"Do you mean you will go to Piurifayne a second time?"

"That would only fail a second time. All the same, I see it as essential that I negotiate with the Metamorphs. The Danipiur must comprehend that I am not like the kings of the past, that I recognize new truths. That I believe we can no longer repress the Metamorph in the soul of Majipoor, but must recognize it, and admit it to our midst, and incorporate it in us all."

"And this can only be done while you are Coronal?"

"So I am convinced, mother."

"Examine your convictions again, then," said the Lady, in an inexorable voice. "If indeed they are convictions, and not merely a loathing for the Labyrinth."

"I detest the Labyrinth, and make no secret of it. But I will go to it, obediently if not gladly, when the time comes. I say the time is not yet at hand. It may be close, but it is not yet here."

"May it not be long in coming, then. Let Tyeveras sleep at last, Valentine. And let it be soon."

5

It was a small triumph, Faraataa thought, but one well worth savoring, this summons to meet with the Danipiur. So many years an outcast, flitting miserably through the jungle, so many years of being mocked when he was not being ignored; and now the Danipiur had with the greatest of diplomatic courtesy invited him to attend her at the House of Offices in Ilirivoyne.

He had been tempted at first to reverse the invitation, and tell her loftily to come to *him* in New Velalisier. After all, she was a mere tribal functionary whose title had no pre-Exile pedigree, and he, by the acclamation of multitudes, was the Prince To Come and the King That Is, who spoke daily with water-kings and commanded loyalties far more intense than any the Danipiur could claim. But then he reconsidered: how much more effective it would be, he told himself, to march at the head of his thousands into Ilirivoyne, and let the Danipiur and all her flunkeys see what power he held! So be it, he thought. He agreed to go to Ilirivoyne.

The capital in its newest site still had a raw, incomplete look. They had as usual chosen an open place in the forest for it, with an ample stream nearby. But the streets were mere hazy paths, the wicker houses had little ornamentation and their roofs looked hastily woven, and the plaza in front of the House of Offices was only partially cleared, with vines still snaking and tangling everywhere. Only the House of Offices itself afforded any connection with the former Ilirivoyne. As was the custom, they had carried the building with them from the old site, and reerected it at the center of town, where it dominated everything: three stories high, fashioned of gleaming poles of bannikop with polished planks of swamp mahogany for its facade, it stood out above the crude huts of the Piurivars of Ilirivoyne like a palace. But when we cross the sea and restore Velalisier, Faraataa thought, we will build a true palace out of marble and slate that will be the new wonder of the world, and we will decorate it with the fine things that we will take as booty from Lord Valentine's

Castle. And then let the Danipiur humble herself before me!

But for now he meant to observe the protocols. He presented himself before the House of Offices and shifted himself through the five Changes of Obeisance: the Wind, the Sands, the Blade, the Flow, the Flame. He held himself in the Fifth of the Changes until the Danipiur appeared. She seemed startled, for the barest brief moment, by the size of the force that had accompanied him to the capital: it filled the plaza and spread out beyond the borders of the city. But she recovered her poise swiftly and welcomed him with the three Changes of Acceptance: the Star, the Moon, the Comet. On that last, Faraataa reverted to his own form, and followed her into the building. Never before had he entered the House of Offices.

The Danipiur was cool, remote, proper. Faraataa felt the merest flicker of awe—she had held her office during the entire span of his life, after all—but quickly he mastered it. Her lofty style, her supreme self-possession, were, he knew, mere weapons of defense.

She offered him a meal of calimbots and ghumba, and to drink gave him a pale lavender wine, which he eyed with displeasure, wine not being a beverage that had been used among the Piurivars in the ancient times. He would not drink it or even raise it in a salute, which did not pass unnoticed.

When the formalities were done the Danipiur said brusquely to him, "I love the Unchanging Ones no more than you do, Faraataa. But what you seek is unattainable."

"And what is it that I seek, then?"

"To rid the world of them."

"You think this is unattainable?" he said, a tone of delicate curiosity in his voice. "Why is that?"

"There are twenty billion of them. Where are they to go?"

"Are there no other worlds in the universe? They came from them: let them return."

She touched her fingertips to her chin: a negative gesture carrying with it amusement and disdain for his words. Faraataa refused to let it irritate him.

"When they came," said the Danipiur, "they were very few. Now they are many, and there is little travel in these times between Majipoor and other worlds. Do you understand how long it would take to transport twenty billion people from this planet? If a ship departed every hour carrying ten thousand of them, I think we would never be rid of them all, for they must breed faster than the ships could be loaded."

"Then let them stay here, and we will continue to wage war against them. And they will kill one another for food, and after a time there will be no food and the ones who remain will starve to death, and their cities will become ghost places. And we will be done with them forever."

Again the fingertips to the chin. "Twenty billion dead bodies? Faraataa, Faraataa, be sensible! Can you comprehend what that means? There are many more people in Ni-moya alone than in all of Piurifayne—and how many other cities are there? Think of the stench of all those bodies! Think of the diseases of corruption let loose by so much rotting flesh!"

"It will be very sparse flesh, if they all have starved to death. There will not be so much to rot."

"You speak too frivolously, Faraataa."

"Do I? Well, then, I speak frivolously. In my frivolous way I have shattered an oppressor under whose heel we have writhed for fourteen thousand years. Frivolously I have hurled them into chaos. Frivolously I—"

"Faraataa!"

"I have achieved much in my frivolous way, Danipiur. Not only without any aid from you, but in fact with your direct opposition much of the time. And now—"

"Attend me, Faraataa! You have set loose mighty forces, yes, and you have shaken the Unchanging Ones in a way that I did not think possible. But the time has come now for you to pause and give some thought to the ultimate consequences of what you have done."

"I have," he replied. "We will regain our world."

"Perhaps. But at what a cost! You have sent blights out into their lands—can those blights be so easily called back, do you think? You have devised monstrous and frightful new animals and turned them loose. And now you propose to let the world be choked by the decaying corpses of billions of people. Are you saving our world, Faraataa, or destroying it?"

"The blights will disappear when the crops they feed on, which are mainly not anything of any use to us, have perished. The new animals are few and the world is large, and the scientists assure me that they are unable to reproduce themselves, so we will be rid of them once their work is done. And

I am less fearful of those decaying corpses than you. The scavenger birds will feed as they have never fed before, and we will build temples out of the mounds of bones that remain. Victory is ours, Danipiur. The world has been regained."

"You are too confident. They have not yet begun to strike back at us—but what if they do, Faraataa, what if they do? I ask you to remember, Faraataa, what Lord Stiamot accomplished against us."

"Lord Stiamot needed thirty years to complete his conquest."

"Yes," said the Danipiur, "but his armies were small. Now the Unchanging Ones outnumber us greatly."

"And now we have the art of sending plagues and monsters against them, which we did not have in Lord Stiamot's time. Their very numbers will work in their disfavor, once their food supplies run out. How can they fight us for thirty days, let alone thirty years, with famine pulling their civilization apart?"

"Hungry warriors may fight much more fiercely than plump ones."

Faraataa laughed. "Warriors? What warriors? You speak absurdities, Danipiur. These people are soft."

"In Lord Stiamot's day—"

"Lord Stiamot's day was eight thousand years ago. Life has been very easy for them ever since, and they have become a race of simpletons and cowards. And the biggest simpleton of all is this Lord Valentine of theirs, this holy fool, with his pious abhorrence of violence. What do we have to fear from such a king as that, who has no stomach for slaughter?"

"Agreed: we have nothing to fear from him. But we can use him, Faraataa. And that is what I mean to do."

"In what way?"

"You know that it is his dream to come to terms with us."

"I know," said Faraataa, "that he entered Piurifayne foolishly hoping to negotiate with you in some way, and that you wisely avoided seeing him."

"He came seeking friendship, yes. And yes, I avoided him. I needed to learn more about your intentions before I could enter into any dealings with him."

"You know my intentions now."

"I do. And I ask you to cease spreading these plagues,

and to give me your support when I meet with the Coronal. Your actions threaten my purposes."

"Which are?"

"Lord Valentine is different from the other Coronals I have known. As you say, he is a holy fool: a gentle man, with no stomach for slaughter. His loathing of warfare makes him pliant and manipulable. I mean to win from him such concessions as no previous Coronal would grant us. The right to settle once again in Alhanroel—possession once more of the sacred city Velalisier—a voice in the government—complete political equality, in short, within the framework of Majipoori life."

"Better to destroy the framework entirely, and settle where we choose without asking leave of anyone!"

"But you must see that that is impossible. You can neither evict twenty billion people from this planet nor exterminate them. What we *can* do is to make peace with them. And in Valentine lies our opportunity for peace, Faraataa."

"Peace! What a foul lying word that is! *Peace!* Oh, no, Danipiur, I want no peace. I am interested not in peace but in victory. And victory will be ours."

"The victory you crave will be the doom of us all," the Danipiur retorted.

"I think not. And I think your negotiations with the Coronal will lead you nowhere. If he grants such concessions as you mean to ask, his own princes and dukes will overthrow him and replace him with a more ruthless man, and then where will we be? No, Danipiur, I must continue my war until the Unchanging Ones have vanished entirely from our world. Anything short of that means our continued enslavement."

"I forbid it."

"Forbid?"

"I am the Danipiur!"

"So you are. But what is that? I am the King That Is, of whom the prophecies spoke. How can you forbid me anything? The Unchanging Ones themselves tremble before me. I will destroy them, Danipiur. And if you oppose me, I will destroy you as well." He rose, and with a sweep of his hand he knocked aside his untouched wine-bowl, spilling its contents across the table. At the door he paused and looked back, and briefly allowed his shape to flicker into the form known as the River, a gesture of defiance and contempt. Then he resumed his own form. "The war will continue," he said.

"For the time being I permit you to retain your office, but I warn you to make no treasonous approaches to the enemy. As for the holy Lord Valentine, his life is forfeit to me. His blood will serve to cleanse the Tables of the Gods on the day of the rededication of Velalisier. Be wary, Danipiur. Or I will use yours for the same purpose."

6

"The Coronal Lord Valentine is with his mother the Lady at Inner Temple," said the hierarch Talinot Esulde. "He asks you to rest here this night at the royal lodging-place in Numinor, Prince Hissune, and to begin your journey toward him in the morning."

"As the Coronal wishes," said Hissune.

He stared past the hierarch at the vast white wall of First Cliff rising above Numinor. It was dazzling in its brightness, almost painfully so, nearly as brilliant as the sun itself. When the Isle first had come into view some days before on the voyage from Alhanroel, he had found himself shading his eyes against that powerful white glare and wanting to look away altogether, and Elsinome, standing beside him, had turned in terror from it, crying, "I have never seen anything so bright! Will it blind us to look at it?" But now, at close range, the white stone was less frightening: its light seemed pure, soothing, the light of a moon rather than of a sun.

A cool sweet breeze blew from the sea, the same breeze that had carried him so swiftly—but not nearly swiftly enough to still the impatience that day after day mounted and surged in him—from Alaisor to the Isle. That impatience still rode him now that he had arrived in the Lady's domain. But yet he knew he must be patient, and adapt himself to the unhurried rhythms of the Isle and its serene mistress, or he might never be able to accomplish the things he had come here to accomplish.

And indeed he felt those gentle rhythms settling over him as he was conducted by the hierarchs through the small quiet harbor town to the royal lodging known as the Seven Walls. The spell of the Isle, he thought, was irresistible: it was such a tranquil place, serene, peaceful, testifying in every aspect of itself to the presence of the Lady. The turmoil now wracking Majipoor seemed unreal to him here.

That night, though, Hissune found it far from easy to get to sleep. He lay in a magnificent chamber hung with splendid dark-hued fabrics of an antique weave, where, for all he knew, the great Lord Confalume had slept before him, or Prestimion, or Stiamot himself; and it seemed to him that those ancient kings still hovered nearby, speaking to one another in low whispers, and what they were saying was in mockery of him: *upstart, popinjay, peacock*. It is only the sound of the surf against the rampart below, he told himself angrily. But still sleep would not come, and the harder he sought it the wider awake he became. He rose and walked from room to room, and out into the courtyard, thinking to rouse some servitor who might give him wine; but he found no one about, and after a time he returned to his room and closed his eyes once again. This time he thought he felt the Lady lightly touch his soul, almost at once: not a sending, nothing like that, merely a contact delicate as a breath across his soul, a soft *Hissune, Hissune, Hissune*, which calmed him into a light sleep and then into a deeper one beyond the reach of dreams.

In the morning the slender and stately hierarch Talinot Esulde came for him and for Elsinome, and led them to a place at the foot of the great white cliff, where floater sleds were waiting to carry them to the high terraces of the Isle.

The ascent of the vertical face of First Cliff was awesome: up and up and up, as though in a dream. Hissune did not dare open his eyes until the sled had come to rest in its landing pad. Then he looked back, and saw the sun-streaked expanse of the sea stretching off to distant Alhanroel, and the twin curving arms of the Numinor breakwater jutting out into it directly below him. A floater-wagon took them across the heavily wooded tableland atop the cliff to the base of Second Cliff, which sprang upward so steeply it seemed to fill all the sky; and there they rested for the night in a lodge at a place called the Terrace of Mirrors, where massive slabs of polished black stone rose like mysterious ancient idols from the ground.

Thence it was upward once more by sled to the highest and innermost cliff, thousands of feet above sea level, that was the sanctuary of the Lady. Atop Third Cliff the air was startlingly clear, so that objects many miles away stood out as though magnified in a glass. Great birds of a kind unknown to

Hissune, with plump red bodies and enormous black wings, circled in lazy spirals far overhead. Again Hissune and Elsinome traveled inward over the Isle's flat summit, past terrace after terrace, until at last they halted at a place where simple buildings of whitewashed stone were scattered in seeming randomness amidst gardens of a surpassing serenity.

"This is the Terrace of Adoration," said Talinot Esulde. "The gateway to Inner Temple."

They slept that night in a quiet secluded lodge, pleasant and unpretentious, with its own shimmering pool and a quiet, intimate garden bordered by vines whose thick ancient trunks were woven into an impenetrable wall. At dawn, servitors brought them chilled fruits and grilled fish; and soon after they had eaten, Talinot Esulde appeared. With her was a second hierarch, a formidable, keen-eyed, white-haired woman. She greeted them each in a very different way: offering Hissune the salute befitting a prince of the Mount, but doing it in a strangely casual, almost perfunctory manner, and then turning to Elsinome and clasping both of her hands in her own, and holding them a long moment, staring warmly and intently into her eyes. When at last she released Elsinome she said, "I bid you both welcome to Third Cliff. I am Lorivade. The Lady and her son await you.

The morning was cool and misty, with a hint of sunlight about to break through the low clouds. In single file, with Lorivade leading and Talinot Esulde to the rear, no one uttering a word, they passed through a garden where every leaf was shimmering with dew-sparkles, and crossed a bridge of white stone, so delicately arched that it seemed it might shatter at the most gentle of footfalls, into a broad grassy field, at the far end of which lay Inner Temple.

Hissune had never seen a building more lovely. It was constructed of the same translucent white stone as the bridge. At its heart was a low flat-roofed rotunda, from which eight long, slender, equidistant wings radiated like starbeams. There was no ornamentation: everything was clean, chaste, simple, flawless.

Within the rotunda, an airy eight-sided room with an octagonal pool at its center, Lord Valentine and a woman who was surely his mother the Lady were waiting for them.

Hissune halted at the threshold, frozen, overcome by bewilderment. He looked from one to the other in confusion, not knowing to which of these Powers he should offer the first obeisance. The Lady, he decided, must take precedence. But in what form should he pay his homage? He knew the sign of the Lady, of course, but did one make that sign to the Lady herself, as one made the starburst sign to the Coronal, or was that hopelessly gauche? Hissune had no idea. Nothing in his training had prepared him for meeting the Lady of the Isle.

He turned to her, nevertheless. She was much older than he had expected her to be, face deeply furrowed, hair streaked with white, eyes encircled by an intricate network of fine lines. But her smile, intense and warm and radiant as the midday sun, spoke eloquently of the vigor and force that still were hers: in that astonishing glow Hissune felt his doubts and fears swiftly melting away.

He would have knelt to her, but she seemed to sense what he intended before he could make the gesture, and halted him with a quick little shake of her head. Instead the Lady held forth her hand to him. Hissune, somehow comprehending what was expected of him, lightly touched the tips of his fingers to hers for an instant, and took from her a startling, tingling inrush of energy that might have caused him to leap back if he had not been holding himself under such taut control. But from that unexpected current he found himself gaining a surge of renewed assurance, strength, poise.

Then he turned to the Coronal.

"My lord," he whispered.

Hissune was astonished and dismayed by the alteration in Lord Valentine's appearance since he last had seen the Coronal, so very long ago in the Labyrinth, at the beginning of his ill-starred grand processional. Then Lord Valentine had been in the grip of terrible fatigue, but even so his features had displayed an inner light, a certain irrepressible joyousness, that no weariness could altogether dispel. Not now. The cruel sun of Suvrael had darkened his skin and bleached his hair, giving him a strangely fierce, almost barbaric look. His eyes were deep and hooded, his face was gaunt and lined, there was no trace whatever of that amiable sunniness of spirit that was his most visible trait of character. He seemed altogether unfamiliar: somber, tense, remote.

Hissune began to offer the starburst sign. But Lord Valentine brushed it away impatiently and, reaching forward, seized Hissune's hand, gripping it tightly a moment. That too was unsettling. One did not shake hands with Coronals. And at the contact of their hands Hissune again felt a current flowing into him: but this energy, unlike that which had come from the Lady, left him disturbed, jangled, ill at ease.

When the Coronal released him Hissune stepped back and beckoned to Elsinome, who was standing immobile by the threshold as though she had been turned to stone by the sight of two Powers of Majipoor in the same room. In a thick, hoarse voice he said, "My lord—good Lady—I pray you welcome my mother, the lady Elsinome—"

"A worthy mother for so worthy a son," said the Lady: the first words she had spoken, and her voice seemed to Hissune to be the finest he had ever heard: rich, calm, musical. "Come to me, Elsinome."

Breaking from her trancelike state, Elsinome advanced across the smooth marble floor, and the Lady advanced also toward her, so that they met by the eight-sided pool at the room's center. There the Lady took Elsinome in her arms, and embraced her closely and with great warmth; and when finally the two women parted, Hissune saw that his mother seemed like one who has for a long while been in darkness, and who now has emerged into the full brightness of the sun. Her eyes were shining, her face was flushed, there was no sign of timidity or awe about her.

She looked now toward Lord Valentine and began to make the starburst sign, only to have the Coronal reject it as he had from Hissune, holding out the palm of his hand to her and saying, "That is not necessary, good lady Elsinome."

"My lord, it is my duty!" she replied in a firm voice.

"No. No longer." The Coronal smiled for the first time that morning. "All that gesturing and bowing is stuff designed for public show. There's no need of such pomp in here."

To Hissune then he said, "I would not have recognized you, I think, had I not known it was you who was coming here today. We have been apart such a long time that we have become strangers, or so it feels to me."

"Several years, my lord, and not easy years," Hissune replied. "Time always works changes, and years like these work great changes."

"So they do." Leaning forward, Lord Valentine studied Hissune with an intensity that he found disconcerting. At length the Coronal said, "Once I thought that I knew you well. But the Hissune I knew was a boy who hid shyness behind slyness. The one who stands here today has become a man—a prince, even—and there is a little shyness left in him, but not much, and the slyness, I think, has turned into something deeper—craftiness, perhaps. Or even statesmanship, if the reports I have of you are true, and I would believe that they are. I think I still can see the boy I once knew, somewhere within you. But recognizing him is far from easy."

"And it is hard for me, my lord, to see in you the man who hired me once to be his guide through the Labyrinth."

"Am I changed that much, then, Hissune?"

"You are, my lord. I fear for you."

"Fear for Majipoor, if you must fear. Waste none on me."

"I do fear for Majipoor, and greatly. But how can you ask me not to fear for you? You are my benefactor, my lord. All I am I owe to you. And when I see you grown so bleak, so wintry—"

"These are wintry times, Hissune. The weather of the world is reflected on my face. But perhaps there is a springtime ahead for us all. Tell me: what is the news from Castle Mount? I know the lords and princes have been hatching great plans there."

"Indeed, my lord."

"Speak, then!"

"You understand, my lord, that these schemes are put forth subject to your ratification, that the Council of Regency would not presume to undertake—"

"So I assume. Tell me what the Council proposes."

Hissune drew his breath in deeply. "First," he said, "we would situate an army encircling all borders of Piurifayne, so that we may prevent the Metamorphs from exporting any further plagues and other horrors."

"To encircle Piurifayne, did you say, or to invade it?" asked Lord Valentine.

"Primarily to encircle it, my lord."

"*Primarily?*"

"Once we have established control of the borders, the plan is to enter the province in search of the rebel Faraataa and his followers."

"Ah. To capture Faraataa and his followers! And what will be done to them if they are captured, which I very much doubt they will be, considering my own experiences when I wandered in that jungle?"

"They will be confined."

"Nothing more? No execution of ringleaders?"

"My lord, we are not savages!"

"Of course. Of course. And the aim of this invasion will be strictly to take Faraataa?"

"No more than that, my lord."

"No attempt to overthrow the Danipiur? No campaign of general extermination of the Metamorphs?"

"Those ideas were never suggested."

"I see." His voice was curiously controlled, almost mocking: much unlike any tone Hissune had ever heard him use before. "And what other plans does the Council propose?"

"An army of pacification to occupy Piliplok—without bloodshed, if bloodshed can be avoided—and to take control of any other cities or provinces that may have seceded from the government. Also, neutralization of the various private armies established by the false Coronals now infesting many areas, and, if possible, the turning of those armies toward the service of the government. Finally, military occupation of any provinces that refuse to take part in a newly instituted program for sharing food supplies with afflicted zones."

"Quite a comprehensive scheme," Lord Valentine said, in that same odd detached tone. "And who will lead all these armies?"

"The Council has suggested dividing the command between my lord Divvis, my lord Tunigorn, and myself," replied Hissune.

"And I?"

"You will of course have supreme command over all our forces, my lord."

"Of course. Of course." Lord Valentine's gaze turned within, and for a long span of silence he appeared to be contemplating all that Hissune had said. Hissune watched him closely. There was something deeply troublesome about the Coronal's austere, restrained manner of questioning him: it seemed clear that Lord Valentine knew as well as Hissune himself where the conversation was heading, and Hissune found himself dreading the moment when it must get there. But that moment, Hissune realized, was already at hand. The Coronal's eyes brightened strangely as his attention turned once again toward Hissune, and he said, "Was anything else proposed by the Council of Regency, Prince Hissune?"

"One thing more, my lord."

"Which is?"

"That the commander of the army that will occupy

Piliplok and other rebellious cities should be one who bears the title of Coronal."

"The Coronal, you have just told me, will be the supreme commander."

"No, my lord. The *Pontifex* must be the supreme commander."

The silence that followed seemed to endure for a thousand years. Lord Valentine stood almost motionless: he might have been a statue, but for the slight flickering of his eyelids and the occasional quiver of a muscle in his cheek. Hissune waited tensely, not daring to speak. Now that he had done it, he felt amazed at his own temerity in delivering such an ultimatum to the Coronal. But it was done. It could not be withdrawn. If Lord Valentine in his wrath were to strip him of his rank and send him back to beg in the streets of the Labyrinth, so be it: it was done, it could not be withdrawn.

The Coronal began to laugh.

It was a laughter that began somewhere deep within him and rose like a geyser through his chest to his lips: a great bellowing booming laugh, more the sort of sound that some giant like Lisamon Hultin or Zalzan Kavol might make than anything one would expect the gentle Lord Valentine to let loose. It went on and on, until Hissune began to fear that the Coronal had taken leave of his senses; but just then it ceased, swiftly and suddenly, and nothing remained of Lord Valentine's bizarre mirth but a strange glittering smile.

"Well done!" he cried. "Ah, well done, Hissune, well done!"

"My lord?"

"And tell me, who is the new Coronal to be?"

"My lord, you must understand that these are only proposals—for the sake of the greater efficiency of the government in this time of crisis—"

"Yes, of course. And who, I ask you again, is to be brought forward in the name of greater efficiency?"

"My lord, the choice of a successor remains always with the former Coronal."

"So it does. But the candidates—are they not proposed by the high counsellors and princes? Elidath was the heir presumptive—but Elidath, as I think you must know, is dead. So, then—who is it to be, Hissune?"

"Several names were discussed," said Hissune softly. He

could scarcely bear to look directly at Lord Valentine now. "If this is offensive to you, my lord—"

"Several names, yes. Whose?"

"My lord Stasilaine, for one. But he at once declared that he had no wish to be Coronal. My lord Divvis, for another—"

"Divvis must never be Coronal!" said Lord Valentine sharply, with a glance toward the Lady. "He has all the faults of my brother Voriax, and none of his merits. Except valor, I suppose, and a certain forcefulness. Which are insufficient."

"There was one other name, my lord."

"Yours, Hissune?"

"Yes, my lord," said Hissune, but he could get the words out only in a choking whisper. "Mine."

Lord Valentine smiled. "And would you serve?"

"If I were asked, my lord, yes. Yes."

The Coronal's eyes bore down intensely on Hissune's, who withstood that fierce inquiry without flinching.

"Well, then, there is no problem, eh? My mother would have me ascend. The Council of Regency would have me ascend. Old Tyeveras surely would have me ascend."

"Valentine—" said the Lady, frowning.

"No, all is well, mother. I understand what must be done. I can hesitate no longer, can I? Therefore I accept my destiny. We will send word to Hornkast that Tyeveras is to be permitted at last to cross the Bridge of Farewells. You, mother, you finally may put down your burden, as I know you wish to do, and retire to the ease of the life of a former Lady. You, Elsinome: your task is only beginning. And yours, Hissune. See, the thing is done. It is as I intended, only sooner, perhaps, than I had expected." Hissune, watching the Coronal in astonishment and perplexity, saw the expression on his face shift: the harshness, the uncharacteristic ferocity, left his features, and into his eyes came the ease and warmth and gentleness of the Valentine he had once been, and that eerie rigid glittering smile, so close almost to a madman's, was replaced by the old Valentine-smile, kind, tender, loving. "It is done," said Valentine quietly. He raised his hands and held them forth in the starburst sign, and cried, "Long life to the Coronal! Long life to Lord Hissune!"

7

Three of the five great ministers of the Pontificate were already in the council-chamber when Hornkast entered. In the center, as usual, sat the Ghayrog Shinaam, minister of external affairs, his forked tongue flickering nervously, as though he believed that a death sentence was about to be passed not on the ancient creature he had served so long, but on himself. Beside him was the empty seat of the physician Sepulthrove, and to the right of that was Dilifon, that shriveled and palsied little man, sitting huddled in his thronelike chair, gripping its armrests for support; but his eyes were alive with a fire Hornkast had not seen in them for years. On the other side of the room was the dream-speaker Narrameer, radiating dark morbidity and terror from behind the absurdly voluptuous sorcery-induced beauty with which she cloaked her century-old body. How long, Hornkast wondered, had each of these three been awaiting this day? And what provision had they made in their souls for the time of its coming?

"Where is Sepulthrove?" Hornkast demanded.

"With the Pontifex," said Dilifon. "He was summoned to the throne-room an hour ago. The Pontifex has begun to speak once more, so we have been told."

"Strange that I was not notified," said Hornkast.

"We knew that you were receiving a message from the Coronal," Shinaam said. "We thought it best you not be disturbed."

"This is the day, is it not?" Narrameer asked, leaning tensely forward, running her fingers again and again through her thick, lustrous black hair.

Hornkast nodded. "This is the day."

"One can hardly believe it," said Dilifon. "The farce has gone on so long it seemed it might never end!"

"It ends today," said Hornkast. "Here is the decree. Quite elegantly phrased, in truth."

Shinaam, with a thin rasping laugh, said, "I would like to know what sort of phrases one uses in condemning a reigning Pontifex to death. It is a document that will be much studied by future generations, I think."

306

"The decree condemns no one to death," said Hornkast. "It issues no instructions. It is merely a proclamation of the Coronal Lord Valentine's grief upon the death of his father and the father of us all, the great Pontifex Tyeveras."

"Ah, he is shrewder than I thought!" Dilifon said. "His hands remain clean!"

"They always do," said Narrameer. "Tell me, Hornkast: who is the new Coronal to be?"

"Hissune son of Elsinome has been chosen."

"The young prince out of the Labyrinth?"

"The same."

"Amazing. And there is to be a new Lady, then?"

"Elsinome," said Hornkast.

"This is a revolution!" cried Shinaam. "Valentine has overturned Castle Mount with a single push! Who can believe it? Who can believe it? Lord Hissune! Can it be? How do the princes of the Mount accept it?"

"I think they had little choice," Hornkast replied. "But let us not concern ourselves with the princes of the Mount. We have our own tasks to carry out, on this our final day of power."

"And thanks be to the Divine that it is," said Dilifon.

The Ghayrog glared at him. "You speak for yourself alone!"

"Perhaps I do. But I speak also for the Pontifex Tyeveras."

"Who seems to be speaking for himself this day, eh?" said Hornkast. He peered at the document in his hand. "There are several curious problems that I must call to your attention. For example, my staff has so far been unable to locate any description of the proper procedure for proclaiming the death of a Pontifex and the ascension of a new one, it having been so long since such an event has occurred."

"Very likely no one now alive has any experience of such things," said Dilifon. "Except the Pontifex Tyeveras himself."

"I doubt that he will aid us in this matter," Hornkast said. "We are searching the archives now for details of the proclamation of the death of Ossier and the ascension of Tyeveras, but if we can find nothing we will have to invent our own ceremony."

Narrameer, eyes closed, said in a low, faraway voice, "You forget. There is one person who was present on the day of the ascension of Tyeveras."

Hornkast looked at her in amazement. Ancient she was,

that everyone knew; but no one knew *how* ancient, except
that she had been the imperial dream-speaker as far back as
anyone recalled. But if she had indeed survived out of the
reign of Tyeveras as Coronal, she was older even than he
imagined; and he felt a shiver go down his back, he who had
thought he was himself far beyond the age when anything
could cause surprise.

"You remember it, then?" he asked.

"I see it through the mists. It is announced first in the
Court of Columns. Then in the Court of Globes, and then in
the Place of Masks; and after that, it is declared in the Hall of
Winds and the Court of Pyramids. After which, it is announced
one final time at the Mouth of Blades. And when the new
Pontifex arrives at the Labyrinth, he must enter at the Mouth
of Blades and journey down through the levels on foot. That I
remember: Tyeveras striding with immense vigor through
huge crowds that called his name, and he walked so fast that
no one could keep pace with him, and he would not halt until
he had traversed the whole Labyrinth to its lowest level. Will
the Pontifex Valentine display such energy, I wonder?"

"That is the second curious matter," said Hornkast. "The
Pontifex Valentine has no immediate plans for taking up
residence in the Labyrinth."

"What?" Dilifon blurted.

"He is now at the Isle, with the former Lady and the
new Coronal and the new Lady. The Pontifex informs me that
it is his intention to go next to Zimroel, in order to bring the
rebellious provinces under his control. He expects this process to be a lengthy one, and he urges me to postpone any
celebration of his ascension."

"For how long?" Shinaam asked.

"Indefinitely," said Hornkast. "Who knows how long this
crisis will last? And while it does he will remain in the upper
world."

"In that case," said Narrameer, "we may expect the crisis
to last as long as Valentine lives."

Hornkast glanced toward her and smiled. "You understand him well. He detests the Labyrinth, and I think will
find every pretext to avoid dwelling in it."

Dilifon shook his head slowly. "But how can that be? The
Pontifex *must* dwell in the Labyrinth! It is the tradition!
Never in ten thousand years has a Pontifex lived in the upper
world!"

"Never has Valentine been Pontifex, either," Hornkast said. "I think there will be many changes forthcoming in his reign, if the world survives this war the Shapeshifters wage against it. But I tell you it matters little to me whether he lives in the Labyrinth or in Suvrael or on Castle Mount. My time is over; as is yours, good Dilifon, and yours, Shinaam, and perhaps even yours, my lady Narrameer. Such transformations as may come hold little interest for me."

"He *must* dwell here!" said Dilifon again. "How can the new Coronal assert his power, if the Pontifex is also apparent to the citizens of the upper world?"

"Perhaps that is Valentine's plan," Shinaam suggested. "He makes himself Pontifex, because he can no longer avoid it, but by remaining above he continues to play the active role of a Coronal, reducing this Lord Hissune of his to a subordinate position. By the Lady, I never thought him so crafty!"

"Nor I," said Dilifon.

Hornkast said, shrugging, "We have no idea what his intent may be, except that so long as the war continues, he will not come to this place. And his court will follow him about: for we are all relieved of our posts, in the moment when the succession occurs." He looked slowly about the room. "And I remind you that we have been speaking of Valentine as Pontifex, when in fact the succession has not yet occurred. That is our final responsibility."

"Ours?" said Shinaam.

"Would you shirk it?" Hornkast asked. "Then go: go, take to your bed, old man, and we will do our work without you. For we must move on to the throne-room now, and discharge our duty. Dilifon? Narrameer?"

"I will accompany you," Shinaam said dourly.

Hornkast led the way: a slow procession, a parade of antiquities. Several times it was necessary to wait while Dilifon, leaning on the arms of two burly aides, paused for breath. But at last they stood outside the great door of the imperial chamber; and once more Hornkast slipped his hand into the recognition glove and touched the door-opening device, a task that he knew he would never perform again.

Sepulthrove stood beside the intricate life-support globe that housed the Pontifex.

"It is very strange," the physician said. "After this long silence, he speaks again. Listen: he stirs now."

And from within the sphere of blue glass came the whistling and gurgling sounds of the voice of Tyeveras; and then, plainly, as he had once before done, he could be heard to say, *"Come. Rise. Walk."*

"The same words," said Sepulthrove.

"Life! Pain! Death!"

"I think he knows," Hornkast said. "I think he must."

Sepulthrove frowned. "Knows what?"

Hornkast indicated the decree. "This is Lord Valentine's proclamation of grief upon the loss of Majipoor's great emperor."

"I see," said the physician, and his hawk-featured face turned dark with congested blood. "So it finally must come."

"Indeed."

"Now?" Sepulthrove asked. His hands trembled. He held them poised above a bank of controls.

From the Pontifex came one last burst of words:

"Life, Majesty. Death. Valentine Pontifex of Majipoor!"

There was a terrible silence.

"Now," Hornkast said.

8

Endlessly back and forth across the sea, now sailing once more from the Isle to Zimroel: it was beginning to seem to Valentine that in one of his former lives he must have been that legendary ancient captain Sinnabor Lavon, who had set out to make the first crossing of the Great Sea and given up the voyage after five years, and who perhaps for that had been condemned to be reborn and sail from land to land without ever halting for rest. But Valentine felt no weariness now, and no yearning to give up this life of wandering that he had undertaken. In a way—a strange and unexpected way—he was still making his grand processional.

The fleet, sped westward by favorable winds, was nearing Piliplok. There had been no dragons in the sea this time to menace or delay the journey, and the crossing had been swift.

From the masts the banners stood out straight toward Zimroel ahead: no longer the green-and-gold colors of the Coronal, for now Lord Hissune sailed under those as he made his separate voyage to Zimroel. Valentine's ships bore the red-and-black of the Pontifex, with the Labyrinth symbol blazoned upon them.

He had not yet grown accustomed to those colors, nor to that symbol, nor to those other alterations that had come. They did not make the starburst sign to him any longer when they approached him. Well, so be it; he had always thought that such salutes were foolishness, anyway. They did not address him as "my lord" now when they spoke with him, for a Pontifex must be called "your majesty." Which made little difference to Valentine except that his ear had long since grown accustomed to that oft-repeated "my lord" as a kind of punctuation, a way of marking the rhythm of a sentence, and it was odd not to hear it. It was with difficulty that he got people to speak to him at all, now: for everyone knew that the custom since ancient times had been to address one's words to the high spokesman of the Pontifex, never to the Pontifex himself, though the Pontifex was right there and perfectly capable of hearing. And when the Pontifex replied, why, he must do it by indirect discourse also, through his spokesman. That was the first of the Pontifical customs that Valentine had discarded; but it was not easy to get others to abide by the change. He had named Sleet his high spokesman—it seemed a natural enough appointment—but Sleet was forbidden to indulge in any of that antique mummery of pretending to be the Pontifex's ears.

For that matter no one could comprehend the presence of a Pontifex aboard a ship, exposed to the brisk winds and the bright warm sunlight. The Pontifex was an emperor shrouded in mystery. The Pontifex belonged out of sight. The Pontifex, as everyone knew, should be in the Labyrinth.

I will not go, Valentine thought.

I have passed along my crown, and someone else now has the privilege of putting "Lord" before his name, and the Castle now will be Lord Hissune's Castle, if ever he has the chance to return to it. But I will not bury myself in the ground.

Carabella, emerging on deck, said, "Asenhart asks me to tell you, my lord, that we will be within range of Piliplok in twelve hours, if the wind holds true."

"Not 'my lord,'" Valentine said.

She grinned. "I find that so hard to remember, *your majesty*."

"As do I. But the change has been made."

"May I not call you 'my lord' even so, when we are in private? For that is what you are to me, my lord."

"Am I? Do I order you about, and have you pour my wine for me, and bring me my slippers like a servant?"

"You know I mean otherwise, Valentine."

"Then call me Valentine, and not 'my lord.' I was your king, and I am your emperor now, but I am not your master. That has always been understood between us, so I thought."

"I think perhaps it has—your majesty."

She laughed, and he laughed with her, and drew her close and held her against him. After a moment he said, "I have often told you I feel a certain regret, or even guilt, for having taken you away from a juggler's free life, and given you in its place all the heavy responsibilities of Castle Mount. And often you have told me, No, no, nonsense, there is nothing to regret, I came of my own will to live by your side."

"As in all truth I did, my lord."

"But now I am Pontifex—by the Lady, I say those words, and they sound like another language in my mouth!—I am Pontifex, I am indeed Pontifex, and now I feel once more that I must rob you of the joys of life."

"Why, Valentine? Must a Pontifex give up his wife, then? I've heard nothing of that custom!"

"A Pontifex must live in the Labyrinth, Carabella."

"You come back to that again!"

"It never leaves me. And if I am to live in the Labyrinth, why, then you must live there also, and how can I ask that of you?"

"Do you ask it of me?"

"You know I have no wish to part from you."

"Nor I from you, my lord. But we are not in the Labyrinth now, and it was my belief you had no plan for going there."

"What if I must, Carabella?"

"Who says *must* to a Pontifex?"

He shook his head. "But what if I must? You know as well as I how little love I have for that place. But if I must—if for reasons of state I must—if the absolute necessity of it is forced upon me, which I pray the Divine will not happen, but if indeed there comes a time when I am compelled by the logic of government to go down into that maze—"

"Why, then I will go with you, my lord."

"And give up all fair winds, and bright sunny days, and the sea and the forest and the mountains?"

"Surely you would find a pretext for coming forth now and then, even if you found it necessary to take up residence down there."

"And if I can't?"

"You pursue problems too far beyond the horizon, my lord. The world is in peril; mighty tasks await you, and no one will shove you into the Labyrinth while those tasks are undone; there is time later to worry about where we will live and how we will like it. Is that not so, my lord?"

Valentine nodded. "Indeed. I foolishly multiply my woes."

"But I tell you this, and then let us talk no further of it: if you find some honorable way of escaping the Labyrinth forever, I will rejoice, but if you must go down into it I will go with you and never give it a second thought. When as Coronal you took me as consort, do you imagine I failed to see that Lord Valentine must one day become Valentine Pontifex? When I accepted you, I accepted the Labyrinth: just as you, my lord, accepted the Labyrinth when you accepted the crown your brother had worn. So let us say no more on these matters, my lord."

"'Your majesty,'" said Valentine. He slipped his arm again about her shoulders, and touched his lips lightly to hers. "I will promise to do no more brooding about the Labyrinth," he said. "And you must promise to call me by my proper title."

"Yes, your majesty. Yes, your majesty. Yes, your majesty!"

And she made a wondrous sweeping salutation, swinging her arms round and round in a flamboyantly exaggerated mockery of the Labyrinth symbol.

After a time Carabella went below. Valentine remained on deck, studying the horizon through a seeing-tube.

What kind of reception, he wondered, would he have in the free republic of Piliplok?

There was hardly anyone who had not opposed his decision to go there. Sleet, Tunigorn, Carabella, Hissune—they all spoke of the risk, the uncertainty. Piliplok, in its madness, might do anything—seize him, even, and hold him hostage to guarantee its independence. "Whoever enters Piliplok," Carabella said, as she had said months before in Piurifayne, "must do so at the head of an army, and you have no army, my lord!"

From Hissune had come the same argument. "It was agreed on Castle Mount," he said, "that when the new armies are organized, it is the Coronal who should lead troops against Piliplok—while the Pontifex directs the strategy at a safer remove."

"It will not be necessary to lead troops against Piliplok," said Valentine.

"Your majesty?"

Valentine said, "I had much experience during the war of restoration in pacifying rebellious subjects without bloodshed. If you were to go to Piliplok—a new Coronal, untried, unknown, with soldiers at his back—it would be sure to stir armed resistance in them. But if the Pontifex himself appears—who can remember a time when a Pontifex was seen in Piliplok?—they will be awed, they will be cowed, they will not dare to raise a hand against him even if he enter the city alone."

Though Hissune had continued to voice strong doubts, in the end Valentine overruled him. There could have been no other outcome, Valentine knew: this early in his Pontificate, having only just handed over the temporal power of the Coronal to the younger man, he could not yet relegate himself wholly to the kind of figurehead position that a Pontifex might be expected to assume. Power, Valentine was discovering, was not easily relinquished, not even by those who once thought they had little love for it.

But it was not wholly a matter of contending for power, Valentine realized. It was a matter of preventing bloodshed where bloodshed was needless. Hissune plainly did not believe that Piliplok could be retaken peacefully; Valentine intended to demonstrate that it could be. Call it part of the new Coronal's education in the arts of government, Valentine thought. And if I fail, he thought—well, then, call it part of mine.

In the morning, as Piliplok burst into view high above the dark mouth of the great river Zimr, Valentine ordered his fleet to form two wings, with his flagship, the *Lady Thiin*, at their apex. And he placed himself, clad in the richly hued Pontifical robes of scarlet and black that he had had made for himself before departing from the Isle, at the prow of his vessel, so that all of Piliplok might see him clearly as the royal fleet approached.

"Again they send the dragon-ships to us," Sleet said.

Yes. As had been done the last time, when Valentine as Coronal had come to Piliplok on what was to have been the beginning of his grand processional through Zimroel, the fleet of dragon-hunters was sailing forth to meet him. But that other time they had had bright Coronal-ensigns of green and gold fluttering in their riggings, and they had greeted him with the joyous sounds of trumpets and drums. Now, Valentine saw, the dragon-ships flew a different flag, a yellow one with a great crimson slash across it, as somber and sinister as the spike-tailed vessels themselves. It was surely the flag of the free republic that Piliplok now deemed itself to be; nor was this fleet coming to hail him in any friendly way.

Grand Admiral Asenhart looked uneasily toward Valentine. He indicated the speaking-tube he held, and said, "Shall I order them to yield and escort us into port, majesty?" But the Pontifex only smiled, and signaled to him to be calm.

Now the mightiest of the Piliplok vessels, a monstrous thing with a horrifying fanged figurehead and bizarrely elaborate three-pronged masts, moved forward from the line and took up a position close by the *Lady Thiin*. Valentine recognized it as the ship of old Guidrag, the senior among the dragon-captains: and yes, there she was, the fierce old Skandar woman herself on the deck, calling out through a speaking tube, "In the name of the free republic of Piliplok, stand forth and identify yourselves!"

"Give me the tube," Valentine said to Asenhart. Putting it to his lips, he cried, "This is the *Lady Thiin*, and I am Valentine. Come aboard and speak with me, Guidrag."

"I may not do that, my lord."

"I did not say *Lord* Valentine, but Valentine," he responded. "Do you take my meaning? And if you will not come to me, why, then I will go to you! Prepare to take me on board."

"*Majesty!*" said Sleet in horror.

Valentine turned to Asenhart. "Make ready a floater-basket for us. Sleet, you are the high spokesman: you will accompany me. And you, Delíamber."

Carabella said urgently, "My lord, I beg you—"

"If they mean to seize us," he said, "they will seize us whether I am aboard their ship or mine. They have twenty ships for each of ours, and well-armed ones at that. Come, Sleet—Deliamber—"

"Majesty," said Lisamon Hultin sternly, "you may not go unless I accompany you!"

With a smile Valentine said, "Ah, well done! You give commands to the Pontifex! I admire your spirit: but no, I will take no bodyguards this time, no weapons, no protection of any sort except these robes. Is the floater ready, Asenhart?"

The basket was rigged and suspended from the foremast. Valentine clambered in, and beckoned to Sleet, grim-faced and bleak, and to the Vroon. He looked back at the others gathered on the deck of the flagship, Carabella, Tunigorn, Asenhart, Zalzan Kavol, Lisamon, Shanamir, all staring at him as though he had at last taken complete leave of his wits. "You should know me better by this time," he said softly, and ordered the basket lifted over the side.

Out over the water it drifted, skimming lightly above the waves, and climbing the side of the dragon-ship until snared by the hook that Guidrag lowered for it. A moment later Valentine stepped out onto the deck of the other vessel, the timbers of which were dark with the ineradicable stains of sea-dragon blood. A dozen towering Skandars, the least of whom was half again Valentine's size, confronted him, and at their head was old Guidrag, even more gap-toothed than before, her thick matted fur even more faded. Her yellow eyes gleamed with force and authority, but Valentine detected some uncertainty in her features as well.

He said, "What is this, Guidrag, that you offer me so unkind a welcome on this visit?"

"My lord, I had no idea it was you returning to us."

"Yet it seems I have returned once again. And am I not to be greeted with more joy than this?"

"My lord—things have changed here," she said, faltering a little.

"Changed? The free republic?" He glanced about the deck, and at the other dragon-ships arrayed on all sides. "What is a free republic, Guidrag? I think I have not heard the term before. I ask you: what does it mean?"

"I am only a dragon-captain, my lord. These political things—they are not for me to speak of—"

"Forgive me, then. But tell me this, at least: why were you sent forth to meet my fleet, if not to welcome us and guide us to port?"

Guidrag said, "I was sent not to welcome you but to turn you away. Though I tell you again that we had no idea it was you, my lord—that we knew only it was a fleet of imperial ships—"

"And imperial ships are no longer welcome in Piliplok?"

There was a long pause.

"No, my lord," said the Skandar woman lamely. "They are not, my lord. We have—how do I say this?—we have withdrawn from the empire, my lord. That is what a free republic is. It is a territory that rules itself, and is not governed from without."

Valentine lifted his eyebrows delicately. "Ah, and why is that? Is the rule of the imperial government so burdensome, do you think?"

"You play with me, my lord. These matters are beyond my understanding. I know only that these are difficult times, that changes have been made, that Piliplok now chooses to decide its own destinies."

"Because Piliplok still has food, and other cities have none, and the burden of feeding the hungry is too heavy for Piliplok? Is that it, Guidrag?"

"My lord—"

"And you must stop calling me 'my lord,'" said Valentine. "You must call me 'your majesty' now."

The dragon-captain, looking more troubled than ever, replied, "But are you no longer Coronal, my lord—your majesty—?"

"The changes in Piliplok are not the only changes that have occurred," he said. "I will show you, Guidrag. And then I will return to my ship, and you will lead me to the harbor, and I will speak with the masters of this free republic of yours, so that they can explain it to me more thoroughly. Eh, Guidrag? Let me show you who I am."

And he took Sleet's hand in one of his, and a tentacle of Deliamber's in the other, and moved easily and smoothly into the waking sleep, the trance-state that allowed him to speak mind to mind as though he were issuing sendings. And from his soul to Guidrag's there flowed a current of vitality and power so great that it caused the air between them to glow; for he drew now not only on the strength that had been growing in himself throughout this time of trial and turmoil, but on that which was lent him by Sleet and the Vroon, and by his comrades aboard the *Lady Thin*, and by Lord Hissune and Hissune's mother the Lady, and by his own mother the former Lady, and by all others who loved Majipoor as it had

been and as they wished it would be again. And he reached
forth to Guidrag and then beyond her to the Skandar dragon-
hunters at her side, and then to the crews of the other ships,
and then to the citizens of the free republic of Piliplok across
the waters; and the message that he sent them was a simple
one, that he had come to them to forgive them for their errors
and to receive from them their renewed loyalty to the great
commonwealth that was Majipoor. And he told them also that
Majipoor was indivisible and that the strong must aid the
weak or all would perish together, for the world stood at the
brink of doom and nothing but a single mighty effort would
save it. And lastly he told them that the beginning of the end
of the time of chaos was at hand, for Pontifex and Coronal and
Lady and King of Dreams were striding forth together to set
things to rights, and all would be made whole again, if only
they had faith in the justice of the Divine, in whose name he
reigned now as supreme monarch.

He opened his eyes. He saw Guidrag dazed and swaying
and sinking slowly to her knees on the deck, and the other
Skandars beside her doing the same. Then she threw up her
hands before her eyes as though to shield them from a
terrible light, and murmured in a stunned, awestruck way,
"My lord—your majesty—your majesty—"

"Valentine!" someone cried, farther back on the deck.
"Valentine Pontifex!" And the cry was taken up by one sailor
after another: "Valentine Pontifex! Valentine Pontifex!" until it
went echoing from ship to ship, all across the waters and
even to the ramparts of distant Piliplok:

"Valentine! Valentine Pontifex! Valentine Pontifex!"

FIVE

The Book
of the Reunion

1

When the royal expeditionary force was some hours yet downriver from Ni-moya, Lord Hissune called Alsimir to him and said, "Find out whether the great house known as Nissimorn Prospect still exists. If it does, I mean to requisition it as my headquarters while I'm in Ni-moya."

Hissune remembered that house—remembered all of Ni-moya, its white towers and glittering arcades—as vividly as though he had dwelled there half his life. But he had never set foot on the continent of Zimroel at all before this voyage. It was through the eyes of another that he had seen Ni-moya. Now he cast his mind back to that time in his boyhood when he had covertly peered at the memory-readings on file in the Register of Souls in the depths of the Labyrinth. What was her name, the little shopkeeper from Velathys who had married the duke's brother, and came to inherit Nissimorn Prospect? Inyanna, he thought. Inyanna Forlana. Who had been a thief in the Grand Bazaar, until the course of her life so amazingly changed.

All that had happened at the end of Lord Malibor's reign—only some twenty or twenty-five years ago. Very likely she was still alive, Hissune thought. Still living in her wondrous mansion overlooking the river. And then I will go to her and I will say, "I know you, Inyanna Forlana. I understand you as well as I understand myself. We are of the same kind, you and I: fortune's favorites. And we know that the true favorites of fortune are those who know how to make the best use of their own good luck."

Nissimorn Prospect still stood, rising splendidly on its rocky headland above the harbor, its cantilevered balconies and porticos floating dreamlike in the shimmering air. But Inyanna Forlana no longer lived there. The great house was occupied now by a brawling horde of squatters, packed five

321

and six to a room, who had scrawled their names on the glass
wall of the Hall of Windows and built smoky campfires on the
verandas facing the garden and left smeary fingerprints on
the shining white walls. Most of them fled like morning mists
the moment the Coronal's forces came through the gates; but
a few remained, sullenly staring at Hissune as if he were an
invader from some other world.

"Shall I clear the last of this rabble out, my lord?"
Stimion asked.

Hissune nodded. "But give them some food and something to drink first, and tell them that the Coronal regrets
that he must have their place for his lodging. And ask them if
they know of the Lady Inyanna, whose house this once was."

Grimly he went from room to room, comparing what he
beheld to the radiant vision of this place he had had from the
memory-reading of Inyanna Forlana. The transformation was
a saddening one. There was no part of the house that was not
in some way soiled, spoiled, stained, blemished, ravaged. It
would take an army of craftsmen years to restore it to what it
had been, Hissune thought.

As with Nissimorn Prospect, so too with all of Ni-moya.
Hissune, disconsolately wandering the Hall of Windows with
its sweeping views of every part of the city, looked out upon a
scene of horrifying ruination. This had been the wealthiest
and most resplendent city of Zimroel, equal to any of the
cities of Castle Mount. The white towers that had housed
thirty million people now were blackened with the smoke of
scores of great fires. The Ducal Palace was a shattered stump
atop its magnificent pedestal. The Gossamer Galleria, a mile-
long span of suspended fabric where the finest shops of the
city had been, had been cut loose from its moorings at one
side and sprawled like a discarded cloak across the avenue
below it. The glass domes of the Museum of Worlds were
broken, and Hissune did not want to think of what must have
become of its treasures. The revolving reflectors of the Crystal Boulevard were dark. He looked toward the harbor and
saw what must have been the floating restaurants, where
once it had been possible to dine elegantly on the rarest
delicacies of Narabal and Stee and Pidruid and other distant
cities, capsized and turned bottomside up in the water.

He felt cheated. To have dreamed so long of seeing
Ni-moya, and now at last to be here and find it like this,
perhaps beyond repair. . . .

How had this happened? he wondered. Why had the people of Ni-moya, in their hunger and panic and madness, turned against their own city? And was it like this all across the heartland of Zimroel, all the beauty that it had taken thousands of years to create tossed away in a single paroxysm of mindless destruction? *We have paid a heavy price*, Hissune told himself, *for all those centuries of smug self-satisfaction*.

Stimion came to him to report the news of the Lady Inyanna that he had learned from one of the squatters: she had fled Ni-moya more than a year ago, he said, when one of the false Coronals had demanded her mansion from her to serve as his palace. Where she had gone, whether she was still alive at all—no one knew that. The Duke of Ni-moya and all his family had fled, too, even earlier, and most of the other nobility.

"And the false Coronal?" Hissune asked.

"Gone also, my lord. All of them, for there was more than one, and toward the end there were ten or twelve, squabbling among themselves. But they ran like frightened bilantoons when the Pontifex Valentine reached the city last month. There is only one Coronal in Ni-moya today, my lord, and his name is Hissune."

Hissune smiled faintly. "And is this my grand processional, then? Where are the musicians, where are the parades? Why all this filth and destruction? This is not what I thought my first visit to Ni-moya would be like, Stimion."

"You will return in a happier time, my lord, and all will be as it was formerly."

"Do you think so? Do you truly think so? Ah, I pray you are right, my friend!"

Alsimir appeared. "My lord, the mayor of this place sends his respects and asks leave to call upon you this afternoon."

"Tell him to come this evening. We have more urgent things to do just now than meet with local mayors."

"I will tell him, my lord. I think the mayor feels some alarm, my lord, over the size of the army that you intend to quarter here. He said something about the difficulty of supplying provisions, and some problem of sanitation that he—"

"He will supply provisions as required, Alsimir, or we will supply ourselves with a more capable mayor," said Hissune. "Tell him that also. You might tell him, also, that my lord

Divvis will shortly be here with an army nearly as great as this, or perhaps greater, and my lord Tunigorn will be following, and therefore he can consider his present efforts as merely a rehearsal for the real burdens that will be placed upon him soon. But let him know, also, that the overall food requirements of Ni-moya will be somewhat lessened when I leave here, because I will be taking several million of his citizens with me as part of the army of occupation going to Piurifayne, and ask him what method he proposes for choosing the volunteers. And if he balks at anything, Alsimir, point out to him that we have come here not to annoy him but to rescue his province from chaos, though we would much prefer to be jousting atop Castle Mount just now. If you think his attitude is inappropriate after you have said all that, put him in chains and see if there is a deputy mayor who is willing to be more cooperative, and if there is not, find someone who is." Hissune grinned. "So much for the mayor of Ni-moya. Has there been any news of my lord Divvis?"

"A great deal, my lord. He has left Piliplok and is following us up the Zimr as swiftly as he can, gathering his army as he goes. We have messages from him from Port Saikforge, Stenwamp, Orgeliuse, Impemonde, and Obliorn Vale, and the last word we have is that he is approaching Larnimisculus."

"Which as I recall is still some thousands of miles east of here, is it not?" said Hissune. "So we have no little while yet to wait for him. Well, he will get here when he gets here, and there can be no hurrying it, nor do I think it wise to set out for Piurifayne until I have met with him." He smiled ruefully. "Our task would be three times as simple, I think, if this world were half as big. Alsimir, send messages of our highest regard to Divvis at Larnimisculus, and perhaps to Belka and Clarischanz and a few other cities along his route, telling him how eager I am to see him once again."

"And are you, my lord?" Alsimir asked.

Hissune looked closely at him. "That I am," he said. "Most genuinely I am, Alsimir!"

He chose for his headquarters the grand study on the third floor of the building. Long ago when this had been the home of Calain, brother to the Duke of Ni-moya—so Hissune recalled out of his acquired memory of the place—the huge room had housed Calain's library of ancient books bound in the hides of uncommon animals. But the books were gone the study was a vast empty space with a single scarred desk in its center. There he spread out his maps and contemplated the enterprise that lay before him.

It had not pleased Hissune to be left behind at the Isle of Sleep when Valentine sailed to Piliplok. He had meant to handle the pacification of Piliplok himself, by force of arms; but Valentine had had other ideas, and Valentine had prevailed. Coronal might indeed Hissune be, yes, but it became clear to him at the time of that decision that his situation was for some time going to be an anomalous one, for he would have to contend with the existence of a vigorous and active and highly visible Pontifex who had no intention whatever of retreating to the Labyrinth. Hissune's historical studies provided him with no precedent for that. Even the strongest and most ambitious of Coronals—Lord Confalume, Lord Prestimion, Lord Dekkeret, Lord Kinniken—had yielded up their place and gone to their subterranean abode at the completion of their time at the Castle.

But there was no precedent, Hissune conceded, for anything that was happening now. And he could not deny that Valentine's voyage to Piliplok—which to Hissune had seemed to be the maddest sort of folly—had in fact been a brilliant stroke of strategy.

Imagine: the rebellious city meekly hauling down its flags and submitting without a whimper to the Pontifex, precisely as Valentine had predicted! What magic did he have, Hissune wondered, that allowed him to carry off so bold a coup with such self-assurance? But he had won back his throne in the war of restoration with much the same tactics, had he not? His mildness, his gentleness—they concealed a temperament of remarkable strength and determination. And yet, thought Hissune, it was not a mere cloak conveniently put on, that gentleness of Valentine: it was the essential nature of his character, the deepest and truest part of it. An extraordinary being—a great king, in his curious fashion. . . .

And now the Pontifex proceeded westward along the Zimr with his little entourage, traveling from one broken land to another, gently negotiating a return to sanity. From Piliplok he had gone to Ni-moya, arriving some weeks before Hissune. False Coronals had fled at his approach; vandals and bandits had ceased their maraudings; the dazed and impoverished citizens of the great city had turned out by the millions, so went the report, to hail their new Pontifex as if he could with one wave of his hand restore the world to its former state. Which made matters far simpler for Hissune, following in Valentine's wake: instead of having to expend time and resources bringing Ni-moya under control, he found the city quiet and reasonably willing to cooperate in whatever must be done.

Hissune traced a path with his finger over the map. Valentine had gone on to Khyntor. A tough assignment; that was the stronghold of the false Coronal Sempeturn and his private army, the Knights of Dekkeret. Hissune feared for the Pontifex there. Yet he could take no action to protect him: Valentine would not hear of it. "I will not lead armies into the cities of Majipoor," he had said when they debated the point on the Isle; and Hissune had had no choice but to yield to his will. The authority of the Pontifex is always supreme.

And after Khyntor, for Valentine? The Rift cities, Hissune assumed. And then perhaps onward toward the cities of the sea, Pidruid, Tilomon, Narabal. No one knew what was happening on that far coast, where so many millions of refugees from the troubled Zimroel heartland had gone. But in the eye of his mind Hissune could see Valentine marching tirelessly on and on and on, bringing chaos into order by the glowing force of his soul alone. It was, in effect, a weird sort of grand processional for the Pontifex. But the Pontifex, Hissune thought uneasily, is not the one who is supposed to be making grand processionals.

He turned his mind away from Valentine and toward his own responsibilities. Wait for Divvis to get here, first. A ticklish business that would be. But Hissune knew that all the future success of his reign would depend on how well he handled that brooding and jealous man. Offer him high authority, yes, make it clear that among the generals of this war he is second only to the Coronal himself. But contain him, control him, at the same time. If it could be done.

Hissune sketched quick lines on the map. One army under Divvis, swinging out west as far as Khyntor or Mazadone to make certain that Valentine had really reestablished order there, and levying troops as it went: then looping back to the south and east to take up a position along the upper reaches of the Metamorph province. The other main army, under Hissune's own command, cutting down from Ni-moya along the banks of the Steiche to seal Piurifayne's eastern border.

The pincers tactics: inward then from both sides until the rebels were taken.

And what will those soldiers eat, Hissune wondered, in a world that is starving to death? Feed an army of many millions on roots and nuts and grass? He shook his head. We will eat roots and nuts and grass, if that is all there is. We will eat stones and mud. We will eat the devilish fanged creatures that the rebels hurl against us. We will eat our own dead, if need be. And we will prevail; and then this madness will end.

He rose and went to the window and stared out over ruined Ni-moya, more beautiful now that twilight was descending to hide the worst of the scars. He caught sight of his own reflection in the glass. Mockingly he bowed to it. *Good evening, my lord! The Divine be with you, my lord!* Lord Hissune: how strange that sounded. *Yes, my lord; no, my lord; I will do it at once, my lord.* They made the starburst at him. They backed away in awe. They treated him, all of them, as though he really *were* Coronal. Perhaps he would become used to it before long. It was not as though any of this had come as a surprise, after all. And yet it still felt unreal to him. Possibly that was because he had spent his entire reign thus far journeying about Zimroel in this improvised way. It would not become real, Hissune decided, until he finally returned to Castle Mount—to Lord Hissune's Castle!—and took up that life of signing decrees and making appointments and presiding over grand ceremonies that was, he imagined, the true occupation of a Coronal in peacetime. But would that day ever come? He shrugged. A foolish question, like most questions. That day would come on the day that it came; in the meantime there was work to do. Hissune returned to his desk and for an hour more continued to annotate his maps.

After a time Alsimir returned. "I have spoken with the mayor, my lord. He promises complete cooperation now. He waits downstairs in the hope that you will allow him to tell you how cooperative he plans to be."

Hissune smiled. "Send him to me," he said.

2

When he reached Khyntor at last Valentine directed Asenhart to make his landfall not in the city proper, but across the river in the southern suburb of Hot Khyntor, where the geothermal wonders were, the geysers and fumaroles and simmering lakes. He wanted to enter the city in a slow and measured way, giving the so-called "Coronal" who ruled it full warning that he was coming.

Not that his arrival could be any surprise to the self-styled Lord Sempeturn. During his voyage up the Zimr from Ni-moya Valentine had made no secret of his identity, nor of his destination. He had halted again and again at the larger river towns along the way, meeting with whatever municipal leadership still survived in them, and obtaining pledges of backing for the armies that were being recruited to meet the Metamorph threat. And all along the river, even at towns where he did not stop, the populace turned out to see the imperial fleet pass by on its way to Khyntor, and to wave and shout, "Valentine Pontifex! Valentine Pontifex!"

A dismal journey that had been, too, for it was apparent even from the river that those towns, once so lively and prosperous, were mere ghosts of themselves, their dockside warehouses empty and windowless, their bazaars deserted, their waterfront promenades choked with weeds. And wherever he went ashore he saw that the people who remained in these places, for all their shouting and waving, were utterly without hope: their eyes dull and downcast, their shoulders slumped, their faces forlorn.

But when he had landed in that fantastic place of booming geysers and hissing, gurgling thermal lakes and boiling clouds of pale green gas that was Hot Khyntor, Valentine saw something else on the faces of the crowds that had gathered at the quay: an alert, curious, eager look, as though they were anticipating some sort of sporting event.

They were waiting, Valentine knew, to see what sort of reception he would receive at the hands of Lord Sempeturn.

"We'll be ready to go in just a couple of minutes, your

majesty," Shanamir called. "The floaters are coming down the ramp right now."

"No floaters," said Valentine. "We'll enter Khyntor on foot."

He heard Sleet's familiar gasp of horror, saw the familiar exasperated look on Sleet's face. Lisamon Hultin was red-faced with annoyance; Zalzan Kavol wore a brooding scowl; Carabella too was showing alarm. But no one dared to remonstrate with him. No one had for some time now. It was not so much that he was Pontifex now, he thought: the exchange of one gaudy title for another was really a trivial matter. It was, rather, as though they regarded him as moving deeper and deeper each day into a realm they could not enter. He was becoming incomprehensible to them. As for himself, he felt beyond all trifling concern with security: invulnerable, invincible.

Deliamber said, "Which bridge shall we take, your majesty?"

There were four in view: one of brick, one of stone arches, one that was slender and gleaming and transparent, as though it had been made of glass, and one, the closest at hand, that was an airy thing of light swaying cables. Valentine looked from one to another, and at the distant square-topped towers of Khyntor far across the river. The bridge of stone arches, he observed, seemed to be shattered in midspan. One more task for the Pontifex, he thought, remembering that the title he bore had meant, in ancient times, "builder of bridges."

He said, "I knew the names of these bridges once, good Deliamber, but I have forgotten them. Tell them to me again."

"That is the Bridge of Dreams to our right, your majesty. Nearer to us is the Bridge of the Pontifex, and next to it is Khyntor Bridge, which appears to be damaged beyond use. The one upstream is the Bridge of the Coronal."

"Why, then, let us take the Bridge of the Pontifex!" said Valentine.

Zalzan Kavol and several of his fellow Skandars led the way. Behind them marched Lisamon Hultin; then Valentine, at an unhurried pace, with Carabella by his side; Deliamber and Sleet and Tisana walked just behind them, with the rest of the small party bringing up the rear. The crowd, growing

larger all the time, followed alongside, keeping back of its
own accord.

As Valentine was nearing the threshold of the bridge, a
thin, dark-haired woman in a faded orange gown detached
herself from the onlookers and came rushing toward him,
crying, "Majesty! Majesty!" She managed to get within a
dozen feet of him before Lisamon Hultin stopped her, catching her by one arm and swinging her off her feet as though
she were a child's doll. "No—wait—" the woman murmured,
as Lisamon seemed about to hurl her back into the throng. "I
mean no harm—I have a gift for the Pontifex—"

"Put her down, Lisamon," Valentine said calmly.

Frowning suspiciously, Lisamon released her, but remained
close beside the Pontifex, poised at her readiest. The woman
was trembling so that she could barely keep her footing. Her
lips moved, but for a moment she did not speak. Then she
said, "You are truly Lord Valentine?"

"I was Lord Valentine, yes. I am Valentine Pontifex now."

"Of course. Of course. I knew that. They said you were
dead, but I never believed that. Never!" She bowed. "Your
majesty!" She was still trembling. She seemed fairly young,
though it was hard to be certain, for hunger and hardship had
etched deep lines in her face, and her skin was even paler
than Sleet's. She held forth her hand. "I am Millilain," she
said. "I wanted to give you this."

What looked like a dagger of bone, long, slender, tapering
to a sharp point, lay in her palm.

"An assassin, see!" Lisamon roared, and moved as if to
pounce once again.

Valentine held up his hand. "Wait," he said. "What do
you have there, Millilain?"

"A tooth—a holy tooth—a tooth of the water-king
Maazmoorn—"

"Ah."

"To guard you. To guide you. He is the greatest of the
water-kings. This tooth is precious, your majesty." She was
shaking now. "I thought at first it was wrong to worship them,
that it was blasphemy, that it was criminal. But then I
returned, I listened, I learned. They are not evil, the water-
kings, your majesty! They are the true masters! We belong to
them, we and all others who live on Majipoor. And I bring
you the tooth of Maazmoorn, your majesty, the greatest of
them, the high Power—"

Softly Carabella said, "We should be moving onward, Valentine."

"Yes," he said. He put forth his hand and gently took the tooth from the woman. It was perhaps ten inches long, strangely chilly to the touch, gleaming as though with an inner fire. As he wrapped his hand about it he thought, only for a moment, that he heard the sound of far-off bells, or what might have been bells, though their melody was like that of no bells he had ever heard. Gravely he said, "Thank you, Millilain. I will treasure this."

"Your majesty," she whispered, and went stumbling away, back into the crowd.

He continued on, slowly across the bridge into Khyntor.

The crossing took an hour or more. Long before he reached the far side Valentine could see that a crowd had gathered over there to await him: and it was no mere mob, he realized, for those who stood in the vanguard were dressed identically, in uniforms of green and gold, the colors of the Coronal. This was an army, then—the army of the Coronal Lord Sempeturn.

Zalzan Kavol looked back, frowning. "Your majesty?" he said.

"Keep going," said Valentine. "When you reach the front row of them, step back and let me through, and remain at my side."

He felt Carabella's hand closing in fear on his wrist.

"Do you remember," he said, "early in the war of restoration, when we were coming into Pendiwane, and found a militia of ten thousand waiting for us at the gate, and there were just a few dozen of us?"

"This is not Pendiwane. Pendiwane was not in rebellion against you. There was no false Coronal waiting at the gate for you, but only a fat terrified provincial mayor."

"It is all the same," Valentine said.

He came to the bridge's end. The way was blocked there by the troops in green and gold. An officer in the front line whose eyes were glittering with fear called out hoarsely, "Who are you that would enter Khyntor without leave of Lord Sempeturn?"

"I am the Pontifex Valentine, and I need no one's leave to enter a city of Majipoor."

"The Coronal Lord Sempeturn will not have you come further on this bridge, stranger!"

Valentine smiled. "How can the Coronal, if Coronal he be, gainsay the word of the Pontifex? Come, fellow, stand aside!"

"That I will not do. For you are no more Pontifex than I."

"Do you deny me? I think your Coronal must do that with his own voice," said Valentine quietly.

He began to walk forward, flanked by Zalzan Kavol and Lisamon Hultin. The officer who had challenged him threw uncertain glances at the soldiers to his right and left in the front line; he drew himself up rigidly, and so did they; their hands went ostentatiously to the butts of the weapons they carried. Valentine continued to advance. They stepped back half a pace, and then half a pace more, while continuing to glare sternly at him. Valentine did not halt. The front line was melting away to this side and that, now, as he marched steadfastly into it.

Then the ranks opened and a short stocky man with rough reddish cheeks emerged to face Valentine. He was clad in a Coronal's white robe over a green doublet, and he wore the starburst crown, or a reasonable likeness of it, in his great wild tuft of black hair.

He held up both hands with his palms outstretched and cried loudly, "Enough! No further, impostor!"

"And by whose authority do you issue such orders?" Valentine asked amiably.

"My own, for I am the Coronal Lord Sempeturn!"

"Ah, you are the Coronal, and I am an impostor? I had not understood that. And by whose will are you Coronal, then, Lord Sempeturn?"

"By the will of the Divine, who has appointed me to rule in this time of a vacancy on Castle Mount!"

"I see," said Valentine. "But I know of no such vacancy. There is a Coronal, Lord Hissune by name, who holds office by legitimate appointment."

"An impostor can make no legitimate appointments," Sempeturn rejoined.

"But I am Valentine who was Coronal before him, and who now is Pontifex—by will of the Divine also, so it is generally believed."

Sempeturn grinned darkly. "You were an impostor when you claimed to be Coronal, and you are an impostor now!"

"Can that be so? Was I acclaimed wrongly, then, by all

the princes and lords of the Mount, and by the Pontifex Tyeveras, may he rest always at the Source, and by my own mother the Lady?"

"I say you deceived them all, and the curse that has descended on Majipoor is best proof of that. For the Valentine who was made Coronal was a dark-complected man, and look at you—your hair is bright as gold!"

Valentine laughed. "But that is an old story, friend! Surely you know of the witchery that deprived me of my body and put me into this one!"

"So you say."

"And so the Powers of the realm agreed."

"Then you are a master of deceit," said Sempeturn. "But I will waste no more time with you, for I have urgent tasks. Go: get you back into Hot Khyntor, and board your ship and sail yourself off down the river. If you are found in this province by this hour tomorrow you will regret it most sorely."

"I will leave soon enough, Lord Sempeturn. But first I must ask a service of you. These soldiers of yours—the Knights of Dekkeret, do you call them?—we have need of them to the east, on the borders of Piurifayne, where the Coronal Lord Hissune is assembling an army. Go to him, Lord Sempeturn. Place yourself under his command. Do what he asks of you. We are aware of what you have accomplished in gathering these troops, and we would not deprive you of leadership over them: but you must make yourself part of the greater effort."

"You must be a madman," Sempeturn said.

"I think otherwise."

"Leave my city unguarded? March off thousands of miles to surrender my authority to some usurper?"

"It is necessary, Lord Sempeturn."

"In Khyntor I alone decide what is necessary!"

"That must change," said Valentine. He slipped easily into the waking trance, and sent forth the merest tendril of his mind toward Sempeturn, and played with him, and brought a frown of confusion from the red-faced man. He sent into Sempeturn's mind the image of Dominin Barjazid, wearing the body that once had been his own, and said, "Do you recognize that man, Lord Sempeturn?"

"He—he—he is the former Lord Valentine!"

"No," said Valentine, and hurled a full jolt of his mental force at the false Coronal of Khyntor.

Sempeturn lurched and nearly fell, and clutched at the men in green and gold about him, and the color of his cheeks deepened until it was the purple of overripe grapes.

"Who is that man?" Valentine asked.

"He is the brother of the King of Dreams," whispered Sempeturn.

"And why does he wear the features of the former Lord Valentine?"

"Because—because—"

"Tell me."

Sempeturn sagged until his knees were bent and his quivering hands hung almost to the ground.

"Because he stole the Coronal's body during the time of the usurpation, and wears it yet—by the mercy and dispensation of the man he would have overthrown—"

"Ah. And who am I, then?"

"You are Lord Valentine," Sempeturn said miserably.

"Wrong. Who am I, Sempeturn?"

"Valentine—Pontifex—Pontifex of Majipoor—"

"Indeed. At last. And if I am Pontifex, who is Coronal?"

"Whoever—you—say, your majesty."

"I say he is Lord Hissune, who waits for you in Ni-moya, Sempeturn. Go: gather your knights, take your army east, serve your Coronal as he wishes. Go, Sempeturn! *Go!*"

He sent one last thrust of force toward Sempeturn, who reeled and swayed and shook, and at last fell to his knees. "Majesty—majesty—forgive me—"

"I will spend a night or two in Khyntor," said Valentine, "and see to it that all is in order here. And then I think I must move on toward the west, where more work awaits me."

He turned and saw Carabella staring at him as though he had sprouted wings or horns. He smiled at her and lightly blew her a kiss. This is thirsty work, he thought. A good bowl or two of wine, now, if they have any in Khyntor, eh?

He glanced down at the dragon-tooth that he had held in his hands all this time and ran his fingers lightly over it, and heard once more the sound of bells, and thought that he felt the stirring of mighty wings within his soul. Carefully he wrapped the tooth in a piece of colored silk that he took from Carabella, and handed it to her, saying, "Guard this well, my lady, until I ask you for it again. I will have some great use for it, I think." He looked into the crowd and caught sight of the woman Millilain who had given the tooth to him. Her eyes were fixed on his; and they blazed with a frightening intensity, as though she were staring with awe and rapture at some godlike being.

3

What sounded like a loud argument seemed to be going on just outside the door of his bedchamber, Hisuune realized. He sat up, scowled, blinked groggily. Through the great window to his left he saw the red daybreak glow of the sun low on the eastern horizon. He had been awake far into the night preparing for the arrival this day of Divvis, and he was hardly pleased to be roused from sleep so soon after sunrise.

"Who's out there?" he growled. "What in the name of the Divine is all that racket?"

"My lord, I have to see you at once!" Alsimir's voice. "Your guards say you must not be awakened under any circumstances, but I absolutely must speak with you!"

Hissune sighed. "I seem to be awake," he said. "You may as well come in."

There was the sound of unbolting of the doors. After a moment Alsimir entered, looking greatly agitated.

"My lord—"

"What's going on?"

"The city is under attack, my lord!"

Suddenly Hissune was fully awake. "Attack? By whom?"

"Strange monstrous birds," Alsimir said. "With wings like those of sea dragons, and beaks like scythes, and claws that drip poison."

"There are no birds of such a kind."

"These must be some evil new creatures of the Shape-shifters that began entering Ni-moya shortly before dawn from the south, a great hideous flock, hundreds of them, perhaps thousands. Already they have taken fifty lives or more, and it will get much worse as the day goes on." Alsimir went to the window. "See, my lord, there are some of them now, circling above the old palace of the duke—"

Hissune stared. A swarm of ghastly shapes soared and hovered in the clear morning sky: huge birds, bigger than gihornas, bigger even than miluftas and far more ugly. Their wings were not bird-wings but rather the sort of black leathery things, supported on outstretched fingerlike bones, that sea dragons had. Their beaks, wickedly sharp and curved, were flaming red, and their long outstretched claws were bright green. Fiercely they dived in quest of prey, swooping and rising and swooping again, while in the streets below people ran desperately for cover. Hissune watched one unwary boy of ten or twelve years, with schoolbooks under his arm, emerge from a building directly into the path of one of the creatures: it swept downward until it was no more than nine or ten feet above the ground, and its claws flicked out in a quick powerful assault that slashed through his tunic and ripped a bloody track up his back. As the bird swung swiftly upward again the boy went sprawling, hands slapping the pavement in wild convulsions. Then, almost at once, he was still, and three or four of the birds plummeted like stones from the sky, falling upon him and at once beginning to devour him.

Hissune muttered a curse. "You did well to awaken me. Have any countermeasures been taken yet?"

"We have some five hundred archers heading for the rooftops already, my lord. And we're mobilizing the long-range energy-throwers as fast as we can."

"Not enough. Not nearly enough. What we have to avoid is a general panic in the city—twenty million frightened civilians running around trampling each other to death. It's vital to show them that we're bringing the situation under control right away. Put five thousand archers up on the roofs. Ten thousand, if we have them. I want everybody who knows how to draw a bow up there taking part in this—all over the city, highly visible, highly reassuring."

"Yes, my lord."

"And issue a general command to the citizens to stay indoors until further orders. No one is to go outside: no one, regardless of how urgent he thinks his business is, while the birds are still a menace. Also: have Stimion send word downriver to Divvis that we're having a little trouble here and he'd better be on guard if he's still planning to enter

Ni-moya this morning. And I want you to send for that old man who runs that rare-animal zoo in the hills, the one I spoke with last week—Ghitain, Khitain, something like that. Tell him what's been going on this morning, if he doesn't already know, and bring him here under careful guard, and have someone collect a few of the dead birds and bring them here too, for him to examine." Hissune turned to the window again, glowering. The boy's body was wholly hidden by the birds, nine or ten of them now, that fluttered greedily about it. His schoolbooks lay scattered in a pathetic sprawl nearby. "Shapeshifters!" he exclaimed bitterly. "Sending monsters to make war on children! Ah, but we'll have them pay dearly for this, Alsimir! We'll feed Faraataa to his own birds, eh? Go, now: there's much that needs doing."

More detailed reports arrived in a steady stream as Hissune had his hasty breakfast. More than a hundred deaths now were attributed to the aerial onslaught, and the number was mounting rapidly. And at least two more flocks of the birds had entered the city, making, so far as anyone had been able to reckon, at least fifteen hundred of the creatures so far.

But already the rooftop counterattack was producing results: the birds, on account of their great size, were slow and graceless fliers and made conspicuous targets for the archers—of whom they showed virtually no fear. So they were being picked off fairly easily, and eliminating them seemed mainly a matter of time, even if new hordes of them were still en route from Piurifayne. The streets of the city had largely been cleared of civilians, for word of the attack and of the Coronal's orders to stay indoors had by now spread to the farthest suburbs. The birds circled morosely over a silent, deserted Ni-moya.

In midmorning word came that Yarmuz Khitain, the curator of the Park of Fabulous Beasts, had been brought to Nissmorn Prospect and was presently at work in the courtyard dissecting one of the dead birds. Hissune had met with him some days earlier, for Ni-moya was infested with all sorts of strange and lethal creatures spawned by the Metamorph rebels, and the zoologist had had valuable advice to offer on coping with them. Going downstairs now, Hissune found Khitain, a somber-eyed, hollow-chested man of late middle years, crouching over the remains of a bird so huge that at first Hissune thought there must be several of them outspread on the pavement.

"Have you ever seen such a thing as this?" Hissune asked.

Khitain looked up. He was pale, tense, trembling. "Never, my lord. It is a creature out of nightmares."

"Metamorph nightmares, do you think?"

"Beyond doubt, my lord. Plainly it is no natural bird."

"Some kind of synthetic creature, you mean?"

Khitain shook his head. "Not quite, my lord. I think these are produced by genetic manipulation from existing life-forms. The basic shape is that of a milufta, that much seems clear—do you know of it? The largest carrion-feeding bird of Zimroel. But they have made it even larger, and turned it into a raptorial bird, a predator, instead of a scavenger. These venom glands, at the base of the claws—no bird of Majipoor has those, but there is a reptile of Piurifayne known as the ammazoar that is armed in such a way, and they seem to have modeled them after those."

"And the wings?" Hissune said. "Borrowed from sea dragons, are they?"

"Of similar design. That is, they are not typical bird-wings, but rather the kind of expanded fingerwebs that mammals sometimes evolve—dhiims, for instance, or bats, or sea-dragons. The sea dragons, my lord, are mammals, you know."

"Yes, I know," said Hissune drily. "But dragons don't use their wings for flying. What purpose is served, would you say, by putting dragon wings on a bird?"

Khitain shrugged. "No aerodynamic purpose, so far as I can tell. It may have been done merely to make the birds seem more terrifying. When one is designing a life-form to use as an instrument of war—"

"Yes. Yes. So it is your opinion without any question that these birds are yet one more Metamorph weapon."

"Without question, my lord. As I have said, this is no natural life-form of Majipoor, nothing that has ever existed in the wild. A creature this large and dangerous could certainly not have gone undiscovered for fourteen thousand years."

"Then it is one more crime we must add to their score. Who could have supposed, Khitain, that the Shapeshifters were such ingenious scientists?"

"They are a very ancient race, my lord. They may have many secrets of this sort."

"Let us hope," Hissune said, shuddering, "that they have nothing nastier than this ready to launch at us."

But by early afternoon the assault seemed all but over. Hundreds of the birds had been shot down—the bodies of all that could be recovered were dumped in the great plaza outside the main gate of the Grand Bazaar, where they made an enormous foul-smelling mound—and those that survived, at last comprehending that nothing better than arrows awaited them in Ni-moya, had mainly flown off into the hills to the north, leaving only a scattered few behind in the city. Five archers had perished in the defense of Ni-moya, Hissune was dismayed to learn—struck from behind as they searched the skies for the birds. A heavy price, he thought; but he knew it had been a necessary one. The greatest city of Majipoor could not be allowed to be held hostage by a flock of birds.

For an hour or more Hissune toured the city by floater to assure himself that it was safe to lift the restrictions on going out of doors. Then he returned to Nissimorn Prospect, just in time to learn from Stimion that the forces under the command of Divvis had begun to arrive at the docks of Strand Vista.

Through all the months since Valentine had given him the crown at Inner Temple, Hissune had looked forward apprehensively to his first encounter as Coronal with the man he had defeated for the office. Show any sign of weakness, he knew, and Divvis would see it as an invitation to shove him aside, once this war was won, and take from him the throne he coveted. Though he had never once heard an overt hint of such treason from Divvis, Hissune had no reason to place much faith in his good will.

Yet as he made ready to go down to Strand Vista to greet the older prince, Hissune felt a strange calmness settling over himself. He was, after all, Coronal by true succession, the free choice of the man who was now Pontifex: like it or not, Divvis must accept that, and Divvis would.

When he reached the riverfront at Strand Vista Hissune was astounded by the vastness of the armada that Divvis had gathered. He seemed to have commandeered every rivergoing vessel between Piliplok and Ni-moya, and the Zimr was choked with ships as far as Hissune could see, an enormous fleet stretching halfway out toward the distant confluence—a colossal freshwater sea—where the River Steich flowed south from the Zimr.

The only vessel that had tied up thus far at its pier, Stimion said, was Divvis's flagship. And Divvis himself waited aboard it for Lord Hissune's arrival.

"Shall I tell him to come ashore and greet you here, my lord?" Stimion asked.

Hissune smiled. "I will go to him," he said.

Dismounting from his floater, he walked solemnly toward the arcade at the end of the passenger terminal, and out onto the pier itself. He was in his full regalia of office, and his counsellors also were bedecked at their most formal, as were the members of his guard; and a dozen archers flanked him on either side, in case the deadly birds should choose this moment to reappear. Though Hissune had elected to go to Divvis, which perhaps was in violation of protocol, he knew that the image he projected was a lordly one, that of a king deigning to confer an unusual honor upon a loyal subject.

Divvis stood at the head of his ship's entranceway. He too had taken care to make himself look majestic, for he was clad—despite the heat of the day—in a great black robe of fine haigus hides and a splendid gleaming helmet that seemed almost to be a crown. As Hissune went upward onto the deck, Divvis loomed above him like a giant.

But then at last they were face to face, and though Divvis was by far the bigger man, Hissune regarded him with a steadiness and coolness that did much to minimize the difference in their size. For a long moment neither spoke.

Then Divvis—as Hissune knew he must do, or be in open defiance—made the starburst gesture and went down to one knee, and offered his first homage to the new Coronal:

"Hissune! Lord Hissune! Long life to Lord Hissune!"

"And long life to you, Divvis—for we will have need of your bravery in the struggle that lies before us. Get up, man. Get up!"

Divvis rose. His eyes unhesitatingly met Hissune's; and across his features there played such a succession of emotions that Hissune could hardly interpret them all, though it seemed to him that he saw envy there, and anger, and bitterness—but also a certain degree of respect, and even a grudging admiration, and something like a tinge of amusement, as if Divvis could not resist smiling at the strange permutations of fate that had brought them together in this place in these new roles.

Waving a hand behind him at the river, Divvis said, "Have I brought you sufficient troops, my lord?"

"An immense force, yes: a brilliant accomplishment, recruiting an army of such size. But who knows what will be sufficient, Divvis, in fighting an army of phantoms? The Shapeshifters will have many ugly surprises for us yet."

With a light laugh Divvis said, "I heard, my lord, of the birds they sent you this morning."

"No laughing matter, my lord Divvis. These were dread monsters of a most frightful sort that struck down people in the streets and fed upon their bodies before they were cold. I saw that done to a child, myself, from the window of my own bedroom. But I think we have slain them all, or nearly. And in due course we will slay their makers, too."

"It surprises me to hear you so vengeful, my lord."

"Am I vengeful?" Hissune said. "Why, then, if you say it, I suppose it must be so. Living here for weeks in this shattered city makes one vengeful, perhaps. Seeing monstrous vermin turned loose upon innocent citizens by our enemies makes one vengeful. Piurifayne is like some loathsome boil, from which all manner of putrescence comes spilling out into the civilized lands. I intend to lance that boil and cauterize it entirely. And I tell you this, Divvis: with your help I will impose a terrible vengeance upon those who have made this war on us."

"You sound very little like Lord Valentine, my lord, when you speak of vengeance that way. I think I never knew him to use the word."

"And is there any reason why I should sound like Lord Valentine, Divvis? I am Hissune."

"You are his chosen successor."

"Yes, and Valentine is no longer Coronal, by that very choice. It may be that my way of dealing with our enemies will not be much like Lord Valentine's way."

"Then you must tell me what your way is."

"I think you already know it. I mean to march down into Piurifayne by way of the Steiche, while you go around from the western side, and we will squeeze the rebels between us, and take this Faraataa and bring a halt to his loosing of monsters and plagues against us. And afterward the Pontifex can summon the surviving rebels, and in his more loving way negotiate some resolution of the Shapeshifters' valid grievances against us. But first we must show force, I think. And if we must shed the blood of those who would shed ours, why, then we must shed their blood. What do you say to that, Divvis?"

"I say that I have not heard greater sense from the lips of a Coronal since my father held the throne. But the Pontifex, I think, would answer otherwise, if he had heard you speaking so belligerently. Is he aware of your plans?"

"We have not yet discussed them in great detail."

"And will you, then?"

"The Pontifex is currently in Khyntor, or west of there," said Hissune. "His work will occupy him there some time; and then it will take him a very long while to come this far east again, and I will be deep into Piurifayne, I think, by that time, and we will have little opportunity for consultation."

A certain slyness entered Divvis's eyes. "Ah, I see how you deal with your problem, my lord."

"And what problem is that?"

"Of being Coronal, while your Pontifex remains at large, marching about the countryside, instead of hiding himself decently out of sight in the Labyrinth. I think that could be a great embarrassment to a new young Coronal, and I would like it very little if I faced such a situation myself. But if you take care to keep a great distance between the Pontifex and yourself, and you credit any differences between your policies and his to that great distance, why, then, you could manage to function almost as though you had a completely free hand, eh, my lord?"

"I think we tread now on dangerous ground, Divvis."

"Ah. Do we?"

"We do indeed. And you overestimate the differences between my outlook and Valentine's. He is not himself a man of war, as we all well understand; but perhaps that is why he has removed himself from the Confalume Throne in my favor. I believe we understand each other, the Pontifex and I, and let us not carry this discussion any further in that direction. Come, now, Divvis: it would be proper, I think, to invite me to your cabin to share a bowl or two of wine, and then you must come with me to Nissimorn Prospect to share another. And then we should sit down to plan the conduct of our war. What do you say to that, my lord Divvis? What do you say to that?"

4

The rain was beginning again, washing away the outlines of
the map Faraataa had drawn in the damp mud of the riverbank. But that made little difference to him. He had been
drawing and redrawing the same map all day, and no need for
doing any of that, for every detail of it was engraved in the
recesses and contours of his brain. Ilirivoyne here, Avendroyne
there, New Velalisier over here. The rivers, the mountains.
The positions of the two invading armies—

The positions of the two invading armies—

Faraataa had not anticipated that. It was the one great
flaw in his planning, that the Unchanging Ones should have
invaded Piurifayne. The coward weakling Lord Valentine
would never have done anything like that; no, Valentine
would rather have come groveling with his nose in the mud
to the Danipiur and begged humbly for a treaty of friendship.
But Valentine was no longer the king—or, rather, he had
become the other king, now, the one with the greater rank
but the weaker powers—how could anyone understand the
mad arrangements of the Unchanging Ones?—and there was
a new king now, the young one, Lord Hissune, who appeared
to be a very different sort of man....

"Aarisiim!" Faraataa called. "What news is there?"

"Very little, O King That Is. We are awaiting reports
from the western front, but it will be some while."

"And from the Steiche battle?"

"I am told that the forest-brethren are still being
uncooperative, but that we are at last succeeding in compelling their assistance in laying the birdnet vine."

"Good. Good. But will it be laid in time to stop Lord
Hissune's advance?"

"That is most likely, O King That Is."

"And do you say that," Faraataa demanded, "because it is
true, or because it is what you think I prefer to hear?"

Aarisiim stared, and gaped, and in his embarrassment
his shape began to alter, so that for a moment he became a
frail structure of wavy ropes that blew in the breeze, and
then a tangle of elongated rigid rods swollen at both ends;

and then he was Aarisiim once again. In a quiet voice he said, "You do me great injustice, O Faraataa!"

"Perhaps I do."

"I tell you no untruths."

"If that is true, then all else is, and I will accept it that that is true," said Faraataa bleakly. Overhead the rain grew more clamorous, battering against the jungle canopy. "Go, and come back when you have the news from the west."

Aarisiim vanished amidst the darkness of the trees. Faraataa, scowling, restless, began drawing his map once again.

There was an army in the west, uncountable millions of the Unchanging Ones, led by the hairy-faced lord whose name was Divvis, that was a son of the former Coronal Lord Voriax. *We slew your father while he hunted in the forest, did you know that, Divvis? The huntsman who fired the fatal bolt was a Piurivar, though he wore the face of a Castle lord. See, the pitiful Shapeshifters can kill a Coronal! We can kill you also, Divvis. We will kill you also, if you are careless, as your father was.*

But Divvis—who surely had no knowledge of how his father had died; there was no secret more closely guarded than that among the Piurivar folk—was not being at all careless, Faraataa thought gloomily. His headquarters was tightly protected by devoted knights, and there was no possibility of slipping an assassin through that line, no matter how shrewdly disguised. With angry stabbing gestures of his keenly honed wooden dirk Faraataa dug the lines of Divvis's march deeper and deeper into the riverbank. Down from Khyntor, and along the inside wall of the great western mountains, making roads through wild country that had been roadless since the beginning of time—sweeping everything before him, filling Piurifayne with his innumerable troops, closing off the countryside, polluting the sacred streams, trampling the sacred groves. . . .

Against that horde of troops Faraataa had been compelled to unleash his army of pilligrigorms. He regretted that, for they were very nearly the nastiest of his biological weapons, and he had been hoarding them to dump into Ni-moya or Khyntor at some later phase of the war: land-dwelling crustaceans the size of a fingertip, they were, with armored shells that could not be crushed with a hammer, and a myriad busy fast-moving legs that Faraataa's genetic artists had altered so that they were as sharp as saws. The appetite of a pilligrigorm was insatiable—it demanded fifty times its own weight in meat each day—and its method of satisfying that appetite was to carve openings in any sort of warm-blooded animal life that lay in its path, and devour its flesh from the inside out.

Fifty thousand of them, Faraataa had thought, could bring a city the size of Khyntor into total turmoil in five days. But now, because the Unchanging Ones had chosen to invade Piurifayne, he had had to release the pilligrigorms not within a city, but on Piurifayne's own soil, in the hope that they would drive Divvis's immense army into confusion and retreat. No reports had come in yet, though, on the success of that tactic.

On the other side of the jungle, where the Coronal Lord Hissune was leading a second army southward on another impossible route along the west bank of the Steiche, it was Faraataa's plan to string a net of the infinitely sticky and impenetrable birdnet vine for hundreds of miles in their path, so that they were forced to take wider and ever wider detours until they were hopelessly lost. The difficulty with that strategem was only that no one could handle birdnet vine effectively except the forest-brethren, those maddening little apes who secreted in their perspiration an enzyme that rendered them immune to the vine's stickiness. But the forest-brethren had little reason to love the Piurivars, who had hunted them for centuries for the rich flavor of their flesh, and gaining their assistance in this maneuver was apparently not proving easy.

Faraataa felt the rage rising and boiling over within him.

It had all gone so well, at first. Releasing the blights and plagues into the farming districts—bringing agriculture into collapse over such a wide region—the famine, the panic, the mass migrations—yes, all according to plan. And setting loose the specially bred animals had worked nicely too, on a smaller scale: that had intensified the fears of the populace, and made life more complicated for the city-dwellers. . . .

But the impact had not been as strong as Faraataa had hoped. He had imagined that the blood-hungry giant miluftas would terrorize Ni-moya, which had already been in a state of chaos—but he had not expected that Lord Hissune's army would be in Ni-moya when the miluftas reached the city, or that his archers could dispose of the deadly birds so easily.

And now Faraataa had no more miluftas, and it would take five years to breed enough to make any impact. . . .

But there were pilligrigorms. There were gannigogs by the millions in the holding tanks, ready to be set loose. There were quexes; there were vriigs; there were zambinaxes; there were malamolas. There were new plagues: a cloud of red dust that would sweep over a city in the night and leave its water supply poisonous for weeks, and a purple spore from which came a maggot that attacked all grazing animals, and even worse. Faraataa hesitated to let some of these loose, for his scientists had told him it might not be so simple to bring them under control after the defeat of the Unchanging Ones. But if it seemed that the war would go against his people, if there appeared to be no hope—why, then, Faraataa would not hesitate to release whatever could do harm to the enemy, regardless of the consequences.

Aarisiim returned, approaching timidly.

"There is news, O King That Is."

"From which front?"

"Both, O King."

Faraataa stared. "Well, how bad is it?"

Aarisiim hesitated. "In the west they are destroying the pilligrigorms. They have a kind of fire that they throw from metal tubes, which melts their shells. And the enemy is advancing rapidly through the zone where we have let the pilligrigorms loose."

"And in the east?" said Faraataa stonily.

"They have broken through the forest, and we were not able to erect the birdnet vines in time. They are searching for Ilirivoyne, so the scouts report."

"To find the Danipiur. To make an alliance with her against us." Faraataa's eyes blazed. "It is bad, Aarisiim, but we are far from finished! Call Benuuiab here, and Siimii, and some of the others. We will go to Ilirivoyne ourselves, and seize the Danipiur before they can reach her. And we will put her to death, if need be, and then who will they make their alliance with? If they seek a Piurivar with the authority to govern, there will be only Faraataa, and Faraataa will not sign treaties with Unchanging Ones."

"Seize the Danipiur?" said Aarisiim doubtfully. "Put the Danipiur to death?"

"If I must," Faraataa said, "I will put all this world to death, before I give it back to them!"

5

In early afternoon they halted at a place in the eastern Rift called Prestimion Vale, which Valentine understood had once been an important farming center. His journey across tormented Zimroel had taken him through scenes of almost unrelieved grimness—abandoned farms, depopulated cities, signs of the most terrifying struggles for survival—but this Prestimion Vale was surely one of the most disheartening places of all.

Its fields were charred and blackened, its people silent, stoic, stunned. "We were growers of lusavender and rice," said Valentine's host, a planter named Nitikkimal, who seemed to be the district mayor. "Then came the lusavender smut, and everything died, and we had to burn the fields. And it will be two years more, at least, before it is safe to plant again. But we have remained. Not one of us from Prestimion Vale has fled, your majesty. We have little to eat—and we Ghayrogs need very little, you understand, but even we do not have enough—and there is no work for us to do, which makes us restless, and it is sad to look at the land with these ashes upon it. But it is *our* land, and so we stay. Will we ever plant here again, your majesty?"

"I know that you will," said Valentine. And wondered if he were giving these people false comfort.

Nitikkimal's house was a great manor at the head of the valley, with lofty beams of black ghannimor wood, and a roof of green slate. But it was damp and drafty within, as though the planter no longer had the heart to make repairs as they became necessary in Prestimion Vale's rainy and humid climate.

That afternoon Valentine rested alone for a while in the huge master suite that Nitikkimal had turned over to him, before going to the municipal meeting-hall to speak with the citizens of the district. A thick packet of dispatches from the east had caught up with him here. Hissune, he learned, was deep within Metamorph country, somewhere in the vicinity of the Steiche, searching for New Velalisier, as the rebel capital was known. Valentine wondered if Hissune would have better luck than he himself had had in his quest for the wandering city of Ilirivoyne. And Divvis had assembled a

347

second and even greater army to raid the Piurivar lands from the other side. The thought of a warlike man like Divvis in those jungles troubled Valentine. *This is not what I had intended,* he thought—*sending armies marching into Piurifayne. This was what I had hoped to avoid. But of course it had become unavoidable,* he knew. *And the times called for Divvises and Hissunes, not for Valentines:* he would play his proper role, and they would play theirs, and—the Divine willing—the wounds of the world would someday begin to heal.

He looked through the other dispatches. News from Castle Mount: Stasilaine was Regent now, toiling over the routine tasks of government. Valentine pitied him. Stasilaine the splendid, Stasilaine the agile, sitting now at that desk scribbling his name on pieces of paper—*how time undoes us all!* Valentine thought. *We who thought life on Castle Mount was all hunting and frolic, bowed now under responsibilities, holding up the poor tottering world with our backs. How far away the Castle seemed, how far away all the joys of that time when the world apparently governed itself, and it was springtime all the year round!*

Dispatches from Tunigorn, too—moving through Zimroel not far behind Valentine, handling the day-by-day chores of relief activities: the distribution of food, the conservation of remaining resources, the burial of the dead, and all the other various anti-famine and anti-plague measures. *Tunigorn the archer, Tunigorn the famous slayer of game*—now did he justify, now do we all justify, Valentine thought, *the ease and comfort of our playful boyhoods on the Mount!*

He shoved the dispatches away. From the case in which he kept it, now, he drew forth the dragon's tooth that the woman Millilain had so strangely put into his hand as he entered Khyntor. From his first moment of contact with it he had known that it was something more than a mere bizarre trinket, an amulet for the blindly superstitious. But it was only as the days unfolded, as he devoted time to comprehending its meaning and uses—secretly, always secretly, not letting even Carabella see what he was doing—that Valentine had come to realize what kind of thing it was that Millilain had given him.

Lightly he touched its shining surface. It was a delicate-looking thing, so thin as to be nearly translucent. But it was as hard as the hardest stone, and its tapered edges were sharp as fine-honed steel. It was cool in his hand, but yet it seemed to him there was a core of fire within it.

The music of the bells began to resound in his mind.

A solemn tolling, slow, almost funereal, and then a more rapid cascade of sound, a quickening of rhythm that swiftly became a breathless mixing of melodies, one rushing forth so hastily that it covered the last notes of the one that preceded it, and then all the melodies at once, a complex mind-baffling symphony of changes: yes, he knew that music now, understood it for what it was, the music of the water-king Maazmoorn, the creature that land dwellers knew as Lord Kinniken's dragon, that was the mightiest of all this huge planet's inhabitants.

It had taken Valentine a great while to realize that he had heard the music of Maazmoorn long before this talisman had come into his possession. Lying asleep aboard the *Lady Thinn*, so many voyages ago, as he was first crossing from Alhanroel to the Isle of Sleep, he had dreamed a dream of a pilgrimage, white-robed worshipers rushing toward the sea, and he had been among them, and in the sea had loomed the great dragon known as Lord Kinniken's, with its mouth yawning open so that it might engulf the pilgrims as they were drawn toward him. And from that dragon as it came near the land and clambered even onto the shore had emanated the pealing of terrible bells, a sound so heavy it crushed the air itself.

From this tooth came the same sound of bells. And with this tooth as his guide, he could, if he drew himself to the center of his soul and sent himself forth across the world, bring himself into contact with the awesome mind of the great water-king Maazmoorn, that the ignorant had called Lord Kinniken's dragon. That was Millilain's gift to him. How had she known what use he and he alone could make of it? Or had she known at all? Perhaps she had given it to him only because it was holy to her—perhaps she had no idea he could use it in this special way, as a focus of concentration. . . .

—*Maazmoorn. Maazmoorn.*

He probed. He sought. He called. Day after day he had come closer and closer to actual communication with the water-king, to a true conversation, a meeting of individual identities. He was almost there now. Perhaps tonight, perhaps tomorrow or the day after that. . . .

—Answer me, Maazmoorn. It is Valentine Pontifex who calls you now.

He no longer feared that vast terrifying mind. He was beginning to learn, in these secret voyages of the soul, how greatly the land-dwellers of Majipoor had misunderstood these huge creatures of the sea. The water-kings were fearsome, yes; but they were not to be feared.

—Maazmoorn. Maazmoorn.

Almost there, he thought.

"Valentine?"

Carabella's voice, outside the door. Startled, he broke from his trance with a jump that nearly threw him from his seat. Then, regaining control, he slipped the tooth into its case, calmed himself, went to her.

"We should be at the town hall now," she said.

"Yes. Of course. Of course."

The sound of those mysterious bells still tolled in his spirit.

But he had other responsibilities now. The tooth of Maazmoorn must wait a little while longer.

At the municipal meeting-hall an hour later Valentine sat upon a high platform and the farmers filed slowly before him, making their obeisance and bringing him their tools to be blessed—scythes, hoes, humble things like that—as though the Pontifex could by the mere laying on of hands restore the prosperity that this blight-stricken valley formerly had known. He wondered if that were some ancient belief of these rural folk, nearly all of them Ghayrogs. Probably not, he decided: no reigning Pontifex had ever visited Prestimion Vale or any other part of Zimroel before, and there was no reason why any would have been expected to. Most likely this was a tradition that these people had invented on the spur of the moment, when they had learned that he would pass their way.

But that did not trouble him. They brought him their tools, and he touched the handle of this one and the blade of that one and the shaft of another, and smiled his warmest smile, and offered them words of heartfelt hope that sent them away glowing.

Toward the end of the evening there was a stirring in the hall and Valentine, glancing up, saw a strange procession coming toward him. A Ghayrog woman who, judging by her almost colorless scales and the drooping serpents of her hair,

must have been of the most extreme old age, was walking up
the aisle slowly between two younger women of her race. She
appeared to be blind and quite feeble, but yet she stood
fiercely erect, and advanced step by step as though cutting
her way through walls of stone.

"It is Aximaan Threysz!" whispered the planter Nitikkimal.
"You know of her, your majesty?"

"Alas, no."

"She is the most famous lusavender planter of them
all—a fount of knowledge, a woman of the highest wisdom.
Near to death, so they say, but she insisted on seeing you
tonight."

"Lord Valentine!" she called out in a clear ringing tone.

"Lord Valentine no longer," he replied, "but Valentine
Pontifex now. And you do me great honor by this visit,
Aximaan Threysz. Your fame precedes you."

"Valentine—Pontifex—"

"Come, give me your hand," said Valentine.

He took her withered, ancient claws in his, and held
them tightly. Her eyes met his, staring straight into them,
although he could tell from the clearness of her pupils that
she saw nothing.

"They said you were a usurper," she declared. "A little
red-faced man came here, and told us you were not the true
Coronal. But I would not listen to him, and went away from
this place. I did not know if you were true or false, but I
thought he was not the one to speak of such things, that
red-faced man."

"Sempeturn, yes. I have met him," Valentine said. "He
believes now that I was the true Coronal, and am the true
Pontifex these days."

"And will you make the world whole again, true Pontifex?" said Aximaan Threysz in a voice of amazing vigor and
clarity.

"We will all of us make it whole together, Aximaan
Threysz."

"No. Not I, Pontifex Valentine. I will die, next week, the
week after, and none too soon, either. But I want a promise
from you that the world will be what it formerly was: for my
children, for my children's children. And if you will promise
me that I will go on my knees to you, and if you promise it
falsely may the Divine scourge you as we have been scourged,
Pontifex Valentine!"

"I promise you, Aximaan Threysz, that the world will be entirely restored, and finer than it was, and I tell you that this is no false promise. But I will not have you go on your knees to me."

"I have said I would, and I will do it!" And, amazingly, brushing aside the two younger women as if they were gnats, she dropped herself down in deep homage, although her body seemed as rigid as a slab of leather that has been left in the sun a hundred years. Valentine reached down to lift her, but one of the women—her daughter, certainly her daughter—caught his hand and pulled it back, and then stared at her own hand in horror, for having dared to touch a Pontifex. Slowly but unaided she stood again, and said, "Do you know how old I am? I was born when Ossier was Pontifex. I think I am the oldest person in the world. And I will die when Valentine is Pontifex: and you will restore the world."

It was probably meant as a prophecy, Valentine thought. But it sounded more like a command.

He said, "It will be done, Aximaan Threysz, and you will live to see it done."

"No. No. Second sight comes upon us when first sight goes. My life is almost over. But the course of yours unfolds clearly before me. You will save us by doing that which you think is impossible for you to do. And then you will seal your deed by doing that which you desire least to do. And though you do the impossible and then you do the undesirable, you will know that what you have done is right, and you will rejoice in it, Pontifex Valentine. Now go, Pontifex, and heal us." Her forked tongue flickered with tremendous force and energy. "Heal us, Pontifex Valentine! Heal us!"

She turned and proceeded slowly back the way she had come, disdaining the help of the two women beside her.

It was an hour more before Valentine was able to disengage himself from the last of the Prestimion Vale folk—they crowded round him in a pathetically hopeful way, as though some Pontifical emanation alone would transform their lives, and magically return them to the condition of the years prior to the coming of the lusavender blight—but at last Carabella, pleading fatigue on his behalf, got them out of there. The image of Aximaan Threysz continued to glow in his mind on the journey back to Nitikkimal's manor. The dry hissing of her voice still resonated in his mind. *You will save us by doing that which you think is impossible for you to do. And*

*then you will seal your deed by doing that which you desire
least to do. Go, Pontifex, and heal us. Yes. Yes. Heal us,
Pontifex Valentine! Heal us!*

But also within him there resounded the music of the
water-king Maazmoorn. He had been so close, this time, to
the ultimate breakthrough, to the true contact with that
inconceivably gigantic creature of the sea. Now—tonight—

Carabella remained awake for a while to talk. That
ancient Ghayrog woman haunted her, too, and she dwelled
almost obsessively on the power of Aximaan Threysz's words,
the eerie compelling force of her sightless eyes, the mysteries
of her prophecy. Then finally she kissed Valentine lightly on
the lips and burrowed down into the darkness of the enormous bed they shared.

He waited a few endless minutes. Then he took forth the
tooth of the sea dragon.

—*Maazmoorn?*

He held the tooth so tightly its edges dug deep into the
flesh of his hand. Urgently he centered all the power of his
mind on the bridging of the gulf of thousands of miles
between Prestimion Vale and the waters—where? At the
Pole?—where the sea-king lay hidden.

—*Maazmoorn?*

—*I hear you, land brother, Valentine-brother, king-brother.
At last!*

—*You know who I am?*

—*I know you. I knew your father. I knew many before
you.*

—*You spoke with them?*

—*No. You are the first for that. But I knew them. They
did not know me, but I knew them. I have lived many
circlings of the ocean, Valentine-brother. And I have watched
all that has occurred upon the land.*

—*You know what is occurring now?*

—*I know.*

—*We are being destroyed. And you are a party to our
destruction.*

—*No.*

—*You guide the Piurivar rebels in their war against us.
We know that. They worship you as gods, and you teach
them how to ruin us.*

—*No, Valentine-brother.*

—*I know they worship you.*

—Yes, that they do, for we are gods. But we do not support them in their rebellion. We give them only what we would give anyone who comes to us for nourishment, but it is not our purpose to see you driven from the world.

—Surely you must hate us!

—No, Valentine-brother.

—We hunt you. We kill you. We eat your flesh and drink your blood and use your bones for trinkets.

—Yes, that is true. But why should we hate you, Valentine-brother? Why?

Valentine did not for the moment reply. He lay cold and trembling with awe beside the sleeping Carabella, pondering all that he had heard, the calm admission by the water-king that the dragons were gods—what could that mean?—and the denial of complicity in the rebellion, and now this astounding insistence that the dragons bore the Majipoori folk no anger for all that had been committed against them. It was too much all at once, a turbulent inrush of knowledge where before there had been only the sound of bells and a sense of a distant looming presence.

—Are you incapable of anger, then, Maazmoorn?

—We understand anger.

—But do not feel it?

—Anger is beside the point, Valentine-brother. What your hunters do to us is a natural thing. It is a part of life; it is an aspect of That Which Is. As am I, as are you. We give praise to That Which Is in all its manifestations. You slay us as we pass the coast of what you call Zimroel, and you make your uses of us; sometimes we slay you in your ships, if it seems to be what must be done at that moment, and so we make our uses of you; and all that is That Which Is. Once the Piurivar folk slew some of us, in their stone city that is now dead, and they thought they were committing a monstrous crime, and to atone for that crime they destroyed their own city. But they did not understand. None of you land-children understand. All is merely That Which Is.

—And if we resist now, when the Piurivar folk hurl chaos at us? Are we wrong to resist? Must we calmly accept our doom, because that too is That Which Is?

—Your resistance is also That Which Is, Valentine-brother.

—Then your philosophy makes no sense to me, Maazmoorn.

—It does not have to, Valentine-brother. But that too is That Which Is.

Valentine was silent once again, for an even longer time than before, but he took care to maintain the contact.

Then he said:

—*I want this time of destruction to end. I mean to preserve the thing that we of Majipoor have understood as That Which Is.*

—*Of course you do.*

—*I want you to help me.*

6

"We have captured a Shapeshifter, my lord," Alsimir said, "who claims he bears an urgent message for you, and you alone."

Hissune frowned. "A spy, do you think?"

"Very likely, my lord."

"Or even an assassin."

"That possibility must never be overlooked, of course. But I think that is not why he is here. I know that he is a Shapeshifter, my lord, and our judgments are all risky ones, but nevertheless: I was among those who interrogated him. He seems sincere. *Seems.*"

"Shapeshifter sincerity!" said Hissune, laughing. "They sent a spy to travel in Lord Valentine's entourage, did they not?"

"So have I been told. What shall I do with him, then?"

"Bring him to me, I suppose."

"And if he plans some Shapeshifter trick?"

"Then we will have to move faster than he does, Alsimir. But bring him here."

There were risks, Hissune knew. But one could not simply turn away someone who maintains he is a messenger from the enemy, or put him to death out of hand on mere suspicion of treachery. And to himself he confessed it would be an interesting diversion to lay eyes on a Metamorph at last, after so many weeks of tramping through this sodden jungle. In all this time they had not encountered one: not *one.*

His camp lay just at the edge of a grove of giant dwikka-trees, somewhere along Piurifayne's eastern border not far from the banks of the River Steiche. The dwikkas were impressive indeed—great astounding things with trunks as wide as a large house, and bark of a blazing bright red hue riven by immense deep cracks, and leaves so broad that one of them could keep twenty men dry in a soaking downpour, and colossal rough-skinned fruits as big around as a floater, with an intoxicating pulp within. But botanical wonders alone were small recompense for the dreariness of this interminable forced march in the Metamorph rain-forest. The rain was constant; mildew and rot afflicted everything, including, Hissune sometimes thought, one's brain; and although the army now was deployed along a line more than a hundred miles in length, and the secondary Metamorph city of Avendroyne was supposedly close by the midpoint of that line, they had seen no cities, no signs of former cities, no traces of evacuation routes, and no Metamorphs at all. It was as if they were mythological beings, and this jungle were uninhabited.

Divvis, Hissune knew, was having the same difficulty over on the far side of Piurifayne. The Metamorphs were not numerous and their cities appeared to be portable. They must flit from place to place like the filmy-winged insects of the night. Or else they disguised themselves as trees and bushes and stood silently by, choking down their laughter, as the armies of the Coronal marched past them. These great dwikkas, for all I know, might be Metamorph scouts, thought Hissune. Let us speak with the spy, or messenger, or assassin, or whatever he may be: we may learn something from him, or at the very least we may be entertained by him.

Alsimir returned in moments with the prisoner, who was under heavy guard.

He was, like those few Piurivars whom Hissune had seen before, a strangely disturbing-looking figure, extremely tall, slender to the point of frailness, naked but for a strip of leather about his loins. His skin and the thin rubbery strands of his hair were an odd pale greenish color, and his face was almost devoid of features, the lips mere slits, the nose only a bump, the eyes slanted sharply and barely visible beneath the lids. He seemed uneasy, and not particularly dangerous. All the same, Hissune wished he had someone with the gift of seeing into minds about him now, a Deliamber or a Tisana or Valentine himself, to whom the secrets of others seemed often to be no secrets at all. This Metamorph might yet have some disagreeable surprise in mind.

"Who are you?" Hissune asked.

"My name is Aarisiim. I serve the King That Is, whom you know as Faraataa."

"Did he send you to me?"

"No, Lord Hissune. He does not know I am here." The Metamorph trembled suddenly, quivering in an odd convulsive way, and for an instant the shape of his body seemed to change and flow. The Coronal's guards at once moved forward, interposing themselves between the Metamorph and Hissune in case these movements were the prelude to an attack; but in a moment Aarisiim was under control and restored to his form. In a low voice he said, "I have come here to betray Faraataa."

In astonishment Hissune said, "Do you mean to lead us to his hiding place?"

"I will, yes."

This is much too good to be true, Hissune thought, and stared about the circle, at Alsimir, at Stimion, at his other close advisers. Obviously they felt the same way: they looked skeptical, guarded, hostile, wary.

He said, "Why are you willing to do this?"

"He has done something unlawful."

"Only now does that occur to you, when this rebellion has been going on since—"

"I mean, my lord, unlawful by our beliefs, not by yours."

"Ah. And what is that, then?"

Aarisiim said, "He has gone to Ilirivoyne and taken the Danipiur captive, and he means to have her slain. It is not lawful to seize the person of the Danipiur. It is not lawful to deprive her of her life. He would listen to no advice. He has seized her. To my shame, I was among those who was with him. I thought he only wanted her a prisoner, so that she could not strike up an alliance against us with you Unchanging Ones. That was what he said, that he would not kill her unless he thought the war was entirely lost."

"And does he think that now?" Hissune asked.

"No, Lord Hissune. He thinks the war is far from lost: he is about to release new creatures against you, and new diseases, and he feels he is on the threshold of victory."

"Then why kill the Danipiur?"

"To ensure his victory."

"Madness!"

"I think so too, my lord." Aarisiim's eyes were open wide, now, and burned with a strange harsh gleam. "He sees her, of course, as a dangerous rival, one whose inclinations are more toward peace than war. If she is removed, that risk to his power is gone. But there is more than that. He means to sacrifice her on the altar—to offer her blood to the water-kings, for their continued support. He has built a temple after the design of the one that was at Old Velalisier; and he will put her upon the stone himself, and take her life with his own hands."

"And when is this supposed to happen?"

"Tonight, my lord. At the Hour of the Haigus."

"*Tonight?*"

"Yes, my lord. I came as quickly as I could, but your army was so large, and I feared I would be slain if I did not find your own guards before your soldiers found me—I would have come to you yesterday, or the day before, but it was not possible, I could not do it—"

"And how many days' journey from here is New Velalisier?"

"Four, perhaps. Perhaps three, if we do it very swiftly."

"Then the Danipiur is lost!" Hissune cried angrily.

"If he does not sacrifice her tonight—"

"You said tonight was the night."

"Yes, the moons are right tonight, the stars are right tonight—but if he loses his resolve, if at the last moment he changes his mind—"

"And does Faraataa lose his resolve often?" Hissune asked.

"Never, my lord."

"Then there is no way we can get there in time."

"No, my lord," said Aarisiim darkly.

Hissune stared off toward the dwikka grove, scowling. The Danipiur dead? That left no hope of coming to any accommodation with the Shapeshifters: she alone, so he understood it, might soften the fury of the rebels and allow some sort of compromise to be negotiated. Without her it must be a battle to the end.

To Alsimir he said, "Where is the Pontifex today?"

"He is west of Khyntor, perhaps as far west as Dulorn, certainly somewhere in the Rift."

"And can we send word to him there?"

"The communications channels linking us to that region are very uncertain, my lord."

"I know that. I want you to get this news through to him somehow, and within the next two hours. Try anything that

might work. Use wizards. Use prayers. Send word to the
Lady, and let her try dreams. Every imaginable channel,
Alsimir, do you understand that? He must know that Faraataa
means to slay the Danipiur tonight. Get that information to
him. Somehow. Somehow. And tell him that he alone can
save her. Somehow."

7

For this, Valentine thought, he would need the circlet of the
Lady as well as the tooth of Maazmoorn. There must be no
failures of transmission, no distortions of the message: he
would make use of every capacity at his command.

"Stand close beside me," he said to Carabella. And to
Deliamber, to Tisana, to Sleet, he said the same thing.
"Surround me. When I reach toward you, take hold of my
hand. Say nothing: only take hold."

The day was bright and clear. The morning air was crisp,
fresh, sweet as alabandina nectar. But in Piurifayne, far to the
east, night was already descending.

He donned the circlet. He grasped the tooth of the
water-king. He drew the fresh sweet air deep into his lungs,
until he was all but dizzied with it.

—*Maazmoorn?*

The summons leaped from Valentine with such power
that those about him must have felt a backlash from it: Sleet
flinched, Carabella put her hands to her ears, Deliamber's
tentacles writhed in a sudden flurry.

—*Maazmoorn? Maazmoorn?*

The sound of bells. The slow heavy turnings of a giant
body lying at rest in cold northern waters. The faint rustlings
of great black wings.

—*I hear, Valentine-brother.*

—*Help me, Maazmoorn.*

—*Help? How shall I help?*

—*Let me ride on your spirit across the world.*

—*Then come upon me, king-brother, Valentine-brother.*

It was wondrously easy. He felt himself grow light, and
glided up, and floated, and soared, and flew. Below him lay
the great curving arc of the planet, sweeping off eastward into
night. The water-king carried him effortlessly, serenely, as a

giant might carry a kitten in the palm of his hand. Onward, onward over the world, which was altogether open to him as he coursed above it. He felt that he and the planet were one, that he embodied in himself the twenty billion people of Majipoor, humans and Skandars and Hjorts and Metamorphs and all the rest, moving within him like the corpuscles of his blood. He was everywhere at once; he was all the sorrow in the world, and all the joy, and all the yearning, and all the need. He was everything. He was a boiling universe of contradictions and conflicts. He felt the heat of the desert and the warm rain of the tropics and the chill of the high peaks. He laughed and wept and died and made love and ate and drank and danced and fought and rode wildly through unknown hills and toiled in the fields and cut a path through thick vine-webbed jungles. In the oceans of his soul vast sea dragons breached the surface and let forth monstrous bleating roars and dived again, to the uttermost depths. He looked down and saw the broken places of the world, the wounded and shattered places where the land had risen and crashed against itself, and he saw how it all could be healed, how it could be made whole and serene again. For everything tended to return to serenity. Everything enfolded itself into That Which Is. Everything was part of a vast seamless harmony.

But in that great harmony he felt a single dissonance.

It screeched and yawped and shrieked and screamed. It slashed across the fabric of the world like a knife, leaving behind a track of blood. It ripped apart the wholeness.

Even that dissonance, Valentine knew, was an aspect of That Which Is. Yet it was—far across the world, roiling and churning and roaring in its madness—the one aspect of That Which Is that would not itself accept That Which Is. It was a force that cried a mighty *no!* to all else. It rose up against those who would restore the harmony, who would repair the fabric, who would make whole the wholeness.

—*Faraataa?*

—*Who are you?*

—*I am Valentine the Pontifex.*

—*Valentine the fool. Valentine the child.*

—*No, Faraataa. Valentine the Pontifex.*

—*That means nothing to me. I am the King That Is!*

Valentine laughed, and his laughter showered across the world like a rainfall of drops of golden honey. Soaring on the wings of the great dragon-king, he rose almost to the edge of the sky, where he could look across the darkness and see the tip of Castle Mount piercing the heavens on the far side of the world, and the Great Sea beyond it. And he looked down into the jungle of Piurifayne, and laughed again, and watched the furious Faraataa writhing and struggling beneath the torrent of that laughter.

    —*Faraataa?*

    —*What do you want?*

    —*You may not kill her, Faraataa.*

    —*Who are you to tell me what I may not do?*

    —*I am Majipoor.*

    —*You are the fool Valentine. And I am the King That Is!*

    —*No, Faraataa.*

    —*No?*

    —*I see the old tale glistening in your mind. The Prince To Come, the King That Is: how can you lay such a claim for yourself? You are not that Prince. You can never be that King.*

    —*You clutter my mind with your nonsense. Leave me or I will drive you out.*

    Valentine felt the thrust, the push. He warded it off.

    —*The Prince To Come is a being absolutely without hatred. Can you deny that, Faraataa? It is part of your own people's legend. He is without the hunger for vengeance. He is without the lust for destruction. You are nothing* except *hatred and vengeance and destruction, Faraataa. If those things were emptied from you, you would be a shell, a husk.*

    —*Fool.*

    —*Your claim is a false one.*

    —*Fool.*

    —*Let me take the anger and the hatred from you, Faraataa, if you would be the king you claim you are.*

    —*You talk a fool's foolishness.*

    —*Come, Faraataa. Release the Danipiur. Give your soul over to me for healing.*

    —*The Danipiur will die within the hour.*

    —*No, Faraataa.*

    —*Look!*

    The interwoven crowns of the jungle trees parted, and Valentine beheld New Velalisier by the gleam of torchlight. The temples of interwoven logs, the banners, the altar, the pyre already blazing. The Metamorph woman, silent, dignified, chained to the block of stone. The faces surrounding

her, blank, alien. The night, the trees, the sounds, the
smells. The music. The chanting.

—*Release her, Faraataa. And then come to me, you and
she together, and let us establish what must be established.*

—*Never. I will give her to the god with my own hands.
And with her sacrifice atone for the crime of the Defilement,
when we slew our gods and were laden with you as our
penance.*

—*You are wrong even about that, Faraataa.*

—*What?*

—*The gods gave themselves willingly, that day in Velalisier.
It was their sacrifice, which you misunderstand. You have
invented a myth of a Defilement, but it is the wrong myth.
Faraataa, it is a mistake, it is a total error. The water-king
Niznorn and the water-king Domsitor gave themselves as
sacrifices that day long ago, just as the water-kings give
themselves yet to our hunters as they round the curve of
Zimroel. And you do not understand. You understand nothing
at all.*

—*Foolishness. Madness.*

—*Set her free, Faraataa. Sacrifice your hatred as the
water-kings sacrificed themselves.*

—*I will slay her now with my own hands.*

—*You may not do it, Faraataa. Release her.*

—*NO.*

The terrible force of that *no* was unexpected: it rose like
the ocean in its greatest wrath and swept upward toward
Valentine and struck him with stunning impact, buffeting
him, swaying him, sweeping him for a moment into chaos. As
he struggled to right himself Faraataa hurled a second such
bolt, and a third, and a fourth, and they hit him with the
same hammerblow power. But then Valentine felt the power
of the water-king underlying his own, and he caught his
breath, he regained his balance, he found his strength once
more.

He reached out toward the rebel chieftain.

He remembered how it had been that other time years
ago, in the final hour of the war of restoration, when he had
gone alone into the judgment hall of the Castle and found the
usurper Dominin Barjazid there, seething with fury. And
Valentine had sent love to him, friendship, sadness for all that
had come between them. He had sent the hope of an
amicable settlement of differences, of pardon for sins commit

ted, of safe conduct out of the Castle. To which the Barjazid
had replied with defiance, hatred, anger, contempt, belliger-
ence, a declaration of perpetual war. Valentine had not forgotten any of that. And it was the same all over again now, the
desperate hatred-filled enemy, the fiery resistance, the bitter
refusal to swerve from the path of death and destruction,
loathing and abomination, scorn and contempt.

He expected no more of Faraataa than he had of Dominin
Barjazid. But he was Valentine still, and still he believed in
the possibility of the triumph of love.

—Faraataa?

—*You are a child, Valentine.*

—*Give yourself over to me in peace. Put aside your
hatred, if you would be who you claim to be.*

—*Leave me, Valentine.*

—*I reach to you.*

—*No. No. No. No.*

This time Valentine was prepared for the blasts of nega-
tion that came rolling like boulders toward him. He took the
full force of Faraataa's hatred and turned it aside, and offered
in its place love, trust, faith, and had more hatred in return,
implacable, unchanging, immovable.

—*You give me no choice, Faraataa.*

With a shrug Faraataa moved toward the altar on which
the Metamorph queen lay bound. He raised high his dirk of
polished wood.

"Deliamber?" Valentine said. "Carabella? Tisana? Sleet?"

They took hold of him, grasping his hands, his arms, his
shoulders. He felt their strength pouring into him. But even
that was not enough. He called out across the world and
found the Lady on her Isle, the new Lady, the mother of
Hissune, and drew strength from her, and from his own
mother the former Lady. And even that was not enough. But
in that instant he went elsewhere. "Tunigorn! Stasilaine! Help
me!" They joined him. He found Zalzan Kavol. He found
Asenhart. He found Ermanar. He found Lisamon. Not enough.
Not enough. One more: "Hissune? Come, you also, Hissune.
Give me your strength. Give me your boldness."

—*I am here, your majesty.*

Yes. Yes. It would be possible now. He heard once more
the words of old Aximaan Threysz: *You will save us by doing
that which you think is impossible for you to do.* Yes. It
would be possible now.

Faraataa!

A single blast like the sound of a great trumpet traveled out from Valentine across the world to Piurifayne. It made the journey in the smallest part of a moment and found its target, which was not Faraataa but rather the hatred within Faraataa, the blind, wrathful, unyielding passion to avenge, destroy, obliterate, expunge. It found it and expunged it, draining it from Faraataa in one irresistible draught. Valentine drank all that blazing rage into himself, and absorbed it, and took from it its power, and discarded it. And Faraataa was left empty.

For a moment his arm still rose high above his head, the muscles still tense and poised, the weapon still aimed at the Danipiur's heart. Then from Faraataa came the sound of a silent scream, a sound without substance, an emptiness, a void. Still he stood upright, motionless, frozen. But he was empty: a shell, a husk. The dirk dropped from his lifeless fingers.

—Go, said Valentine. *In the name of the Divine, go. Go!*

And Faraataa fell forward and did not move again.

All was silent. The world was terribly still. *You will save us,* said Aximaan Threysz, *by doing that which you think is impossible for you to do.* And he had not hesitated.

The voice of the water-king Maazmoorn came to him from far away:

—*Have you made your journey, Valentine-brother?*

—*Yes. I have made my journey now.*

Valentine opened his eyes. He put down the tooth, he took the circlet from his brow. He looked about him and saw the strange pale faces, the frightened eyes: Sleet, Carabella, Deliamber, Tisana.

"It is done now," he said quietly. "The Danipiur will not be slain. No more monsters will be loosed upon us."

"Valentine—"

He looked toward Carabella. "What is it, love?"

"Are you all right?"

"Yes," he said. "I'm all right." He felt very tired, he felt very strange. But—yes, he was all right. He had done what had to be done. There had been no choice. And it was done now.

To Sleet he said, "We are finished here. Make my farewells to Nitikkimal for me, and to the others of this place, and tell them that all will be well, that I promise it most solemnly. And then let us be on our way."

"Onward to Dulorn?" Sleet asked.

The Pontifex smiled and shook his head. "No. Eastward. To Piurifayne, first, to meet with the Danipiur and Lord Hissune, and bring into being the new order of the world, now that this hatred has been thrust from it. And then it will be time to go home, Sleet. It will be time to go home!"

8

They held the coronation ceremony outdoors, in the great grassy courtyard by Vildivar Close, where there was a fine view of the Ninety-Nine Steps and the uppermost reaches of the Castle. It was not usual to hold the ceremony anywhere but in the Confalume throne-room, but it was a long while since anyone had given much heed to what was usual; and the Pontifex Valentine had insisted that the ceremony take place outdoors. Who could gainsay the express wish of a Pontifex?

So they all had gathered, by the express wish of the Pontifex, under the sweet springtime sky of Castle Mount. The courtyard was lavishly decorated with flowering plants— the gardeners had brought in halatinga trees in bloom, miraculously potting them into huge tubs without disturbing their buds, and down both sides of the courtyard their crimson-and-gold flowers cast an almost luminescent glow. There were tanigales and alabandinas, caramangs and sefitongals, eldirons, pinninas, and dozens more, everything in full bloom. Valentine had given orders that there be flowers on all sides; and so there were flowers on all sides.

It was the custom, at a coronation ceremony, to arrange the Powers of the realm in a diamond-shaped pattern, if all four of them had been able to attend: the new Coronal at the head of the diamond, and the Pontifex facing him, and the Lady of the Isle to one side, and the King of Dreams to the other. But this coronation was different from all other coronation ceremonies that Majipoor had ever known, for this time there were five Powers, and a new configuration had had to be devised.

And so it was. Pontifex and Coronal stood side by side. To the right of the Coronal Lord Hissune there stood, some distance away, his mother Elsinome the Lady of the Isle. To the left of the Pontifex Valentine, at an equal distance, stood

Minax Barjazid, the King of Dreams. And at the farthest end of the group, facing the other four, stood the Danipiur of Piurifayne, fifth and newest of the Powers of Majipoor.

All about them were their closest aides and counsellors, the high spokesman Sleet on one side of the Pontifex and the lady Carabella on the other, and Alsimir and Stimion flanking the Coronal, and a little cluster of hierarchs, Lorivade and Talinot Esulde and some others, about the Lady. The King of Dreams had brought his brothers Cristoph and Dominin, and the Danipiur was surrounded by a dozen Piurivars in shining silken robes, who clung close together as though they could not quite believe they were honored guests at a ceremony atop Castle Mount.

Farther out in the group were the princes and dukes, Tunigorn and Stasilaine and Divvis, Mirigant and Elzandir and all the rest, and delegates from the far lands, from Alaisor and Stoien and Pililplok and Ni-moya and Pidruid. And certain special guests, Nitikkimal of Prestimion Vale and Millilain of Khyntor and others like them whose lives had intersected that of the Pontifex in his journey across the world; and even that little red-faced man Sempeturn, pardoned now for his treason by his valor in the campaign in Piurifayne, who stared about in awe and wonder and again and again made the sign of the starburst toward Lord Hissune and the sign of the Pontifex toward Valentine, acts of homage that appeared to be uncontrollable in their frequency. And also there were certain people of the Labyrinth, childhood friends of the new Coronal, Vanimoon who had been almost a brother to the Coronal when they were boys, and Vanimoon's slender almond-eyed sister Shulaire, and Heulan, and Heulan's three brothers, and some more, and they too stood stiffly, eyes wide, mouths agape.

There was the usual abundance of wine. There were the usual prayers. There were the usual hymns. There were the traditional speeches. But the ceremony was by no means even at its halfway point when the Pontifex Valentine held up his hand to indicate that he meant to speak.

"Friends—" he began.

At once there were whispers of astonishment. A Pontifex addressing others—even Powers, even princes—as "friends"? How strange—how Valentine-like. . . .

"Friends," he said again, "Let me have just a few words now, and then I think you will very rarely hear from me

thereafter, for this is Lord Hissune's time, and this is Lord
Hissune's Castle, and I am not to be conspicuous here after
today. I want only to give you my thanks for attending us here
this day"—whispers again: did a Pontifex give thanks?—"and to
bid you be joyful, not only today, but in all the time of
reconciliation that now we enter. For on this day we confirm
in office a Coronal who will govern you with wisdom and
mercy for many years to come as our time of rebuilding this
world goes forth; and we hail also as a new Power of the realm
another monarch who was of late our enemy, and who will be
our enemy no longer, the Divine willing, for now she and her
people are welcomed into the mainstream of Majipoori life as
equal partners. With good will on all sides, perhaps ancient
wrongs can be redeemed and atonement can begin."

He paused and took from a bearer a bowl brimming with
glistening wine, and held it high.

"I am almost done. All that remains now is to ask the
blessing of the Divine upon this festivity—and to ask, also,
the blessing of our great brothers of the sea, with whom we
share this world—at whose sufferance, perhaps, we inhabit a
small part of this huge world—and with whom, at long last,
we have entered into communion. They have been our
salvation, in this time of making of peace and binding of
wounds; they will be our guides, let us hope, in the time to
come.

"And now—friends—we approach the moment in the
coronation ceremony when the newly anointed Coronal dons
the starburst crown and ascends the Confalume Throne. But
of course we are not in the throne-room now. By my request:
by my command. For I wished one last time this afternoon to
breathe the good air of Castle Mount, and to feel the warm
sun upon my skin. I leave this place tonight—my lady
Carabella and I, and all these my good companions who have
stayed by my side through so many years and so many
strange adventures—we leave for the Labyrinth, where I
mean to make my home. A wise old woman who is now dead
said to me, when I was in a place far away called Prestimion
Vale, that I must do that which I think is impossible for me to
do, if we are to be saved—and so I did, because it was
necessary for me to do it—and then I would have to do that
which I least desired to do. And what is it I least desire to
do? Why, I suppose it is to leave this place, and go down into
the Labyrinth where a Pontifex must dwell. But I will do it.

And not bitterly, not angrily. I do it and I rejoice in it: for I am Pontifex, and this Castle is mine no longer, and I will move onward, as was the intent of the Divine."

The Pontifex smiled, and gestured with the wine-bowl toward the Coronal, and toward the Lady, and toward the King of Dreams, and toward the Danipiur. And sipped the wine, and gave it to the lady Carabella to sip.

And said, "There are the Ninety-Nine Steps. Beyond them lies the innermost sanctuary of the Castle, where we must complete today's rite; and then we will have our feast, and then my people and I will take our leave, for the journey to the Labyrinth is a lengthy one and I am eager to reach my home at last. Lord Hissune, will you lead us within? Will you lead us, Lord Hissune?"

ABOUT THE AUTHOR

ROBERT SILVERBERG was born in New York and makes his home in the San Francisco area. He has written several hundred science fiction stories and over seventy science fiction novels. He has won two Hugo awards and four Nebula awards. He is a past president of the Science Fiction Writers of America. Silverberg's other Bantam titles include *Lord Valentine's Castle, Majipoor Chronicles, The Book of Skulls, Born With the Dead, The World Inside, Thorns, The Masks of Time, Dying Inside, Downward to the Earth, The Tower of Glass, World of a Thousand Colors* and *Valentine Pontifex*.